DOWN
TO MY
SOUL

SOUL SERIES BOOK TWO
KENNEDY RYAN

Cover Art:
Kari March Designs

Cover Photos:
iStock, Dollar photo

Editing:
Lisa Christman, Adepts Edits

Proofreading:
Kara Hildebrand

Interior Design & Formatting:
Perfectly Publishable
www.perfectlypublishable.com

This book is a continuation of book 1, My Soul to Keep, and should be read after that one.
Thank you for reading!

Acknowledgments

FIRST I'LL THANK GOD. MAYBE AN odd way to kick off a romance novel, but the prayer I learned as a child, *"Now I lay me down to sleep, I pray the Lord, my soul to keep . . ."* was an inspiration, not only for the heroine's tattoo, but was a kernel of thought when I started this book. It grew into Rhys and Kai's journey. I don't take imagination for granted, and believe it is not only sublime, but in many ways, divine.

Thank you to my little tribe of author sisters who answer my dumb questions, talk me off ledges when I'm on the verge of quitting, and best of all, make me laugh!

Thank you to all the bloggers, tooooo many to name, who have supported this series and me personally. I don't take it or you for granted—ever. Your passion for and dedication to books is astounding and appreciated.

Thank you to my beta readers who put up with so much on this one! The re-reads and second . . . third . . . fourth passes at the same passages, sometimes only slightly different from the last! LOL! Your honesty and enthusiasm for this story, for this series, buttressed me so often.

Thank you for all your feedback and constructive love.

To my ladies in Kennedy Ryan Books on Facebook! You guys make me smile every day. You are my happy place. The ones always shouting for me and yelling at the top of your lungs for my books. Thank you for being awesome.

And I must always acknowledge the ones who sacrifice the most every time I write a book. Who deal with me being lost in my head for months on end, neglecting too much and paying attention not enough. My lifetime lover and husband of 19 years. All we need is a couple of forevers, baby. And to my son who is the most beautiful challenge I've encountered in this life. I'm a better person for raising you.

"Deep calls out to deep . . ."—Psalm 42:7

Glory Falls

8 Years Old

DADDY'S ALWAYS WORKING.

His head is bent over the Bible. It takes him all week to get ready for his Sunday sermons, and Mama says leave him be 'cause Daddy does the most important work in the world. He shepherds God's flock.

"Baaaaaaa," I say softly from the door to his study.

I'm Daddy's favorite sheep, and when I need him, all I have to say is . . .

"Baaaaaaa." Louder now 'cause Mama says Daddy gets lost in the Word sometimes. Daddy says that's the only place where he's found. He looks up from his work, frown disappearing as soon as he spots me in the door.

"Look at you, baby girl." His dark eyes—Cocoa Puff brown—smile at me over the rims of his reading glasses. "I thought the recital wasn't for a few days. You're already dressed up."

I pluck at the layers of the lavender tutu, fluffy as cotton candy, and wriggle my toes in my new ballet slippers.

"I wanted you to see." My feet shuffle me quickly over to his big, messy desk.

He motions for me to scoot the last few inches forward and sit on his lap, running his hand over the long braids hanging down to my waist.

"Prettiest little thing in Glory Falls." He kisses my forehead like he does every night before bed. "You're gonna dance for Daddy at this fancy recital?"

"Yes, sir." I nod and lean back, hoping he won't make me go just yet. Sometimes if I sit real quiet, he'll let me stay while he studies. I hold my breath until he turns back to the Bible, tucking our legs under the desk.

Yellow and pink highlight the thick columns of words on the pages. I want to ask him what he's working on, but stay quiet because I want to stay.

"I know you want to know, little preacher girl, so go ahead and ask."

"Why do you call me 'little preacher girl'?" I smile, flashing the little hole where my front tooth used to be. "I'm gonna be a dancer."

"Last week it was a singer."

"I gonna be both! Like Cher."

A laugh shakes in his chest at my back.

"Your Aunt Ruthie oughta be whooped for making you watch them old tapes. Cher, of all people. Anybody as interested in sermons as you are oughta be a preacher."

I could tell him that it's not so much the sermons that interest me as it is him. Spending time with him. Being his favorite sheep, but I don't. He loves to think of me as his little preacher. And it's true that the sermons interest me, just not as much as Daddy does.

"What's this one about?" I point to a line of scripture tucked in the middle of one column, circled and highlighted and surrounded by stars. "*Deep calls out to deep.* What's that mean?"

"One of my favorites. That's about . . . well, it's like . . ." He looks down at me, his eyebrows pulling together. "It's hard to explain."

"Mama says you make the hard stuff easy, Daddy."

Everybody knows he's the best preacher in town. People squeeze into Glory Falls Baptist's wooden pews every Sunday to hear him.

"She does, does she? Well, I try." His face lights up in that way Mama says tells you he's on to something. "It means that God has a way of connecting the deepest parts of Himself with the deepest parts of us. We try to run. We let things get in the way, but His love is so deep that it can get past everything to reach us."

His voice drops off and I hear him swallow.

"Even when we make mistakes and we try to hide, his love has a way of finding us."

"Can people love like that?" I look up at him, past his strong chin and nose that was broken once in a fight before he met the Lord, and straight in the eyes. "I mean, can people love you no matter what? In the deep calls out to deep kinda way?"

Daddy tilts his head, his eyes squinching at the corners, a little bit of a smile on his face.

"Well, we're made in His image, so I guess we can, baby girl."

"That's how you love me?" The thought makes me smile and my heart feels all big and warm behind the tight stretch of my leotard.

"Absolutely." He tugs one of my braids.

"And Mama? That's how you love Mama?"

It's quiet behind me for a few seconds 'til Daddy clears his throat.

"There's all kinds of love. I have a real special kind for your mama."

"But it's not the deep calls out to deep kind?" My lip starts trembling for no reason, and I think I might cry if he doesn't love my mama that way. "You don't love her like that?"

"'Course I do," he finally says, so low I almost don't hear him.

I look up and over my shoulder, unsure for the first time in my life that he's telling me the truth, but he looks like Daddy. I lean into his neck and sniff. Smells like Daddy, and Daddy always tells the truth.

"It's like that song they taught us in Sunday school," I tell him.

"What song? How's it go?" His voice isn't low anymore. It teases me the way I'm used to. "Why don't you sing it for me?"

I know he knows. He just always wants me to sing.

"Your love goes past the heart," I sing, barely remembering the melody, but knowing the words for sure. "Your love goes to the deepest part. Your love, Your love, Your love, Your love. Your love goes all the way down to my soul."

"Yep. That's it." He brushes my bangs back. "You'll be in the choir soon, baby girl, and—"

"Excuse me, Pastor," a soft voice comes from the door. Daddy's secretary, Carla, stands there, holding a stack of folders. "Sorry to interrupt, but I need, um . . . your signature."

"Of course." Daddy slides back from the desk and sets me on my feet, patting my shoulders. "We got some work to do. You go on now, baby girl. Come get me when dinner's done."

"But, Daddy, I—"

"You heard your father, Kai." Carla walks over to the desk, plopping the folders into a pile. "You hurry on now. We got work to do."

I look up and over the skirt, just short of her knees, past the blonde hair around her shoulders to meet her blue eyes. She helps Daddy. He says he doesn't know what he'd do without her. Indispensable. That's what he calls her, so I should like anyone who helps my daddy like that

But I don't. I don't like Carla at all.

"Kai, come on now," Mama says from the hall. "Let your daddy work. Come help me snap these peas."

I walk slowly past Carla, looking her up and down like I've seen Aunt Ruthie do a few times. I don't think Aunt Ruthie likes Carla either.

"You staying for dinner, Carla?" Mama asks, the smile on her face she always has for everyone. Even Carla.

"Um, I'm not sure." Carla's eyes go to Daddy. He shakes his head, a small frown on his face. "Maybe next time."

Mama frowns a little, too, asking Daddy questions with just her eyes the way I've seen her do when she doesn't want me to know what they're talking about.

"Well, there's plenty and you're always welcome." Mama takes my hand once I make it into the hall outside the study. I don't want to leave, so I look for something else that will give me a few more minutes before Daddy goes back to work.

"Mama, Daddy thinks I'm gonna be a preacher," I say loud enough for him to hear, grinning up at her and then over at Daddy, but I've already lost his attention. He and Carla are working, their heads close together over the stack of papers she brought. Mama leans down to whisper in my ear.

"We know he's wrong, though." She pulls back, her dark, tilted eyes warm and smiling. Making me smile back. "We both know what you're gonna be when you grow up, Kai Anne."

"What am I gonna be, Mama?" I whisper, even though Daddy and Carla don't seem to be paying us much mind.

She kisses my nose and pats my bottom, leading me toward the kitchen and the peas that need snapping.

"Baby, you're gonna be a star."

Chapter ONE

Kai

THAT WEARINESS DOING WHAT YOU LOVE kind of loses its novelty around the second week of eighteen-hour days. Dub, the choreographer, and I expend so much energy working on my opening act for the second leg of the tour, I barely have energy for the show each night. It's just singing easy BGV parts for Luke's set. When Luke performs his hit single, I join him onstage to simulate the lap dance from the video. It's a show-stopper.

The whole plan is getting me lots of face time, lots of exposure. It's a brilliant strategy, but it's wearing me down. I can't let on, though. I don't want Mr. Malcolm to think I can't pull this off. I can. I've waited too long for this. Nothing will get in my way. Certainly not my own body.

I keep hearing Rhyson's warning about John Malcolm. It's galling that I kind of already see what he means. Mr. Malcolm's not tyrannical, but he definitely focuses on the bottom line, and requires the talent to do whatever it takes to meet it.

It's been a week since Rhyson called or texted me. We have a fifteen-minute break from rehearsal, so I sit on the stage step and pull out my phone to look at his last text. It was a long one, but I almost have it memorized, I've read it so many times. It starts, of course, with a movie quote.

R. Geritol: *"So I'm single now, and everything's changed. I hate it."*—*Say Anything*

I know you're mad at me. It was a dick move. I know that, but don't give up on us, Pep. San told me you're on tour for three months. I've started my tour, too. We can take this time to clear our heads and do what we need to do, but you know I can't let you go. Please don't see me not coming after you as giving up. When you get back, you have to give me another chance. You have to. I thought I was doing what was best for you. I wanted to protect you. I'm sorry I went about it the wrong way. Please forgive me, and PLEASE TAKE CARE OF YOURSELF! You know I don't trust John Malcolm, but this is a great opportunity, so kill it. Your whole life is about to change, because when the world sees what I see, they won't be able to get enough of you. I can't. Don't forget I'm yours and you're mine.

I LIVE you.

I fight the smile forcing its way onto my face when I see our "auto correct" way of saying I love you. It's too soon to smile. I'm too close to what happened, to what he did, but I can't deny he affects me even with just words on a screen. A new text comes in as I'm reading the last line of Rhyson's message.

My heart patters in case it's him. Stupid heart. After all he did—the manipulation, the deception, the out and out betrayal—a chain still hooks my heart to Rhyson's, stretching from wherever I am to wherever he is in the world. I have no idea how to break it. When it comes down to it, in spite of everything, I'm not sure I want to.

The text is not from him. It's an unknown number. Odd.

There's a link, and I open it, which is probably stupid, but I'm curious. It's to a *Spotted* post detailing our very public fight. And breakup. Okay. Old news. Even my tour mates have stopped looking at me funny by now. Their curiosity has waned, and thank God, so has the public's.

Another text comes in.

> *Unknown: You and Rhyson Gray don't belong together. I advise you to keep things this way.*

What the hell?

> *Me: Who is this?*

> *Unknown: Don't worry about who I am. Worry about what I have.*

A video file comes over. This can't be good. Finger hovering over the screen, I tap the file. Sounds of loud panting and grunting come from my phone. Two naked bodies in profile, a man and a woman, fucking hard, doggy-style. The man at the back turns his head to grin right into the camera like he's giving the performance of his life. My heart skids to a halt, burning rubber and slamming on the brakes in my chest. Horror and disgust war in my belly, churning dark emotion until it leaks out through my sweaty palms and under my arms. I can't process what I'm seeing. How did he . . . How could it . . . It can't be. The handsome face smeared with a devil grin is Drex. Even though I know it's not possible, I feel like those malevolent eyes are looking right at me—taunting and toying with me.

My brain is still catching up to what my eyes are seeing, when I focus on the woman. She's on all fours, her face forward and turned away, but I know her. I see the words hugging her ribs. Lost in the iniquitous sight, buried in the lusty sounds, the prayer looks out of place.

My soul to keep.

As if I needed further confirmation, the woman turns her head just enough for me to see her face clearly. I'm ashamed of my face, looking so much like my mother in a situation she would never have allowed to compromise her.

I tap the screen to stop the video, doing a frantic sweep of the stage to see if anyone heard or saw. Sweat covers my body, slicking my palms and dampening my forehead. My heart rages and rattles inside of me. My hands tremble so badly I drop the phone.

Ohmygodohmygodohmygod.

On the brink of my big break, the girl who wanted no distractions could be ruined by the biggest distraction of all.

A sex tape.

But it's not the buying public I consider, who'd probably be titillated and maybe even more intrigued than ever. It's not the good people of Glory Falls Baptist, who'd be scandalized to see Mai's little girl getting herself plowed from behind. It isn't Aunt Ruthie, who might not judge, but would probably never see me quite the same way. It's none of those people, none of those responses that strike fear right down the center of my heart.

It's Rhyson.

He didn't even want to *hear* the details of what went on with Drex, the vermin who has been a pain in his ass and a thorn in his side since high school. The man screwed Rhyson's girlfriend behind his back and sabotaged his first album release. How would he handle *seeing* me with Drex that way in dirty, living color? Could he ever scrub his mind completely free of it? Would it change how he saw me? How he loved me? Even if he said it wouldn't?

All these weeks I thought his transgression was the thing that might irreparably break us.

Turns out it may be mine.

Chapter TWO

Kai

IF I NEVER WEAR ANOTHER PAIR of fake eyelashes again, it'll be too soon.

I gently bat away the slim hand poised to apply the ridiculously long falsies.

"Not today, Ella." I meet the makeup artist's bright blue eyes in the mirror of my hotel bathroom. "I think my normal human-size lashes will be fine. It's not the tour. It's just radio."

"One of the biggest radio shows in the country." Ella sets the lashes aside and picks up her go-to mascara. "And it's streaming to millions online so it may as well be your first TV appearance. Why do you think Malcolm insisted on hair and makeup for it?"

"Because 'insist' is the only gear Malcolm knows." I grimace over his demands, which have only continued to increase. "He insists on my wardrobe. He insists on extra rehearsals. He insists that I get on Instagram and Snap Chat."

"He knows what he's doing, kid." Ella rakes a hand through her short, crimson hair before scooping up a chunk of mine. "I have to disagree with his suggestion that you go blonde, though. This hair is gorgeous just as it is."

"Me? Blonde? I can't even—"

The chirp of Ella's phone interrupts.

"That's him." Ella rolls her eyes and digs into the pocket of her plain black smock. "I assigned him his own tone so I'll know when he's trying to reach me. Look in your jewelry box to see if you've still got those big hoop earrings. They'll be great with this outfit."

While she responds to Malcolm's text, I walk over to my jewelry box tucked in the corner of the bathroom counter. A sprig of fresh mistletoe rests right on top of the earrings Ella asked me to find. It's delivered to my dressing room at every stop.

Rhyson.

Damn that man. Using my grandfather's habit of keeping mistletoe for my grandmother to win me back. Clever? Evil? Sweet? The typical conundrum of contradictions I face with him. Most days I want to strangle him because of the control freak stunt he pulled with *Total Package*. A tangle of emotions paralyzes me. Hurt is right in front of me, and I still ache from his betrayal. Fear to my right, I'm afraid that contacting him could trip a wire and set off that bomb of a sex tape. To my left, that persistent desire that gets stronger every day to say screw it all and take him back. And where does that leave me? With my back against the wall. Trapped, and even though I'm in a different city every day, frozen in place. Unsure of what I should do.

So I've done nothing.

I twist the mistletoe between my fingers, memories of Rhyson in Glory Falls for the holidays crowding out everything else. Of singing Mama's favorite carol with him on Christmas Eve and laughing over Christmas sweaters at the dinner table. We shared our first kiss on the front porch, steam rising from our lips into the cold night air. Every day these memories erode my anger. Every time the mistletoe comes, my fury ebbs a little more. I can't forget what he did to jeopardize the thing I've worked for my whole life. He lied and manipulated me. But these memories . . . they make me miss him. If he were here now, I'd smack him one second and kiss him the next.

God, if he were here now . . .

"That from him?" Ella pockets her phone and nods toward the mistletoe trapped between my fingers.

"What?" I drop the mistletoe back into my jewelry box, grab the earrings and slam the lid. "Is what from who?"

"Wow." Ella raises her over-plucked eyebrows. "You're real subtle. There's two people you can't, or shouldn't keep secrets from. Your priest and your stylist. So 'fess up. I'm guessing the mistletoe's from Rhyson Gray."

Leaning one hip against the granite counter top, I study Ella in the harsh light of my hotel bathroom and arrange my face into the mask I've worn since the sex tape exploded into my life. It's not a guard I let slip. I have no idea who to trust. San is the only person I've told about the tape. I had to tell someone. San's been my someone since we were kids. He's always known what to do, and I'm praying that he can help me figure this out. He's doing what he can on his end to unravel this web while I'm touring. Since that first text message six weeks ago, the blackmailer has been suspiciously quiet, but it hasn't lulled me. If anything I live on high alert, braced for his next jab. I have no idea who knows about that sex tape, who's behind it, and until I do, I'm giving nothing away to anyone. Not even sweet Ella.

"How should I know who's sending the mistletoe?" I re-take my seat in front of the mirror, waiting for Ella to resume the makeup and hair rituals we've gone through together on this tour. "There's never a card."

"Probably because there doesn't need to be one." Ella goes back to scooping up my hair, but doesn't leave this dangerous subject alone. "Everyone knows you were dating him and everyone saw things go bad on that video. You telling me he's not trying to win you back?"

I'm telling you nothing.

A knock at the door saves me from having to avoid more questions.

"That'll be Malcolm." Ella heads out of the bathroom, calling back to me. "Forgot he said he was coming up."

"For what?" I ask the girl in the mirror since Ella's gone. The girl I've seen every day of my life, but sometimes barely recognize after only two months on the road. Same dark hair and tilted eyes, traces of her Asian ancestry. Same petite figure, maybe a little slimmer now. But that's where the similarities end. Something behind those eyes has changed. Beyond the surface I'm a collection of reordered molecules making me a new creature I wouldn't know in a crowd. I'm guarded in a fundamentally different way than when I first moved to LA. Maybe because I shared myself with Rhyson and he betrayed the trust it took me so long to give. Maybe I'm afraid to open up because I'm in an industry of takers who would usurp my place in a heartbeat if I slack off even a little. On days like today when I'd rather be cuddled in bed than putting on false eyelashes at five a.m., all I want to do is let up, but I can't. I don't want to gain everything I've dreamed of only to lose everything I am, but I feel that happening in some ways, and it all starts behind the eyes.

"You ready?" John Malcolm asks from the doorway.

Ella takes her place behind me again, swiveling me on the stool so she can apply a creamy foundation.

"I'm ready."

"Always." Malcolm leans his back against the wall, a smile creasing his puffy face, making him look like a happy blowfish. "Always the professional."

"Thanks," I murmur, barely parting the lips Ella is lining.

"This appearance is a big deal, Kai." Malcolm watches the makeup motions Ella goes through. "*Morning Hype* isn't just one of New York's biggest shows. It's one of *the* biggest shows. And even though Luke was the original draw, your performance on tour is creating enough buzz for them to ask you to come along."

I just nod since Ella's filling in my lips with our favorite red matte. This isn't my first radio appearance with Luke. Yeah, it's the biggest, but why do I get the feeling there's more to it? Probably because Malcolm is rubbing his chin in the way that means he's broaching a touchy subject.

"They have this segment called No Holds Barred." Malcolm leans forward the tiniest bit, making sure he looks right into my eyes even though Ella is brushing shadow across my eyelids. "They'll have questions about Gray."

It takes a nanosecond to sink in. I've scrupulously avoided all questions and discussion of my relationship with Rhyson. Maybe it would have been smart for me to talk about it. To blast in every interview that I'm done with Rhyson Gray. That there's no hope for us. Maybe that would have bought me some breathing room with my blackmailer. I just never could do it. Never could say we're kaput. Every time I consider his betrayal, it's like a fresh blow to my heart. He held me when *Total Package* turned me down. He was the one who kissed away my tears. If I fell for that, what else was a lie?

If something is built on a lie, can it still be real?

I can't make myself believe that what Rhys and I shared wasn't real, that it was all somehow a fabrication. He was the realest thing I've ever had.

And, even with the lies, I still miss him.

"I'm not talking about Rhyson." I lower my real lashes, wishing now for the falsies to hide behind.

"It's No Holds Barred." Irritation pinches Malcolm's bushy eyebrows together. "Everyone who agrees to go on the show understands that's part of the deal."

"Well, I didn't agree." I give him a steady stare. Calm resolve is the best way to handle Malcolm. "You booked this, not me, and it's the first I've heard of answering questions about Rhys."

"Kai, the public is still fascinated with that video fiasco. It's got millions of hits."

"That 'video fiasco' as you call it was my real life. A real relationship."

"I hate to say it, but talking about it could make you an even hotter prospect."

"No, you don't." I shake my head, ignoring Ella's warning look to keep still.

"No, I don't what?" Malcolm asks.

"You don't hate to say it. You've wanted me to talk about this from day one."

"Because I've always understood the public's fascination with you and Gray. We should use it to your advantage."

To my advantage? Or yours?

"I won't use my relationship that way."

Interest piques the look Malcolm gives me.

"So there's still a relationship?"

"No, that's not what I mean." I smile my thanks to Ella in the mirror when she pats my shoulder to signal she's done. "It's my private life. I'll give it all up on the stage, you know that. But I have to keep something for myself."

I reach for my black leather Converse with the rhinestone shell toe.

"Not those." Malcolm runs his eyes over the wardrobe choices Ella brought in before pointing to a pair of stacked high heels. "Those work better."

"I wasn't aware you were a fashion designer *and* a manager." I slip the stacked heels on instead.

Malcolm shrugs and slides his hands into his pockets.

"Image is everything."

Another lie. Image is a conscious, deliberate projection. It's not everything. Without substance to back it up, it's nothing.

"Just be ready to deal with their questions." Malcolm straightens from the wall and smoothes his already-wrinkle-free suit jacket. "I know it's been a long two months, and you're tired, but you're so close to some R&R. Just knock this interview out of the park, get through these last few shows, and you get a break."

I get a week off before we start our last month of the tour. I've thought about going back to Glory Falls instead of LA. Rhyson and me in the same city. I can't imagine he'll stay away. Not to mention Grady's getting married next week, and I'm pretty sure Rhys is the best man. It won't be possible to avoid him. I can only hope to resist him, and my track record with that ain't great.

"The car's downstairs waiting." Malcolm turns and leaves.

I study myself in the mirror. My own Madonna t-shirt with red rhinestone lips is paired with an expensive black leather jacket that is definitely *not* my own. I search beneath the makeup and the designer jeans and the high-end leather for the girl who waited tables at The Note just months ago. There's no sign of her. There's this person that Malcolm is making a star, and even she looks a little lost.

"You ready?" Ella runs a brush through the hair hanging around my shoulders one last time.

A tiny spark of rebellion flares inside of me. I toe off the high heels, reaching for my Converse. As soon as I'm done tying them, I look up at Ella's smirking face, smirking in return.

"I am now."

Chapter THREE

Kai

LUKE AND I ARE THUMB WRESTLING in the greenroom when the door leading to the studio opens. A girl wearing an Intern t-shirt ushers through a heavy-set man I don't recognize and a woman I do. It's Qwest, one of the hottest female rappers in the game. I don't really listen to her music and have only seen her in a few videos, but she's as compelling and beautiful in real life as she is onscreen. Black braids twist into a knot to crown her head. Her skin, the color of nutmeg, is absolutely flawless. I know the wonders of makeup. I rely on them every day. But there is a naturalness to her that I didn't expect. She wears the same red matte shade on her lips as I do.

Our eyes catch and hold. She grabs the elbow of the heavy-set man, whom I presume is her body guard.

"Hold up, Ace." She comes to stand in front of us, tilting her head to study me more closely. "Nice lipstick."

I grin up at her from my seat, dropping Luke's hand.

"Yours, too."

"Erika." She extends her hand to me. "Kai Pearson, right?"

It's so odd for someone as famous as she is to know me. I'm not sure if it's because of my relationship with Rhyson or because of my short stint on tour. Maybe a little of the latter. Probably mostly the former.

I stand to shake her hand, realizing how much taller she is.

"Hi, Erika. Yeah, I'm Kai."

"You Rhyson Gray's girl?" Her almond-shaped eyes probe mine for a second before inspecting me from head to toe.

Who knows? I wake up every morning alone in a new hotel room wondering if I'm still Rhyson Gray's girl. Having to answer that publicly, even between just the two of us, disconcerts me.

"Um . . ."

"I mean, ex-girl." Qwest . . . Erika . . . shrugs. "Whatever."

"Yeah, whatever." I offer a shrug of my own.

"I ask because I'm wondering if you know Grip." She slides her hands into her back pockets, a small smile tugging at the corners of her mouth. "He's dope. I wanna collab, but having trouble getting to him. No manager. No agent. Nothing."

"Yeah, he's kind of grass roots."

"That's what I love about him." She cups her neck and tilts her head back a little, covering the rose tattoo at her throat, a purely feminine appreciation in her eyes. "And he's fine as hell. That don't hurt."

I'm not sure what she wants me to say or do here. I look at Luke, but he's no help, surfing Instagram.

"How should I get to him? He and Rhyson are best friends, right? So I figured you might know a good angle."

The word angle makes me uncomfortable, but I think she and Grip working together could be fire. And I know just the person to make it happen.

"Bristol Gray." I give Erika a quick smile. "Have your people contact her. She's Rhyson's sister, not Grip's manager, but she'd love to make something happen, and she probably can."

"Nice. I'll do that."

We both turn when the door opens and the intern comes back

through.

"Mr. Foster, Ms. Pearson, they're ready for you.

"Hey." Luke stands and smiles at Qwest, offering a hand. "I'm a fan."

Erika's eyes flick from his hand to his All-American face.

"Aiight. Thanks." She gives his hand a quick shake. "Nice to meet you."

Luke nods and goes on ahead. I'm turning to follow when Erika stops me with her words.

"You know they're gonna try to eat you alive, right?" she asks, dark brows up. "I mean about Rhyson Gray and all that. That No Holds Barred segment is a trip."

I glance at the intern holding the door open, who shifts from one booted foot to the other, waiting for me.

"They won't get anything I don't want to give," I assure her, setting my mouth in a hard line.

"I can see that." Erica grins. "And if they come at you, tell 'em pucker up and kiss on these."

She reaches back to grab the two globes of her ample ass. It takes a second for what she's saying to compute, but once it does, I love it. And I think I love her. She's based in New York and I'm in LA, but I think I could be friends with someone this genuine in a landscape of phonies.

I grab my round, if not-as-ample ass, and grin up at her.

"Got it."

"Ms. Pearson, we need to go," the intern says. "They're ready for you."

Erika and I exchange one last look, one last smile before I follow the intern into the studio.

Five minutes later, Luke and I sit around a huge table with Randy May, *Morning Hype's* host, and his two co-hosts. I adjust the headphones piping in the intro package music as Randy comes back from the last commercial.

"One of today's hottest performers is in the building," Randy says into the mic. "We've got Luke Foster in studio this morning.

Reminder we are streaming, and you're gonna wanna tune in online because he brought his beautiful tourmate Kai Pearson with him. Let's give them both a *Morning Hype* welcome."

The show's theme music plays over canned applause while Randy glances down at a small sheaf of papers in front of him. The other two hosts, a Black guy and a girl I'm guessing is Puerto Rican, murmur their welcomes, too.

"Luke, you've been to the show a few times since you won *Total Package* last season." Randy gives Luke a brief smile. "Good to have you back."

"Always love rolling through when I'm in New York," Luke says with enviable ease. He's such a people person this all comes naturally to him. I want to perform. I live to entertain, but get me offstage and that switch flips off. I'm afraid the millions listening are in for a snooze fest when Randy turns his attention to me.

"And you brought us a treat." Curiosity and speculation mingle in Randy's eyes when he considers me. "Kai Pearson, welcome to the show."

"Thanks," I say softly in the vicinity of the mic.

The producer catches my eye on the other side of the glass wall, gesturing for me to lean closer to the mic when I speak.

"Um, I mean." I press my lips to the mic. "Glad to be here."'

"You two are selling out arenas all over the country," Lola, the only girl in their hosting trio pipes in. "Kai, about halfway through, you became Luke's opening act. Really exceptional for a back-up singer new on the scene to get such a prominent role so quickly."

All I hear between the lines of what she actually says is "What makes you so special?" Maybe I'm paranoid, but I'm not a fool. It's no secret that a lot of people think I got this chance because of my relationship with Rhyson. The thing I hate, the thing I *really* hate, is that I can't know for sure whether or not they're at least a little right. Before I can respond, Luke jumps in.

"Kai's an exceptional talent." Luke flashes me a grin across the table littered with wires and notes. "I'd worked with her on my first video for this album, so we knew she could dance. We found out later what a great singer she was. Bringing her on tour and then expanding her role was a no brainer."

I give him a tiny smile, hoping he knows how grateful I am. He's a real class act. Every time a reporter or blogger implies that I'm not here on the merit of my talent, he very subtly and convincingly defends me. It didn't take long for me to understand why he's in Rhyson's small circle of friends.

We answer questions about the tour for a few minutes and take a short station break. All I can think about is the breakfast Malcolm promised me after this interview. I'd love to do some sightseeing, but there's not time. We're going straight into rehearsals and then it'll be show time. And then tomorrow the next city, the next show.

"We're back." Randy elevates his voice just a little to be heard over the transition package music. "If you're just tuning in, we have Luke Foster and Kai Pearson. They're at Barclays tonight, and we're the only ones with any tickets left. We'll give a pair away in just a second. First, we want to get into my favorite part of the show."

He looks right at me, the anticipation evident in his expression.

"Time for No Holds Barred." Randy leans back in his chair, dragging his adjustable mic on its stand with him. "We've seen Luke's rise over the last couple of years, but you, Kai, appeared out of nowhere. Where did you come from?"

"Georgia." It slips out before I can think of anything witty to say.

Something sharp embedded in Randy's laugh grates on my ears and on my nerves.

"I didn't mean that literally, sweetheart." He chuckles again, eyes trained on my face. "In just a few months you went from being someone we'd never heard of to the girl we're all talking about. It's something thousands dream about, and you did it. Congratulations."

His words feel more like an accusation than anything, so I just stare back at him, bending my lips into a hard curve while I wait. I know Malcolm wants me sparkling and fun, but Randy doesn't look like he's ready to play. Or if he is, it's hard ball.

Well, two can play that game.

"We've loved hearing all about the tour," Randy continues. "But,

Kai, we gotta talk about the elephant in the room."

"Elephant?" I sweep the small studio with a quick glance before looking back to Randy. "I don't see any elephant."

"Oh, he's here, all right." Randy looks to Lola. "Right, Lo? You see the elephant, don'tcha?"

For a moment, Lola's eyes meet mine, and I see kindness or sympathy. Something softer than what's in Randy's eyes, but she looks away quickly and nods.

"I see him."

"His name is Rhyson Gray." Randy leans forward.

"I don't think Rhyson would appreciate the comparison." I manage a smile I hope looks easier than it feels.

"Maybe he'll come on the show and take me to task for it." Randy grins. "We'd love that. We've asked him more than once, but he's never come on. Now you've heard of our No Holds Barred segment, yeah?"

Everything leading up to this was just small talk. This is what he wanted, and he's going straight for the jugular. I'm not giving him anything. He'll have to come and get it, and even then he won't get much more from me than the blank look I'm giving him right now.

"Everyone knows you were in a very public relationship with Rhyson Gray," Randy says.

"Actually I was in a very private relationship with Rhyson." I twist my fingers in my lap beneath the table where no one can see them. "And we had one very public argument."

"Yes, very public." Randy glances down at his little stack of notes and then back up again. "The video's been viewed a helluva lot, but no one knows what the fight was actually about. The audio was kind of muffled."

Small mercies. I look at him, brows all the way in the air.

Dude, if you have a question, ask. Doesn't mean I'll answer.

"Care to shed any light on that for us?" Randy asks in that way that tells me he doesn't expect me to.

"Rhyson and I are both entertainers." I run one finger along the ridges of Gram's necklace at my throat. "We give everything to the people who come to see us perform, but I think we deserve to keep some things private."

"Can you tell us if you've spoken to him?"

What'll it hurt? Maybe if I give them this worthless bone, it'll appease Malcolm. And my blackmailer, if they're listening.

"No, we haven't spoken." I move a little in my seat, hoping it looks more like a shift than the squirm it actually is.

"He was on a tour of his own, right, for the last few weeks?" Don, the other host asks.

I just look back at him and nod.

"There's a lot of speculation that you two have gone your separate ways for good." Randy leans back, one elbow draped over the chair. "Petra Andreyev was on tour with Rhys, and Dub Shaughnessy is on tour with you. Rumor has it that maybe you both have new flames."

I'm so tired of people pairing me with Dub. Couldn't be further from the truth. We're just friends. Actually we've become really good friends since he's one of the few people I knew before the tour started, and he's been my bridge to befriend the other dancers. I've missed the camaraderie of a dance crew, and he gave that back to me. I'm not telling Randy that. I'm taking the no comment route, just smiling serenely.

As for Rhyson and Petra . . . just the thought of it is like a spiked ball rolling right over my heart, flattening and tearing at the flesh as it goes. Just because he's sending mistletoe to my dressing room at every stop and texting and calling doesn't mean he's not screwing the more-than-willing Russian. On the one hand, wouldn't that make things simple for me? But on the other hand . . . well, I don't have enough hands to hold the hurt that would inflict.

"Nothing to say to that, Kai?" Randy demands in a follow up. "You and Dub a thing?"

Butthole.

"Dub is the most gifted choreographer in the business, and we're lucky to have him on the tour." I sit back, crossing one leg over the other. "That's all there is to it. As for Rhyson and Petra, like I said, we haven't spoken."

"All right, then I got another question for ya." Randy narrows his eyes a little more. "I'm sure you're aware that a lot of people look at your meteoric rise and wonder if you have the talent to back it up."

He pauses to see if I will respond. I don't with any more than a set of raised eyebrows while I wait for his question.

"What would you say to people who think you wouldn't be where you are now if it wasn't for Rhyson Gray?"

Luke clears his throat and begins to speak before I can.

"I think Kai—"

"It's okay, Luke," I hold up a hand, eyes never leaving Randy's. "I'd love to answer this question."

I lick my suddenly dry lips before going in.

"I would tell them that no one finds success without the help of others along the way." I look down at the hands in my lap for a second before looking back up. "I wouldn't be here without my mother, who sacrificed all my life to make sure I had dancing and singing lessons. I wouldn't be here without my best friend, Santos, who dragged me out to LA to pursue my dreams. I wouldn't be here without my vocal coach, Grady, who took me under his wing in a strange new city."

I pause, swallowing back unexpected emotion I hope I'm hiding well.

"And, yes, I wouldn't be here without Rhyson, whose music and work ethic inspired me years before I even met him when I was just a fan. So in that sense, they're right."

I lean forward, elbows propped on the table, lips pressed close to the mic like the producer told me to.

"But I would also invite those people out to see me on the road because, though so many have helped me, I'm the one who has to perform night in, night out, and no one does that for me. I'd offer them a ticket, but my shows are all sold out."

Randy's mouth hangs open a little. Guess he thought this little country bumpkin was gonna roll on over under his line of questioning. I wait for his follow up question, but it's Lola who breaks the silence that follows my words.

"Well, um, you've said a lot, Kai, and thanks for sharing." She offers me a smile. "I'm sure you understand the public's fascination with it all since Rhyson's never had a girlfriend that we know of. "

"I get that," I nod, smiling in return. "I do, but he's a very private man. I think it's that space he creates just for himself that fuels him to offer so much to us onstage, so we should let him keep it."

"I can respect that." Lola's eyes hold the interest, the fascination Rhyson effortlessly inspires in people. "But isn't there *one* thing you could tell us that few people know?"

I draw a shallow breath before speaking.

"Yeah. There is one thing." I pause for effect, leaning forward like I'm about to share a secret. Anticipation lights their faces, and they lean forward to catch the inside information I'm about to drop. "He *loves* hummus."

Chapter FOUR

RHYSON

APPARENTLY A SQUIRREL HAS TAKEN UP residence in my mouth. That thick, furry thing moving around in there can't be my tongue. In my current state—stretched out under my piano with a bean bag for a pillow, sledgehammer going in my head, and my eyes blearily barely cracked open against the morning light—I can't come up with a better explanation.

Something pointy nudges between my ribs. What the hell?

"Rhys, get up." Jimmi, one of my best friends since high school and one of the few people who can get into my house, stands over me, hands on her hips and frown firmly on her face. Her boot connects with my stomach again, and I grab her foot.

"You got one more time to jab me with that knife-shoe thing you're wearing." The words scratch in my throat, and I drag myself into a sitting position, bumping my head against the piano.

"Careful," Jimmi says, wincing on my behalf.

Now she tells me.

"What's up, Jim?" I rub at the sore spot on my forehead. "Did you . . . wait, if this is about that song, I'm almost done. I promise it'll be ready by Thursday."

"And what do you think today is?"

"Tuesday?" I ask cautiously, looking around my music room for clues among the instruments shelved and displayed on the walls.

"Gah! *Today* is Thursday." Jimmi cocks one hip, resting her hand there. "And I've been calling you to check on your progress with the song."

She holds up my phone, her expression exasperated.

"This was upstairs on the kitchen counter. Dead."

"I wondered where that was." I run a hand through the hair hanging past my ears and around my neck. God, I need a haircut. And a shave. And a shower. A toothbrush wouldn't hurt.

"Not doing you much good dead." Jimmi tosses the phone to me.

"My charger's here somewhere." I sift through the blanket of music sheets beneath me until I find the small wire. "Here we go."

I drag myself to my feet and plug the phone into the wall, leaving it to charge on top of the piano.

"What's all this?" Jimmi bends, picking up several composition sheets, narrowing her eyes over the notes I barely remember chicken scratching out. "You wrote all these?"

Her eyes wander around the room, taking in the composition paper, napkins, and receipts littering every surface, all covered with music I vaguely remember writing over the last two weeks since I got off tour.

"This is some *Beautiful Mind* shit." Jimmi holds up a napkin to the light to read the song I scrawled there. "Have you been in here drunk? High?"

"Something like that." I squeeze a spot at the back of my neck tight from sleeping on the floor. "Great movie, by the way. Some of Russell Crowe's finest work."

It only took one stint in rehab for me to understand what an addictive personality I have. My gift comes at a price, near obsession. Unchecked, I'm nothing but a wave of extremes. I barely drink alcohol and I never do drugs, so music is my drug of choice. And I've been on a bender ever since I got off tour. Since I came home to this empty house and faced the fact that Kai isn't coming back any time soon.

If ever.

"Is this symphony orchestra stuff?" Jimmi peels at the edges of the music sheet plastered to the wall, a frown puckering her brows. "It won't come off."

"Here, lemme see." I lean forward to rub at the edges, finally barking out a harsh laugh. "Great. It won't come off because I wrote it *on* the wall. Sarita's gonna kill me."

"I'm gonna kill you myself unless one of these songs is mine." Jimmi leans against the piano.

"I got your song, Jim." I kick a few music sheets out of the way, squinting at the floor to see where the hell her song could be. "It's here somewhere."

"Also," Jimmi says, holding one finger under her nose. "You reek."

"You're saying I stink?" I lift my arm to take an investigative sniff. "Hmmm. So *that's* where the smell is coming from."

I take a step in her direction, thrusting a handful of my two-day-old t-shirt into her nose.

"Rhys, stop it!" Jimmi laughs, backing up, stumbling and slipping on the papers under our feet.

"Couldn't resist." I grin, feeling less like microwaved shit than when I woke up. Jimmi and I used to play pranks on each other in high school. She was always good for a laugh. I feared that misbegotten one-night stand on the road had ruined our friendship. I'm glad we still have this.

"Gimme ten." I back out of the room, gesturing to a stack of papers on the piano. "I'm seventy-five percent sure your song is in that pile right there. Look while I take a shower, and then we can head to the studio."

I'm actually more like forty-five percent sure, but that'll keep her busy while I scrub the grunge away. I'm looking and feeling pretty nineties Seattle right now. I rush up the steps and to my bed-room, pausing when I cross the threshold.

That bed.

That cold, empty bed is the reason I've spent the last week of nights under my piano. The sheets, void of Kai's warmth, of the small curvy shape of her body, hold no appeal. The loneliness of that bed chases me into my dreams, and not even in sleep can I escape the fact that she's not here. Kai was in my house just a few weeks, but it only took one night for me to crave her beside me every morning when I wake up.

I leave a trail of dirty clothes on the bathroom floor on my way to the jets of life coming from the showerhead. Rivulets rush over my head and down my body, washing away all my defenses and all my distractions, leaving me nothing to keep my mind off how royally I fucked things up. Nothing to hide this deep, raw, self-inflicted wound that's been bleeding out ever since Kai left LA without a word.

I rest my forehead against the water-slick tile and bang one fist into the wall. All I want is Kai. I miss the way we laughed togeth-er and talked so easily the hours felt like minutes. God, I miss her hot-honey voice and the sweet taste of her. Feeling her moving un-der me, our bodies in perfect synch. I miss being inside of her, feeling the desperate grip of her body around me.

Shit. Now I'm hard and my own hand's the only thing gripping me. I tighten my fingers around my cock, ready to handle this the only way I know how until Kai comes back to me.

"Let me get that for you," Jimmi says at my back, her hand reaching around to hold me tightly.

I jerk away, turning to face her. What the hell? She's in my damn shower wearing nothing but lust and mischief.

"Jimmi, go." I grit the words out, pointing to the opening lead-ing out of the shower. "Now."

"Come on, Rhys."

She reaches for me again, this time stepping closer until our bodies are flush and her naked tits press into my chest. Celibacy isn't exactly a habit for me, so of course my dick gets harder. It's what it *does*. She feels me swelling in her hand and grins up at me.

"Somebody's on my side. Maybe you don't remember much about the night we had together, but your dick sure does."

I don't want her. I don't want this. I've messed things up enough with Kai without adding this to the list of shit she might not forgive me for. I met Jimmi on my first day at the School of the Arts, and we've been through a lot, but she's not worth losing Kai. Nothing is. I shove at her shoulder, maybe harder than I intended because she stumbles back against the wall, almost falling. I grab her arm to steady her, but she captures my hand and drags it to her breast, the nipple pressing into my palm.

"Nothing's holding you back, Rhys," she whispers so low I barely hear it over the water.

I jerk my hand away and step out of the shower. If she won't go, I will. I grab a towel and tie it around my hips before turning to face her. She's still standing under the spray of water darkening her hair. She runs her fingers over her breasts and slides them down her stomach to stroke between her legs.

"Rhyson, come on." Jimmi drops her head back, heavily-lidded eyes snaring mine through the rising steam. "You want me to handle this myself?"

"That's up to you." I turn away from this scene before my body does something every other part of me will regret. "Be downstairs in five minutes ready to get outta here, or you get no song from me."

I stalk off to my closet, quickly snagging briefs, jeans and a t-shirt. When I come back through to brush my teeth, Jimmi's gone. A relieved breath pushes from my chest. This is beyond awkward. I feel sick, nauseated by the memory of her touching me, of her breast under my hand. I would never cheat on Kai, but do I tell her what just happened? Does it matter? Would she care? Is it cheating when she won't even return my calls? I could even rationalize that technically Kai walked out on me and ended things, but there's no rationalizing with my heart that insists she's *it*, and no one else has the right to touch me. If she were in a shower naked with some other guy who touched her like that, I wouldn't care if we'd been apart for two months or two years. I'd dice him into microscopic chunks, and fuck Kai blind until her body remembered nothing but me.

The closer I get to the music room, the slower my steps become. I don't want to have this conversation with Jimmi. Actually, we've had this conversation before, but it didn't take. I need it to take. I need for what just happened upstairs to never happen again, or I'll have to cut her out of my life as ruthlessly as I cut out my parents.

Here's the problem. And to say it aloud sounds dickish, so I'll just say it to myself. Marlon's Uncle Jamal put it best. I think he's the one who got my best friend categorizing pussy in the first place. Uncle Jamal is the OG. Compton's original arbiter of pussy. He said most girls think they have that magic pussy, but one day you meet that *one* girl who makes you realize just how basic everyone else has been. And that's Kai. And it wasn't even the pussy. It was a look. It was her laugh. It was the way she smells. The way she carries herself. The way she cares about people . . . about me. The way she works hard and expects only what she earns. It's a dozen things about her that make her *not* basic. She was Taj Mahal before I even slept with her. I knew she wasn't basic. I knew she would shatter my world and I'd never be the same. And that's what happened. And maybe I fucked it up, but I'm gonna fix it.

And there's no way I'm explaining that I slipped and fell into some basic pussy while she was on tour.

So how do you tell one of your best friends she's just basic?

Jimmi looks up from the piano, elbows resting on the closed top, and holds a sheet of music up in the air.

"Found my song." She glances away, chewing at her bottom lip, wet hair hanging around her shoulders and dampening her t-shirt. "Look about what happened up there, I—"

"Let's just forget it, okay?" I grab the paper from her hands, giving it a quick once over. "Yeah, this is it. Let's go."

"I don't want to forget it." Jimmi plants her hands on the piano, meeting my eyes boldly. "I've told you that before. That night happened, and we can't pretend it didn't."

"I didn't say pretend." I sit down on the piano bench, bracing myself for the conversation I was hoping to get out of one more time. "I said forget. There's nothing there, Jimmi."

"Your dick was hard." Her smile holds some satisfaction. "I know when a guy wants me."

"That's right, I'm a guy." I nod, a self-deprecating laugh escaping. "A swift wind gets me hard. It doesn't mean anything. My heart's nowhere near it."

"Oh, and where is your heart?" She reaches in her jeans pocket and pulls out a small harmonica that she's got no right touching. "Here?"

I stand, snatching the harmonica out of her hands, gripping it between my fingers.

"Keep your hands off my shit, Jim."

"I read the inscription. I know it's from Kai."

"Oh, and she reads, too. Gold star for you."

I glance at the harmonica Kai gave me for Christmas, just a few months ago. It feels like an eternity. I'd never even made love to her when she gave me this, but I was certain we'd be connected deeply and forever.

"She's moved on, you know." Jimmi takes my spot on the piano bench.

"You don't know what the hell you're talking about." I slip the harmonica into my back pocket and start walking toward the door. "If you want that studio time, come on."

"I take it you haven't been on Kai's Instagram lately, huh?" Jimmi asks from her spot behind my favorite piano.

"Did I *look* like I've been on Instagram?" I turn back to face her. "Kai doesn't even have it."

"Tell that to the quarter million people following her."

"A quarter million . . . a quarter *million* followers?" I frown and freeze in my tracks. "In two months?"

"The world's a big place with a lot of people. Doesn't take long." Jimmi rolls her eyes. "And I'm sure most of them are following her hoping she'll post about you. Hoping she'll post something about that disaster of a relationship you guys had."

She unplugs my phone and walks it over to me.

"Check for yourself."

"I don't even have it on my phone." I shake my head. "And I really don't care what social media has to say about Kai and me."

"Oh, so you don't care that Dub is all over Kai's Instagram?" Jimmi pulls out her phone, pressing a few keys and pulling up the app. "I guess you don't want to see?"

I hate myself for this weakness I can't hide from Jimmi. I hold my hand out for her phone, bracing my inner idiot not to flip about what I'm about to see.

Shit. It's not working. That metronome of fury ticks in my head. Blood pounds in my ears and sweat sprouts out all over my freshly-showered body.

Dub and Kai at some carnival. A cream-colored beanie stark against her dark hair, tilted eyes bright and a red-tinted smile on her face.

Dub and Kai at a 7-Eleven drinking Slurpees with their crew of dancers, hamming it up and making faces.

A video of Dub and Kai at rehearsals, his hands at her waist, adjusting her execution of a move.

Fuck. Fuck. Fuck.

I can't fake nonchalance. Rage pebbles under my skin, buckling my straight face. Jimmi watches me too closely not to see, but I can't look away from this screen. I can't give the phone back to her. This is the closest I've come to Kai in two months, and she's with this motherfucker in every post.

"Like I said, moved on." Jimmi takes her phone from my clenched hand, pushing her fingers up into my hair. "So there's nothing holding us back, Rhys."

I step back, jerking away from her touch.

"This not happening," I gesture between her and me, "has nothing to do with Kai."

Jimmi gives me a look that calls BS.

"I mean, yeah. There's Kai." I sit down on the bench, preferring to look at the phone flipping back and forth in my hands to looking at Jimmi. "But even if she weren't in the picture, what happened between you and me was a mistake. I knew that the morning after. Hell, I knew it before it happened. But me plus Ketel One equals bad decisions."

"It hurts that what was so special to me was a mistake to you." Jimmi blinks at tears. "It wasn't the first time I'd thought about it. I've been crushing on you since high school, Rhys."

I blow out a weary breath.

"Jimmi, you're great." I look her straight in the eye. She deserves my frankness. "You know that. You know I think that, but I'm not the one for you."

"And she's the one for you?" Jimmi turns her phone to me, the screen still splattered with tiles of Kai and Dub. "Maybe she missed that memo."

I clamp my lips over an expletive. I know Kai. She wouldn't do that to me. Even with things the way they are between us, I refuse to believe someone else has been inside of her. I refuse to believe someone else has her heart. But I also know she's oblivious sometimes when it comes to guys. What they want and how they go about getting it.

Before I can respond to Jimmi's provocation, Bristol walks in. She flicks a look between Jimmi and me, and a frown dents her forehead.

"Hey, guys." She sits on the couch and crosses her long legs. "You working on the song?"

"Don't you have a life of your own to tend to?" I cross over to flop beside her on the couch, tugging at the dark hair she has pulled into a sleek ponytail. "Or do you basically just obsess over every detail of mine?"

"It's what you pay me the big bucks for, brother." She grins at Jimmi. "And now I can obsess over Jimmi's, too."

"For real?" I stretch my eyebrows up, glad to have something to talk to Jimmi about other than her misplaced and ill-fated desire for me. "You crossing over to the dark side, Jim?"

Jimmi smiles, but it barely takes.

"On my way to world domination. Got things in the works for her already," Bristol says, a quick grin spreading over her face. "Speaking of which, did you look at those offers I sent over, Rhys? Those artists who want to work with you?"

"Dammit." I snap my fingers. "I keep forgetting to give a fuck."

"Rhys." Bristol laughs and shakes her head. "One of them could be the next big thing."

"I'd rather have a great thing than a big thing. I want to be *interested*. Give me something interesting."

"Do the Boston Pops interest you?"

Hmmmm . . . She knows they do.

"Whatchya got?" I give her the satisfaction of asking.

"The Boston Pops called."

"Let me guess." My interest starts waning. "They want me and Petra to bring our dancing bear act to Boston."

"Actually they just want you. As a guest pianist next season." She pauses for effect, one brow lifted to provoke me. "Think you still got it, brother?"

Something flickers inside of me that has lain dormant for a long time. I glance at the symphony orchestra piece I sketched onto the wall. That might be fun. That might interest me.

"Let me think about it."

"Of course. I told them you'd need some time to consider." Bristol pulls the hair hanging around my ears and scrapes at the scruff on my jaw. "Btdubs, you look like Grizzly Adams."

"You should have smelled him." Jimmi offers her first natural smile since Showergate.

"That's what you get for sniffing under my piano." I laugh a little, hoping the air will keep loosening between us.

"True that." Jimmi leans back and watches me for a minute before giving me a short nod. "It won't happen again."

I guess that's the closest she'll come to conceding the point for now. Hopefully she won't be naked and groping me in my shower any time soon.

"So what's the deal with you guys?" Bristol asks, predictably nosy. "You both have wet hair, and the vibe was all weird when I came in. So are my two megastar clients fighting, fucking, or both?"

Jimmi and I exchange a quick look. Bristol is mulish. She won't let up until we give her something.

"Just a difference of opinion," I say with a shrug.

"About?" Bristol persists.

See? Mule.

"If you must know." A speck of defiance returns to Jimmi's eyes. "I was trying to convince Rhys that Kai has moved on."

"But you don't believe it?" Bristol shifts enough to see my face clearly.

"No, I don't." I shake my head. "Definitely not with Dub."

"Well, she said as much yesterday when she and Luke were on *Morning Hype.*"

Calm the hell down, Gray.

"Kai said she and Dub are together?" My voice somehow sounds strong, but it feels like little more than a breeze in my throat.

Bristol just stares at me for a few elongated seconds like a beast toying with its food before taking the first bite.

"Don't lose a lung. She said the opposite, actually." Bristol's eyes never leave my face. "She said she and Dub are just friends. Who knows the truth?"

I do. She's not with that dude. She can't be. It would break me in half to see her with someone else, especially knowing I'm the one who pushed her there.

"They asked her about you, too." Bristol says.

We're not your typical twins, all telepathically connected and shit, but Bristol knows me well enough to figure I'm not sure I want to hear Kai's response. I nod for her to go ahead and tell it.

"They asked if she'd spoken to you, and she said no." Bristol laughs a little, something as close as she'll come to admiration on her face. "They pressed her for more intel, but she didn't budge. When they asked for a big secret of yours, she told them you like hummus."

I can't help but chuckle. God, I miss my girl. I'd eat a bowlful of her hummus that tastes like butt if I could see her. Maybe she lied to the radio host and she is seeing Dub. I don't know. Doesn't matter. If she is seeing him, that shit ends as soon as she gets home. She'll forgive me and we'll go back to normal. We have to. That's the only option.

"You should listen to the whole thing online. Fascinating interview. She held her own." Bristol's smug smile gives me pause. "She also directed Qwest to reach out to me about working with Grip."

"But you're not Marlon's manager." I lift one brow. "I wasn't under the piano that long. You're not repping him yet, are you?"

"Ah, the operative word being 'yet.'" Bristol leans back and links her hands behind her head. "He loves Qwest. If I bring her to the table, maybe he'll reconsider."

It's not gonna happen, but I just nod. The only thing Marlon wants from Bristol is a date, and it's the one thing she won't give him. So . . . impasse. I'll let them work it out. I'm trying to salvage my own relationship. I can't be bothered with theirs.

"So you guys are cool?" Bristol bounces a look from me to Jimmi, her sharp eyes not missing a thing.

"Cool as three Fonzies," I say.

Both girls give me blank faces.

"Come on." I look between them. "You know. Cool like three little Fonzies."

"Saying it again doesn't make it less obscure," Bristol says. "We still have no idea what you're talking about."

"*Pulp Fiction*." I check both their expressions for some recognition. Nada. "It's near the end. They're in the diner during the stick up, and the girlfriend comes out of the bathroom and pulls a gun. Samuel Jackson says we're gonna be cool like three little Fonzies."

"I've never actually watched *Pulp Fiction* all the way through," Jimmi admits.

"You've never . . ." I re-order my world to accommodate having friends who haven't seen *Pulp Fiction*. "Never?"

"Never, Tarantino." Bristol stands. "Come on. You both need to get to the studio."

I let the girls walk up the steps ahead of me, slowing until I'm standing still, holding my newly charged phone. There's dozens of missed calls and text messages from everyone except the one person I'd give anything to hear from. Supposedly the definition of insanity is doing the same thing over and over again and expecting different results. Even knowing this, I do what I've done almost every day for the last fifty-seven days. Send a text to Kai that will probably get deleted or ignored, but I have to try. To keep trying until she's back in that bed, warming my sheets again.

> Me: *"That's when you know you've found somebody really special. When you can just shut the fuck up for a minute and comfortably share silence."*

I send the movie quote and stare at the screen, but it remains stubbornly

mute. No beeping alert. No trail of bubbles telling me she's responding. I hold the phone for a few more seconds, fooling myself that we're sharing one of those silences between people who are special to each other, instead of the frigid wall of nothingness she's used to freeze me out for the last two months. It doesn't really matter. Even if she deletes every message, she'll know I never stop trying. This is just a pause, a comma, but our relationship runs on.

I'm digging around in my pocket for the keys to the Cayenne when the phone beeps. I know it's probably just weird timing. Probably Marlon texting me a picture of him riding his new Segway or some shit, but my heart still grinds to a halt in my chest at the possibility . . .

Pepper: "Pulp Fiction." Come harder, Gray.

Fuck me sideways. It's Kai.

Is there a guidebook for this conversation? I've proven that I'm really good at screwing things up badly. I medaled in it. After two months of text messages, voice mails, and mistletoe, I have no idea why it's Quentin Tarrantino that convinced her to finally respond. The phone rests in my hand like a bomb with a convolution of rainbow wires. Blue? Yellow? Red? Which wire to cut? What do I say? I should probably not come on too strong. Shouldn't ask her about Dub, even though the pictures on that Instagram account splatter in my head like brains blown onto the wall. I for sure shouldn't demand that she come home to me as soon as she steps off that damn tour bus. Just play it cool like this isn't twisting my stomach into roller coaster loops.

Do something, Gray. Say something, you pussy.

Me: I want to hear your voice. Call me.

Dammit, did that sound like an order? That'd be the last thing I'm in a position to give after I went all Captain Control Freak with her career. That was the wrong thing to say, obviously, since I stand at the door for a full minute holding a quiet phone.

"You coming, or what?" Bristol yells from behind the wheel of her Audi convertible in the circular driveway. "Jimmi's already on her way."

May as well lose myself in music again. It's the only thing that's gotten me through the last two months. I may not know what day it is, but I know I made it through one more day without her. Music is all I have right now. It's not all I want, but it's all I have. I lock up, climbing into the truck as Bristol pulls away.

Disappointment cements into the resolve I somehow find every day to send another message, knowing I'll get the same response.

Nothing.

I'm adjusting my mirror ready to pull out of the driveway, when I'll be damned if the phone doesn't ring.

Chapter FIVE

Kai

"PEP?"

The silence puddles over the phone between us like water, waiting for me to dive in. It's a plunge I can't un-take. Once I make contact with Rhyson, that chain linking our hearts, the one I've spent the last two months figuring out how to break, only tightens.

"Pep, you there?" It's in his voice. The same ache, the same need, the same desperation that compelled me to answer his text today. To finally surrender to the pull I've resisted since I left LA. Since I left him. And just the sound of his voice reminds me of what we had, makes me want to find a way to save it, even though right now I'm not sure how.

"Yeah, I'm here." I take a few steps away from the stage, putting some distance between this conversation and any possible eavesdroppers.

"So . . . I heard you've been sharing State secrets," he says, forcing some humor into the conversation.

"What?" Panic overtakes me for just a moment. Irrationally, the word "secrets" sets off an alarm system all over my body. I immediately think of the sex tape and my blackmailer. "What secrets? What-what do you mean?"

"Relax." Rhyson chuckles at the other end. "The radio show yesterday. Telling the whole world I love hummus. What'd you think I meant?"

Relief drains the tension away, and I slump against a wall backstage. Just the thought that someone got to Rhyson with that tape, that he saw me with Drex that way . . . I can't even speak for a minute.

"Kai, you still there?" Uncharacteristic uncertainty colors Rhyson's voice on the other end.

"Yeah, um yeah. Just came backstage to talk."

"I can't believe you called. I wish I'd known all it took was Tarantino."

Despite the tension that has me gripping the phone like a lifeline, I have to smile just a bit. He sent one of my favorite lines from *Pulp Fiction*. It *would* be a film with grit and blood and Samuel Jackson that reconnected us.

"What made you finally call?" he asks.

Because I'm a fool. Because I miss you. Because . . .

"Because you asked me to."

"And that's it?" Tamped-down frustration creeps into his voice. "So me texting and calling for the last two months didn't let you know I'd like to hear your voice?"

"I just . . . I guess it was time."

"Past time, Pep. We need to talk. We've *needed* to talk."

"Yeah. I know." I notice a stagehand clearing some props away and I take a few more steps back. "Things are crazy right now, though. I'm in the middle of a rehearsal. We're on break, so I can't talk long. I picked a bad time to call."

"You picked the perfect time to call, even if it's for just a few minutes. I'll take it."

"Well, like I said, we're in rehearsal." I hesitate before plowing on, completely unsure of the words that will come out. "I know we have a lot to talk through, but things are hectic on the road."

"I'll come to you." He keeps his voice soft, but I know Rhyson too well not to hear the steel determination behind it. He's not dropping this. Me calling gave him an inch. He's fully prepared to take a mile.

"Rhys, I'm all the way across the country."

"Chicago is only halfway across the country."

I'm not surprised he knows exactly where I am. There's a trail of mistletoe dotting my tour schedule that says as much. There was mistletoe last night in New York. I'm sure there will be some waiting for me in my dressing room tonight.

"Thanks for the mistletoe, by the way."

"Hey, it worked for your Pops with Grams." He releases a laugh that on anyone else would sound nervous. "I figured . . ."

He trails off, and the silence between us remains uncertain. Neither of us knows where to step next. A real conversation between us could be a patch of briars and thorns. I'm certainly not going to be the one taking the next step. I'm not sure I should have taken this one.

"I fucked up," he finally says. "I know that, Pep."

A fresh wave of hurt and humiliation washes over me as I remember crying in his arms on his pool table after *Total Package* passed on me. As I remember standing in the wings watching Rhyson perform while John Malcolm told me how my boyfriend had betrayed me. I felt like a fool. As much as missing him compelled me to answer that text, hurt still holds parts of me back.

"Yeah, ya did." I choke out. "That's an understatement."

"I know I said it in my text and on a dozen voice mails, but I'm sorry. Baby, you've gotta know how sorry I am."

"I know, Rhys, I just . . . what you did, it was one of the most hurtful things anyone has *ever* done to me."

"I thought I was doing what was best. I know now I should have handled it differently, but we've gotta get past this. I can't undo it. It's behind us, so there's only forward. We have to figure out forward."

"There's a lot to figure out." I shake my head even though he can't see me. "It won't be easy."

"What are you saying, Pep?" His voice lowers and hardens, and I see how easily this could become a fight.

"I'm just saying the hurt doesn't simply disappear. The issues behind what you did don't just go away. Don't make assumptions, Rhys."

"What exactly do you think I'm assuming?" He doesn't check his frustration before it leaks through. "That you'll still love me even though I screwed up? 'Cause, yeah. My bad. I did assume that."

"Love's not our problem. It takes more than love, Rhyson."

"Since when?"

"Since always. There's lots of people who love each other and don't make it because it's not enough."

"Well, I feel sorry for those people. We're not them."

"We're no different."

"We're no different? Oh, so their private arguments are put on blast for millions of people on TMZ? These people that we're just like, they have to disguise themselves just to hang out with their girl-friends, too? They face the same pressures we do?"

"That's not what I meant, and you know it."

"What I know is that I'm fine with not being these people who think love isn't enough. Whatever it is that gives me the capacity to do what I do, to manage this impossible life I live, it makes me all kinds of not normal. And I'm fine with the fact that I love you in a way that isn't normal. I love you so hard and so much that it makes me do dumb shit sometimes. I just need you to forgive me when that happens because I don't know another way."

He draws a quick, shallow breath.

"Baby, I don't know another way, and I need you to tell me I can come to you. That we'll work this out because the prospect of not having you . . ."

The very real possibility that we might not overcome it all thickens between us across the miles like quicksand, and I feel us sinking. Maybe he does, too.

"Shit, Pep." His voice shakes a little and it unravels my resolve and my anger and anything that would hold me back from him. I want to comfort him even though I'm the one causing his pain. Even though he's the one who caused mine. "Tell me what I have to do to make this right and I will. Just tell me when you come back, it'll be to me. I *need* to know that."

"Rhys, I . . . we . . ." The emotion soaking his voice short circuits my thoughts, and I can't form words. It doesn't help to have Dub barreling toward me from the stage, sporting a wide grin. As soon as he gets close enough he dips at my waist and hauls me up and over his shoulder. My legs dangle across his chest and I almost drop the phone.

"Dub, I'm on the phone," I screech, banging lightly on his back. He always does this, but it's the absolute worst time for his horseplay, as Aunt Ruthie used to call it.

He gently lowers me to the floor, the shock of platinum hair bright against the rich caramel of his skin.

"Sorry." He grins and holds up two fingers. "We're back in two minutes. Get that fine little ass of yours onstage so we can run through that last number."

"Okay." My answering smile is stiff and unnatural because I know as soon as he walks away, I've got a mess to clean up. "I'll be right there."

The silence on the other end of the phone weighs about two tons. So heavy I'm not sure how to move it, how to break it.

"Rhys, I—"

"What the fuck was that?" Anger powers Rhyson's words across the distance, and I feel it like he's standing right here, scowling at me.

"Um, well . . ."

"Don't 'um well' me, Pep. What's happening on the road? I will crush him. You know that, right? If he touches you, I'll have his Irish ass on a boat back home before he knows what hit him. I didn't believe the rumors about Dub because I know you wouldn't do that to me, but if you've let that motherfucker touch you—"

"Then what?" I fire back, finding my own anger. "You'll do what? You did this, Rhys. You're the one who broke us, and we aren't together. That's what I'm telling you. We aren't mended. We aren't *fixed*, and we have things to work out."

"The hell we aren't together. Even when we're apart we're together," he says. "I'm all for mending and fixing and whatever shit you think it takes to get us back, but in the meantime he *does not touch you*."

I don't answer. Not because I want to deliberately torture him the way the thought of him with Petra or some groupie has tortured me for the last two months, but because I don't know what to say. Our first conversation has blown up in my face, and I'll be picking shrapnel out of my heart for the next two days. Somehow I thought just hearing his voice would make it better. Would make it right, but it won't happen that way. And I'm so afraid the next thing I say will only make things more wrong between us that I don't say anything at all.

"Pep, have you and Dub . . ." Rhyson draws and releases a stuttering breath. "Has he . . . did you let him?"

How could I when all I've thought about is Rhyson? Can I forgive him? Who's blackmailing me? How will I resolve this without Rhyson ever finding out? Will it even matter if we can't fix what's broken between us? It's a never-ending equation of x's and y's, and nothing adds up, but I know I don't want anyone else.

"No."

Relieved air rushes at me across the line, and I envision Rhyson, eyes closed, hand wandering over his face and through his wild hair.

"I'm coming to Chicago."

"We're leaving Chicago tonight after the show." I nod at Dub who waves me over to the circle of back-up dancers assembled center stage. "I gotta go."

"You're in Cincinnati tomorrow and Detroit the next night. Should I go on? I'm coming to wherever you are."

"Don't." The dancers line up for Dub's run-through. "I really have to go. I have a show tonight, and I need to focus."

"And what? We just go back to not talking? To not resolving this?"

"Rhys, I think we—"

"I'm coming so we can hash this out."

"No, you're not." I turn my back on the stage, holding my hand over my ear to block out the music that just started. "Can I just have this? Can I just do my job and prove to everyone that I'm more than just Rhyson Gray's ex-girlfriend from that viral video?"

"You're not my ex. You're my always."

Damn him for saying things like that when I need to hold on to this anger long enough to get me through this tour and to the bottom of why he did what he did. Long enough to make sure he never does it again.

"I'll be home for a few days next week, but I'm sure you know that." I don't wait for him to confirm or deny. "I'll see you at Grady's wedding. It worked out perfectly that it fell during my break."

"You actually think that was a coincidence?" His voice lightens.

"You didn't make him have his wedding when I'd be home, did you?"

"No, but he did ask me when you had a break." I can almost see him shrugging those broad shoulders of his. "I told him. He and Em wanted you there, so it was an easy call."

"It was quick. They weren't even engaged when I left and already a wedding."

"I guess when you know you know." Rhyson pauses. "Will we talk before the wedding?"

"I think it's best if we don't."

Please don't push. Please don't push. Please don't push.

Between Rhyson's dogged determination and my weakness for him, if he pushes, he'll be in my bed tomorrow night in Cincinnati. And all the issues we need to settle will bow to the power of the pull that breathes between us.

"Okay." That one word sounds like it's wrung from his lips, and I know it's taking everything in him to let me have my way. "If that's how you want it. I'll see you at the wedding."

"Kai! *Now*, sweetheart," Dub yells from stage, his slight frown telling me he's feeling less playful the closer we get to show time.

"Sweetheart?" Rhyson says it like a curse from the other end.

"I gotta go."

"Remember what I said about that overgrown breakdancer keeping his hands to himself."

"Rhys, I really have to go."

"You're not leaving that wedding without talking to me."

"I know. Gotta go."

"Pep, wait."

I clutch the phone, knowing I should just hang up, but feeling tethered to his voice as long as it's on the other end.

"I live you." His voice is a deliberate caress over the three words.

Those words, *our words*, slip right under the armor I've been wearing to keep him out as long as I can. Saying it back will unlock a door between us that I'm not ready to walk through.

"Did you hear me?" He knows it. He understands the power those words carry. He wants me to say it so he feels like we're on our way back to normal. But our version of normal is what got us here in the first place, so I don't give him those words. I can't. Not yet.

"I gotta go," I say.

And hang up.

Chapter SIX

Kai

"YOU READY FOR THIS?" SAN FLICKS a quick glance from the road to me in the passenger seat.

"Of course. You know I love weddings." I stroke the ribbon on the gift in my lap, avoiding San's eyes. "And I love Grady and Em."

"You didn't answer the *real* question." San gives me a wry look. "Are you ready to see Rhyson?"

There are things we need to get straight. Things we need to fix. Our last conversation wasn't great. I've been angry at him. He's been frustrated with me. But I know we still love each other. That chain still linking our hearts tells me that. But what do I want to do about it? I've spent the last two months sorting through this pile of hurt, seeing if I can get past it and back to him. And even if I can, how am I going to be with him and keep that tape from coming out?

"Kai?" San presses.

"Yeah, I heard you," I answer. "Even if we can work things out, there's still the tape."

My eyes wander to the gorgeous ocean view alongside this

narrow, curving road, not really seeing it. Too caught up in what, or rather who, waits for me at Grady's wedding.

"I still have no idea who's behind that video. I assume Drex is connected to it, but why the anonymous text?" I clamp the inside of my jaw between my teeth. "Until we get to the bottom of it, find that video, convince them to destroy it if I can, I need everyone to at least believe that Rhyson and I are done."

San opens his mouth, and I can already tell by the look in his eyes what he'll say. He wants me to tell Rhyson. We've gone back and forth about this, but I won't budge. God, how can I? Before he gets to make his case again, my phone comes to life in my lap with a text from an unknown number. I swipe to see the full message. A gasp rushes past my lips, and my fingers tremble around the phone. I drop it like it's on fire and it falls by my feet.

"Oh my God," I whisper, my hand covering my mouth to catch the words. "He released the tape."

"What?" San's eyes swing away from the twisting road to search my face. The truck swings dangerously close to the edge. "Shit."

He pulls off to the narrow shoulder, kills the engine and un-snaps his seat belt, reaching to the floor to retrieve my phone.

If you can be numb and electrified all at once, I am. Every cell of my body buzzes with shock even as shame numbs me piece by piece, a slow, steady creep until I can't feel my fingers or toes. But I feel my heart, and it throbs as if it's suffered a blow. I don't even think about the millions of people who will now see that tape. I can only think of one. I can only think of Rhyson.

"Kai, I don't think . . ." San's forehead furrows as he considers the phone screen. Irritation presses his lips together. "He's fucking with you. It's not real."

"What?" The question dies on my lips when he turns the phone for me to look again.

The picture hasn't changed. It's a still of the tape, my face clear-ly visible, Drex leering over my back and shoulders. There's a post accompanying it, the headline proclaiming "Rising Star, Rhyson's Ex, Caught In The Act!"

Seeing it, reading it a second time only turns my stomach more, and I reach for the door handle because I think I need to puke. I'll dump what little is in my stomach right here in the dirt of this oceanside road.

"Look closer." San tosses the phone to my lap. "Actually read it."

I cautiously pick up the phone and scan the graphic and post again. The picture is exactly what I thought it was—me and Drex in the most compromising position imaginable. But the post, when I read it, is just gibberish. Letters thrown together and making no actual words. I'm still processing what this means when a second text comes over.

> Unknown: This could so easily be real. Remember that when you see Rhyson at the wedding today. Remember what I said. It's over between you two, or this goes LIVE.

Before I think better of it, my fingers zoom over the keys.

> Me: Drex, is this you? Why are you doing this? I need to talk to you. Please.

I call the number, but it just rings. No voice mail. No answer. Nothing.

I hold the phone, waiting for it to vibrate in my hand with a response, an explanation, anything that will help this make sense and show me how to make it all go away. San and I sit there on the side of the road for minutes, quiet and waiting, but apparently my black-mailer is done tormenting me for now.

"Just tell Rhys." Concern weights the look San gives me. "That takes all the power away from this son of a bitch."

"Are you out of your ever-loving mind?" I turn as far as my seat belt will allow to face him, back pressed to the door. "This isn't some game, San. This is my life. My relationship, if I can still salvage it. My reputation. Rhyson can't *ever* see that video. No one can. I only told you because I knew you were the only one I could trust to help me."

"I know, but I remember the way Rhys was the night of the

fight. The night you left. The guy was . . . despondent. He loves you. He wouldn't let something like that from your past ruin your future together."

"And you didn't see his face when I tried to tell him everything about that night with Drex. He couldn't hear it. He said the only reason he can get past it is because he doesn't know the details." I hold up the phone with the trashy still splattered over the screen. "And doesn't ever want to."

"Yeah, he cut me off when I tried to explain, too."

"See! If he can't even *hear* about me being with Drex, imagine him watching . . ." The image of Drex pounding into me from behind invades my mind, his grunts and gasps stinging my ears. "Oh, God. If Rhyson sees that tape, I don't know if he can get past it. He and Drex hate each other so much."

"Speaking of which, there's still no sign of Drex. It's like he's disappeared into thin air. He's not anywhere. He's even sublet his apartment." San gives me a quick apologetic glance before starting the engine again. "I'm trying. I've been discreet, but I'm using every resource at my disposal through *Spotted*. It's hard to quietly investigate something like that when it involves two rock stars."

"I'm not a rock star yet." I give a little bark of a laugh. "And I'm not sure I'd classify Drex as one, either."

"Well, he's famous enough, and between your relationship with Rhys and the tour, now so are you. If I poke around too much, and the wrong people get a whiff of it, they'll go digging and maybe figure things out before we do. And that you don't want."

No, *that* I can't have.

"How does he just disappear?" I knot my hands in my lap. "He may not be an A-lister, but he *is* a celebrity. No sightings of him? Nothing? We have to find him, San. I need to talk to him. He has to want something else. Just Rhyson and me not being together? It doesn't make sense."

"And why the anonymity of the text message from some burner phone when he's obviously involved?"

"Did your guys find out anything from the cell number?"

"It's in the name of some corporation that, as far as we can tell," San says, sparing me a quick glance, "doesn't really exist. I mean, on paper it does, but nothing that has lead us to a real person once you sort through the maze of paperwork covering up the identity. No apparent link to Drex that I've found."

I swallow the fear that churns in my belly, rises past my chest, and splashes into my throat when I think of the threats.

"If he wants to blackmail you, he's not being very stealth about it. He's the obvious person to have that video, since he made it and would presumably have access that no one else would." San shakes his head, dark brows squeezed together in a frown. "And then he disappears right after you receive the threat."

"I have no idea what he's thinking." I glance out the window, taking in the ocean bordering the winding road. "I just know he's making my already complicated situation with Rhyson that much harder."

"I hear ya about Rhyson not getting past it, but I think you're wrong." San takes one hand off the wheel to grab mine even though his eyes don't leave the road. "You should trust him."

"Trust?" I blow my anxiety out in a long puff of air. "That's the one thing we don't have a lot of right now after what he did."

"Well, you can't say he hasn't been trying to make up for it. You've been ignoring him for two months."

"I couldn't deal." Though none of it is funny, a laugh breezes past my lips. "Between the demands of the tour and the huge learning curve, and being threatened with a sex tape, I just couldn't deal with everything. My time on tour was the best thing for us, I think, though I know he doesn't agree. I wasn't ready."

"And now?" San asks.

"I miss him. You know I do." I close my eyes tightly. "I love him. It would be a lot to work through under normal circumstances. This tape only makes it harder."

"And you won't even consider telling him about it?"

The question reminds me of that loose end I have to tie up before I can be with Rhyson, free and clear and out in the open. The loose end that is on my phone, coiling in my lap like a noose. If I can keep him from ever seeing that sex tape, I will. I have to try. Because what if that tape, not our fight, is the very thing that makes me lose him for good?

"Let's keep trying this my way for now and see what we find."

San goes quiet, still not looking convinced that my way is the right way when we pull up to the venue, formerly a private estate that now hosts weddings and other events. The cream-colored lime-stone house with its circular steps and wide veranda welcome us as warmly as the wedding hostesses.

San hands the keys to his shiny new Tahoe over to the valet. Steady work at *Spotted* is paying off. We've both moved up fast in the world. He's even in a new apartment downtown, where I'm crashing for my one week off tour. I'll figure out living arrangements when I'm done in another month. Maybe by then, I'll have the whole video problem solved. Maybe by then I'll have the whole Rhyson problem solved, too.

My problem is standing in the slab-stoned foyer where guests gather as they wait to be ushered into the backyard. Rhys wears a dark suit and a sky blue tie, eyes dark and intense and set on me, wait-ing for me. I could never forget the pewter eyes that barrel through my defenses, or the hair, dark but dappled with deep copper streaks, or the beautifully rugged symmetry of his features. I didn't forget, but everything about him impacts me like it's the first time, trapping the breath in my throat. Our eyes haven't even met yet, and I already feel the tug of that chain. I was a fool to underestimate this pull. It's only now that he's within touching distance that I realize how foolish I was to think I could resist him.

He steps into my path so there's no avoiding him, his eyes lick-ing heat over my body in the periwinkle dress molding to my torso, clinging to my arms from shoulder to elbow, and belling out from my waist to stop just above my knees. For a moment, we just stare at one another, drinking in the details until I can't take it another second and free my eyes from his, looking instead at the simple flats on my feet.

"Kai, hey." He flicks a dismissive look at San by my side. "San."

"Rhyson, good to see you." San smirks, standing there when he knows good and doggone well Rhyson wants to talk to me alone. He just pokes Rhys sometimes to watch him jerk. Rhys levels an annoyed look at San.

"Dude, take a walk."

San slides his glance to me, brows raised, silently asking me if it's okay to leave.

"It's fine." I assure him with a smile. "I'll catch up."

San saunters off, finding someone I don't know to chat with a few feet away, leaving Rhyson and me alone. The air charges with every breath we draw, both of us waiting for the other to speak. Rhyson finally goes first.

"I see you still have your guard dog." He frowns over at San before returning his attention to me.

"We've been taking care of each other a long time." I still don't, can't quite fully meet his eyes.

Whatever small talk I thought we might make disintegrates as soon as I brave a glance up at him. The space between our eyes, our bodies, pulses with tension and heat.

"Pep, you've *got* to stop looking at me like that," Rhyson says, voice strung low and tight.

"Like what? I . . ."

He dips his head, looking up from beneath the dark brows in a way that tells me I know exactly how I'm looking at him. Like he's a wall I want to scale and devour everything on the other side of. That's how it feels, assaulting me without warning. The desire to reclaim, repossess him.

"You're looking at me like you wanna get fucked in this foyer," he answers softly.

His husky words set my cheeks on fire, and I lower my eyes so he won't see just how accurate that statement is. Maybe a little time and distance dulled my memory of this connection that vibrates between us like a physical thing exploding onto my senses. Our passion sprinkles across my tongue. Our lust hovers like a torch just shy of my skin. Our love—an ultrasonic boom, out of frequency for everyone but the two of us.

"I-I guess I didn't really think about how it would be seeing you again." I glance up at him once I have my body set to simmer.

"And I haven't been able to think of anything else." His eyes never leave my face, and I can't look away for the life of me. We've trapped each other, and less and less I want to wiggle free.

"It's good to see you," I manage.

"Is it?"

He takes my hand, pulling me subtly closer inch by inch. His thumb brushing over my wrist electrifies the skin, jolting me back to my surroundings. A glance around confirms that several people watch us closely, probably waiting for a replay of the last scene Rhyson and I entertained the world with. Is one of them keeping tabs on me for my blackmailer? Could one of them be . . . *him*? I jerk my hand away, slipping it into the slit pocket of my skirt.

Rhyson stiffens, eyes narrowing.

"So I can't touch you now?"

"It's not that." I step back, allowing myself room to catch my breath and patch my composure back together. "Or maybe it is that, at least not in front of all these people itching to grab their camera phones."

"You're not leaving this wedding without talking to me." He captures my eyes with his. "I can't trust that you'll answer my calls or text me back or see me, and you only have a week off tour."

I glance uneasily at the clusters of wedding guests milling around the spacious foyer.

"I'm not sure, Rhys."

"Well, I am, and I don't care who hears or sees, so if you want to avoid attention, I suggest you listen."

I don't put it past him to make a scene. What if Drex isn't working alone? Whoever sent that mock up knew I was coming to the wedding today. Somehow they know my schedule. The last thing I need is to tip off the crazy person holding that disgusting video over my head. I have to be careful.

"Okay, what are you thinking?" I ask.

"You want to know what I'm thinking right now?" A grin quirks his full lips. "Well, in my mind, you're not wearing any clothes and—"

"Rhyson." I close my eyes, hating the insistent heat flooding my face. "I mean about us . . . talking. What are you thinking?"

"There's my blush." He dusts his knuckles across my cheekbone. Despite the eyes I feel on us, I can't pull back. Finally, his hand falls away. "There's an orchard that borders the yard out back where the ceremony's being held. Through that orchard, on the other side, is an old barn."

"When?" I flick an anxious glance over the small crowd around us, my voice barely reaching a whisper.

"I have all kinds of responsibilities today." A smile softens the firm line of his mouth. "Best man stuff."

He shrugs, running a hand through his hair, longer than I've ever seen it, falling past his neck, riotous, thick and dark. My fingers itch to get in there, to twist into it.

"So the last thing I have to do is the best man toast." His words draw my attention from the affair I'm having with his hair in my head. "After that, slip away to the barn."

My mind catches up to his plan for us to talk. It's reckless. Foolhardy. Any hint that Rhyson and I are together could set off a salacious fire I won't be able to put out. Even standing here with him now so close is dangerous. But seeing him, being so close that his familiar scent lures me to lean in, I hurl caution far to the wind. I'll slip away. I have to.

Before I get the chance to tell him so, Bristol strides over to us, her dark hair up and elegant. Her tall frame sheathed in a dress the same blue as Rhyson's tie.

"Rhys, we need you." She doesn't even look at me or acknowledge my presence. "They want to make sure the piano is still tuned the way you want it. Something about the weather affecting it outdoors."

"Yeah, I need to check that." He looks back to me, eyes intent.

"I'll give you a shout out during the song I'm playing."

I'm used to this by now, so I know he means he'll tug his ear like he usually does during performances.

"You wrote a song for them?" I ask.

He leans in until his breath touches my ear, until his fingers touch my elbow, so his words can touch my heart.

"No, I wrote a song for *you*."

He pulls back, studying the effect his words have on me. I know what he must see. The blush heating my face again. The deep breath lifting my chest. The lashes I drop to hide from him. He sees it all, I'm sure. What he doesn't see, the only thing I can hide is how my heart twists around inside of me. How anticipation speeds my pulse.

"Rhyson, we need to go." Bristol looks at me for the first time. "Hey, Kai, thanks for pointing Qwest my way. Hopefully I can hook her up with Grip."

"Hopefully." I give her a tentative smile. "She seemed sweet."

"Sweet?" Bristol lets out a rough laugh. "Not that I noticed, but she doesn't need to be. Anyway, you'll have to excuse us. We need to get in there."

"After the toast." Rhyson waits for me to confirm.

I nod wordlessly. I've barely lost sight of his broad shoulders in the dark, well-tailored jacket when San rejoins me. I just shake my head, warning him not to ask any questions now. We're ushered through a room where long tables hold wedding gifts. When San and I drop off our gifts, he starts a conversation with a student from one of Grady's music classes. I'm turning away, about to walk through the French doors into the backyard when a slim, cool hand on my arm stops me.

"Kai, so good to see you again," Angela Gray says, her eyes disconcertingly similar to Rhyson's and Bristol's. "I'm glad you could make it."

"You are? I mean . . . yes, ma'am." I lick my lips, hoping I don't say anything to make her like me less than she did the last time we met. "It's good to see you again, too. How's Mr. Gray?"

Angela allows her sculpted brows a tiny frown.

"He had a small setback, or he'd be here today. Open heart surgery recovery can be difficult, and it's only been a few months, but we found an excellent facility here and have been very pleased."

"Rhyson mentioned you were moving to LA." I keep my smile polite. "I hope the transition hasn't complicated Mr. Gray's recovery at all?"

"Oh, no." Angela waves her hand. "Gorgeous weather and finally on better terms with our son, he couldn't be happier."

"I'm glad to hear it."

"And we're coming back together as a family," she says. "Did Rhyson tell you we may be starting family counseling soon?"

"Oh, we haven't . . ." I reach up to touch the nameplate necklace Rhyson gave me out of habit, but it's not there, so my hands drop to my sides. "Rhyson and I aren't together anymore, Mrs. Gray. I thought you knew."

Surely everyone knows after that video.

"Yes, I knew." Something that is probably the closest she can come to sympathy enters her eyes. "I just assumed . . . well, the two of you seemed to be friends even before you were . . . more, so I wasn't sure if you still talk."

"We were." I look around to find San still deep in conversation. "We are. It's just . . . complicated."

"Believe me. I know how difficult Rhyson can be."

"He's not difficult." I blurt the defense before I can stop it. "I mean, he's complex, yes, but not difficult. At least I wouldn't say so."

"I see you still have feelings for him." She pulls her thin lips into a matte red moue.

I smooth the belled skirt of my dress, running my fingers over the raised flowers embroidered into the material. Caution slows my response. There's nothing maternal about Angela Gray. If anything I hate how she's hurt Rhyson in the past. She's the one who got him hooked on prescription drugs when he was still just a boy so he could perform under pressure. She doesn't trust me with her son, and I certainly don't trust her with him.

"Let's just say Rhyson's not an easy guy to get over." I look up from my skirt and offer a smile that tells her nothing more.

She pats my hand, that supposed sympathy evident in her eyes again.

"I'm sure you'll manage, dear. There's someone out there for you."

The thought of being with anyone other than Rhyson nauseates me, but I just wax a smile onto my face. I wish she'd rip away the thin layer of pleasantry and voice what is so apparent beneath her polite smiles and condescending words. I wish she'd just say I'm not good enough for her son. That someone like Petra is better suited, is her preference. But she's not prepared to be that sincere at her brother-in-law's wedding in front of two hundred guests, and neither am I. I'm saved from responding to her candy-coated gibe when San walks up.

"Sorry to interrupt." San smiles at Mrs. Gray before looking back to me. "But they're seating now."

"Of course." I gesture to Mrs. Gray. "San, this is Mrs. Gray, Rhyson and Bristol's mother. Mrs. Gray, my friend, Santos."

"Nice to meet you." San's smile doesn't slip, but his eyes chill a degree or two. He knows the history between Rhyson and his parents as well as I do. As well as everyone does.

"Yes, nice to meet you, too." Her eyes flit from me to my good-looking best friend, speculating about a relationship between us. Maybe it's best I let her believe that.

"Ready if you are." I link my arm through San's, smiling up at him warmly. "Let's go."

We're a few feet ahead of her when San leans down to whisper in my ear.

"What was that all about?"

"Nothing. She doesn't like me, at least not for Rhyson. It was all she could do not to jump up and down that we aren't together anymore."

"She must not have seen you *together* when we first got here." San lets out a low whistle. "You could have boiled an egg between the two of you."

"He wants me to meet him."

"I just bet he does," San says with a chuckle. "Two months is a long time. Wedding fucks are the best."

"Not for . . . not for *that*, San."

"I'd bet my next check it *is* for that."

I ignore all the tingly places his suggestion ignites, and don't bother responding since we've reached our seats. Instead, I settle into the white folding chair and absorb the beauty of this day. Not the green carpet of grass under our feet, vibrant, verdant. Or the canopy of cloud and cerulean sky overhead, with the sun glowing bright and gold. Not the trees, Spring heavy on their branches, blossoms scenting the air. No, the beauty of a man who has always sought good for others, finally finding so much good for himself.

Grady didn't have to take me under his wing when I moved here, a country bumpkin fresh off the truck, green as a watermelon. But he did. He looked out for me, for San, and so many of his other students. He looked out for Rhyson, when his parents should have but didn't, and for that I'm more appreciative than a beautifully wrapped gift from Williams-Sonoma could ever express.

I cry a little when Grady takes his place at the front under an arch of crimson roses. So much of the good I see in Rhyson is because of Grady. Seeing Rhsyon standing beside the man who's been more of a father to him than his natural father only stirs the emotion more. I reach into my little clutch where I stuffed Kleenex. I thought that was all the preparation I'd need, but wiping away the tears doesn't wipe away the emotion that goes even beyond Grady.

I want this.

It hits me out of nowhere, as incongruous as rain would be on this bright, sunny day, but that doesn't make it less true. Even with all we still have to work out, even with the tape threatening me, even when right now I'm not even sure I *trust* him, I know I love him. And I want this. A gorgeous day with Rhyson standing there waiting for me at the end of a path of roses like the one Emmy's walking down now, with a crowd of family and friends standing when I enter. I want an impractical white dress that I'll only wear once and that costs entirely too much. Something I can save for our girls just in case one of them wants to wear it one day. With all the crap we still have to sort, that feels like an improbable light at the end of an impossible tunnel, but I want this more than I ever wanted to perform. The idea that one lonely, careless night with an asshole who hates the man I love could ruin those possibilities for me, for us, chokes me. Lodges emotion in my throat too thick to swallow past.

"You okay?" San whispers.

"Yeah." I give a jerky nod, sniffling and patting at the corners of my eyes as the minister tells us we can take our seats again. "You know how I am at weddings."

San studies my profile, but I refuse to look at him. The man sees enough without looking into my eyes. And then Rhyson's voice makes me forget San is even there.

"Thank you for celebrating this great day with Grady and Em," Rhyson says from behind a piano on a slightly raised dais. "This is a day I've been really looking forward to. Probably not as much as Grady has, though."

The crowd laughs, and Rhyson smiles into the mic.

"For as long as I can remember, Grady and I have shared the songs we're working on. When he heard this song for my next album, he asked me to sing it today. And even though I wrote it for *my* girl, today it's from Grady to his. It's called *My Soul To Keep*."

I keep a straight face, even though several sets of eyes swing in my direction, watching for a response. Wondering if I'm still "his girl." Wondering if he wrote this song for me. My expression remains impassive, but heat and pleasure combust in my chest, setting fire to every part of me waiting to hear my song.

Rhyson looks up from the piano, and a moment of déjà vu transports me back to the first time we met in Grady's studio, when I saw only a sliver of him at the piano, just enough to fascinate me. Only this time he's searching for me. I know it. He scans the crowd, looking methodically up and down rows until he finds me. Eyes locked with mine, he tugs his ear before launching into the first words.

I was lost before you found me, or maybe I found you
Maybe it was fate or kismet, or something much more true
It could have been an answered prayer, a sacred certainty
All I know is what we have now. I've got no plans to leave

Not an ocean, not forever
Nothing wide or deep
Will ever end this love between us
My soul is yours to keep

To have the full power of Rhyson's gift fixed on me, his talent with words, the nimble fingers loving the keys, the force of his charisma turned on me, is overwhelming. I sit up straight, but inside I'm slumped over from the force of these intimate moments between him and me with a crowd looking on.

From there, things blur. Grady and Em tearfully pledge themselves to each other. By the end of their vows, my Kleenex is a limp, damp useless blob in my fist. I have vague impressions of food in my mouth. I'm sure it's delicious, but I barely taste it. I don't look at Rhyson, and I don't think he looks at me much either. He's giving Grady and the reception his full attention, and I love him for that.

Grady and Em make their rounds, greeting guests. When they come to our table, I almost lose it again because Emmy has always been beautiful, but today she's something different—that blissed-out beauty that must be reserved for the special day when you marry your soul mate.

"I'm so glad you could make it, Kai." Grady pulls me close, bending to whisper in my ear. "You-know-who made sure you'd be here."

"He told me." I pull back to look in his eyes, offering him a smile. "I'm so happy for you, Grady. You deserve this more than anyone I know."

"Thank you." He glances at Emmy, who's chatting with San. "She's something else."

"So are you." I lean up to kiss his cheek.

"Have you and Rhys worked things out? He's driving me crazy. Our honeymoon is basically an excuse to get away from him."

I smother a chuckle with my palm, shaking my head. I catch Rhyson's eyes across the room, watching us. Watching me. The smile dies because as much as I want him, I have to protect him. I have to protect *us* from whoever wants to keep us apart.

"We still have some things to work out, but it'll be okay, Grady."

"He handled things badly," Grady says, eyes sober. "Believe me. I made sure he knew how badly he messed up, but he loves you, Kai. You know that."

"I know that, yes."

"And you love him, too, right?"

I drop my eyes to the bright green grass under our feet.

"You know I do, Grady."

"Then you'll be fine. It might be hard, but if there's two people who know how to get through hard things, it's the two of you."

I wag a finger up at him.

"Will you forget about us? Today is your day. We'll figure it out."

Even after he and Emmy have moved on to the next table, his words stay with me. I wish it was just hard. The tape is a complication I never saw coming. It's a mess I made, a bad spill I'm determined to clean up before it reaches Rhyson.

The closer we get to the toasts, the slicker my palms become. The faster my heart races. The shorter my breath comes.

"Could I have your attention?" Rhyson finally clinks his champagne flute. "Me again. I promise it's the last time."

The crowd laughs, eating up all this face time with Rhyson, who they so rarely see in intimate settings like this. This isn't him onstage or begrudgingly doing some interview, but it's him with his family. With his friends, relaxed, joking, happy for Grady. It's rare, and they love it. So do I.

"I have to go back to the beginning." Rhyson looks at Grady with a small smile. "When I was really young, I used to get Grady confused with my father all the time because they're twins."

He finds Bristol in the crowd and points to her.

"There's my twin, Bristol. Twins run pretty hard in our family."

Bristol raises a glass, an enduring smile on her face until the attention shifts back to her brother.

"Anyway, I often ran to him when he was around, if I got hurt or needed something because he looked just like my dad." Rhyson's face sobers, and he drops his gaze to the champagne glass in his hand. "In a lot of ways, he's been a second father to me. He taught me so many important things. Not tying my shoes or riding a bike. He taught me about being kind to people, though sometimes I'm still not very good at that."

Rhyson gives half a chuckle before looking right at Grady.

"You taught me that I'm more than my music. More than talent, and that I could be loved for who I am, not for all the other stuff."

Something so special and private passes between Grady and Rhys, I can barely watch. It's the moment Rhyson should have had with his father, but maybe never will. I'm kind of glad his father isn't here to see what he forfeited with such a special man. My eyes drift to Angela Gray just a few rows ahead of me. Her posture stiff, her lips tight in profile, her hands clenched in her lap. She *is* here witnessing that. I don't know if it's anger or hurt or some helix of the two, but emotion comes off her like an echo. I don't hear it, but I feel it the way a clanging cymbal vibrates in your chest.

Emmy's sister does her toast, and my eyes seek Rhyson out immediately, blood pounding at my wrists. He's talking to Grip, who has wrangled his dreads into a long, winding trail down his back. Grip nods, and Rhyson catches me looking at them. He flicks his head toward the orchard before returning his eyes to his best friend, concentrating on what he's saying.

There are so many people eating, dancing, talking, I'm confident I can slip off unnoticed, but of course one person does notice.

"You got protection?" San grins at me over his almost-empty champagne flute.

Exasperation rolls my eyes and twists my lips, but I just shake my head.

"I won't need it."

"Oh, that's right, you get the shot."

"Would you stop?" I hiss at him, glancing around to make sure no one nearby heard him publicly declaring my chosen method of birth control. "I really am gonna stop telling you girl stuff."

"You been saying that since seventh grade." His eyes comb the crowd like mine have done so many times since we arrived. "And be careful. We don't know who's watching."

The reminder of today's text message weighs me down for a second and makes me wonder if I should meet Rhyson after all, though I don't have much choice. He really might make a scene if I don't follow through on my promise. But like he has so many times before, San distracts me with his warped humor.

He takes a sip of his champagne and gives me a lazy grin. "And don't stain that dress."

"I . . . you . . . ugh." I turn to walk away, tossing my last words over one shoulder. "I'll be back."

San's laugh chases me all the way to the edge of the yard. Step by tiny, discreet step, I inch my way toward a small opening in the thicket. I pick through the orchard, which is so thick with apple and pear trees that sunlight barely peers through. At one point, the path forks, and I'm not sure which way to turn. I just stand in the cool orchard shade, looking from left to right.

A wall of muscle warm at my back steals my breath.

"Are you lost?" Rhyson whispers into my ear, linking our hands.

No. After two months, finally found.

I look up at him over my shoulder, and can't help but think about the song we first bonded over. The lyrics of *Lost*, track number nine, mark his body and touch my heart. I guard my eyes, hoping he won't see how good it feels to be this close to him again.

"Where's the barn?" I look back over the path I followed to reach this point. "No one followed you?"

"We're not secret agents, Kai." Rhyson starts moving down the left path, pulling me along. "You're the one who cares if people know about us. I certainly don't."

"There isn't an 'us' again yet, Rhys." My hand gripping his as we rush toward the light breaking through the thick overgrowth makes a lie of my words.

He looks at me, eyes narrowed and mouth compressed into a flat line.

"There's always an 'us,' Kai. You know that."

I drag my eyes away from his and look at the clearing we've reached. Just ahead stands a red barn that looks like it's seen better days, but still holds a certain charm. The heavy door falls back when Rhyson pushes, and he pulls me in behind him, letting the door slam shut. He gestures ahead to a ladder leading up to a loft above.

"After you."

I climb up ahead of him, but pause when his hands circle my waist from behind. His fingers splay over my stomach, and he presses his head to my back, drawing a deep breath.

"Keep going," he says, voice heavy and husky.

The ladder only takes us a few feet above the ground, so I know it isn't altitude making me lightheaded and breathless. It's his touch. His breath ruffling the hair at my neck when we reach the top. His hands on my shoulders, squeezing. His thumb tracing sensuous circles over my collarbone. I'm struggling to hold on to my composure, to my resolve, when I take the last step up and onto the top floor.

A tablecloth, I presume from the caterer since it looks like the ones from the reception, covers a small patch of hay. A bucket filled with ice and a bottle of champagne grace the middle of the white cloth. Two huge chunks of wedding cake under glass sit beside it.

"This is nice." I clear my throat. "How'd you pull it off when they haven't even cut the cake yet?"

"I left it to Marlon and didn't ask. He may have slept with the caterer to get this. It's better if we don't know." Rhyson chuckles. "We don't have much time before Grady and Em leave. I want to see them off, so let's sit and eat."

He traps my eyes with a determined look.

"And talk."

I drop to the cloth, arranging the skirt over my knees. For a few minutes, we eat in silence, reacquainting ourselves with the solitude of each other. We never needed small talk. Never needed other people. Just each other. I think we're poking around in this silence to make sure that hasn't changed. I'm halfway through my mammoth piece of cake before I slow down and actually taste it.

"I love wedding cake," I mumble, passing my fingers over my lips to rid them of crumbs.

"I see that," he says with a straight face, even though his eyes tease me.

I give him my evil eye, but my lips twitch.

"You can afford it, though." His eyes lose their humor as they run over me. "You've lost weight."

"Dancing twelve hours a day for two months'll do that." I gather a dollop of icing from the plate and slide it into my mouth.

"And you look tired."

"Gee, thanks, Rhys." I grab a napkin to wipe the sweet icing residue from my fingers.

"I'm just saying." He pushes his clear glass plate of cake away. "And you sound tired, too. Is Malcolm building vocal rest into your schedule?"

"Let's not do this." I push away what's left of my cake, too. "Talking about my career certainly won't get us far."

"Just don't come into the studio tomorrow sounding like that."

"Tomorrow?" I frown, clueless about what he means. Luke and I are recording a song for his new album tomorrow, but I'm not sure what that has to do with Rhyson.

"Luke didn't tell you?" Rhyson runs a hand over the back of his neck. "I wrote that duet you're recording tomorrow with Luke."

"Oh," is all I manage before he follows up with even better news.

"And I'm producing it. He may be keeping my involvement low key because he knows Malcolm and I aren't exactly best buds. Malcolm might try to interfere if he knew."

"Oh."

"Yeah, oh." Rhyson takes a sip of the champagne. "I'm not easy in the studio."

"You're not easy out of it, either."

Maybe his mother was right about him being difficult, because none of this feels easy. My first time in the studio recording professionally? Not a demo, but a real track that will be heard everywhere? And Rhyson's producing? I knew we were recording at Wood, the studio Rhys co-owns, but Luke always records there, so I thought nothing of it. Why didn't Luke at least tell *me*?

"I'm not going easy on you because you're my girl."

"You keep saying I'm your girl like we're not apart."

"Because we're not." Displeasure chisels his features. "Have you been out on tour acting like we're apart?"

"What do you mean?"

Rhyson stands, walking over to the small window letting in light. Back to me, hands shoved into his pockets, shoulders stiff, eyes trained on the landscape.

"How would you feel if I fucked someone else, Pep?"

I'd set that woman on fire.

I go completely still, my heart frantic as a hummingbird's. Every fiber of my body violently rejects the thought of him inside another woman. Was it Petra? Was it on tour? Was it good?

"No answer?" Rhyson nods, still facing the sun. "Then I'll go first. Even if you married someone else, I wouldn't acknowledge it. Every night you slept with him I'd call you a liar and a cheat."

The words slap me across the face like an open palm.

"Rhyson, I—"

"I don't need a ceremony or a ring or a license." He turns back around, eyes lit with emotion. "You know there's already a vow between us that goes beyond all of that, and for you to be with anyone else would be adultery of the soul."

The intensity of his words frightens me because I feel the same way. Despite every damn thing that would keep us apart, I feel the same way.

"Why are you saying all of this?" I gather enough breath to ask.

"Is there something going on between you and Dub?"

If I really wanted to put him off until I figure out this video thing, I'd say yes, but I can't do that. It would violate too much. Make him question something that isn't the question at all.

"I told you no," I say softly.

"You sure?" His eyes don't leave me. "'Cause it looks like it. Everyone seems to think you're with him."

"I know, but you should know—"

"I should know what?" He takes his jacket off, tossing it to the corner of the loft. "What am I supposed to think when you won't even talk to me, and I see you all over the place with *him*?"

"You're supposed to think he's my choreographer. That he's my friend." I pause before going on. "And what about you and Petra? Did anything happen on tour with her?"

He scowls, huffing his irritation out in a quick exhale.

"Don't ask me dumb questions."

"So it's dumb when I ask, but perfectly valid when you do?"

"I'm not the one who left and shut you out." Rhyson slams his fist into his palm. "Not a day has gone by that you didn't know I still wanted this. That I still wanted you. And from you? Nothing."

"I needed that time to pursue this opportunity." The memory of his betrayal, the pain blowing a hole in me like a twelve-gauge shotgun when I found out what he took from me, returns full force. "And to get over what you did. Rhyson, you hurt me. What you did hurt me."

"I know that." He growls under his breath, and I know this anger is directed at himself, not at me. "I was dumb. I was an asshole and handled it all wrong. You know I know that, but that doesn't mean it's over. Ever. And you've been acting like it's over."

"At first I thought maybe it was." I snap a stalk of hay between my fingers.

"At first?" Rhyson looks up from the barn floor, eyes alert. "Does that mean you've forgiven me?"

Growing up, Mama always reminded me that love keeps no record of wrongs. I didn't know until now that true love, pure love, the *right* love, doesn't keep that record because it *can't*. I can't. I have to forgive Rhyson because I have to be with him. I just want it to be right. I want *us* to be right. To resolve the things that broke us in the first place. And as much as I want to just pick right back up where we left off, that might take some time.

"Pep." As hard as I know he's trying to keep his tone even, desperation puckers it. "I asked if you've forgiven me."

If I say yes, he'll be all over me. Not just physically, though he's like a tuning fork vibrating, and my body the instrument helplessly aligning itself to him. He'll be all over me to be with him. God help me, I want him all over me.

"Yeah, I've forgiven you." Emotion whittles my words down to a whisper. "I have to."

The words have barely left my mouth and he's across the space, dropping to his haunches in front of me, palms at the back of my head, thumbs caressing my cheeks and running over my lips.

"Thank God." He presses his forehead to mine, standing on his knees. "Baby, come home."

I release a sigh, a breath between our lips.

"I kind of don't have a home right now."

He rubs our noses together, his words cool on my lips.

"This *is* home. Us is home. Come back."

"I . . ." A ragged breath climbs my throat. "I just . . ."

"You just what?" he whispers, so close the words float across my mouth.

"It's not that simple to fix, Rhys." I close my eyes tightly against the emotion reflected in his. "I don't even know if I trust you right now."

"I'll earn it back." He sprinkles kisses over my cheeks, his fingers creeping into the hair at my nape to draw me closer. "Give me the chance to earn it back, baby."

"But you can't control me, Rhys." I allow myself a quick kiss before finishing my point. "Love isn't control."

"You're right. I've got control issues." He sucks my bottom lip between his like he can't help himself before he goes on. "I'll work on 'em. I swear."

"Yes, but . . ." I pull his top lip between mine, sucking and groaning into the contact I've missed so much. "We need to—"

"We're doing what we need to do."

He fuses our lips together, stoking the passion higher with every second we touch. It's even better than I remember, kissing him. His tongue brushes inside my jaw, over my teeth, licking the roof. Repossessing me with every stroke. I taste his desperation, his regret. I know he must taste my forgiveness because I can't hold it back. It rushes up to meet him, burning my throat and streaking tears down my face.

"I'm so sorry I hurt you." His voice wavers as he wets his lips with my tears. "I won't do it again. I promise. Not like that."

"I want to believe you." I slide my fingers into the cool, silky hair.

"Then believe me. I miss you so fucking much, Kai," he breathes the words over my neck. "I need . . . I have to . . . baby . . ."

He gives up on words, pressing me back onto the soft hay. He dips his nose into the shallow cleft barely visible between my breasts, inhaling.

"Pear and cinnamon," he whispers, continuing down my torso, past my waist. His hands slide the dress up my legs, and I'm already gasping just from his palms caressing behind my knees. His head disappears under my dress. He pushes my panties aside, and his lips close over me. My back arches up, pressing my breasts into the air like an offering. He slides the panties off altogether, pulling my legs over his shoulders. He nibbles at the lips, separating me with his tongue. Spreading his mouth over me as his hands traverse the backs of my thighs to grip my bare butt, pulling me into his hunger.

"This is mine," he says hotly against the wet flesh. "And I'm yours, Kai. Nothing changes that. Ever. You know that, right?"

"I know," I pant, twisting the tablecloth beneath us between my fingers, gale force pleasure ripping through me. "Oh, God. I know."

He keeps worshiping me with his lips and tongue until my legs spasm, my body stiffening with the intensity of it. My fingers twine in his thick hair, trapping him against me, pushing him deeper into me. My hips rock into his urgent kisses. He's eating me like I'm so good, his moans vibrating against me, layering sensation on top of sensation until I'm nothing more than a wave beautifully cresting, violently crashing; a tide pulled in, licking at the sand. I'm limp and sated, arms fallen to my sides, head lolling back, drained of all movement, but he's still tasting me like he can't stop, his lips and tongue warm and compulsive.

Steps below startle us, still us.

"Rhys," Grip calls up. "It's almost time. They're leaving soon."

From between my knees, Rhyson's eyes burn a possessive trail up my body and to my face, his hands venturing over the sensitized skin of my inner thighs as he presses me open wider. He looks between my legs like he wants more. Like I'm something sweet in the store window he's not sure he can walk past.

"Okay," he calls down, voice hoarse. "Be down in a minute."

Grip chuckles from below.

"Wrap that shit up and get back out there before you miss the send off."

As I slip my panties on, I can't even manage embarrassment that Grip knows. The love, the tenderness in Rhyson's eyes, in his touch as he pulls me to my feet, crowd out everything else until we reach the floor below. As soon as my feet touch the barn floor, all the reasons I have to slow this down, to control it, come rushing back, chief among them a sex tape I can't risk Rhsyon seeing. Maybe San is right. Maybe Rhyson *can* get past it. Or maybe he can't, and he'd never see me the same again. And the thought of losing this, the way he's looking at me right now, isn't worth the risk. If there's one thing I've seen for myself, one thing I learned from my father, even in a love this deep, there are no guarantees.

My back to the ladder, I tighten my fingers around his, pulling him in for a moment to face me. He stands on one foot and rests the other on a rung of the ladder behind me, pressing into my belly, so I can't escape feeling him hard and long and ready.

"Come home with me," he whispers near my ear, one hand above our heads on the ladder, the other wandering beneath my dress to squeeze my butt. Just that gentle squeeze has me clenching again in my panties. With reason my only weapon, I fight my way back through the fog.

"Rhyson, we need to talk about how this will be."

He drops his lips to mine, feeding the scent of my body to me in light kisses.

"Better than cake," he whispers against my lips. "You taste better than cake. Come home. I need to be inside you, Pep, so bad."

I squeeze my thighs together against the pleasure his words dart through me. His words stroke me as surely as his lips and tongue. I tuck my head under his chin and grip his elbows.

"If I go home with you, I'll end up in your bed."

Laughter rumbles deep in his chest, and he pulls me so close it reverberates through me. He pulls back just far enough to tip up my chin.

"Can't say it didn't cross my mind." He drops a quick kiss on my lips.

"If we make love . . . have sex . . ." I falter, not sure how to articulate what I'm thinking. "If we sleep together—"

"Is this conversation supposed to be making me less horny? Because that's not what's happening."

"Rhyson." I laugh up at him, happy to be with him, even with all the complications. Even with the threat of exposure. "I'm just saying we haven't seen each other in two months. We haven't resolved anything. Sex is always right between us, and it'll only give us a false sense that *everything* is right, when it's not yet. Let's just take it slow."

"Slow." He pulls a breath in through his nose, expels it in a rush. "We can do slow."

"And not public." I glance up at him. "For now it would help me a lot if people don't know we're back together."

He stiffens against me, his arm dropping from overhead, his booted foot leaving the ladder to hit the barn floor.

"Not public?" Irritation clouds his face. "Why?"

"I'm back on tour in just a few days." I touch the lapel of the jacket he retrieved. "All the crazy viralness is just now dying down from that fight everyone saw. I'm starting to make my mark, and people are paying attention for the *right* reasons. For my music, my performance on tour. Can I just have the rest of this tour to let it be that without all the speculation about us? To prove myself before it becomes about us again?"

There was a time when everything I just said would be the truth, and to a degree, it *is* true. Those are all valid reasons, but if it wasn't for this video, I honestly wouldn't care if the whole world speculated about Rhyson and me. I'd do my thing on tour and proudly be his girl. But there *is* the video, and I have to find out who's behind it.

"So you don't want to be public?" His eyes fall to the barn floor. "You don't want people to know we're back together?"

"Just 'til I'm done with the tour," I rush to say, cupping his chin. "Just give me this next month. We won't be together anyway 'cause I'll be on the road."

He clears his throat and steps away from me, sliding his hands into his pockets.

"I've done enough to set you back." He looks up, wearing his disappointment and his acceptance on his face. "If that's how you want it for now, then okay."

"Just until I get off tour. I promise."

If I haven't found out who's blackmailing me by then, I'll have to confess, but I've at least bought myself another month to work on this. I tip up on my toes, one hand gripping the back of his neck and the other wandering into his hair as I open his lips with mine. Our tongues tangle, our bodies swaying into each other while I lose myself for precious seconds in this kiss, as intimate and as binding as a covenant. His hands tighten at my waist, lifting me up higher until my toes barely brush the ground.

"We need to go," he says against my lips. "We don't want to miss Grady and Em."

We walk back to the orchard, our fingers linked until we reach the edge. I know he'll hate it as much as I do, but I drop his hand before we arrive at the small clearing leading back to the wedding and to the guests and to the speculation and to the camera phones. To exposure. Back to the world we've escaped for the last half hour.

"You go first." I hang back in the shade of an apple tree. "I'll see you tomorrow at the studio."

"I hate this," he says through tight lips. "I don't care who knows."

"Just 'til I come off tour, Rhyson. Please."

He bites the inside of his jaw for a second before nodding abruptly and turning to leave. He disappears into the thicket, broad shoulders pressing through the foliage. It sounds stupid, but I miss him already. My resolution to find out who's behind that tape calcifies into absolute necessity.

Chapter SEVEN

RHYSON

I CAN'T REMEMBER A TIME WHEN I've been nervous in the studio. Producing is something I learned, a skill I've honed over years. So much of my talent with the piano was just there, a natural foundation my parents built on. Producing is different. My time at Full Sail, years in the studio producing for other artists when I took a break from performing, even the lessons I learned at The School of the Arts—it's all converged to make me a sought-after producer. I don't do it as much as I used to, but for friends like Luke, or for projects that excite me, I will.

And nothing excites me more than Kai. It's because of her that, for the first time, I'm nervous behind the board. I booked Cherry, my favorite studio here at Wood. They all have state of the art equipment and boards, of course, but this one adjoins a room that holds nothing but one of my pianos. I can slip in there and add the things in my head on the spot.

I should be thanking my lucky stars, if I have any, that she's forgiven me. But, no. Hard-to-please bastard that I am, I spent the night under my piano again, instead of in that cold bed, resenting the fact that she doesn't want people to know. There's this tiny, insistent voice somewhere deep down that keeps asking me if there's more to it. Is it really her career she's concerned with? Does it have anything to do with Dub? Does she not want *anyone* to know? Or does she not want *him* to know?

"Ready, boss?" Our receptionist Amber asks from the door, smiling at the other guys in the studio. Two engineers already sit at the large soundboard, checking levels and prepping for Luke and Kai's arrival.

"Yeah, I'm good." I give Amber a quick nod. "You seen Marlon?"

"He's in Birch." Amber grins, flicking a fall of tawny dreadlocks over her shoulder. "Gettin' high."

"Should've known." I take my seat behind the board. "At least it's somewhat legal now."

"The law finally caught up to Grip . . . somewhat." Amber laughs. "I'm up front all night. Let me know if you need anything."

I swivel my chair to consider her. She's here all times of the day, but especially when Marlon's here. All the girls like him, and he only likes one girl. Not that he lets that stop his dick.

"Don't you have class in the morning?" I ask.

"Yeah, but I gotta close."

"Nah." I wave my hand at her. "I'll close up. You hang as long as you want, of course, but leave when you need to. I got this."

Kai's laugh from the hall cuts our conversation short. I turn my head to watch her through the door. She's talking to Luke, her back to the studio. Her t-shirt, knotted just below her shoulder blades, leaves the golden skin between the shirt and the waistband of her leggings bare. All her hair is gathered high on her head, pierced by chopsticks. Her petite frame is slim and fit, soft and curved.

"Holy shit," Gus, one of the engineers whispers to the other. "Who is *that*?"

"Dayummmmm. I've only seen her from the back," Monty, the other, whispers back, "and I already know I'd hit that . . . from the back."

"Not and live to tell it, you wouldn't," I mutter without looking up from the knobs I'm twisting.

"What?" Gus frowns. "Dude, I—"

Kai looks down the hall to smile at someone, her delicate profile clearly visible for the first time.

"Oh, hell." Monty wide eyes me, genuine regret all over his freckled face. "I didn't know that was Kai, Rhys. Sorry, man."

I nod, but just go back to my knobs. I have enough to handle tonight without throwing in a jealous fit.

"It's fine." I glance toward the hall, my attention snagged and held by her still standing there. "I mean, don't say that shit again, but I get it."

Luke and Kai come in, both smiling. Luke gives out fist pounds to everyone in the studio. He grins at me, blue eyes excited.

"This song is the shit, Gray." He leans against the board. "Thanks for doing this, man. I know you got your own stuff you're working on. This is gonna blaze right out of the gate."

"Happy to do it. I didn't envision it as a duet when I wrote it." My eyes shift to Kai at his side, who's taking in her surroundings and smiling at the two engineers. "But I think it'll work."

"Yeah, and Kai's gonna be so hot by the time this song drops, if Malcolm's got anything to do with it. It'll be perfect timing."

He hooks an elbow around her neck, and I can see the fraternal affection he's developed while they were on tour, but I still don't like him touching my girl. I've heard about the lap dance she gives him every night on stage as part of the show. I have *so* many reasons to be glad when this tour is over.

She glances at me nervously, moving from under Luke's arm. She knows me well.

"Let's do this." I pull out the charts I marked up, handing one to each of them. "I think you both got my notes, but I had some other thoughts today."

We talk through the changes I'm proposing to the bridge. Kai nods, dark brows pulled together in concentration. She wears no makeup, and I could just stare at her all day, especially after two months of not seeing her at all. She looks up, catching my eyes on her, smiles a little before looking back to the chart.

"Let's lay Luke's verse first." I roll out a chair for Kai. "You listen, Kai, to the things I tell him because a lot of it will hold for your verse, too."

Luke's good. Always has been, but the fatigue in his voice is evident. Maybe it wasn't such a good idea to record this while they're on tour. We're professionals, used to singing through anything, but Malcolm sets a much more bruising pace than I would set for myself, or anyone else.

The raspiness fatigue lends Luke's voice actually works for his verse, deepening it and adding grit. He's a seasoned pro, so he takes guidance well and adjusts easily. He and I have worked together ever since I accompanied him for his performance piece junior year, so we know each other. He knows I don't settle. I push. He's prepared for it, and doesn't push back, but just gives me what I need to make the song work.

I hope Kai's watching because she's up next.

She looks back at me from inside the booth, headphones looped around her neck. By now I know Kai like the first Bach symphony I ever learned. Literally I could play it half asleep. I anticipate Kai like my next heartbeat, and I can tell she's nervous, though I doubt anyone else can.

"Let's take it from the top of verse two, Kai," I say through the system so she can hear me in the booth.

She nods and the track starts. From the first note I know this won't go well. As much as I love her . . . *because* I love her . . . I can't tolerate less than the best I've heard from her. She can do better. I feel Luke and the other engineers watching me, seeing if I'm going to give her special treatment because she's my girl, or used to be, in their minds. They've seen me press until I hear from that booth what I'm hearing in my head.

"Hey, Kai," I cut in over her singing. "You're flat."

She blinks a few times, her mouth dropping open.

"Oh, I'm sorry. I—"

"Lift your eyebrows." I keep my tone impersonal. "You're just barely under the note, especially at the top of the verse. I need that first note clarion clear. Dead on."

"Okay. I can do that." She adjusts the headphones, closes her eyes and waits for the track to begin again.

It's still not what I'm looking for. I wrote this ballad before I met Kai, so to my ears, the lyrics about love lack a certain intimacy. I wrote about an idea of love. Kai brought it to life for me. The lyrics hold power if delivered properly, though.

"Still flat," I interrupt, my voice sharpening with the impatience I always feel when an artist isn't getting it. "And I need more from you. Tonally and in the delivery. It's emotionally flat right now. Again."

Kai looks back at me, crimson flooding her cheeks. She bites her lip and nods.

"Sorry. I-I'll do better. Can we take it again from the middle of the verse?"

"No, we need to take it from the top. None of it was right."

"Got it." She lowers her lashes, pulling the chopsticks from her hair so it falls past her shoulders. "I'm sorry, Rhys."

"I don't need an apology. I need you on top of that note."

She nods, the fine bones of her jaw clenching.

"Amber." I turn to find her standing in the door, eyes wide, probably over the way I'm talking to the woman I introduced as my girlfriend not too long ago. "Go make that throat coat tea concoction for Kai. Her voice sounds ragged."

Gus clears his throat and Luke shifts in the seat next to me.

"It's not that bad, Rhys," Luke says.

"Yeah, man. We can fix some of that in post," Monty says. "Give her a break."

"A break?" My voice whips at them both. "You want the first track you release to be mediocre and flat, Luke? Because right now that's all she's giving us. And, Gus, if you could stop admiring her for two minutes, you'd realize she's a professional and can take direction. Or at least she usually can. I have no idea why she can't tonight."

"Your finger's still on the button," Luke whispers.

"What?" I look into the booth and realize that Kai heard everything I said. Hurt gathers in her eyes, but she looks down before I see it fully formed.

Shiiiiiit.

"Gimme ten." I stand. "Grab a coffee, a blunt, whatever it takes you to survive me tonight. I think Marlon's getting high over in Birch. Go keep him company."

All three guys get up and head out, and I step into the booth. Kai doesn't look up from the small square Persian rug she's standing on. She slides her hands into her back pockets, waiting.

"I'm sorry about that." I lean against the door, crossing one ankle over the other. "I didn't mean—"

"You didn't know I was listening, so I know you meant it." She finally looks at me, her eyes still hurt, but inlaid with resolve. "Just tell me how to fix it."

"Vocal rest, for one." I walk over to her, and unlike that time all those months ago in Grady's studio, I don't ask permission to touch her. I lay my hand against the muscles of her stomach with the ease of possession because now she's mine.

"You're not thinking about your breathing, so your phrasing is off." My index finger strokes across her belly ring. "The phrasing is a huge part of the delivery on this song, so it's not convincing. I don't believe it."

"Okay." Her eyes fix on my finger still stroking the smooth skin at her waist. "That's not helping my breathing."

I smile, slipping my hand down her arm and over hers in her back pocket. I step closer, bending my knees until I can press our foreheads together.

"I'm sorry for being a jerk."

"You're not. You weren't." She shakes her head against mine. "You're right. If I want to be a professional, I have to perform like one."

"Yeah, you do." I pull back, leveling a sober look at her. "Your voice is ragged, Kai. I know what you sound like rested. You need vocal rest."

I brush a thumb over the dark circles under her eyes I didn't notice yesterday when makeup camouflaged them.

"You need rest, period. I'm concerned."

"I'm fine." She grips my wrist. "What else?"

"I know I wrote that first phrase ending on the G, but resolve it. It's not working the way I wrote it."

"Got it. Anything else?"

"The biggest thing, and this is an intangible, but it's the most important part. Emotion." I grip her hips and catch her eyes. "You're delivering this song with zero emotion. I know you know about love, so sing like you do."

"I guess I am tired." She runs a hand through her hair. "I'm having trouble connecting to the lyrics. Having trouble communicating it."

"Sing it for me," I say softly.

My suggestion would seem presumptuous if I didn't know how deep our connection goes. Her dark eyes warm and soften when she looks up at me. I pull her into me, close enough to smell her hair and feel the heat of her body.

"Will you sing it for me, Pep?" I whisper in her ear, spreading my hand over the silky skin of her back. "Pour everything you feel for me into it."

She lays her head against me, her breath quickening against my neck.

"Can you do that for me?"

She nods, sliding her hand up to grip my neck, fingers piercing into my hair. The booth door opens, and she jerks back, turning away and linking her hands behind her head.

"Sorry." Amber glances between Kai and me. "Thought you'd want this."

I take the tea from her and give it to Kai.

"Drink this, Pep."

She takes the mug, sipping and smiling gratefully at Amber.

"Thanks. It's good."

"That'll help your voice some." I turn to Amber. "The guys back?"

"Yeah, they're in the studio."

I look through the plexiglass, and sure enough, they're back behind the board. I take one more look at my girl when Amber leaves. She already seems more confident.

"You got this." I turn just before I exit the booth, connecting our eyes. "For me. Sing for me."

I hear the difference immediately. I don't know if it's Amber's miracle tea that has saved more than one voice on a rough night, or if it was our pep talk, but Kai nails it. She measures her breathing, every phrase spaced as it should be. Every note, properly supported. And emotion . . . God, as jaded as I am, it takes a lot for me to get goosebumps, but my goosebumps have goosebumps when she sings the lyrics this time. I don't stop her once. I'm afraid to, scared I'll ruin something magnificent by meddling with it.

And when I told her to sing for me, I didn't expect her to sing *to* me, but she does, stretching a live wire between her eyes and mine. I'm not only transfixed, but also painfully aroused by the whole thing. It's so incredibly personal to have my words in her mouth. It's almost an erotic experience to see something that came from my mind, from my heart, dwelling inside of her. I scoot under the board as far as I can so these guys can't tease me about getting a hard on for a second verse.

My synesthesia is in overdrive. I close my eyes, trapping all the colors the music shows me beneath my eyelids, not sharing them with anyone. Bright gold mixed with blue and green, a musical paisley splashed across the palette of my mind, splashed across my senses.

When she's done, the studio stays completely silent. They feel it, too. It was only a verse, but it was so perfect it felt sacred, and they're as scared to ruin it as I am.

"Was that better, Rhys?" she asks, voice husky, eyes wide, skin flushed like we've been touching each other in front of everyone for the last few minutes. And maybe we have.

How she can think anyone would see us in the same room and not know we're together is beyond me. The heat between us, even separated by several yards, could melt the plexiglass wall of the studio.

"Much better." I clear my throat and turn to Luke. "You wanna get in there for the chorus? If you guys can give me a couple of good passes, we'll just stack the vocals to fill that sound out some."

The rest of the song goes relatively smoothly. They knock out the chorus and the bridge. We lay some background vocals they do themselves. Kai guzzles a steady stream of Amber's magical tea, and her voice, though tired, holds for the night.

It's two o'clock in the morning when we're done. So much of this industry happens in studios while everyone else sleeps. I'm exhausted, but color still swirls in my mind. I keep hearing new things that came to me while Kai sang, notes that will enrich the song. Everyone else packs up, but I'll stay and hammer out the parts I want to add.

The energy from Kai's verse still churns inside of me. Were it up to me, I know exactly where this energy would go. I'd pour it into my sweet girl. In our bed. Between our sheets. But she wants slow so that we get this right. And I want this right even more than I want what's between those beautiful legs of hers. So for now, my piano will be my release, as it has been so often over the last two months.

I'm about to get started in the small piano room adjoining Cherry, when I look up to see Kai standing at the entrance. I wasn't even sure she would say goodbye because I have no idea how "not public" she wants us. I'll follow her lead on it because, left to me, she'd be wearing a *Property of Rhyson Gray* sign. I'd write it in the sky if she'd let me.

I gesture for her to come in, and she walks over to stand right in front of me.

"You got a ride home?" I lean against the piano and push the hair over her shoulder, my hand dropping to palm her waist. She'll have to pull away if she's concerned about someone seeing us because I can't *not* touch her.

"Yeah." She looks up at me, the same restrained energy in her eyes that churns inside of me. "I've got San's truck."

Gus and Monty come through to wave a final goodnight, their speculative eyes bouncing between Kai and me. After what they've probably read about us being apart, they must be as confused as I am half the time. With them leaving and Amber long gone, it's just Kai and me in the studio. When she leaves it'll be just me like it's been so many nights since she left.

"I should go," she whispers, stepping back.

"You were amazing." I tighten my hand at her waist, hoping I can keep her for a few more minutes.

"Thank you." She smiles. "I mean that. Thank you for bringing something so much better out of me than I thought I had."

She opens her mouth like there's more she would say, but she bites her lip and drops her gaze to the floor. I lift her chin with one finger until I have her eyes again.

"What is it, Pep?"

A breath stutters over her lips and emotion deepens the rich brown of her eyes to sable.

"Did you feel it?" The heat in her eyes mesmerizes me. "When I sang for you? Did you feel it?"

I don't bother answering her question. I just haul her into me, hands cupping her ass and tongue in her mouth before she can waste time with more words. Who needs words when we have this? This living, panting thing that ignites every second we're together. Lust and love rub against each other vigorously like two sticks making sparks fly, the first sign of fire. I feather kisses down her soft cheeks until I reach her lips again. She opens for me, warm and eager. My hands glide past her waist and up her body until I cup either side of her face, holding her still so I can plunder that sweetness over and over until I'm satisfied. Only there's no satisfaction, just more hunger. It claws out of my belly and drags her closer.

"Rhyson, oh God," she husks against my lips. "I-I . . . need . . ."

Her arms wrap around my neck, pressing our bodies so close not even a breath would dare intrude. But her words intrude. What she said yesterday in the barn about going slow and getting it right, it intrudes as much as I don't want it to.

I pull back, hands at her hips, to look down at her.

"Pep, you know where this goes." I shake my head. "If we don't stop, I *won't* stop. You know that, right?"

The hunger in her eyes answers me.

"Yeah." She blinks rapidly, her hand tightening behind my neck, fingers plowing into my hair.

"You know I want this." I feel the window closing, that window where I give her a choice in this, where I let her go home. "But you said slow, baby. I just . . . I don't want you to regret this, or see it as a setback for us. It wouldn't be to me."

"I just . . ." Her eyes pick up where her words leave off, telling me that I'm not the only one lonely or needy tonight after so long apart. "What we felt tonight in the studio, I need that."

"What are you saying?" I know what she's saying, but she's gonna have to *say* it. And once she does, that's it. The timetable, the slow pace—all of it goes poof, and good riddance.

"I'm saying you can have me, we can have each other tonight." She seals her fate by tipping up on her toes to lay a soft kiss on my lips.

That may be the last soft thing between us for a while because what burns in me isn't soft or slow or gentle. I'm done questioning this. I'm not asking for permission or waiting another minute. Her singing my lyrics tonight, holding my words so close they became a part of her—I'm still hard from that. There's only one way to satisfy this hunger.

I spin her around and bend her over the side of the piano, with frantic hands peeling her leggings and panties down over her hips. I can't even wait for her to get them off, leaving them bundled around her ankles. I fumble with my zipper, want making my hands tremble.

"Hurry, Rhys." Her voice shakes with need. "Please hurry."

I drop my pants, align our bodies and plunge into her tightness as deeply as her body will take me. I slide my hand up her back, pushing her neck, her cheek into the piano. I'm as gentle as I can be while

I grind into the curve of her ass.

"You don't ever keep this from me again." I thrust into her roughly, watching the blush wash over the downy skin of her neck and cheeks. "I can't . . . I can't be without you, Kai."

"I know." Her voice shakes.

I can't speak, the force of the pleasure too intense. I want to savor being with her, inside of her again, but it's been too long. I thought our first time together again would be long, leisurely love in my bed, or by my pool, naked with the cameras off. Instead we steal this rough fuck in the back of my studio. One hand grips her hip and the other presses into the fragile line of her spine. Dammit, I don't want to hurt her, but I'm pounding into her, my hips out of control, shaking the piano, the superb acoustics of the studio echoing back my grunts and groans. But she takes it, wants more.

"Deeper, Rhys," she pants, eyes closed, bottom lip captive between her teeth. "Baby, don't hold back. I can take it."

Then I can give it. I push impossibly deeper, harder until she's up on her tiptoes. My hand shoves the knotted t-shirt up her back. She reaches behind her, hurriedly unhooking the bra, and my hand slips under her to squeeze one plump nipple.

She groans, slamming one palm to the piano, pulling it into a fist and banging until she's matching the rhythm of my thrusts, mixing with our erratic breaths and the guttural sounds of our pleasure, an erotic symphony with just our bodies and our love as instruments.

"Damn, this is good, Pep." I bend my knees, sinking into her more, painting her back with the sweat falling from my face and shoulders.

"Yes, don't stop. I'm almost . . ." The words strangle in her throat.

"Touch yourself, baby."

Her hand disappears between her legs, and the sight of her touching herself, the sound of her release wrenched from her lips, the clench of her body around me when she comes, sets me off so hard my body jerks rough and rapid until I'm coming, jetting into her body. And for the first time, it's so intense it's the same as my synesthesia, colors overtaking my mind, red wrapping around green, pink fusing with yellow, purple interspersing with blue. Vibrant hues coalescing into an aurora borealis that takes my breath, revealing to me the color of love.

Chapter EIGHT

Kai

SO MUCH FOR SLOW.

The pull between Rhyson and me at the studio was loco-motive, and we rode it all night. My lofty intentions of taking things slow, of not letting sex cloud our issues, crashed and burned after what we shared while I was singing in the booth. I've never felt any-thing like that before. The words to his song burned my tongue, ca-ressed my lips and slid down my throat, searching out my deepest places. I thought I could just say goodnight, but as soon as I walked into that piano room, the pull was too strong. Inescapable. I knew we wouldn't be going our separate ways.

And now it's morning. For the first time in two months, I'm waking up with Rhyson warm and solid behind me. He doesn't feel like a mistake. Not with his arm a heavy, welcome claim draped over my stomach. Not with the comfort of each deeply drawn breath in his sleep rustling my hair.

I turn over slowly so I won't wake him. On the road, Malcolm made sure I experienced so many things I never thought I would.

Expensive suites. Champagne. Gorgeous clothes I'd never buy for myself. But this is the luxury no tour or check could ever provide. The luxury of waking up with Rhyson. Him on the pillow beside me, his broad chest, lean naked body inked with the music he loves. The long lashes softening his rugged, handsome profile. The dark hair, dusted with autumn, wild, spilling over his closed eyes. Waking up with Rhyson is absolutely decadent.

I don't know how long I study him before he sleepily blinks back at me. A smile tugs the edges of his lips, his hands wandering under the sheets to pull me flush against him, my breasts pressed into his bare chest.

"G'morning," he says, voice still husky with sleep. "It's kind of creepy to wake up with you staring at me like that."

He drops a kiss on my forehead and pushes the hair out of my eyes.

"I could get used to it, though."

I fold my arms against his chest between us, pressing my lips to his throat where his pulse drums beneath the warm, tanned skin.

"Sorry to be a creeper." My laugh is scratchy in my throat. My voice was already a little ragged. Last night's session didn't help. "I guess I missed waking up with you."

I flick a glance up at him, taking in the line of his scruffy jaw.

"You're beautiful, Rhys."

Something melts in his eyes before they start smiling at me.

"I think that's the pot calling the kettle beautiful."

The smile teasing his lips disappears.

"Are you . . ." Rhyson lets the words hang for a second, clears his throat and starts again. "I know you wanted to go slow with this and make sure we get things fixed. I don't want you to think we can't still do that. Work on things, I mean. Do you, well, regret last night?"

I scoot back just enough so he can see me and I can see him clearly, eyes to eyes.

"Not regret, no. It was too perfect to regret." I place two fingers over the smile that instantly sprouts on his face. "*But* my concerns still stand. We can't just jump back in like nothing happened. You really hurt me. We hurt each other."

"I know." His hand drifts down my back under the sheet, fingers spreading over the curve of my butt. "If I could go back and do it differently, I would."

I wiggle away a few inches, dislodging his hand. There's no way I'll get through this conversation with his hand on my ass.

"You'll get plenty of chances, Rhys." I firm the line of my lips. "Over and over again we'll disagree about my career, about the steps I should take and what I should do. You'll have a choice every time to manipulate and control, or to trust me."

An annoying voice whispers in my head that maybe I should trust *him* about the sex tape, but it sounds too much like San for me to pay it any mind. This is different. It *has* to be.

"What can I do to prove I'm serious about this?" His hand moves again under the sheet to grip my hip.

"Since you asked." I give him a careful glance like my next words might set him off. "The family counseling that Grady keeps bringing up? I think you should do it."

He closes his eyes tightly and presses his lips against his teeth.

"Pep, that won't—"

"Hear me out." I tangle my fingers in the thick hair hanging past his ears, holding his eyes with mine. "I know you hate it when I say this, but there's a pattern. The same way your parents controlled you and called it love, you have the potential to do that. Not on purpose, but it's the way you were first loved."

He swallows, lowering his lashes before looking back at me.

"That will prove to you that I'm serious about this? That will make you feel good about coming back to me?"

"*You* make me feel good about coming back to you." I shake my head, cupping his jaw. "Do you think I didn't miss you, too? I did. I just . . . I don't want us to go through that again the next time you don't like a move I'm making."

"Don't ask me to stand by and watch you get hurt or taken advantage of, Kai." His jaw flexes beneath my fingers as he grits his teeth. "No amount of counseling will get me to do that."

"Can we just talk about it? Don't go behind my back. Don't undercut me. Manipulate me." I bite my lip to stop because the more I say, the more the anger and hurt rush back. "The counseling, it's a start. It's a step. That's all."

"All right." Rhyson gives a jerky nod, flipping onto his back and linking his hands behind his head, eyes fixed on the ceiling. "I'll do it. Grady'll set it up."

"Good." I snuggle into his side, slipping my arm across the hard plane of his stomach.

"I have my own conditions." He twists a chunk of my hair around his hand, gently tugging until I have to look at him. "Remember after the tour, we go public."

Fear and anxiety slosh around in my belly. That gives me a month to find Drex. To kill this threat before Rhyson or anyone else sees that sex tape. There has to be more we can do. I'll have San redouble his efforts and press his contacts a little harder. Last night proved I can't stay away from Rhyson, but if I'm giving us just this slice of time together before I go back on the road, I'll have to be extra careful.

"Kai?" Rhyson asks. "You agree? Once the tour is over, everyone knows about us."

"Yeah." I nod and meet his eyes. "I said so yesterday."

"I need you to mean it."

"Okay. Of course. After the tour. "

"It's like we're hitting the reset button." He smiles the tiniest bit. "This is our fresh start. Our clean slate. No more lies. No more secrets."

I stare at him for long seconds, and that last secret, which blossoms every day into a full-blown lie, gathers between us like an invisible storm cloud. I want to reset so badly. And after this tape is settled I will.

If something is built on a lie, can it still be real?

The question I asked myself so many times when I was trying to forgive Rhyson comes back to mock and challenge me.

"Yeah." I drop my eyes from the eager light in his. "We'll reset."

"Thank you for forgiving me." He tips my chin back so our eyes reconnect. "Nothing but trust from here. Promise."

"Promise," I whisper.

"In case I haven't told you." He brushes a thumb over my lips. "I'm so damn proud of you. You're doing amazing. Everyone's falling for you just like I knew they would. I want you to have that without all the speculation and the drama about me distracting from what should be *your* time."

I didn't expect the tears that burn my eyes when I hear him say he's proud of me. Maybe I didn't realize how much that meant to me until he said it. It means the world. Emotion stifles my words, so I just nod and manage a watery smile.

"In the meantime, we've got today." Rhyson drags himself to sit up, back against the headboard, smiling down at me. "I wanna take you out."

I frown, pulling myself up to sit beside him, sheet tucked beneath my arms, dropping my head to his shoulder.

"Doesn't sound very low key to me, us being out in public together."

"Ah, I have a plan, ye of little faith. I have a plan."

"A plan, huh?" I pull my knees up to my chest under the sheet.

He tugs on the sheet gently at first, but then with a wicked grin, jerks it away and tosses it to the floor. I stand to my knees in the middle of the bed naked, scooting to the foot, and dive for the sheet. His hand nudging my shoulder stops me. He grips both my arms, inspecting my body.

"I did that?" He traces a finger over a black and blue bruise belting my waist.

I have bruises in unusual places. It's not every day a girl gets bent over a piano and screwed out of her mind. I wanted it, needed it rough in the moment, but I'm paying for it now.

"No, the piano you bent me over last night did that." I take his wrists and place them on my shoulders, pushing into him. "It doesn't hurt, and it was worth it."

"And your tired voice and weight loss." He thumbs under my

eyes where I know he'll see shadows. "Exhaustion. Is that all worth it?"

"Don't." I pull back, jump off the bed to gather the sheet and toss it onto the rumpled bed. "I told you it's the dancing that has me losing weight. Every day, every night, all the time. I can't keep weight on."

"And the voice? And the—"

"Rhys, stop." I walk toward the bathroom and turn on the shower, looking at him over my shoulder. "You've been on tour. You know the toll it takes."

"But I don't like it taking a toll on *you*."

"I'll be fine. The worst of it's over. I'm back on the road, and then only another month. I don't wanna fight, okay?"

He nods, walking toward me, a tall, lean, naked distraction.

"No fighting." He backs me into the shower until I'm flush against the wet tiles. "We have to make the most of the time we have. Starting now."

He's gentle with me, mindful of my bruises, until he can't be anymore. Until the time we've spent apart, wanting and needing, takes over, and he's rough and fast, taking me hard with my slippery arms and legs wrapped around him and barely hanging on. Every powerful thrust slamming me into the shower wall. Our grunts, groans, and moans echoing off the walls, the love slick between our bodies until I'm coming so hard, I just know my heart will stop. I just know I won't ever catch my breath again. Every time he loves me, I'm changed. Every time he takes me, I die a little and am born again.

I've missed the intimate rituals of living with him almost as much as everything else. Dressing together. The privacy of our nakedness where no one else can see. Our eyes meeting in the mirror to reminisce about what we just shared.

"So this date we're going on." I tighten the belt of my robe, one of the many things I left behind when I went on tour. "Tell me more."

"Music Festival out at Newport Beach." Rhyson shrugs shoulders still damp from the shower. "Marlon says there's a few acts I should scope, possibly for Prodigy."

"Just how do you plan to keep us off the radar?"

"Very simple." He walks backwards toward his closet, pulling me with him by the belt. Once we're in, he turns me to face a small alcove at the back. "Voila."

It basically looks like he raided the nearest Salvation Army. This collection of out-of-date jackets, floral-patterned shirts and polyester pants could only mean one thing.

"You're going in disguise?"

"*We're* going in disguise." He laughs at the expression I can only imagine is on my face. "While you were blow drying all that hair of yours, I had Sarita run out and buy you a few things that should fit."

"I hope it's not polyester."

"No, that's my thing." He opens a small drawer in the panel of built ins. "Let me show you what I was thinking."

He pulls out a jacket that's straight from Goodwill.

"Is that a Member's Only Jacket?" I hold it against my chest. "So what are you, the last Member?"

"*Shallow Hal,*" he says absently, not looking away from the array of horrific shirts he's flipping through to offer the movie reference. "Throwing soft balls this morning, are we?"

I haven't movie stumped him in a long time. Must try harder.

He pulls out a small drawer beneath a row of watches to reveal a disgusting display of fake lip hair.

"You have a mustache collection?" I cackle through the hand covering my mouth. "That's just weird."

"My life is weird." He turns to me, the expression on his face so earnest you'd think this was a matter of national security. "OK. Here's the first option. I usually save this for special occasions. It's the handle bar moustache."

"That thing is not leaving the house with me."

"See? I knew you would say that."

"No, you didn't."

"I did, so I have a back-up." He points to a row of thin moustaches.

"And here we have the Creeper Collection, ladies and gents," I say, disgusted by the little hairy squiggles.

"Is that a no?" His face actually falls.

"Resounding no!"

"What about this one?" He points to an obscenely thick row of hair.

"It's the size of a pregnant caterpillar."

"It's the Magnum P.I. What I like to call full lip coverage. No one ever recognizes me behind this thing."

"That one will do, I guess. Let's just go so we won't miss the first acts."

"Wait." He gives me an I'm-loving-this grin and gestures back toward the array of lip toupees. "You have to choose yours."

"Mine?" My mouth drops open. "I'm not wearing a moustache."

"Come on. Get in the spirit. It's like Halloween, but better."

"Is there candy?"

"No."

"Then it's not better."

"I think going full guy will guarantee that no one recognizes you." He grabs me by the hips and does a little shake, his voice cajoling me. "It'll be fun."

Those sound like famous last words to me, but to be with Rhyson after so long, even in this ridiculous get up will be worth it.

Chapter NINE

RHYSON

DAMN, THESE GUYS ARE GOOD. THE band, Kilimanjaro, lives up to all of Marlon's hype. And then some. I especially like the bass player. That's one instrument I consider myself only adequate on, so I envy guys who can make it speak the way this one does. The bass has a soul, a musical undercurrent that, though subtle, anchors everything else. And the bass player is the soul of this band.

"What do you think?" I turn to study Kai, whose eyes haven't left the stage since Kilimanjaro came on.

"They're fantastic." She turns to me, her eyes wide and a huge grin on her face. "The bass player's sick, right?"

I nod, distracted by the peculiar and entrancing picture she makes. Sarita bought her some boy jeans, which fit okay, but I still can't stop staring at her ass. The bulky, hooded sweatshirt does a good job of disguising her breasts, but that face . . . The delicate bones and striking lines, even under the baseball cap, with all her hair hidden, would still stop me in my tracks. Those full, pouty lips look completely kissable under the thin moustache I finally convinced her to wear.

I can't believe she did this—came out in public like this with me. If I wasn't convinced there is only one girl in the world for me before, this did it.

"Rhys?" She frowns and pokes my chest. "I said they're fantastic. Are you listening?"

"Oh, yeah." I force my attention back to the subject at hand. "Think I should sign 'em?"

"Like yesterday." She returns her eyes to the stage. "Before someone else snatches them up."

"Yeah. I was feeling that, too."

"They're almost done with the set. Should we try to see them? Like get backstage?"

"Nah." I grab her fingers, locking them with mine. It feels so good to hold her hand in public again, even if everyone does assume we're just two gay guys in love, taking in the show. "I'll have my people call their people."

"You think they have people?"

"They're booked for a festival this size. Believe me, they have people. They may be unsigned, but they're not unorganized. Somebody's running things."

"So I guess now you have Prodigy's second act."

I push down my irritation. *She* should have been Prodigy's second act. She would have been if John Malcolm hadn't interfered.

"What exactly is your deal with Malcolm? And for how long?" I try to look harmless. "If you don't mind me asking, of course."

"I *do* mind you asking because we said we wouldn't talk about any of that today." She steps close enough for me to smell her mother's soap. "If you're not talking to the band, you have to feed me."

I keep thinking about all the weight she's lost.

"Gladly." I place my hand at the curve of her waist beneath the sweatshirt, my fingers brushing the velvety skin of her back. "What do you want?"

She looks up at me, and I know what she wants because I want it, too. To be as physically close as possible every moment we have together. Since last night's infamous piano encounter, we've been insatiable. It's not just our bodies that can't get enough. I've missed every part of her equally. Her laugh. Her kisses. The silences we fill up with all the things we don't ever have to say aloud. And when I can't find the words to tell her the world is less bright when she's not around, my body speaks for me. Sometimes there's no other way to say it.

And I love that everything I'm feeling, I see reflected back every time she looks at me. She can't hide it.

"Why are you looking at me like that?" Suspicion tinges her voice, even though she's smiling just the tiniest bit.

"Nothing."

"It's not nothing." She narrows her eyes at me. "Tell me what you were thinking."

"I'll sound like a dick."

"Won't be the first time."

Oh, she's got jokes.

"Okay. You asked for it." I heave a longsuffering sigh, preparing myself for a ball busting. "I was thinking that I like seeing the effect I have on you."

Pink crawls over her cheeks, immediately making my case.

"How you . . . what?" Her eyes slide down and to the side. "What do you mean?"

"Well, your cheeks, for one thing." I brush a knuckle over the high slant of one cheekbone. "You blush."

"I do not blush, Rhys," she says unconvincingly.

"Yeah, okay." I laugh because her cheeks just get pinker by the second. "And your breathing changes. Kind of catches."

As if on cue, her breath hitches in her throat. It's incredibly arousing knowing I'm doing this to her in a crowd, like my words are stroking her under her clothes.

"And then," I say, leaning down so my words land right in her ears. "It's like you don't know what to do with your hands. You touch your throat. Put your hands in your pockets. You fidget. After months together, I love seeing that you still respond that way to me."

She lowers her eyes to the sand under our feet, a wry smile crooking her mouth.

"You were right. You do sound like a dick."

I recapture her hands, pulling her into me.

"But it's the same for me." I have to laugh at myself. "Maybe worse. I feel all of that when you walk into a room. Hell, I feel that waking up beside you."

"Well, I can't tell."

"Guys just do a better job at hiding that shit. Only fair since we can't even hide our erections. At least we can hide our feelings. Maybe it's the male's overdeveloped evolutionary response so we don't look like pussies. A mating thing."

I pause, tilting my head to consider my little Southern Baptist girl.

"You *do* believe in evolution, right?"

"I'm a Creationist, actually."

"You've got to be kidding." I shake my head, grinning and on the verge of laughter. "Pep, that's basically a fairy tale."

"Says you."

"Says science."

"I believe that science and faith can peacefully co-exist."

"But you must have questions. I mean, half of it makes no sense. Doesn't even compute."

"Is something less powerful because you have questions about it? Because sometimes you have doubts or you're unsure?"

"Are we still talking about creation?" I frown a little, her question provoking me.

"Among other things. Is it really faith if it doesn't require you to stretch yourself beyond the rational? Past your questions?" The intensity of her eyes holds me completely. "Mama always said faith requires at least a little bit more than you think you have. You should be glad I was raised that way. It may be the only thing holding this dysfunctional relationship together."

"Oh, really?" Now that grabs my attention by the horns. "How do you figure?"

"I was raised with the capacity to believe in something that I can't see and always have questions about, but have no doubt is absolutely real."

She tips up on her toes and hovers over my lips.

"Like us."

She comes in the last few inches to lay those sweet lips on me. I open for her and lose myself in that kiss for long seconds. She draws my tongue in deeper, until with a groan, I squat to grab her butt and lift her up. When my moustache starts slipping and sliding around our lips, she laughs, pulling away.

I catch the eye of a lady over Kai's shoulder watching us intently, who gives me two thumbs up.

"Love is love, my man," she says. "You and your little guy look great together."

I smile and adjust my moustache. I glance back at Kai, whose eyes are still a little dreamy and glazed from our kiss.

"Pep, you keep looking at me like that, I'm dragging you over to one of those ships in the harbor to play rock the boat with my little boy toy."

"No rocking any boats." She pulls back pouting. "Your little guy's hungry. You promised me food. And, no, I'm not having public sex with you."

"Spoilsport." I laugh down at her while we make our way toward a row of food trucks not too far from the main stage.

A few minutes later, I must concede that her weight loss is probably not from lack of food. We've spread a blanket as close to the ocean as we safely can. Kai is chomping her way through a fried feast that would daunt a linebacker. French fries topped with crab meat. Yuck, by the way. Not to mention the pork belly chips, a monster burger and deep fried Oreos. This meal should come with a pacemaker, but my girl, barely able to get her little hand all the way around this mammoth burger, is halfway through hers before I've even dented mine.

"What?" She glances up from her half-empty, grease-laden plate, sauce all around her lips. "You're not hungry?"

"Obviously not as hungry as you are." I reach over to wipe her mouth with my napkin.

"You're not supposed to tease a lady about how much she eats," Kai says, mouth full. "It's impolite."

"Not even when this delicate flower eats me under the table?"

She falls back on the blanket, chewing and laughing, looking up at a cloudless sky. Even after the laugher stops, her smile lingers. With a parade of boats in the harbor, music drifting from the main stage, the sun warming our faces, and the people around us clueless about who we are, I can't think of one thing I wouldn't do to make her smile this way every day. She blurs everything. Erases every line I've drawn in the sand. Forces me to rethink the boundaries of right, wrong, acceptable, never would, and couldn't ever. She's my absolute. It should scare me, but I'm just too damn grateful to have her. I'm just too determined to never screw things up so badly again that she walks away.

Speaking of . . .

"So back on the road tomorrow, huh?" I keep my tone casual, but the voice in my head; that overgrown spoiled boy who wants his way 24/7 stomps around my brain throwing a tantrum. We've only had a few days together. A hundred and one excuses swirl in my head to keep her here with me instead of going back on the road. With Dub.

"Yeah." All traces of her smile evaporate. Her eyes, when they meet mine, are cautious. "Bright and early."

"Can you stay with me tonight?"

"The car's coming at five in the morning to pick me up from San's."

"I could take you to the airport, or the car could pick you up from my place."

"Except." She bites her lip and looks out at the ocean instead of at me. "That kind of defeats the purpose of us keeping our relationship on the low."

My lips clench over the words that want out so badly. That I don't give a damn who knows. That Dub and everyone else *should* know she's mine. That I hate her being out on the road unclaimed. I adjust my Dodgers cap and smooth two fingers over my fake stache.

"Stay with me tonight." I put on my "hear me out" face. "I'll take you to San's as early as you need me to. Unless you don't want to stay?"

Her eyes jerk back to me, a small frown on her face.

"You know I want to stay. I want as much time with you before I leave as possible."

"Then it's settled." I stand, reaching down to pull her up to her feet. "We have tonight."

"And the rest of the day." She leans up, resting her forearms on my chest. "What do you want to do now?"

"Let's walk for a while. It feels good to walk around and not be recognized, bothered for an autograph, have some camera shoved in my face." I bend to grab one end of the blanket, meeting her eyes across it as she takes the other corners and we fold it up. "But you've gotten a taste of that now, too."

"Some." She shakes her head, taking my side to finish the blanket in a neat square she stuffs it into our backpack. "Not anything close to what you deal with."

"It's only a matter of time." I wed our fingers, looking down at not just my girlfriend, but soon-to-be one of the hottest stars out there. I'm struck again by how proud I am of her, despite the fact it isn't the route I would have chosen. Despite the fact I wouldn't trust John Malcolm as far as I could toss his lard ass. She's doing it. Her way, not my way, but she's doing it. And, as hard as I fought it, it kind of makes me love her that much more.

We explore every corner of the festival, abusing our anonymity any way we can. We ride the Ferris wheel bordering the water. At the top, I take her mouth in a kiss as light as meringue and as rich as cream. Kai gets her face painted, sunrays on one side and rainbows on the other. We devour our combined weight in funnel cakes. To the world, just two guys in love. To us, it's everything. It's every date we never got to go on. Every moment we've ever had to steal all squeezed into one sunlit day.

The sun is going down when we come across a guy busking on the boardwalk, guitar slung across his shoulder, hat on the ground. Attention isn't the only thing people aren't paying him. His hat sits empty, which gives me an idea.

I look down at Kai, who's now starting to fray around the edges some. She's held off the exhaustion revealed by the faint lines bracketing her mouth and the shadows under her eyes as long as she could. Now it's starting to show. I want to get her home so she can rest before the tour restarts tomorrow. One last thing will seal this day, and then we'll leave.

"Are you thinking what I'm thinking?" I ask, knowing damn well she can't be.

"I doubt it." She laughs, reaching into her pocket to pull out a dollar and drop it into the busker's hat.

"Hey, dude." I gesture to his guitar. "Lemme hold that for you while you take ten."

"My guitar?" By the look on his face, you'd think I just asked for his kidney. He may not be a great musician, but he definitely loves his guitar like one.

"Ten minutes." I shrug. "I'll be right here. You can even stay and watch to make sure I don't leave. Just give your fingers a rest."

"Man, I gotta make rent." He shakes his head and flexes his fingers. "I'm nowhere close."

"What'll get you there?" I reach for my wallet. I know he'll probably bloat the price, but I don't really care right now. I'm past smart and am pretty much just determined.

"You serious, man?" His wide eyes go from my face to my wallet a couple of times. "My share is two hundred."

"And how much have you made today?"

"Around thirty."

"Like I said, take a break." I offer him two hundred dollar bills. "Ten minutes."

That guitar is off before I've put my wallet away. He hands it to me, a huge smile on his face. I slip the strap over my shoulder, plucking a few strings to see how badly out of tune it is. For my purposes, it'll do. Kai's standing off to the side watching and grinning, arms folded across her chest. I dig around in my mind for the lyrics I want to sing, hoping I don't screw this up since Kai is an expert on this song and this artist.

"They say we're young and we don't know," I sing, strumming the familiar chords. "We won't find out until we grow."

I sing the rest of the first verse and then nod my head, encouraging her to sing what comes next. To my surprise, she darts over and tips up on her toes until she can whisper in my ear.

"That's actually Cher's part. Cher goes first. Then Sonny."

When she pulls back, I expect at least a smile, but no. If there is one thing Kai's serious about, it's her Cher.

"Sooooo . . ." I keep playing and roll my eyes. "Let me guess. You want to sing Cher's part?"

She nods, an infectious grin stretching between her cheeks. So we start over, her singing Cher's part, me singing Sonny's. Our voices tangling up at the chorus, declaring I got you, babe. A small crowd gathers around, and a few dollar bills land in the hat. Some even start to sway with the music we're making.

It is, without a doubt, the simplest, goofiest song maybe ever written, but there is something about the lyrics. Something about the defiant, doubt-us-if-you-dare, naïve hope of a love like the one we're singing about. It grips me. Our eyes hold, and before I know it, our smiles fade. There's no one on this boardwalk but us. The sunset is ours alone, and I'm singing a promise to the only girl I've ever loved. And miraculously, after all I did to destroy it, everything about her says she loves me back. If there's a moment more perfect, I've never had it.

And unless it's with Kai, I don't want it.

Chapter TEN

RHYSON

K AI MAY BE THE ONLY PERSON who would get me in a room
face to face with my parents. I've only seen them a handful of
times outside of a courtroom since I emancipated. One of those
times, last year, I fondly refer to as Bloody Christmas. Another was
necessitated by threat of death when my father had a heart attack.
Even after his apology, my visits to him as he rehabilitated were in-
frequent. A whispered half-apology when he was wired up like Fran-
kenstein and mere heartbeats from death doesn't bridge the chasm
the years have created between us. As for my mother, I've met den-
tures less fake.

"I first want to commend you all for coming today," Dr. Ramirez,
our counselor, adjusts her glasses and leans back in the leather arm-
chair like the ones my parents and I occupy. "Taking the time to repair these relational breeches is a positive step that many never take."

I fix my eyes on her instead of looking at my mother and father.
She has kind eyes behind her glasses. Well-meaning eyes, I'm sure,
but I'm not convinced she can perform a miracle we haven't been

able to achieve in almost fifteen years of enmity.

My father and mother seem as determined to *not* look at me as I am to *not* look at them. Tension clogs the air, that hand gripping my throat the way it always does after more than five minutes with them. I reach to loosen my collar, but there isn't one on my Ramones t-shirt. I'm choking from the inside.

"This is our first session." Dr. Ramirez tucks a dark strand of hair behind one ear. "So we won't go too deep today, but I would like to hear from each of you. Tell me what you hope to get out of this. Why you're here. Rhyson, why don't we start with you? Why are you here today?"

"My girlfriend made me come."

Shit. I should at least try to sound less coerced. Well, cards on the table, I guess.

"What girlfriend?" My mother finally turns her eyes my way. "I thought you and Kai broke up."

Like it's your business.

I just stare back at her for a few seconds, not sure how to respect Kai's wish for secrecy and still be honest. Before I can figure that out, my mother goes on.

"I saw her at Grady's wedding." She shrugs. "We talked briefly."

Remembering how snooty my mother was to Kai at the hospital when my father had his heart attack, I immediately want to figure out how she may have insulted her. Dr. Ramirez doesn't leave time for that, though.

"Why did your girlfriend . . ." She nods to my mother. "Ex-girlfriend want you to come, if you don't mind sharing?"

I could brush this whole process off, just be a body in a comfy seat once a week, but Kai is trusting me to actually try. Her trust isn't something I'll ever take for granted again, so I'll actually try.

"We had a big blow out." I cross an ankle over my knee, shrugging though talking about my fight with Kai feels anything but casual. "I did something stupid that she felt . . . feels . . . might be connected to unresolved issues with my parents."

Interest deepens in Dr. Ramirez's eyes, raises both brows.

"May I ask what that was?" At my sharp glance up she back-pedals a little. "If you don't mind sharing. If you don't want to . . ."

What the hell.

"She's in the business, like me." I give my parents a cursory glance before going on, realizing just how exposed my confession will leave me. How bad it could make me look. "She had an opportunity I didn't feel good about, and I went behind her back to convince them to pass her over."

"To pass Kai over?" my mother asks, a small frown between her neatly arched brows.

"Yeah."

"Why did you do that, Rhyson?" Dr. Ramirez leans forward until her elbows rest on her knees, eyes intent.

"Because I love her." I swallow hard, wishing I hadn't started this. Already wishing I'd held more back.

"You love her so you went behind her back to deny her an opportunity?"

Well, when you put it that way, it sounds ridiculous.

"Maybe not my brightest moment," I admit. "But at the time, it seemed like the best thing."

"The best thing?" Dr. Ramirez presses.

"For her. She's new to all of this and doesn't know the pitfalls like I do." I hold Dr. Ramirez's eyes, hoping she'll see past my asshole actions to my intentions. "I just wanted what was best for her. Honestly. That's the only reason I did that."

"And she didn't agree?" Dr. Ramirez asks.

"No, she thought it was controlling and manipulative." A hoarse laugh barges past my lips. "She might have a point. She thinks control and love get mixed up for me because of everything that happened with my parents."

I don't bother looking at them. My mother, whose hackles I feel rising from across the room, or my father, who's been pretty much on mute the whole time. I look at the counselor. I *need* her to tell me Kai is wrong. I *need* her to tell me what I feel isn't some tainted thing I inherited from my parents because it's the purest thing I've ever felt.

And if this isn't even clean, isn't good, I hold very little hope for my-self to ever be any different from the two people sitting across from me.

And that scares the hell out of me.

"Mrs. Gray," Dr. Ramirez says. "Let's hear from you. What are you hoping to get out of these sessions? Why are you here?"

My mother clears her throat and studies her hands before glanc-ing at Dr. Ramirez and letting her eyes drift to me.

"Well, I have wanted this kind of opportunity for years to make Rhyson understand why we handled things the way we did." The eyes I see every morning when I face myself in the mirror look back at me. "That we only wanted what was best for him."

"So giving me your Xanax when I was twelve," I say, old anger snipping my words. "And once I was obviously addicted, telling me we'd consider rehab after I met my tour obligations, that was best for me, Mother?"

A weighty silence overpowers the room, and Dr. Ramirez's wide eyes skitter between my mother and me. That isn't public knowl-edge. That never came out in court when I emancipated. It was only Grady's threat to expose it that convinced my parents to drop the fight and let me go.

If only my mother would flush with shame. Or maybe betray some guilt with a flurry of blinks. Hell, I'd settle for anger narrow-ing her eyes at me. But her face remains smooth, implacable and un-affected. Her posture stays straight, and she doesn't squirm or shift when she meets my outrage.

"We've been through this before, Rhyson." She sounds like she did when I was a child. Like I was something she had to tolerate, a means to her profitable ends. "Maybe here with Dr. Ramirez I can finally make you see it my way."

I'm not even a therapist and I know that can't be right. The word "make" smacks of control, and is already hitting too close to home. Is that how I sound to Kai? Like selfishness veneered with platitudes? If so, I make myself sick.

"Well, we'll get into those deeper issues later, I'm sure. We're just getting started today." Dr. Ramirez focuses that kind stare on my father for a moment. "Mr. Gray, what about you? You've been very quiet. What did you want today? Why are you here?"

My father clears his throat. He's lost weight since the heart attack. I grew up with him a giant in my mind, but every time I see him, he seems a little smaller.

"What I want," he says, looking me straight in the eyes for the first time, "the only thing I'm here for is to convince Rhys that I'm sorry. That I realize now how badly I mishandled things when we were managing his career. I treated him like a meal ticket instead of a son. It wasn't until I almost died that I realized the damage I'd done. I'm asking him for a second chance. I'm asking him to forgive me."

Emotions wrestle in my chest. I don't want this. I don't want his words to whiz like a dart past my hurt and disillusionment and find a bullseye on my heart, but they do. At the same time, it's what I've always wanted. I've wanted him to see it, to mean it. And there's no way I can look at the sincerity in his eyes, more like Grady's today than I've ever seen them, and not know that he *does* mean it.

I don't say a word, and neither does he. We just stare at one another, blinking and swallowing, holding everything back. Keeping it locked up tight.

"Thank you, Mr. Gray," Dr. Ramirez says softly. "I think we often underestimate the power of a sincere sorry. We think our reasons and excuses somehow make the hurt we've caused make sense, but the damage is done, and the only thing that makes it any better is admitting how wrong we were.

The kindness in Dr. Ramirez's eyes makes its way into her smile.

"Sometimes our best intentions come with our worst decisions," she says. "We're lucky to have people forgive us in situations like that."

I'm grateful for her words, which give me something to focus on besides my father and the awkward, confusing softening his apology imposed on me. I don't know what I feel, but I know I've never felt it before today, before he apologized.

Dr. Ramirez pushes her glasses up her nose with one finger and spreads a considering look between the three of us.

"It may be beneficial to schedule some one-on-one sessions with each of you to supplement our group time." She closes a little pad I hadn't really paid much attention until now. "If you decide that's the direction you should take, the receptionist out front can set that up."

As we're standing at the front desk setting up the next sessions, my father touches my shoulder. I look from his hand to his face carefully.

"I hope things work out with Kai," he says. "I can tell you really care about her."

I nod, allowing the touch to linger for a moment before stepping back.

"I need to go. I've got a session," I lie. "See you next week."

I'm on my way to the elevator, turning everything over in my head when it strikes me how hard it probably was for my father to apologize. I glance back to see him standing off to the side, studying his shoes while my mother consults her calendar with the receptionist.

"Hey, Dad."

He looks up, his expression surprised that I'm still here.

"What you said in there." I falter, unsure of how to finish what I started. "It was . . . well, thanks. It meant a lot."

He doesn't respond, just looks kind of thrown before nodding and giving me a smile that, for the first time in a long time, I find easy to return.

Chapter ELEVEN

Kai

YOU WANTED THIS. YOU WORKED FOR *this. You dreamt of this.*

Those reminders chant in my head as I go through the new routine Dub wants to introduce for the European leg of our tour for what feels like the hundredth time. And I still can't quite get it. I'm a step behind, short of breath. My synapses seem to be misfiring. We've been in London for two days, and we open tomorrow night. All I want to do is go find some fish and chips and ride a double-decker bus. Maybe go see Big Ben. Visit the Poet's Corner in Westminster Abbey.

As much as my feet hurt, as much as my eyes burn, as tired as I am, I'd settle for the inside of my hotel room. I'd settle for my bed.

"Kai, you with us?" Dub leaps down from the platform where two dancers simulate a club scene for this number.

"Huh?" I jump a little when he lands right in front of me. "Yeah, sure."

"Good. 'Cause when we're done here, I had an idea to add to the lap dance for Luke's number."

Can I tap out? I silently beg him not to give me any more new material. I thought the week off would reinvigorate me, for this last month on the road. Re-energize me for Europe. Instead my body just realized what it had been missing and is craving more. Rest. Relaxation. Rhyson.

Mostly Rhyson.

Being back on tour, having this distance between us is ideal for the situation with my blackmailer. There are fewer chances to slip up and provoke him to release that sex tape, but I miss Rhyson. And even though San reports little progress, and the threat still looms, if I were in LA, I'd find a way to be with Rhyson, no matter how much I had to sneak around. Despite the risk.

But I'm not in LA with Rhyson. I'm here. Living the dream.

Some dream.

"Let's catch a quick break before we take it from the top." Dub glances at the countdown clock mounted on the sound booth in the middle of the arena. "Fifteen minutes, guys."

Before Dub can pull me to the side to coach me on a move, or worse, not coach me. Just find an excuse to talk about nothing at all. I skip down the stage steps, barreling down the aisle before anyone stops me.

"Kai!" Dub calls from stage.

"Yeah," I answer, but keep moving forward.

"Kai! Wait up!"

His heavy steps pound behind me. He catches up, gently taking my arm and turning me to face him.

"Wanna go grab a coffee across the street before we get started back?" His eyes travel over my face and down my body. His interest is becoming harder to ignore. I don't want to acknowledge it to myself because eventually I'd have to acknowledge it to Rhyson. I already have a sex tape hanging over my head. With all the stress I'm under, another complication could crush me.

"I need to make a quick call." I step back until his hands fall away. I walk backward, forcing a smile. "I'll be back before we start."

Without waiting for his agreement, I resume my fast pace up

the aisle and out the side door that leads to the loading dock. Not a person in sight right now. Usually crew members and stagehands mill out here prepping props and equipment for the show.

I climb up onto a huge crate, scooting back until my back hits the wall and my feet can't hang over the side. Before I select the contact in my phone, I stare at it for a few seconds.

R. Geritol.

God, so much has happened since that first night when I saved Rhyson's number. I can't help but remember our day at the beach in disguise. We sang "I Got You, Babe." A laugh gurgles in my throat, and before I know it, I'm blinking back tears. Not even a week back on the road and I want to go home. I want to wake up in Rhyson's arms tomorrow morning. I want this sex tape to go away. I want to eliminate the threat to all Rhys and I are building. To all we could have.

It's ringing.

"Come on," I whisper. "Pick up."

I'm eight hours ahead of him, so it's only six in the morning there. I know he's been in the studio constantly and probably only got to bed a few hours ago, but I need his voice.

It's gonna go to voicemail. Disappointment rises in my chest. I bite my lip to keep it from trembling.

"Pep?" His voice comes just as I'm about to give up, sounding weary and half-dead. I should feel guilty that I woke him up.

"Were you asleep?"

Dumb question, but he'll let me get away with it.

"Um, pretty much." He clears his throat, and I can almost see him dragging himself up in bed with his shoulders against the headboard. I can almost smell that space between his neck and shoulder where I tuck my head. "It's cool. I'm glad you called."

"Things were hectic with us just getting to London so I didn't call yesterday." I pull one knee up to my chest. "I wanted to see how your first session with your parents went."

"You remembered." I hear the smile in his voice.

"I kinda made you go. Least I could do is see how it went."

"It was good. We're gonna do some individual sessions, and we may even bring Bristol and Grady in for a few later. Right now we're just focusing on the issues between the three of us."

"That's good, right?" I venture tentatively.

"Yeah, it's good. I just . . . I'm processing a lot after that first session." His sigh comes heavy from the other end. "My dad said he was sorry."

A dry chuckle crosses the line.

"And I believed him."

"That's great, right?"

"I guess, but it's like I can't quite get to the place of actually forgiving him. Ya know? Maybe that's what these sessions will do. I keep feeling like if I forgive him, I'm saying it's okay. Everything they did was okay, and it wasn't."

"That's not what forgiveness is about to me." I lower my voice some in case anyone is lurking. "At least not what I learned about in Sunday school."

"What's that version?" he asks.

"I remember a preacher once saying there's at least two categories of forgiveness. One is just as much about you as it is about the other person because unforgiveness left on its own too long becomes bitterness. And that can creep into every part of your life, end up hurting the people you love who had nothing to do with the person who hurt you."

"And the other category?"

"That's when someone you love has hurt you, and you hold on to it as long as you can until you can't anymore. The hurt of being apart from that person outweighs the hurt of what they did, and you just wanna make it right so you can repair the relationship."

Irony soaks the silent moment while Rhyson processes what I said. That preacher was my father, and I've still never found a way to forgive him.

"So which category did I fall into?" As soft as Rhyson's question is, it jars me.

"What do you mean?"

"When you forgave me? Was it the first or the second?"

"Maybe it was both." My throat is so raw it hurts to laugh. "I just woke up one morning and really needed to hear your voice. It just so happened to be the same day you asked to hear mine."

"Yeah?" The smile is back in his voice.

"Yeah." I'm smiling, too. I knew he could do that. "Sometimes forgiveness is a decision you make with your head that takes a while to reach your heart, and sometimes it's just . . . there. You'll know how to move forward with your dad. Your mom, too."

"Hey, speaking of my mother, she said she saw you at the wedding. Was she rude to you?"

There's always winter in Rhyson's voice when he speaks of his mother. A chill that I never hear for anyone else, not even his dad.

"No, she was cordial. I think she's hoping San and I will hook up and you'll be safe from my clutches."

"San?" His voice predictably hardens. "The hell?"

"Calm down, baby. It was a joke."

Kind of.

"Jokes are funny, Pep."

"I'll try to remember that."

"Hey, can I ask you something stupid?"

"Wouldn't be the first time."

"I'm serious. You know I love you, right?" Something in his voice desperately searches for the answer. "Not some twisted around control thing handed down from my parents, like real love. You know you're the most important thing, right?"

"Baby, why—"

"Just answer me. Just tell me you know."

"Rhys, I know." I close my eyes to savor this sweet moment his words just made for me.

"Good. Yeah, well." He sounds like now he feels silly. "I just wanted to make sure."

A smile stretches over my face as I recall our day at the music festival. "I keep thinking about that day at the beach. It was—"

"Kai!" Dub's voice snatches me away from the conversation.

"There's a blogger Malcolm wants you to talk to. Hurry up so we can get back to the routine as soon as you're done."

He's covered in curiosity. Who am I off talking to by myself with a goofy grin on my face?

"I'll be right there." I wait for him to walk away before speaking. "Hey, I gotta—"

"I heard Dub." Rhyson's tone is stiff as bark. "Duty calls."

"You know there's nothing going on between us." My voice drops to a whisper. "You know it's only you."

"I know how *you* feel. I have my suspicions about *him*."

So do I, but that would inflame this conversation, and I don't want that when we only have seconds left.

"Can I be completely honest with you?" he asks.

"Always."

And I'll be completely honest with him . . . as soon as I figure out how.

"I knew you'd make it big. I just thought I'd be a part of it."

"You are, Rhys. You are."

"I haven't even seen you perform on tour. Not one show. And to know that he gets to . . ."

A harsh breath breaks the silence his words slipped into.

"He's there every step. He gets to share *all* of it with you, and I hate that." He's quiet for just a second. "I want that."

So do I.

"I'd probably be really nervous if I knew you were in the audience and fall on my face anyway," I say to lighten the moment heavy with his honesty. "But I do wish you were here, too."

"The tour's ending in LA, right?"

"Yeah, it was a scheduling nightmare. By all rights, we should have done LA with the North American leg, but Luke wanted to end it all in his hometown with a big bang."

"Maybe I'll catch that last show here in town."

I've been performing for thousands every night, but the thought of this one man in the audience breaks me out in a cold sweat.

"Okay." A nervous laugh breaks free. "Just don't tell me for sure."

"Kai, come on." He chuckles. "Are you serious?"

"As a heart attack. I can't explain it, but knowing you're there would freak me out."

"Okay. I won't tell you if I come. I couldn't come to a show right now even if I wanted to anyway," he says. "I'm helping Jimmi with her album, putting finishing touches on Marlon's, and working on a few of my tracks."

"Yay for yours." I smile. "Seems like you've been working on everyone else's stuff."

"Well, I got quite a bit of material done while you were on tour." There's something in his voice I don't understand, but I don't press.

"Really? That's great."

"Yeah, it was a little bit of a musical bender where I forgot to bathe and groom myself, but some good stuff came out of it."

I wrinkle my nose.

"Sorry I missed that."

"I'm not." He laughs. "So anyway, some of the songs I did are good, but need an edge. You know DJ Kaos?"

"German?"

"Yeah. He lives in Berlin. He's coming to LA in a few days to go in the studio. See if we can sharpen some of the stuff I came up with."

Berlin's not too far. We'll be there soon. Maybe I could stow away in the dee jay's luggage.

"Pep, are you okay?"

The question comes like a flash of lightning, cracking into the conversation with unexpected force. No one has asked me in days how I'm doing. Everyone just assumes this pace, these demands, take no toll, but they have. They do. I don't want to acknowledge how much of a toll the last two months have taken on me. On my body, my voice, my mind. Part of me doesn't want Rhyson to worry. And part of me doesn't want him to know, in many ways, he was right.

"I'm fine. I just gotta go."

He's quiet on the other end, like he's probing between the lines of what I'm saying. Hunting for what I won't say.

"Yeah, the blogger. I heard."

"I love you, Rhys." Stupid tears flood my throat.

"Baby, you know I love you more than anything. If you need me—"

"I'm good. It's just a tour, Rhyson. I'm good. Promise." I clear my throat. "They're gonna come looking if I don't—"

"Yeah. Okay. Bye."

I know that once I say this word, it's over. This conversation, this connection to him, is over, and I'm back to the grind. As much as I love performing and as much as this really is all a dream come true, it's chaos. I'm ready to rest. And there's no greater peace than Rhyson. So I hold off as long as I can until I know I absolutely have to go. And then I say it.

"Goodbye."

Chapter TWELVE

Kai

LONDON. CHECK

Manchester. Check.

Today. Rehearsals.

Tomorrow night, our show here in Berlin.

DJ Kaos' stomping grounds. I guess he's in LA with Rhyson by now. Just three weeks and I go home. I can do this. I realized it might be more than just fatigue weighing me down. I think I'm coming down with something. Like I can afford that.

"Tea?" Ella walks across the stage, steaming mug in hand.

I finish the last of my stretches before rehearsal starts and accept her lemon-scented gift. The first sip soothes my raw throat, coating the rough spots.

"Honey?" I aim a smile at my makeup artist over the brim.

"Of course." Ella grins, leaning against the stage wall. "I know by now how you like it."

She frowns, eyes sharpening on my face.

"And I could tell last night you were a little under the weather."

An ill-timed cough racks my chest before I can respond.

"I'm fine," I say once the little coughing bout passes. "Just tired. I could use some vocal rest, but I don't see that coming with back-to-back shows in front of us. Just glad to have the night off."

"You gonna explore Berlin some?" Ella looks over at a cluster of back-up dancers. "They're hitting the clubs tonight. You going?"

"I think I'll stay in. Try to lose this cold."

"So you *do* have a cold?"

I grin at the little trap she set for me.

"Little bit, but nothing rest and more of your tea won't make better."

Two strident claps draw everyone's attention center stage. Dub stands in the middle, loose jogging pants hanging low on his lean hips, fitted t-shirt clinging to his muscled torso. All the girls love Dub. I hope he'll focus more on the girls who actually want him and less on me.

"Let's hit it, fam." Dub points to the back-up dancers. "Places. Where's Kai?"

"Present and accounted for, sarge." I raise my hand with a grin, which he returns.

"Good. Let's run through those new steps. See if we can nail 'em before the show tomorrow."

For the next two hours, we work without a break. Malcolm got the right one. Dub understands the high expectations Malcolm sets for the whole team, and is more than happy to meet them. Exceed them. He's the best choreographer in the business right now, and I'm so fortunate to have him. I remind myself of that when he snaps at me again because I've missed another step.

What is *wrong* with me? I've always prided myself on being a quick study. Show me a combination once, twice. I got it. But this new routine eludes me. I just can't quite execute it. There's a row of dancers behind me who would kill to be in my place wondering why I can't get it together.

"Okay, fam. I think we got it." Dub looks at me meaningfully. "Well, most of us got it. You guys take off. I know some of you hood rats are planning to get all nasty in Berlin tonight."

Everyone laughs and whoops. I could probably be closer to them all if I went to the clubs they hit in every city. That's never been my thing. I've never been that girl who lets it all hang out. Every time I try, it ends badly.

One-night stand with a D List rock star and a sex tape, anyone?

"Kai, hang back." Dub waves me over. "Let's chop it up for a sec."

The weight of a dozen knowing eyes lands on my back as I cross the stage. Dub glances around, watching them watching me. His frown softens a little.

"Why don't we step into my office for some privacy?" He lightly grasps my wrist and pulls me backstage away from all the eyes.

"I know what you're gonna say," I start before he can. "I'll have it. I'll get it. You know I will."

"But you don't yet, and I've never seen that from you." Concern fills his eyes. "You okay?"

"I think I'm coming down with something." I rush to fix it. "But it's nothing. It's just taking a half step off maybe."

"So I guess I shouldn't ask you to have dinner with me in the city tonight, huh?"

I don't want to look at him, so I study the shoes on my feet, the stage floor between my toes and his.

"Um . . ."

He tips my chin up with one finger, his thumb brushing my cheek. I have no choice but to meet his eyes.

"Hey, I know it's only been a few months since the breakup, and you're still getting over Gray."

"Not exactly." I frown and pull my chin from his grasp.

"But we'd be good together." He dips his head, looks at me from under thick, dark brows. "Give us a chance, Kai."

I shake my head, ready to tell him there is no chance. That we're just friends and that won't change, but he steals my words. Steals my chance.

Steals a kiss.

Before I can get the words out, his hand cups my head and his lips press to mine and his tongue is practically down my throat. One thick arm loops around me until I'm flush against his chest. My hands come up right away, shoving at an immovable force of muscle and bone.

"Stop," I mumble against his lips. "Dub, no."

A throat clearing behind us puts a stop to it. It's only been a few seconds, but it felt like forever trapped in his arms and against his mouth. I touch my lips, throbbing from the brief, but deep, kiss. We both turn to find Luke standing there, his narrowed eyes moving between Dub and me slowly, like he's trying to figure out what he just saw.

"Sorry." Luke focuses his attention on me. "Didn't mean to interrupt."

"You didn't," I say quickly. "There's nothing going on. I mean, we were . . . we . . . It's okay."

"Yeah, I can see that." Luke pushes a hand through his already tousled blond hair. "Your car's outside waiting to take you back to the hotel, Kai. Just letting you know."

"We could still do dinner." Dub looks down at me like he didn't just molest my mouth, pressing his hand to the small of my back. "I can come get you—"

"No." I step away, putting several inches between us, biting back my anger. How dare he grab me like that? Take that kiss from me? "I want an early night. I'll see you in the morning."

Dub fist pounds Luke as he passes him, leaving an unsettled quiet between Luke and me.

"What you saw . . ." I swipe a hand across my forehead. "It wasn't what you think you saw."

"You can do what you like, Kai." Luke turns his lips down at the corners and shrugs his broad shoulders. "I mean, if you were still dating one of my best friends, it would be my business. It would be a problem, but you're not. Right?"

A sheet of sweat wraps around my body like a damp toga. My heart thump thumps in my chest. My feet and my eyes shift. All telltale signs of guilt when I have nothing to feel guilty about. But no one knows Rhyson and I are together, and until San finds Drex and we can torture him a bit, no one will.

"Right." I nod, untying the sweatshirt sleeves from around my waist and slipping it over my head. "Yeah, that's right."

When I look up, I swear disappointment flashes across his face, but it's gone before I can be sure.

"Well, like I said, your car's waiting." Luke gestures back toward the stage. "I'm just talking through some production stuff with the lighting guys for tomorrow night."

"Yeah. Okay." I force a smile. Remind myself that I haven't done anything wrong. "I'll see you tomorrow then."

The venue is only a few minutes from my hotel, but I squeeze in a quick call to Aunt Ruthie from the back seat. We've been missing each other, phone tagging it. I know she's busy with Glory Bee, and I'm busy with all I have going on, but it's been weeks since we spoke voice to voice. How does that happen? How do the people who have always been closely woven into our lives become peripheral so quickly? Become . . . occasional?

"Aunt Ruthie, hi." I clear the scratchiness from my throat before going on with the voice mail, try to sound a little less nasally because I know she'll worry that I'm not taking care of myself. "Just checking in. I hope you got the money I sent. I know you're not really digital, so I mailed it. If you need more, just let me know. I'm making pretty good money with this tour and . . . Well, just let me know. I hope you're doing well. I've been thinking about you a lot."

My mind grapples for something else to say. Even though she's not listening, not there, I feel as connected to her as I have to anyone since I came back on tour.

"Hey, if you see Mama's soap recipe lying around anywhere, let me know. The pear cinnamon. I'm down to my last bar and . . ."

Tears collect at the corners of my eyes as a strong desire to be home overtakes me. To smell biscuits baking first thing in the morning. To sit on the front porch, an evening breeze on my face, the scent of honeysuckle thick in the air. I sniff quickly as we pull up in front of the hotel.

"I'll call back soon." I clench my eyes tight, swiping over my cheeks. "I love you, Aunt Ruthie. So much. I'm gonna try to get home real soon, okay?"

I don't even bother saying goodbye, just hang up the phone, thank the driver, and dash inside. As soon as I enter my hotel room, I peel off my clothes, leaving them in a rumpled pile of cotton at the foot of the bed. I'm too tired to even shower. My footed Jackson Five pajamas are right where I left them, under my pillow. I zip them up over my days of the week panties and pull the elastic from my ponytail, glad to have my hair loose around my shoulders and down my back.

Season three of *New Girl* waits on Hulu. I'm a real party animal. My wild life on the road. I glance at my phone, needing a little music before I join Jess and the gang. I flick through my playlists, but nothing strikes me. Nothing matches my mood until I come to the song that always meets me when I'm feeling adrift or alone.

Track number nine from Rhyson's first album. I drop my phone in the dock, flop onto the bed, throwing my arms over my head, and let the sounds of *Lost* suffuse every aching cell. My eyes close over tears I refuse to let fall. If they start they won't stop for a long time, and it's unreasonable. This is what I wanted. This is what I've worked all my life for. A million girls would give anything to have this shot.

"Who wrote that sad shit?" a voice asks from the bathroom entrance, the person still hidden in a chunk of darkness.

Panic sits me up straight with a hand over my palpitating heart, a river of fear running through me. But as soon as the person steps into the room, into the light, my heart rattles in my chest for a completely different reason.

"Rhys?"

His name rushes from my mouth on a breath, and I'm off the bed, hurling myself at him top speed. Somehow my legs wrap around his waist and my arms tangle behind his neck. I couldn't hold back and play this cool if I wanted to. Every part of me that's been fighting to stay focused, to keep working, to be *on*, collapses against him. Surrenders to the feel of him in my arms and the smell of him. My fingers lace through his hair. I scatter kisses across his face, the sharp angles and taut skin warm beneath my lips.

"So I take it you're happy to see me?" He chuckles, pressing his forehead to mine, hands squeezing my thighs.

"Happy?" I release something that's half a sob, half a laugh, pulling back a few centimeters to let him breathe. "What gave you that idea?"

We stop grinning at the same time, laughter dissolving, our bodies exchanging sensual information. My breasts flattened to his chest. His erection growing and hardening against my core. Our breaths mingling and hearts tattooing beats through our clothes and into the other's skin.

I move first, leaning in to capture his bottom lip between mine, sucking and pulling between my teeth. Licking into his mouth like there's honey hidden inside. He groans into the kiss, walking backward until we reach the bed and dropping me so I bounce a little, his eyes roving over me head to toe.

"Pep, what the hell are you wearing?" Humor and desire tussle in his eyes.

I look down, laughing when I see the young Jackson brothers emblazoned across my chest, my legs ending in the footed bottoms.

"If I'd known you were coming, I could have made sexier arrangements."

"Arrangements?" He quirks a dark brow, placing a knee on either side of my legs, hovering over me like a promise. "Lingerie would have been nice. Other rock stars have girlfriends who wear lingerie."

"Oh, are you referring to *yourself* as a rock star now?" I grin up at him, feeling whole for the first time since he kissed me goodbye a week ago. "That's not egomaniacal at all. Is there a club? You guys have rock star meetings? Does one of you take rock star minutes?"

"You *are* sitting in here listening to my music in the dark." He leans forward to tug at the zipper beneath my chin. "Maybe you're actually one of my crazed fans. Or a groupie. I might even find a Mrs. Rhyson Gray t-shirt around here somewhere. My girlfriend doesn't like those."

"No, she doesn't." I shake my head, eyes never straying from his.

A small frown jerks his brows together. He tugs again at the zipper, but it doesn't budge.

"Pep, it's stuck," he says.

"Sometimes it does that," I answer easily, enjoying the frustration spreading over his expression as he keeps pulling and it keeps staying.

He places my hand over his cock, hard and poking through his jeans.

"Well, it's not exactly a good time for it to *do that.*"

I laugh, grasping my zipper and tugging. Wow, it really is stuck. These are vintage PJs, older than I am and threadbare in places. I'm surprised the zipper hasn't rusted before now. I sit up, bringing our bodies closer as I jiggle the little hook a few times. Nothing.

"Just how attached are you to this Jackson Five onesie?" His glance burns hot across my subtle curves visible through the thin flannel, telegraphing his intentions.

"Well this *is* Michael's original nose." I release a fake exasperated sigh. "But I do have my sewing kit."

"All I needed to hear."

Sorry, boys.

He grabs the two ends of the collar separated by the zip line and pulls until there's a ripping sound, the panels falling back to reveal my naked breasts and my panties. A wicked grin spreads across lips.

"You naughty girl." He runs a finger over the writing on the front of my panties, carrying a current that simultaneously hitches my breath and gets me wet. "Wearing Monday panties on a Thursday. My little rebel."

"Well let's see what *you're* hiding." I hop off the bed, turning him by the shoulders until he's facing me, and push him to sit on the edge of the mattress. I grab the bottom of the Bob Marley hoodie he loves so much, pulling it over his head.

"Ah. What every rock star is wearing this year." I pluck at the shoulder of his t-shirt. "The obligatory wife beater."

"It's called layering." He laughs, hands sliding under my pajamas to push the material over my butt and down my legs. "As much as I'm enjoying all this conversation, I didn't cross time zones for banter. I need this to go faster."

"Faster, huh?" I kick the pajamas to the side and shimmy my panties off, stepping out of them and into the vee of his thighs. "Fast enough for you?"

There's no teasing left in his eyes. He lifts up, sliding his jeans and briefs off, pulling me onto his lap, my knees bordering him on either side.

"Did you miss me?" His hand slips between us, one long finger slowly, deliberately, sliding up and down my hot, wet slit while his eyes lock on mine.

"It's only been a week." My words float on a breath. It's all I can manage with my body begging his fingers to move, to possess me. To penetrate me. "I hardly had time to miss you."

One dark brow lifts, along with the left corner of his mouth. So damn sexy I want to skip all of this and just impale myself on him right now, but the waiting, the taunting of our bodies heightens every sensation.

He circles my clit, the motion stirring heat in my belly. The callus on his finger from playing guitar brushes over the thin, sensitive skin, erotic and rough. My breath is in a holding pattern, trapped in my throat, waiting for his next move.

"You sure you didn't find time to miss me?" His voice, always deep and smooth and dark, roughens with the desire written so clearly in his heavy-lidded eyes.

"That depends. Did you miss me, Rhyson?"

My hands wander over the muscles in his arms, over the lean chest and the ridges in his abdomen, down to grip and slide over his thick cock. He's smooth and hard in my hands, and I'm rewarded by his response. His head falls back, mouth drops open on a gasp. His fingers cover mine, guiding my hand, pacing me to his pleasure.

I lower myself, whispering my love over his chest before taking a nipple into my mouth, rolling my tongue around him. Suckling him hard while steadily gripping and pulling. He braces one hand on the bed behind him while the other cups my neck, his thumb brushing over my lips.

"I missed you." His eyes open, holding mine. "I missed this. You know I did."

"I missed the taste of you." I slip lower until my mouth hovers over him. "Can I taste you, Rhys?"

Without waiting for consent, I take him into my mouth, sliding my lips over him until he pushes against the back of my throat. I'm on the floor, on my knees between his thighs, greedily lapping and sucking at him, my hands gripping his hip, the muscled curve of his butt, the sinewed arm, anything to anchor me when the rich, salty taste of him on my tongue would send me into a tailspin. The longer he's in my mouth, the more desperate I am to taste him. To take him as far as he can go.

"Pep, fuck." He twists my hair around one hand, tugging until only the tip remains in my mouth. "Babe, I'm gonna come."

I nod, asking for it only with my eyes fixed on his. I pull him in deeper, my fingers wandering up his chest to twist his nipple until my name storms past his lips. He sets an erratic rhythm that's almost too much for me. Both his hands cup my head as he pushes deeper into the slippery interior of my mouth.

"Yes, baby. Fuck, Pep." He hauls in jagged breaths, his fist clenched in my hair just shy of pain. "Shit."

Every word pushes me higher, desperate to have him streaming hot and wet and thick down my throat. He's always so strong, but under my hands, in my mouth, he moans, head flung back, vulnerable, every defense stripped away. I can't take my eyes off him as I milk away his inhibitions. He tips his head up, our eyes locked as I watch him become as much mine as I am his in every way. I slow the motion of my mouth to a caress of my lips over him, finally, reluctantly releasing him. I run my tongue over my lips, still wet with his release.

"You didn't have to do that," he says, his voice raw and husky.

I stand, pushing his shoulders back to the bed, shocked by my own aggression.

"Did you enjoy it, though?" I ask unnecessarily. I taste the evidence of how much he enjoyed it.

"There's only one thing I love more than that." He pulls me forward until I'm straddling him, pulling one breast between his lips. My gasp fills the quiet hotel room. "That's being inside you."

He takes my mouth in a kiss, his tongue exploring and plundering. We twist into each other, desperation in every breath, in every brush of our lips. Each of us silently begging the other to go deeper, harder, moaning into the intimate contact. I grasp him, tugging until he's hard again in my hands.

He grabs my hips, poising me over him. "Ride me."

I rise up and down slowly, a raw, hot, wet slide of skin. My body grips him, and it's sweet and hot and tight like the first time. Even better than I remember. The reality of him more fantasy than my dreams.

"I'll never get enough of this." He kisses my throat until he reaches my lips again.

"You say that now," I gasp into our kiss. "We'll see what you think in twenty years."

My words freeze us both, my wide eyes finding his in the dim light of my hotel room. I can't believe I said that. We've never even discussed . . . I mean, you don't just say . . . you don't assume . . . I drop my eyes to the place between us where we're joined, my stomach caressing the muscles in his. He tugs my hair, bringing my eyes back to his face, back to his serious eyes.

"I fully anticipate that in twenty years you'll have me as whipped as I am tonight."

He pulls out, twisting until he's the one standing, and I'm lying down, my butt at the edge of the mattress. He pulls my legs over his shoulders, and the first thrust goes so deep and hard it scoots me up the bed. I grunt from the force of it, clenching the cool sheets between my fingers. I don't want him gentle. I want to still feel him when he's gone. The sensual paradox of his eyes, tender on mine, while his body takes me with rough passion pushes me over the edge.

One of his hands grips my thigh and the other grips the mattress, his handsome face twisting with the same emotion ripping through me as my body gives him the only response he demands, the only response it can.

Complete surrender.

Chapter THIRTEEN

RHYSON

TWENTY YEARS, HUH? MY MASTER PLAN is working. My heart almost fell right out of my chest when she said that. She's never referenced our future that way. In terms of decades spent together. She's thinking marriage, right? I've been thinking marriage since . . . let's just say it isn't a new concept to me. In terms of time, we haven't been together too long.

I know.

How else would I measure how long we've been together other than time? I measure it in terms of every private joke we shared in a roomful of people. In every kiss that feels like the first time over and over again. I measure it in how much better I want to be when she's in my life. In those terms, we've already got eons together.

"You're awfully quiet back there." Kai burrows her back deeper into my chest, looking up over one shoulder, her smile brighter than the dim lamp light.

I fold the length of her hair over one shoulder, baring a stretch of naked skin to feather kisses down her neck and between her shoulder blades. She flips onto her back, reaching up to brush the hair out of my eyes. Without skipping a beat, I shift my kisses to the front, dusting across her collarbone. I open my mouth wide over her breast, laving the nipple with my tongue until she arches up, her breath hitching and her fingers clenching at my scalp.

"Your nipples are absolutely perfect," I mumble into the underside of her breast. "Have I ever told you that?"

"Once, twice, five, maybe seven times." She laughs, her Southern drawl even slower, her breath still jagged, nipples tight and wet under my tongue.

"But that was in the throes of passion." I dip to kiss the tattooed prayer wrapping around her ribs. "I'm saying it completely sober, so you know it's true. Not in the throes."

"Will you stop saying throes? No one say throes."

"I just said it." I lift my head, teasing her with a glance. "You're saying I invented the word throes?"

"No, not invented, just that people don't use the word . . ." She rolls her eyes. "Shut up and get back to my nipples. You were saying?"

My hands roam her flat stomach and one sleekly muscled thigh. This girl and her dancer's legs are gonna be the death of me. I flip her back onto her side and spoon my body around hers until that tight ass is pressed against me as I reach around to cup her breasts. I know she's self-conscious about them.

"How could you ever think these breasts were anything less than perfect?"

"They're tiny," she whispers. "Most men—"

"Don't matter since I'm the only one who'll ever see them." A horrible thought blackens my brain and I turn her onto her back again. "Pep, you still want to act?"

"You know I do. Eventually. Malcolm already has an acting coach lined up."

Fucking Malcolm. Not even going there.

"I mean, you know you can't do nudity, right?"

"Rhyson," she groans. "Don't you dare start with this."

"And no sex scenes." Okay. Compromise. "I mean I guess, kissing is okay. Like *closed-mouthed* kissing."

She turns those tilted eyes my way wearing her "gimme a break" face.

"Name the last movie you saw with closed-mouthed kissing, no nudity, and no sex scenes, Rhys. In recent memory! *A Wonderful Life* doesn't count."

I mull that over because there's gotta be something she can do.

"*Frozen*." I can barely get it around the laugh swelling in my throat. "They had it on the plane."

"Dude, you just said *Frozen*."

"That's it. I just solved our problem. Animation. You'd make a great Pocahontas. Or who was that other one? Mulan?"

"Diverse Disney princesses." Her shoulders shake with the laugh. "That's what you're leaving me? And by the way, you don't have to physically resemble animated characters to play them."

"But it *would* lend a certain authenticity, don't you think?"

"We're not having this discussion any time soon."

"Animation could be a great way to ease into acting, Pep. I think you should consider it. Because if you start acting before you're good, I'll rotten tomato you."

"You would rotten tomato your own girlfriend?"

I shrug, turning down the corners of my mouth and linking my hands behind my head.

"If you suck, you'd leave me no choice."

"If you rotten tomato me, I'll never give you another blow job."

Even knowing she's pulling my chain, my heart stops for a second at the possibility of those lips never wrapped around my cock again.

"You, my lady, are the most powerful woman in the universe."

She laughs so hard she curls her legs up and grips her stomach under the sheet.

"Blow jobs make me the most powerful woman in the whole universe?"

I lift up on an elbow, turned on my side, pushing the hair back from her face.

"Nope. Just in mine."

Our eyes hold until the laughter evaporates.

"You're crazy, but I adore you," she whispers. "You know that?"

When someone says they adore you, it's like love with a heap of cherries on top. You could love someone and kind of hate them. But to *adore* them, you have to like them a lot. And still it seems a pretty flimsy word to describe what I feel for this girl.

She lifts off the pillow far enough to give me a quick kiss that I waste no time taking deeper, licking into her mouth and nudging my thigh between her legs.

"Don't start again," she says, the words husky against my lips. "Or we won't get to talk."

"And that's a bad thing?" My hands skim over a naked hip beneath the sheet.

"Yes." She pulls back to look at me. "You haven't even told me how this happened. How you came to be here with me."

"Maybe if you hadn't started humping my leg as soon as I walked through the door."

"You're so conceited." She chuckles, tracing the musical notes over my ribs. "How long do I have you?"

"Just tonight." We stop smiling as that sinks in. That when we wake up in the morning together, it'll be the last time for a while. "I checked the mistletoe schedule and realized you were headed for Berlin. Since Kaos lives here, I suggested coming to him instead of him flying to LA. I'm going to his home studio in the city tomorrow, and then I gotta fly back to work on Marlon's album."

"I'm glad you came." She drops her eyes from mine, biting one corner of her mouth. "I needed this."

So did I. I had to flip the world upside down and spin it around a couple of times to make this happen, but I'd do it again if it meant having this. Just one night. If anyone had told me a year ago I'd cross continents for one night with a girl, I would have laughed that person out of my face. And yet here I am. One night only and feeling no regret.

"How'd you get into my room?" Kai wears a frown at the top of her face, smile at the bottom.

"Luke told your road manager he was playing a joke or a prank and needed to leave something in your room."

Her fingers go still against my chest, and she looks up, smile gone.

"Luke?" She pulls back. "Luke got you into my room? He knows you're here? Knows we're together?"

"I know you don't want us public right now, but Luke's not public." I brush my thumb over her lips. "We can trust him not to tell anyone."

"Yeah, I know how close you guys are." She closes her eyes briefly before opening them again, finding mine in the half light, reluctance all over her face. "He, um, well, he saw something earlier today that he may have misunderstood. I need to tell you about it."

"What happened?" My hand falls away from her face.

"So he, uh, saw Dub kissing me backstage." She grips my biceps right away, probably because she already knows I'll find Dub and kick his ass all the way back to Ireland's fields of green. "I didn't kiss him back."

Volcanic heat scalds my face and neck, lava red hazing my eyes. She's still talking, but I couldn't tell you what the hell she's saying. I haven't heard a word since she said Dub kissed her.

"What the fuck, Pep?" I toss the sheet back and turn away from her, planting my feet on the floor, squeezing the edge of the mattress. Holding on to my control. My fingers rake through my hair as I struggle to check the rage pumping hot through my veins.

"I didn't kiss him back."

I glance back to see her sitting up against the headboard, eyes wide and lips still swollen from our kisses, from being wrapped around my cock.

"He kissed you? You let him?"

"No, as soon as he grabbed me—"

"*Grabbed* you?" I stand and face the bed, searching her arms for bruises I might have overlooked. "Did he hurt you?"

"No, not like that." She tips her head back to study the ceiling like it might help her get me to understand before she looks at me again. "It happened so fast. One minute he was asking me to dinner and the next—"

"Asking you to dinner?"

Like on a date?

"He asked if I wanted to go out, which wasn't a big deal. Then he said he knew I was still getting over you, but he thought we'd be good together if I would give him a chance."

"What kind of chance?"

"You know what kind of chance, Rhys." She pulls the sheet taut over her legs before looking at me. "He hasn't said anything like that while we've been on tour, and he's never tried anything before. Nothing's been going on. He pulled me in for a kiss and I jerked back immediately, but Luke saw."

I snatch my jeans from the floor, zipping and snapping them, long, swift steps taking me toward the bathroom.

"You're not hearing me," Kai says from the bed behind me. "Nothing really happened. I just didn't want Luke to think something did and tell you and . . . you know."

I look back to see her standing on her knees in the middle of the bed, sheet wrapped haphazardly, barely covering her breasts, dark hair spilling around her shoulders. She looks so damn delicious I want to bury my head between her legs and eat that sweet pussy 'til the sun comes up. I still taste her, and the thought of Dub ever . . .

"Fuck!" Anger sets the expletive off in my mouth, and I walk into the bathroom. "I need a minute."

"Rhys, just listen—"

"When you need space, I give it to you." At the bathroom entrance I face her, arms overhead, gripping the doorframe. "So give me a damn minute."

I close the door with more force than I intend, sitting on the edge of the tub, the insulated quiet of the luxurious bathroom denting my fury. There's nothing to this. I'm sure that's what she's trying to tell me, but I can't hear it right now. Dub kissed her? He grabbed her? He asked her out on a date? A tiny voice in the recesses of my mind warns me not to trust her, tells me there's got to be more to this. That where there's smoke, there's gotta be fire. That voice can shut the hell up. What do I give a damn about smoke? Kai's all I want, and I'm fooling myself if I think as soon as I'm on the other side of that door I'll be able to resist her.

It's not even the kiss. The actual kiss. I can't help but remember those images of the two of them on Instagram having fun on this tour. Just because she loves me, doesn't mean she doesn't like him. They have a lot in common. I've seen them dance together, and their chemistry is undeniable. They're *friends*. I shouldn't begrudge her that connection.

But I do.

He likes her. He *wants* her, and for him to have taken a kiss . . . Every kiss is mine. That's an intimacy he doesn't get. Ever.

Damn thief.

The door cracks open, and Kai sticks her bed-rumpled head in, an unspoken plea loud in her eyes.

"Your minute's up," she whispers. "Can I come in?"

When are you ever out?

I nod, studying the cold tiles under my bare feet. She steps in wearing the wife beater I had under my sweatshirt, so big on her the collar slides off her shoulder, barely covering her breasts, and the hem hangs to mid-thigh. The sight of her in something that still smells like me, may even still hold the heat from my skin, softens the hard knot of rage in my chest.

She sits on the floor, back to the wall, knees pulled up to her chest, hands wrapped around her ankles

"You know I wouldn't kiss Dub, right?" she asks softly. "And you can only blame him for so much because I didn't tell him we're together. If you want to be mad at someone, be mad at me."

She looks up, shoulders tensed like she's braced for a blow.

"I'm not comfortable with this arrangement anymore," I say after a few seconds I use to calm down a little more.

"What arrangement?" Caution takes over her expression.

"You working so closely with Dub."

"Rhyson, I don't get a say about that. It's Luke's tour, not mine."

"It could be. You could come to Prodigy and have your own tour."

"Oh, you mean you could *gift* me a tour out of the goodness of your heart." She shakes her head, dark strands of hair clinging to her shoulders. "When will you get that I don't want you giving me anything. I don't want a hand out because I'm your girlfriend."

"This is a useless conversation because we won't see eye to eye." I grip my knees, holding onto my control. "And I didn't cross the Atlantic to spend the one night I have with you fighting."

She nods, looking up from the floor, the stiff lines of her face softening.

"What do you want, Rhyson?"

I shake my head, a weary sigh crossing my lips.

"Don't ask me that unless you really want to know."

"Tell me."

"Okay." I shove my fingers through my hair, looking her dead in the eye as I lay it all out on the line. "I want Dub out of your life. I want you off this tour that's wrecking you. I want you on my label where I can take care of you. And I don't want to pretend we aren't together. How's that?"

She gives me a look that's half helpless, half frustrated.

"Those are all things I can't change right now, Rhys."

"Won't," I correct. "Things you *won't* change. Not can't."

She presses her forehead to her knees, muffling her words.

"Then I don't know how to make you happy."

I'm not handling this well. Neither of us is. We take turns hurting and pissing each other off. I brush her hair back and cup her chin, bringing her eyes back to me.

"Kai, I have you back. We just had amazing sex, and I get to fall asleep with you in my arms tonight. Believe me—I'm happy." I force a smile. "You asked me what I *want*. That's something different."

"Most of what you want is out of my control." She grabs my hand stroking her hair, turning my knuckles to her lips. "What *can* I give you?"

Such a dangerous offer. If she's not careful, I'll take everything she has just because I can't stand the thought of anyone else having any of it.

"Tell him." I slide down the tub rim until we're close enough for her to rest her head on my knee. "The media is one thing. I get that. We won't go public until the tour is over, but Dub needs to know we're together and that what he wants won't ever happen."

"I can do that." She lifts her head and meets my eyes. "I'll tell him."

"I'm sorry if you think I'm overreacting, but—"

"I don't." Her short laugh bounces off the bathroom walls. "While you were in here taking your minute, I thought of how I'd feel if some other girl kissed you. I'd respond the same way."

"Really?" I never think of Kai as jealous or possessive, but I like it. A lot. It's nice to not be alone in this.

"I'm yours and you're mine, right?" On her knees she crosses the space between us until she's between my legs, her elbows resting on my knees. "No one else gets to touch you either."

She claims me with a look before leaning in to add a kiss. Maybe she means for it to be quick, but I can't let her go. My hands at her hips urge her closer. I deepen the kiss until we lose minutes in one another, our lips clinging, hands clutching, breaths catching. The thought of someone else tasting her like this sends a chill across our passion. I'm chilled another degree when the image of Jimmi naked in my shower a few weeks ago revisits me. If I'm expecting full disclosure from Kai, I can't give her any less.

"Hey, I need to tell you something, too." As much as I'd rather just scoop her up and tuck her in, because the signs of exhaustion show all over her face the later it gets, I need to say this. I owe her that.

"Talk." She yawns, covering her mouth, eyes watering. "Sorry. Early morning. Long day."

"I'll make this quick so you can get some rest." I haul in a breath and dive in. "You know Jimmi and I have been friends a long time, right?"

"Since high school." She nods, coughing a little.

"Yeah, since high school." I slide down off the edge of the tub until I'm on the floor, bare back pressed against the side. "Well, there was one night when we were, uh, more than friends."

I let that sink in before meeting her eyes. She's gone still, a small frown gathering on her face.

"The two of you—"

"It was one night," I cut in. "I was on her tour for some dates last summer. We got drunk, and I barely remember it. It meant nothing."

Better revise that.

"Well, it meant nothing to me, but Jimmi, she . . . it meant something to her."

"You never thought to tell me this before?" she asks quietly, studying the dark paint on her toenails that's started chipping.

"I didn't think it was important." I shrug. "It happened before you and I were even together, and I thought she'd gotten over it."

"But she hasn't?" she comes back right away. "What happened?"

"Couple of weeks ago she came by my place because I was supposed to be working on a song for her. She could see I was, um, missing you."

No need to detail how I was basically off the grid and living under my piano because Kai wouldn't talk to me. A man's gotta maintain *some* self-respect.

"That's when she showed me the pictures of you and Dub on Instagram. Started building a case that we should give it another go since you had moved on with him."

"I don't even manage that account, Rhys. Malcolm wanted me to have a presence on social media. One of his interns posted all that stuff. She took a ton of pictures in a few days and just spread them out over several posts."

"Whatever. Doesn't matter." It really doesn't right now. I need to get this out. "I told her I didn't believe that, and that you and I . . . well, there was still an us."

"As much as I fought it," she says, eyes softening a little. "There was always still an us."

"Glad we can agree on that." I bite the inside of my jaw before continuing. "I went upstairs to grab a quick shower, and she snuck in behind me."

"In the shower?" Kai's eyes go wide. "She was in your shower? Were you naked? Was she? What happened?"

The questions fly past my head, and I try to field them as they come.

"Yeah, in my shower where I was naked and so was she."

"And what happened?" Kai demands.

"Nothing."

Give her all of it, my conscience screams at me.

"Okay, something small happened," I say. "I pushed her away immediately, though."

"You mean like how I pushed Dub away immediately?"

"I don't appreciate the parallel, but yeah. Like that."

"She just kissed you?"

"Um, no, she actually didn't." I hesitate before giving a mental *what the hell* and coming out with it. "She grabbed my dick."

All is quiet for a moment, and I'm not sure she heard me.

"Pep, I said she—"

"No," she cuts me off, wrapping her fingers around my cock through my jeans. "She grabbed *my* dick, and if she does it again, she's gonna get herself slapped. You should convey that to her."

This is so damn hot. It shouldn't be, but yeah.

"I'll make sure to tell her." I barely breathe lest she take her hands away from my very happy place.

"Seriously, Rhys." Kai scoots away, taking my stiffie with her, sitting back against the wall, displeasure in her frown. "Not cool."

"So maybe we'll call it even since she thought we weren't together just like Dub did." I consider her across the small space. "But you'll tell him, right?"

"Right."

"I'm just glad this tour is almost over. I understand you working with him on Luke's tour. It's Luke's right to choose who he wants on his team, but you won't be working with Dub for your project, right?"

She's quiet and avoiding my eyes.

"Kai, right?"

"I don't know." She straightens her legs out in front of her, leaning forward. "Once Dub knows we're together it won't be a problem. I think it'll be okay, Rhys."

"No, it won't." I give an adamant shake of my head. "He still wants you. I'm not cool with you working together beyond the tour."

"He's the best in the business. We've already started brainstorming stuff for my videos."

"Then un-storm. There are other choreographers out there."

"Jimmie went further than Dub did today, and I'm not asking you not to work with her again. For that matter, did I ever ask you not to work with Petra?"

"That's the thing. You could. At any moment you could say 'Hey, Rhys, could you please not work with the girls you've fucked,' and I wouldn't."

"But I trust you, so I don't need to do that."

"Don't make this a trust issue. It's not."

"It absolutely is. If you trust me, then working with Dub shouldn't be a problem."

"I don't trust *him*. It's about eliminating any threat to the most important thing in my life, which is this relationship."

"That's not fair, and you know it."

"No, I don't know it. What I know is that I'm prepared to put you first, and you're not prepared to do the same."

Voicing this hidden frustration is freeing, but I hate the hurt that shadows her expression at my words.

"You think my career is more important to me than this relationship?" Her eyes add a demand to her question. "More important than you are?"

"What am I supposed to think? You want to continue working with a guy who tried to kiss you today because it might help your career."

"A guy who thought I was single. I told you I'll tell him I'm not."

"True. This wouldn't have happened if you would tell people we're back together. Again, a move you're making with your career in mind."

"You said you agreed with that. Understood it, and you're going back to it like it's a strike against me now? If it came down to it, you know I'd choose you. But it doesn't have to come down to it. That's what I'm saying. Dub's not a threat, and everyone will know we're together after the tour. Are you good with that or not?"

I actually am. I don't know why we're fighting. Why I'm pressing this when I don't have to. There's this part of me still aching from the two months when she wouldn't even take my calls. I made one wrong move and almost lost her. That part of me has been left uncertain, afraid I'll make another wrong move. Or that she will. That part of me is afraid our love is as fragile as it is strong. And that part of me is about to fuck things up all over again. It makes me say and do dumb shit that will only keep pushing her away.

"I trust you," I answer after a moment. "I guess I was just thrown by the kiss. I didn't handle this well. I'm sorry."

"Neither did I. If I—" Before she can finish, a rough cough rattles in her chest, making me feel like an inconsiderate asshole.

"Hey, up off that cold floor." I sit on the edge of the tub again, gesturing for her to come to me. She climbs into my lap, looping her arms behind my neck. We've gone from snarling to snuggling in under sixty seconds flat.

"You may not believe it," she says, caressing the back of my neck. "But you're first. In all of this, you're first, Rhys. I've dreamt of this chance, worked for this shot my whole life. I just want to do it right. It's not worth losing you, though. Not worth losing this. You believe that?"

I look down at her, huddled close against my chest, shivering and heavy-lidded. She's done. Exhausted from the rigors of today and the days before it. She has rehearsal in the morning and a show tomorrow night, and I have her up late arguing about shit that doesn't even matter. Is this the lesson I should have learned the last time? Hold something you love too tightly and you'll crush it? I can't go through that again, and I won't put Kai through it either.

I stand up, hoisting her light weight against my chest, walking back into the bedroom.

"I said do you believe that, Rhys?" Kai mutters into my shoulder.

"I do, baby." I lay her down on the bed, crawling in behind her and pulling the down comforter over us both.

"You're not just saying that?"

"Nope." I turn off the lamp, plunging the room into darkness I hope will push Kai over the edge of exhaustion into the deep sleep her body craves. "I believe you."

"Are we done talking?" She turns over to face me, her breathing slowing down to a sigh over my lips. "We can talk some more if we need to."

"Let's try not talking." I pull her in, stroking her back until her body relaxes against me.

"I like it when we don't talk." Her voice gets softer the closer she gets to sleep. "I can be quiet with you."

"Then do it." I drop a kiss into her hair. "Be quiet with me, baby."

And after a few minutes, the only sound in the hotel room is her deeper breathing. I lie perfectly still for a long time, but my thoughts remain in constant motion, our argument replaying in my head. I need to stay out of her business. I know it's best for our relationship, but I can't ignore my need to protect her from sharks like Malcolm and guys like Dub. There has to be a balance. Maybe I'll ask Dr. Ramirez next week in our one-on-one session the best way to find it.

Once I'm sure she's not waking up, I carefully roll out of bed and close the bedroom door, making my way to the front of the suite. Earphones plugged into my phone, I prop my feet up on the coffee table and submerge myself into Schumann. Chopin's unconventional, whimsical compositions always creatively unstick me because he erased so many existing lines and drew his own. Schumann is for soul searching. He was a man divided, who literally created two personalities for himself, the dreamer and the rebel, and would sign his compositions based on which of the two helmed that particular piece. "Davidsbündlertänze" soothes one side of me and incites the other. One faction wants to protect Kai and intervene at every turn, and the other cautions me to give her space, to simply be there when she needs me. I'm still not sure if either side knows best as the song on repeat lulls me to sleep.

A firm knock on the door startles me awake. I gather my bearings, disoriented. I'm not under my piano, but I spent most of our one night on the couch. I'm cursing the waste when I peer through the peephole.

You've got to be kidding me.

According to my watch it's barely eight o'clock, and Dub stands outside Kai's hotel room. My hand is on the knob and turning before I think twice about it. Kai's going to tell him about us anyway, right? She said it last night. Not to mention I can't wait to see his face when I open this door.

This may not have been the right call, but it's so worth it to see the shock, followed quickly by displeasure, his expression gives away.

"Gray." His eyes narrow at the edges, his face pinching into a scowl. "What are you doing here?"

"You mean in Berlin?" I fight a smile, but it might come through just a little. Smugness is so classless, but I can't help it. "Or in Kai's room? I'm thinking neither is any of your business."

Dub visibly stiffens, and I know if he could, he'd wrap those ham-sized hands around my throat.

"Look, I don't mean to be an asshole about this . . ." I lean against the doorjamb.

"You don't *mean* to? Oh, it just comes naturally, does it?" he asks. "So it's a gift."

Enough pleasantries. This son of a bitch kissed my girl yesterday and has the nerve to show up at her room first thing in the morning. Over-eager bastard. He needs to state his business and be on his way.

"What do you want, Dub?"

For a minute the look on his face is so exposed I have the answer to my question even though he doesn't say a word. He wants my girl. Sorry. Shit outta luck, dude.

"I need to talk to Kai."

"She's still in bed."

We watch one another for long seconds while the intimate implications of that statement sink in.

"I didn't know you two were back together," he finally says. "She never mentioned it."

"Yeah, we wanted to avoid the media attention while she's on tour." I shrug. "Like I said, she's still asleep, but I can give her a message for you."

"I don't need you to deliver messages for me." He laughs, crossing his arms over his wide chest. "I assume you'll be leaving soon, and I'll still be here with her. You hate that, don't you?"

"What I hate is the fact that you want my girl." If he wants gloves off, they can come off. "And you can't seem to grasp the fact that it'll never happen."

"Maybe you hate the fact that she just may like me, too." He leans forward, squeezing his thumb and index finger together. "*Just* the tiniest bit. Maybe just enough."

"She's your friend, yeah. No accounting for taste." I turn my mouth down at the corners, outwardly calm, inwardly feral. "But if you think there's more on her end, you're mistaken."

"Ya sure about that, are ya?" His Irish accent thickens and his smile grows wider. "Seems to me you have a habit of foockin' up, and maybe all I have to do is be around at the right time. And maybe I will be, yeah?"

Before I can form words to even tear into this asshole, a sound behind me catches my attention, and I'm sure Dub's too. Kai shuffles into the suite, rubbing her eyes groggily, my wife beater hanging off one shoulder, a perky, rose-tipped breast exposed, dark hair clinging to her arms and shoulders.

"Baby, was someone at the—"

"Kai, get back in the room!" I snap, shifting to block Dub's view.

"Oh, I'm sorry. I didn't know . . . I . . ." Her eyes get wide when she catches a glimpse of her choreographer in the hall. She drags the strap up over her shoulder and turns to dash back into the bedroom, the door slamming behind her.

When I turn back to face Dub, his mouth is set, expression grim. Maybe seeing her drove home that I'm the only one who gets to see her that way, who has her that way, and he never will.

"I hope you enjoyed the view." Irritation still roughens my voice. "'Cause that's the closest you'll ever get. I promise you that."

"Tell Kai I came by in case she wanted to grab breakfast before rehearsal," he says, not addressing my promise. "We have a production meeting at nine, so make sure she's not late."

Without another word, he turns and walks down the hall. I close the door and head back to the bedroom. Kai sits on the edge of the bed, head buried in her hands. She looks up when I enter, cheeks pink.

"I had no idea he was here. Oh my God."

"It's okay." I sit beside her, dragging her onto my lap and pressing a kiss to her lips. "He got an eyeful of what he'll never have."

She pulls back, searching my face.

"So I guess he knows we're together, huh?"

"Sorry. I was asleep and didn't think twice about answering the door. He was gonna find out anyway."

"Yeah." She nods, laying her head against my shoulder. "I'll talk to him later. Explain what's up. He'll be fine."

"He has no choice but to be fine." I pause, looking for a way to say this without sounding insecure and jealous. "I'm serious about you not working with him beyond this tour."

"We'll cross that bridge when we come to it." She slides off my lap, standing at the foot of the bed.

"We're at the bridge, Kai." I wrap my hands around the backs of her thighs, bringing her back to stand between my legs. "He as much as admitted he's just biding his time. Waiting for me to fuck up again so he can make his move."

"He said that?" She frowns, pushing one hand into my hair and cupping my face with the other.

"Pretty much." I lean into her palm. "Look, I can't make you do anything. I've seen where that gets me, but I *can* tell you when someone in your life wants me out of it. And Dub wants me out. You do what you want with that information."

She stares at me unblinkingly for a few moments, and for the first time, I think I may have handled this the right way. I think the wiser part of me won this round because she nods, a thoughtful expression on her face.

"Okay," she says softly. "I'll tell Malcolm we need to find someone new."

There is so much inner fist pumping going on, but I keep a cool front, just nodding like I haven't won this round.

"I overslept." She climbs up on the bed, knees on either side of my legs, her ass in my lap. "I need to shower and get to this production meeting. I guess you have to go?"

"Yeah." I press her back until we're heart to heart. "Supposed to meet Kaos at his place around eleven."

"I can't believe you came all this way for one night." She peers at me, a small smile on her lips. "Was it worth it?"

"You mean were you worth it?" I whisper into her hair.

After a second's hesitation, she pulls back to study my face and nods.

"I'll always move heaven and earth to be with you," I assure her. "When it makes no sense. When it wastes time. When it's hard. Doesn't matter. If you ever wonder if you're worth it, the answer's always yes."

Maybe every time I've said that before, it hasn't gone much further than her ears. It hasn't made it past her head to her heart. For some reason today I think it sinks in that I mean it. That there's nothing in my life I wouldn't forfeit to be with her. As crazy as it sounds, as quickly as it happened, it's just there. It's just true. And there's nothing I would do to change it. Maybe it's that realization that makes her mean it, too, because for the first time I believe her when she answers.

"And there's nothing I wouldn't give up for you." She rests her forehead against mine, her eyes sober and set. "I live you."

I didn't know what it would mean to me when she said it *that* way for the first time again, *our* way, but it unlocks something inside of me. A certainty that I didn't imagine our love the way it was before. No matter what Dub or Jimmi or the media or damn Instagram would lead me to believe, I never lost her. What's between us won't be destroyed by one fight or two months apart or anything else that's thrown at us.

"I live you, too, Pep." I flatten the words between our lips. "God, so much."

And that's all that counts.

Chapter FOURTEEN

Kai

A MERICAN SOIL NEVER FELT SO GOOD beneath my feet. Tonight is the last show, and we're back in LA. We blazed a trail through Europe over the last three weeks. I've visited cities I never thought I would, though I didn't get to see much of them, and seen and done all the things I only dreamt of doing, at least onstage. It would truly feel like a dream if it weren't such hard work. Malcolm wanted me to leave a mark with this tour, to take full advantage of Luke's audience with my opening act, and he seems pleased. At the beginning of the tour, I was a footnote.

Isn't that the girl Rhyson Gray was dating? What's she doing on Luke Foster's tour?

I sang background vocals, danced in the centerpiece of Luke's set, created my own opening act, and went on the grind to build my own following. I've worked my ass off to prove I'm no one's footnote; no one's afterthought. I'm satisfied with what I've accomplished so far. Heck, I think I may even be proud.

We're just wrapping my sound check for tonight when Dub

enters the arena, making his way toward the stage. I'm removing my in-ears and handing them over to the sound tech when Dub leaps onstage, grabbing me by my waist and lifting me up. My head swims a little and not just from the motion. Nothing I've taken for this cold has helped. My cough has only worsened. I'm slightly lightheaded, and if I'm not mistaken, sporting a low-grade fever. But you won't hear me complaining. Not the last night of the tour. I'll get through this final show with no one the wiser and no one disappointed, especially not all the people who paid top dollar for tonight's tickets. But Dub spinning me around isn't helping.

"Put me down." My voice sounds weak to me, so I try to find a bright smile.

I was completely honest with Dub after Rhyson left Berlin. I told him that Rhyson and I were together, but just keeping it under the radar until after the tour. He said he understood, but every once in a while, I think he's holding out hope.

"Sorry about that." Dub sets me down. "You ready for tonight?"

I just nod because I need to rest my voice as much as I can. It feels withered in my throat. I'm surprised every night when it comes out strong for the show.

"I'm gonna let you get through this last show," Dub says, grinning. "But I can't stop thinking about that idea we had for your first video. Dancing in the tunnels. It'll be fire."

That's one thing I haven't done. I haven't told him he won't be choreographing for me going forward. I didn't see the need yet. It would only have made things unnecessarily tense, and I wanted the last leg of the tour to be drama-free. But now we're at the end, and he should know.

"Dub, I know we talked about a few preliminary ideas for my project," I say, walking beside him off the stage and pausing at the front row. "But I think I need to explore some other options for choreography."

His brows bunch together, confusion on his face for a moment before a wry grin quirks his mouth.

"Let me guess," he says. "Your boyfriend doesn't want us

working together."

I'm not sure how to respond without sounding like such a girl, and unprofessional on top of that. I don't have to justify myself to Dub, but he's been a huge part of the success I've had so far. There's no rational reason for us not to continue what has been an incredible partnership.

Except my boyfriend. And I wouldn't call him rational.

"Dub, you're amazing." My voice and my laugh grate in my raw throat. "The best actually, and I can't believe my luck having you for this first tour. Artists would kill for that."

"And you're a once-in-a-lifetime talent, Kai. Your body was made for my moves." His voice drops, his eyes darkening as they run over me in the cut off leotard and half shirt I rehearsed in. "We could be so good together."

"We've been great together." I give him a pointed look. "Professionally. There's nothing else there."

"You don't believe that." He lightly grasps my wrist, pulling me a few inches closer. "If Gray wasn't in the picture, I'd already be in your bed."

I jerk away, setting my jaw now that I see the hand he's never shown this clearly before.

"I don't think so." I make my voice firm and sure. Neutral. "I'm pretty selective about who makes it into my bed. Rhyson's not going anywhere anytime soon, and he wouldn't tolerate company."

"If you'd give us a chance." He gathers my fingers into his, pressing a hand at the curve of my back. "Let me show you how it could be with us."

I step back abruptly, pulling my fingers away.

"I've said no. I've tried to be nice, but you're pushing, Dub. This only confirms that we should go our separate ways professionally."

"What's going on?" Malcolm asks from a few feet away, eyes sharp and darting between Dub and me. "Everything okay here?"

I draw a quick breath and nod. Dub's expression stays hard, not giving the same assurances.

"Kai was just telling me she wants to go in a different

direction creatively for her project," Dub says. "And will be using a new choreographer."

"Nonsense." Malcolm spreads his lips over an unnaturally white smile. "You two are magic together. No need to fix what ain't broken."

"I don't really want to get into it before the last show." I smile at them both, really needing to lie down now. "It's just something I feel strongly about."

Malcolm's smile slips a little before he recovers, turning to Dub.

"Hey, Dub, gimme a minute with my artist, okay?" he asks. "I think production had a lighting question about Luke's set."

Dub glances at me before nodding and walking off.

Dub is barely out of earshot before Malcolm is speaking again, his voice almost arctic.

"You listen here, little girl." His sharp glance slices over my face. "Dub Shaughnessy is the best there is, and we aren't using anyone else until I say so."

I've always suspected Malcolm's slick demeanor hid something hard and cold. Now I know it's a knife.

"I'm not your little girl," I say, my voice only a few degrees warmer. "And I'm the one out there every night performing. If I say I need a new choreographer, I think we should at least explore other options."

"Except you don't get paid to think." Malcolm slides his hands into his pockets and leans close enough for me to smell the garlic he had for lunch. "You get paid to sing and dance and look like every man's fantasy every night. I do the thinking. You stick to that, *little girl*."

"I'm not getting into this." I turn to walk away. "I have a show tonight to prepare for. We'll talk about this later."

His meaty hand around my arm pulls me short. I look from the fingers clamped around my arm to the hard lines of his face, but he doesn't let me go.

"We don't have to talk about it later." His mouth becomes a cold curve, his teeth like icicles in his smile, fat blurring the line of his jaw.

"You should have read your contract a little closer, sweetheart."

Dread creeps over me. I read the contract, but Rhyson and I were fighting, so I didn't run it by him and didn't know anyone else. I just wanted out of LA. I wanted space between Rhyson and me. I wanted this opportunity, so I signed a two-year artist development deal. It seemed pretty standard to me at the time, but maybe there were some fine print details I overlooked.

"I own you, lock, stock, and barrel for the next two years," Malcolm confirms. "According to your contract, all creative decisions are mine, including who choreographs your videos and shows. And I made sure it's so airtight, even your famous ex-boyfriend won't be able to get you out of it without sidelining you until your contract is fulfilled. Even if you won't work for me, you can't work for anyone else."

He drops my arm and straightens his tie.

"You want to wear Converse instead of high heels, go right ahead. I don't give a fuck," he says. "Everything else, I decide."

I don't know if it's my fever or the horror of what I've gotten myself into, but something makes me sweat and sway a little on my feet. Malcolm's hand snakes back out with false solicitation to steady me.

"You really should go get some rest." He offers a warmed over smile. "It's been a long three months, and we have a lot more ahead of us. You go on your way. Don't worry about letting Dub know it was all a misunderstanding."

His eyes land on me like a fist.

"I'll handle that. I'll handle everything."

A hand on my shoulder distracts me from the icy stare down I'm having with Malcolm.

"Hey, drink this." Ella offers me a cup of the magic tea that has kept my voice on life support the last few weeks. She flicks a glance between Malcolm's stony expression and mine. "Everything okay?"

"Yep. I'm off to go find Dub." Malcolm smiles for Ella's benefit, I assume. "You've done an amazing job on the tour, Kai. Kill it one last time for me tonight."

He walks off, leaving me with Ella's questioning eyes.

"You sure it's all good?" Ella glances over her shoulder, watching Malcolm's bulky figure all the way backstage. "Malcolm seemed even creepier than usual."

"It's nothing I can't handle." I sip the hot tea, swallowing my pride. "This is perfect. Thank you for this and a million other things you've done for me on the tour that have nothing to do with makeup."

"Hey, you're a sweet kid." Ella shrugs one slim shoulder. "And you're the real deal. Your tour will be twice as big as Luke's next year. Maybe I'm just getting in on the ground floor of something great."

"Yeah, you're such an opportunist." I roll my eyes because she's the genuine article. Few and far enough between in this business. "You've taken care of me, especially the last few weeks when I've been under the weather. I'll never forget that."

"And you need to get to the bottom of whatever you're under." Ella gives me a stern look. "The lingering cough. The aches."

She presses the back of her hand to my forehead.

"You have a fever. I think we should call a doctor."

"After the show." I start walking toward the exit and the promise of a nap in my dressing room.

"Mistletoe was just delivered." Ella's grin is secretive. "Right on time."

I nod, an irrepressible grin all over my face, despite the achiness of my body. Despite the residual slime of my conversation with Malcolm. Last show. Rhyson didn't miss one stop. I'm sleeping in his bed tonight. I don't care what time we wrap. I don't care if he's in the studio and comes home to find me curled up on his front step. It's happening. Even no closer to figuring out who is behind the sex tape, even knowing Rhyson wants to go public soon, even with the crap revelation Malcolm just dumped on me. All of that makes my life vastly complicated. I'll figure it out. Maybe San made some headway. Maybe Drex will turn up. Maybe I'll find a way to wiggle out of the contractual headlock Malcolm has me in, but tonight I get Rhyson. Right now I can't see beyond that.

"You think he'll come to the show tonight to see you perform?" Ella keeps pace with me, digging a lemon ginger lozenge out of her pocket and pressing it into my hand.

"Who?" I laugh at her "come on now" expression. Rhyson is an unspoken understanding between Ella and me. She's the only one on tour who knows we're together, even though I haven't actually told her so. Besides Dub, of course. "If he comes, he knows not to tell me. I'd rather not know he's out there."

"He'd make you nervous?"

"Uh, yeah." I shake my head, deriding myself. "I know it's silly, but it is what it is."

"I've really tried to play this cool and not be a total fangirl," Ella says, obviously working up to something.

"I hear a 'but' in there." I open my dressing room door and gesture for her to follow me in. "Go on. What is it?"

"He's just so . . . amazing. I mean, obviously, he's hot. Not that I noticed your boyfriend is hot or anything. And he's so talented and mysterious. I just . . . how do you *stand* it?"

I knew Ella loved Rhyson's music, but this is her first full on gush, and it's something to behold.

"He *is* amazing." I stretch out on the couch, grateful to finally surrender to the respite my body has been begging for. "But he's also just a guy. I mean, he's *my* guy."

I can't help but laugh thinking of our day at the beach. Him in his thick moustache singing "I Got You, Babe" by the beach.

"He's a goofball. He's a genius. He makes me laugh."

My lips quirk to a wry angle, memories of our infamous video imprinting my mind.

"He makes me cry sometimes, too." I shrug. "He's not perfect, but then neither am I."

"And all the drama between you two at the beginning of the tour?" Ella settles into the seat in front of the mirror, pulling spikes into her short hair. "All resolved?"

"I don't know if 'resolved' is the right word," I mumble, barely able to keep my eyes open as exhaustion takes me under. "But we're working on it. I have no choice."

"Why's that?" Ella swivels the seat around to stare at me.

I see only a slice of her through sleep-slitted eyes.

"I'm in love with him." My words slur, but I'm sure she heard them. The words I've only ever admitted to a handful of people.

"You're a lucky girl."

I barely manage a sleepy smile, my last conscious thought the truth that's gonna get me through this last show, even though my body doesn't seem able.

Don't I know it.

Chapter FIFTEEN

RHYSON

A S A KID, I COULD BARELY make it through a performance without a healthy dose of Xanax. So much so that it became a crutch I couldn't walk without. The anxiety, the pressure every time I stepped onto the stage overshadowed my early years of performing. So when I reinvented myself as a musician, I did it for me and me alone. Not for my parents or the money or the acclaim, but because I had, for whatever reason, been given a gift that not many people in the world had. I could play just about anything . . . *really* well.

And though my early life left me so cautious I only let a few people past the gate, only lowered my guard by inches, when I take the stage, I hold nothing back. I'm all heart and soul every time, and what the audience gives me in return is like nothing I'd ever imagined I'd experience as a musician. It's a sonic freefall, and those people who love my music, who *get* it, are the net that catches me every time.

So nerves don't really come into play for me anymore when I perform. But tonight, I'm in an arena packed with fans, the air vibrating with their anticipation. My foot bounces a frantic rhythm on the sticky floor. I'm sweating through my t-shirt. My stomach knots up. The nerves, man, the nerves before this performance are like old times. Like everything rides on this next set.

And I'm nowhere near the stage.

I'm halfway back, just in sight of the soundboard so I can geek out over the equipment they're using to mix the show. I'm smack dab in the middle of a row of people, wearing Dickies. I'm carrying glow sticks and drinking flat beer while we wait for the opening act, the only thing I care about tonight. I'm here to see my girl perform, really perform, to a packed house, and this room can barely contain me I'm so high on possibility.

Other people take this for granted, standing in a crowded concert, shoulder to shoulder with thousands of fans. It's wonderfully novel for me, though, to be on this side of the stage. I approached this outing with the stealth and missional strategery of Jason Bourne. I worked out my disguise. I plotted an elaborate plan to get out of my neighborhood, undetected and all plebeian in the used Corolla Marlon secured for me. I parked and walked to the venue like everyone else. On my back, standard issue Luke Foster t-shirt. On my head, my Dodgers cap. I'm wearing the Magnum P.I. moustache, which has never let me down. My own mother would be hard-pressed to recognize me. I'm drinking cheap beer and chomping on a pretzel like everyone else on my row.

It's exhilarating.

All the pre-show stuff is coming to an end, and my heartbeat picks up speed. Is she nervous? Does Kai suspect that maybe, just possibly, I'm in the audience? We spoke earlier, but only briefly. Partially because she was getting ready for the show, and partially because I knew if we spoke too long, I'd give something away and she'd know I was coming.

Tonight she'll be in my bed because finally the longest month of my life comes to an end. Over the last three weeks, Kai and I have texted and Facetimed and talked every day, despite the time difference, but now we're in the same state. She doesn't know it, but we're in the same place. The same arena. She has to at least suspect that I'm coming, but we haven't talked about it at all. The only part of the show I'm not looking forward to is that lap dance she gives Luke during his set. That shit ends tonight, and she won't be anywhere near his lap ever again.

The announcer welcomes everyone to the show before introducing the opening act. The crowd erupts for Kai. In three months she has rocketed to her own prominence. I can't stand John Malcolm, but I have to hand it to him. He knows how to transform a talent into a star.

But at what cost?

The last few Facetime calls, Kai looked worn down, exhausted. That skin-deep sparkle that's always been so much a part of her was absent. As if the tour weren't demanding enough, Malcolm added mall stops along the way. And because of all the hype surrounding Kai, he's had her doing multiple early morning radio and TV interviews in every city. It's too much and it's taken a toll.

She promised me after this tour we wouldn't care who knew we're still together. She promised me we'd be together again. I hope she meant it because I've already booked our vacation from the rest of the world, and it starts as soon as this tour stops.

But not before I get to see her performing live for myself. She's phenomenal. Many singers learn to dance because you kind of have to these days. Unless you're *this* guy, anchored to your piano and not giving a fuck. But Kai *is* a dancer. She's not just competent. She's masterful. Combine that with her incredible voice and magnetic stage presence, along with being gorgeous, which never hurts, and you've got a rare package.

I'm so damn proud of her when she starts her set. I completely get why people want more from her, why she's gained so many fans of her own opening for Luke.

"Rhyson Gray is one lucky son of a bitch," the guy beside me says to the person on the other side of him. It jars me to hear my name when I'm supposed to be knee-deep in anonymity.

Concert-goer number two agrees, eyes fixed on Kai as she

dances across the stage. "Didn't they break up, though?"

"But he got to fuck her first." The guy cackles, licking his lips like he can taste my girl. "How else you think a chick from Nowhere, USA gets here this fast? He probably wasn't the only one she fucked to get on that stage."

I knew there were some people who thought like that. Hell, that was Kai's greatest fear, but to hear someone talk about her that way when she's worked her ass off to get where she is; when she's trained since she was a kid, sacrificed all her life and pressed through every delay, including her mom's illness—it makes me furious. If I give in to this, I jeopardize my disguise and maybe cause a small commotion when people realize who I am. I can see those headlines now. Kai would never let me live that down. I jerk the reins on my control, pulling my own ass in line. I can't resist some retaliation, though, however small.

I bump my shoulder against douchebag's like someone jostled me, dumping my beer into his lap.

"Dude, what the fuck!" He drops his pretzel, patting the huge wet spot on his jeans.

"My bad," I mumble. "Sorry, man."

"Just stay in your lane," he snaps, looking at me an extra minute like he's trying to place me. I pull my hat lower over my brow and bend, pretending to retrieve something from the floor. That wasn't the ass-kicking he deserved, but at least I get to see my girl without causing a brawl.

She's on her second song when I realize something isn't right. She misses a step, and even though she recovers quickly, I know from her face something is wrong. She loses her place in the song, the band and the dancers moving forward without her. It's like I'm watching it all in awful slow motion. One minute she's standing in her skimpy little outfit, small and alone at the center of the huge stage, a choreographed spectacle behind her. The next minute, she presses her hand to her forehead, her face crumpling, her eyes rolling back in her head, her slim body falling into a glittering heap on the floor.

And taking my heart down with it.

I don't make a conscious decision to rush toward the stage, but that's what happens. I'm shoving everyone on my row, barreling down the aisle until I slam into a mass of flesh and bone and muscle. I jerk against two sets of hands gripping my arms on either side.

"Let go," I say through gritted teeth.

"Man, we can do this the easy way or the hard way," one of the security guards says. "Return to your seat or we take you out."

"No, you don't understand." I can barely get the words out because my heart is stuffed in my throat. "That's my girlfriend. I need to get to Kai."

"You and every other guy in this place." The other guard starts dragging me back into the crowd. Onstage, the music still goes on, but the dancers have stopped, several of them running center stage where Kai lies completely still.

"No!" I dig in my heels in. "She is. Why won't you . . . you have to let me . . ."

They're dragging me backward. I've never felt so completely helpless in my life. She's gone. A burly security guard scooped her up, taking her limp body offstage. A few dancers straggle back, but the whole crew is leaving. The announcer asks for everyone's patience. Patience is a completely foreign concept to me right now. I strain against the strength of two massive security guards when it hits me. They don't know who I am.

"I'm Rhyson Gray." My eyes zipline between them. I try to keep my voice low when everything inside of me is rising and surging and clawing to get backstage.

"Geez, man," Guard number one says, shaking his head. "You're taking this fantasy kinda far. You gotta go."

"Listen to me, shithead," I ground out. "I'm Rhyson fucking Gray. I'm wearing a disguise because I wanted to watch the show in peace, but my girlfriend just collapsed, and I need you to get me to her right now, dammit."

Despite the death grip on my arm, I manage to get my hand to my mouth, peel the moustache away, and push my Dodgers cap back just enough for them to see.

Guard number one is still pulling me back, but the other one squints, studying me more closely before his eyes widen, recognition on his face.

"Curt, it's him," he says. "I think he *is* Rhyson Gray."

Curt stops in his tracks, peering at me.

"Shiiiit. You sure?"

"Look." I channel the coldness of my mother's negotiator voice. "I *am* Rhyson Gray, and I promise you that if I'm not backstage in the next minute, both your jobs are mine. I need you as discreetly and quickly as possible to get me to my girlfriend. Now."

They look from me to each other for a few seconds before shrugging in synch and dragging me again, this time toward a side door.

"This'll get you backstage fast," Curt says. "But we'll need to see your license as soon as we get back there to confirm."

"Whatever." I nod, quickening the pace so I'm practically dragging them.

As soon as we're backstage, I dig out my license. With that hurdle behind me, I'm not sure what should be next. There's a flurry of activity as Luke's dancers scramble to go on earlier than anticipated. There's no sign of Luke or Malcolm or anyone I know.

"Where's Kai Pearson?" I demand of one of the dancers rushing past. "Do you know where they took her?"

"To the hospital, I think. Not sure which one." She tilts her head, curiosity clear on her face. "Rhyson Gray?"

I don't answer, but just move on, searching for anyone who might know where I can find my girl. How I can get to her. My car is blocks away, and it'll take me forever to get out of here. I'm frantic and lost. As much as I try to slow my brain down long enough to think clearly, the image of Kai heaped onstage interrupts every functioning synapse.

"Okay, think." I shove my fingers through my hair, dislodging the cap and sending it to the floor. "What's the nearest hospital? Where would they have taken her? How can you get there fast? Think, idiot. Think."

"Rhyson?"

I turn toward my name, bending to retrieve my cap and pushing it back on my head.

"You're Rhyson Gray, right?" The petite girl with short, cherry-red hair asks. "You're looking for Kai?"

The chaos backstage fades to the periphery and I zero in on her face, rushing forward to grip her arms.

"You know where she is?" I demand. "Where? I need to know. I need to . . ."

My voice evaporates. I gulp back the panic, struggling to hold my shit together while the most important thing to me is on her way to some hospital alone. With God knows who, but not with me.

"Can you help me?" I will get down on my fucking knees if I have to. "Please? I need to get out of here. I need to find her."

She nods, her eyes ping ponging from me to the people scurrying to get in place for the show.

"I'm Kai's makeup artist." She gives her head a quick shake and chews on her bottom lip. "I'm her friend, Ella."

"Kai's mentioned you. Do you know which hospital? Is your car here? Is it close?"

"Yeah, there's a lot by the loading dock where some of us parked. They've taken her to Cedars Sinai." She starts walking toward an exit, and for the first time I feel like I might be getting close. "I was on my way there. You can ride with me."

Once we're in the car, my mind starts ordering things, and I realize no one knows where I am or what's going on. I dial the person who always knows what to do in a crisis and stops me from screwing up my life half the time.

"Rhys, hey." There's a smile in Grady's voice. It seems to be there more than ever since his wedding.

"Kai collapsed." I would ease in instead of air striking, but sometimes he's the only one who finds a way to ease my mind. I need that right away. I need that now.

"She what? What do you mean?" Confusion and urgency build in his voice.

"I was at Kai's concert, in the audience, and she collapsed." I draw a deep breath. "I couldn't get to her, Grady. They took her away. She's at the hospital. She—"

"Slow down, son." I can almost feel the staying hand Grady usually places on my shoulder to calm me. "What hospital?"

"Cedars."

"Are you on your way there now?"

"Yeah." I nod even though he can't see me, my heart slowing a little. "Yeah, I'm almost there."

"Em and I are on our way. We'll meet you."

I've no sooner hung up than my phone buzzes with a call from Marlon.

"Dude, twitter is blowing up about Kai," he says. "What's going on?"

"Whatever Twitter says is more than I know."

Marlon and I haven't talked much about Kai over the last few weeks. He's been slammed with his album, in the studio every chance he gets, and I've been tight-lipped about my relationship. He knows that viral video wasn't the end of us, though. He knew I was attending her concert tonight.

"You okay?" he asks after a beat or two.

"No." I rest my temple against the cool glass window of Ella's little car. "Not until I know she is."

"Someone tweeted that she was taken to Cedars. You on your way there?"

"Yeah, and if it's on Twitter, there's probably already press waiting."

"Probably. Bristol's here. She wants to holla at you."

"She's there with you?"

"Yeah, we got business," he says, sounding more guarded than I'm used to.

Any other time I would probe and tease him about Bristol, but not now. Not with that image of Kai crumpled in the middle of the stage still haunting me.

"Rhys," Bristol says. "You okay?"

Everyone keeps asking me that. I want to scream at them, ask them how I can possibly be okay when the girl I love just collapsed.

"I'll be better once I get there and know what's going on."

"What can I do?" Concern rounds the edges of Bristol's normally brisk tone. "What do you need?"

"Um, I think there will be press when I arrive. I don't give a fuck. I'm just going in. Whatever, but it might be good to have Gep with me later."

"I'll call him now. He'll meet you there. What else?"

"Um, shit, Bris." I squeeze the bridge of my nose. Trying to slow my heart. Trying to clear my head, but it's like an entire symphony orchestra tuning before a concert. A dozen players in different keys with discordant notes. A cacophony of instruments and clanging symbols ringing in my ears, cluttering my mind.

"I don't know," I say, my voice as weary as my mind. "I just . . . I can't think straight right now."

"I can come think for you," my sister says softly. "Want me to?"

Emotion crowds my throat because I so rarely see this side of her—the sister who would drop everything, not for her client, but for her twin brother.

"Yeah, that'd be great, Bris. Bring Marlon with you, okay?"

"We're on our way."

Now that I've called the tiny circle of people in my life who matter, I don't know what to do with myself. Silence builds in the car, and I realize just how rude I've been to Ella. She must think I'm the asshat most people assume I am.

"Uh, thanks for the ride. Sorry I had a few calls to make." I glance at Ella, actually seeing her this time. "I remember you."

Her startled eyes swing quickly from the road to me and then back.

"You do?"

"From the set of Luke's video. You took off Kai's robe."

"Don't hold that against me." She flashes me a small smile. "You were pretty pissed that day."

We'd just gotten together. My father was in the hospital, but I couldn't stay away from Luke's set. I had to see my girl, only to find her half naked for Luke's video. Man, I was angry that day, and so was she. Things felt so complex then, but compared to our life now, it was child's play.

"You've been sending the mistletoe, right?" Ella's eyes don't leave the road.

I watch her profile cautiously. Only Kai and I know about that. I don't want to give too much away.

"What do you mean?" I ask.

"The mistletoe that came to her dressing room before every show." She shrugs. "I did her makeup, so I'd see. It always made her smile."

I smile naturally, just the smallest bit, since Kai's collapse.

"Her grandfather kept mistletoe in the house all year so he could kiss Kai's grandmother all the time."

"That's really sweet." Ella steals another quick glance. "You, um, you really love her, huh?"

The short answer would be yes, but that's a pitiful Cliffs Notes to an epic story. If I go into what Kai means to me when I don't even know for sure she's okay yet, I'll lose it, so I give her the simple truth anyone with eyes could see.

"I love her more than everything."

Ella swings a surprised look my way, eyes wide. I remember her saying before that she was a fan of my music. She had tickets to one of my shows. I can't be a celebrity right now. I don't give a damn that she loves my music or about any preconceived notions she may hold. I'm just raw and wide open and grateful that she's taking me to Kai.

"Thanks again, Ella, for driving. I was blocks away. It would have taken me a lot longer."

"I wish I had pressed her more about that cold."

"So do I. She's been coughing for weeks, but she kept saying it was just a cold and that it was okay."

"Yeah, but she had a fever tonight."

"What?" I try to soften my tone, but the thought of her going on tonight sick angers the hell out of me. "Why didn't she pull out?"

"If you love Kai as much as you say you do, then I'm sure you know she'd never do that."

I clench my fists. "Malcolm pushed her too hard on this tour."

"You're certainly right about that." There's a wry twist to Ella's mouth.

We pull to a stop in front of Cedars Sinai emergency entrance before I get to ask her more questions.

"I'll park," Ella says. "You get on in there."

I'm out of the car and slamming the door almost before she's completely stopped. I knew there might be some press, but I didn't anticipate the knot of reporters clustered at the entrance, armed with questions I don't even dignify with a response.

"Rhyson, are you here to see Kai?"

"Are you two back together?"

"What can you tell us about what happened tonight?"

Each question skids across my nerves like pebbles over a pond, disturbing the surface but not sinking in. I pull my Dodgers cap down lower and rush through the door, bracing my heart for whatever lies on the other side.

Chapter SIXTEEN

RHYSON

"I AM HER NEXT OF KIN," I growl at the battle axe nurse blocking me. "Tell me where the hell she is or I will go to every room in this fucking hospital until I find her."

"Our policy—"

"I don't care about your damn policy." I slam my hand onto the front desk. "Her only family isn't here. I'm her . . . we're . . . I have to see her."

"Yes, Mr. Gray." The nurse blinks furiously. "But I can't give you that information. You're not next of kin, and I—"

I'm about to hurl her little clipboard when a hand on my shoulder stops me.

"Rhys," San says from behind me. "Calm down. Come on back."

He looks at the pale-faced nurse.

"He's with me."

I jerk away from him.

"I'm not *with you*," I snap, galled that he got to her and I couldn't. "Where is she?"

"This way." San starts walking down the hall, but my feet adhere to the floor, paralyzed with the emotion I've stuffed under the anger and frustration of getting here, of getting to her.

"Is she . . ." I clear my throat, fists balled at my sides. "Is she okay? Is she gonna be okay?"

He stops and looks over his shoulder, his face giving away nothing.

"I think so. The doctor's with her now. They ran some tests." San starts forward again, and I follow, the fear abating some. "We should know something soon."

"Aunt Ruthie?" I keep pace with him, but my mind races ahead. "You called her?"

"Yeah, she's figuring out a flight now."

"Figuring out a flight? No." I frown, pulling my phone from my pocket. "I'll get Bristol to arrange a private flight. She needs to get here as quickly as possible, and I don't want her worrying about how she'll pay for it."

"That'd be great," San says. "I really appreciate that, man."

I grab his arm to stop him.

"It's not some benevolent act from a rich friend." My voice, despite the restraint I try to exercise, rises. "That's *my* girl in there, San. I don't know how much she's told you, but we're—"

"Together, I know." He bounces a hard look back to me. "And for the record, before she was *your* girl, she was my best friend. I know you hate it, but she and I have been close a lot longer than she's been in love with you. She doesn't need you rolling up in here all possessive and loud and irrational. Keep your shit together. The last thing she needs is you stomping up and down these halls telling everyone she's yours and you're together. Stay out of sight when you can and if anyone asks, the two of you are just friends."

"First of all, I don't hate that you two are close." I try to take the edge off my tone. "If there's anyone I'd trust to protect her besides me, it's you."

"Well, thanks for that." The look on his faces actually says he doesn't give a damn.

"And second of all, why the hell do you care if people know we're together?" I point back to the nurse's station. "I'm not even down as an emergency contact. If you hadn't shown up, I probably still wouldn't even know how the hell to find her in this hospital. I've been sneaking around for the last month to have anything to do with her. And now you tell me to keep it on the low, too. Why?"

San presses his lips against his teeth, like he's biting something back. Holding something in. I can't help but think of the night I found out about Kai's one-night stand with Drex. Something she'd been keeping from me, San already knew.

"Is there something I should know?" My voice drops, not because I'm discreet, but because the thought of her keeping something critical from me, still not trusting me, sobers the hell right out of me. "San?"

For a minute, our eyes connect, and there's no doubt in my mind there is something I should know. I hope he'll tell me, but someone in a white lab coat a few feet up the hall calls his name.

Our eyes stay locked for an extra second before he tips his head in the direction of the doctor.

"I think we got some news," he says. "Let's go find out."

I set my bad feeling aside long enough to focus on whatever the doctor can tell us.

"I'm Dr. Wells." He looks at me, recognition and curiosity flickering in his eyes, before he turns his attention back to San. "I understand you're Ms. Pearson's next of kin?"

"Well, she doesn't really have any kin, but I'm her emergency contact," San says. "Ruthie, the closest she's got to family, should be here soon."

That reminds me we still need to make arrangements for Aunt Ruthie's flight. I fire off a quick text to Bristol asking her to charter something to Georgia. I'm giving her details, but the doctor's words to San pull me into their conversation.

"Did you say pneumonia?" I demand of the doctor. "Kai has pneumonia?"

He looks at San questioningly, silently asking if it's okay to share information with me.

"I'm her—"

"Friend," San cuts in over me. "Rhys and I are both Kai's friends. She doesn't have any blood left, so we're all she's got. You can talk freely to him."

My teeth grind against each other, frustration like a keg of dynamite in my belly, ready to blow at the slightest spark.

"Mr. Gray, right?" Dr. Wells glances down at a chart in his hands. "Yes, Ms. Pearson has pneumonia."

"Dammit." I remove my Dodgers cap, slapping it into my palm. "I should have pushed about that cough."

"Cough?" A frown draws Dr. Wells' silvered brows together. "Any other symptoms you noticed?"

"I mean, she's been on a pretty grueling tour, so I assumed the fatigue was because of that."

"I'm sure it was," Dr. Wells agrees. "But her body was trying to fight this with very few weapons."

"A fever, too," I add. "Ella, her makeup artist, said she had a fever earlier, but went on anyway."

"She still has a fever." Dr. Wells looks between San and me, his expression grave. "Pneumonia is a serious infection. It's in her lungs, and her body is in no shape to fight it very well. We're trying to get the fever down now."

"But she'll be okay, right?" Concern shadows San's face. "I mean, people have pneumonia all the time. She's young and healthy."

"She is both, you're right." Dr. Wells nods, but a frown bends over his eyes. "But it's been complicated by exhaustion and dehydration. Had she not been on tour, it may have been detected sooner. She probably wouldn't have pressed through or missed the signs. An already compromised immune system, an incredibly rigorous schedule, not enough rest. It just all came together in the worst way, but she'll be fine soon. We've started a round of antibiotics. We've actually sedated her because the best thing she can do for her body right now is rest."

"Can I see her?" I rush to assure him because I see hesitation on

Dr. Wells' face. "Not to disturb her or wake her up. I just . . . can I see her?"

"I'm not sure that's a good idea," John Malcolm says from his position in front of the room I assume is Kai's, flanked by a security guard on both sides.

I hadn't noticed him, but now that I see him, before I have time to check it, rage bursts in my head, popping all my caution, propelling me forward, hands already ahead of me and clawing for John Malcolm's throat. I slam him into the wall, his head hitting with a satisfying thud.

"Motherfucker." I dig my forehead into his until it probably hurts me as much as it hurts him, my words landing on his fat, jowly face in angry pants. "You did this to her. You wore her down to nothing overworking her."

San and one of the security guards pull at me until Malcolm's free, slumped against the wall, holding his throat and gasping for air.

"Get him out of here!" he spits, anger shaking his red face.

No one moves. I'm not in disguise anymore, and everyone here knows exactly who I am.

To her.

Nobody's kicking me out.

"If anyone's leaving, it'll be you." I pin him to the wall with a glare. "I hold you responsible for this, Malcolm."

"She's a professional and an ambitious artist." Malcolm coughs, my fingerprints still vibrant against his neck. "She knew what she was getting herself into."

"She has pneumonia." I fire back. "She's exhausted. You pushed her past her limits."

"My job is to stretch her limits. It's what will make her great." He smears a nasty grin across his face. "Not that it's any of your business. Why are you even here?"

"You know why I'm here, you slimy piece of shit. She's done with you." I twist my arms out of the hands holding me back and point to him. "You hear me? Done."

"I have a contract with her that tells a different story. At least for the next two years."

Before they can stop me, I step back into his space, close enough to drill my anger into him. San reaches for me again, but I shake him off.

"You honestly think your little contract can stop me?" I turn my voice down to deadly quiet.

"I know it can." The facsimile of his smile falls away. "But it won't come to that because Kai and I have an understanding, which is more than you have with her anymore."

"If you could both put your dicks away for a second," San says, irritation stamped on his face, "maybe Dr. Wells can tell us what's next."

I don't wait for the doctor to volunteer any more information than he's already given us. I know what's next.

"I need to see her," I tell him. I'm really trying not to be the dictatorial jackass that I know I can be, but every cell in my body aches to be on the other side of the door Malcolm's two goons still stand in front of.

"Technically, you're down as her emergency contact," Dr. Wells says to San, not looking me in the eye. "Would you like to see her first?"

If San says yes, I'll choke him. I suspect he knows that. His eyes flick back to mine, and for a moment I think, just to put me in my place, he'll try to go first. I set my pride aside long enough to silently plead with him. He rolls his eyes, quirking his mouth to the side before shaking his head.

"Nah, Rhyson can go."

"She's my artist," Malcolm says. "I think I should—"

"Fuck you." I give Malcolm one last glare as I shove past him and the goons to enter Kai's room.

It's dark and quiet and empty, except for a nurse jotting down notes on the chart at the foot of Kai's bed.

And except for Kai.

She's asleep in the large bed, the simple hospital gown at odds with the heavy stage make up she still wears. The false eyelashes rest on her cheeks, which are gaunter than even a month ago. The blush and eye shadow seem too ornate for this stark room, for this smaller audience of just the nurse and me.

"Mr. Gray, she's resting." The nurse hangs her chart on a hook at the foot of the bed. "We need her to stay that way."

"Understood." I plant myself in the seat beside her bed, swallowing fear at how still she is. "She's okay?"

"Very tired. She needs a lot of rest, lots of fluids, but once the antibiotics kick in, the infection in her lungs should start to clear soon."

The nurse walks to the door, turning to give me one last instruction.

"Just don't wake her. Sleep will help her recover better than anything else."

Don't wake her. I can manage that. After the fight it's taken to find her, to get to her, it feels anti-climactic to just sit here and wait for her to wake up. I feel pretty damn helpless. This feels completely useless to her, but for me, it's everything. Seeing the steady rise and fall of her chest. Knowing she's going to be okay. Getting to hold her small fingers between mine on the sheets, it's everything.

She's everything.

Seeing her crumble to that stage only solidified that. She's the one thing in my life worth protecting. All the money, the fame, the career, my ambitions—it can all go to hell.

This—she—is the one thing I must have. The one thing I must keep.

Chapter SEVENTEEN

Kai

"**M**AMA, GET UP."

I don't say it loud enough to wake her. I just have to say it. She hasn't left the bed in two days. Not since Daddy left. No one told me he's gone, but I know. Even if I hadn't overheard Aunt Ruthie talking about it, even if I hadn't heard Mama crying, I would know. The house is too quiet. His big laugh isn't filling every room at once. There's a certain way he clears his throat when he's studying, and I haven't heard it in days. His office is empty, his Bible left open to the last passage he taught me about a deep love.

He's never missed a recital because he loves to see me dance, but for the first time, he wasn't there. I didn't know until the end when Mama met me backstage, wearing her worry face, as Daddy always called it.

"Where's Daddy?" I had looked past her and all around at the other girls whose mamas were taking pictures of them in their tutus and ballet slippers.

"He must have gotten held up at the church." Mama grabbed my hand and started toward the exit.

Only he hadn't come home for supper. And when I went into their bedroom, their closet door stood open, half the space empty where his clothes had been.

He's gone. And Mama's gone, too, even though she's huddled under the covers.

A noise from the kitchen makes me jump. A door closing and heavy steps.

Daddy!

It has to be. He's back. He's come home. Mama can get out of bed and cook dinner. I've had nothing but cereal for the last two days. Everything can go back to the way it was. I rush to the kitchen, smiling 'til my eyes squinch at the sides. I round the corner, ready to throw myself up and into his big arms.

Only it's not him.

I skid to a stop at the kitchen door. Aunt Ruthie hangs her coat over the chair at the table and pulls off her work boots, the ones she uses to go out in the garden. She drops a bushel of collard greens into the sink.

"You remember how to clean greens, Kai Anne?" Her voice is quiet, her eyes sadder than I've ever seen.

"Yes, ma'am." I drag one of the chairs over to the sink and climb up onto it.

She reaches into the drawer, searching through the utensils until she finds the dullest knife.

"You remember how we cut 'em off the stem?" She hands me the knife. "Be careful with that."

"Yes, ma'am." I bite my lip, not wanting to ask the question. Not wanting to be a bother. "Am I going to dance class today?"

Aunt Ruthie frowns, her eyes going to the door.

"Where's your mama?"

"Um, she's still in bed."

Her eyes get narrow.

"How was school today?"

"I didn't . . . I didn't go to school." I look down at the dull knife in my hand. "I stayed here. How was church Sunday?"

For the first time in all my years, we didn't go to church on a Sunday. We've never missed except for snow. Once I was sick and I still went. Mama said Jesus died for the sick and the weary. I was sick and she was weary, so we were both dragging ourselves to church. Mama never wanted to miss one of Daddy's sermons. And even though we missed church, she didn't miss his sermon. Because for the first time, Daddy missed church, too.

Where is he? The idea that he actually left us, left me, is too big for my head, so I just start cutting leaves off the stem in the sink.

"Don't you worry about church for a while now, Kai Anne." Aunt Ruthie rubs my hair, straightening out one of the glittery bows still in my hair from Saturday's recital. "Did you take your bath last night, child?"

"No, ma'am." I shake my head. I haven't had a bath since right before Saturday's recital. Not since Daddy left.

Her eyes drift over to the table where my box of Fruit Loops is still open on the table.

"What'd you have for lunch, honey?"

"Cereal," I answer quietly. "It's all right. I love Fruit Loops, Aunt Ruthie."

Even at eight, I know it's not good. I know something's mighty wrong with Mama if I'm eating cereal for every meal, not bathing, and still have bows in my hair from two days ago. Mama's picky about most things, but most of all about me. And for the last two days, she forgot I was even here because Daddy's not.

Aunt Ruthie's lips get thin and a little knot pops up in her jaw.

"You wait here, Kai Anne. I'm gonna go talk to your mama."

I nod, using my little dull knife to pull the leaves away from the stem.

"Mai Lin, you gotta get up." Aunt Ruthie's voice is a distant rumble down the hall. I climb off the chair and tip toe to the door to hear better.

"Go away, Ruthie," Mama moans. "Just go."

"No, I will not go. This ain't right, Mai." I've never heard Aunt Ruthie's voice so hard. Never heard her talk to anyone like that, much less her best friend.

"He's gone." Mama's words come out barely louder than a whisper. "Don't you understand he's left me? With that whore Carla. Oh, God, Ruthie. How could he? Why? What did I do wrong? I thought we . . ."

There are no more words. Only tears. When I cry that hard it makes me sick sometimes. I just throw right up when I cry like that, and I wonder *if Mama will need the trash can by her bed. Or if she'll make it to the bathroom.*

"You did nothing wrong," Aunt Ruthie says. "You were the best wife he could have asked for. You did everything right, and the fault is not with you."

It's quiet except for the sound of Mama sniffling. I haven't heard her cry since Pops passed not too long after Grams died. She told me then Pops couldn't stay in a world without Grams. And now I know Mama doesn't want to stay in a world without Daddy.

"I know it's hard," Aunt Ruthie says. "And you know I'm here. I was here before he came and I'm here now that he's gone. We will get through this. There is a whole congregation behind you. A whole community behind you. But most of all, Mai, there is a little girl in that kitchen who hasn't had a bath in two days and had cereal for dinner yesterday."

"Kai Anne?" Mama says it like I'm a surprise. Like she didn't know I was still here. "Oh, God. I didn't think . . . how long? Two days? Oh, God, Ruthie. I'm so sorry. I would never . . . Ruthie, what am I gonna do? Now that he's gone and I have to raise her by myself? How will I take care of her? I don't even have a job."

"We'll figure it out, Mai. I've told you. I'm here, and you're not alone. But the first thing you have to do, and this is right away right now, is get up."

Chapter EIGHTEEN

Kai

GET UP.

Aunt Ruthie's words sound as clear in my head when I open my eyes as they did in my dream. In the memories buried in my sleep. I glance around a semi-dark room, my brain struggling to compute my surroundings. The starchy gown, the antiseptic smell, the thin sheets. Over the last three months I got used to waking up somewhere different almost every morning, but I never in all my life woke up in a hospital.

And then my memories click like a camera shutter, assembling my last performance in a hazy pictorial. I woke up from a fitful nap in my dressing room, still feverish. Still aching and short of breath. But it was the last show. I kept telling myself I only needed to get through one last show. My routine was going fine until I hit the second song, and then the lights blurred and spun, a glaring kaleidoscope over my head. I stumbled, literally feeling my body shutting down limb by limb, my heartbeat slowing . . . and then oblivion. And now, I have no idea how many hours later, I'm here.

I look to my right, my eyes carving out a shape in the sheer dark of dawn filtering in through the blinds. I have no idea what time it is. I have no idea what day it is. I barely know my own *name*, but I know the man slumped in an awkward, sleeping pretzel, his tall frame squeezed into the small chair by my bed.

"Rhys." My raggedy voice barely pushes the word out, but it abrades my throat. I reach up to touch my neck, like that will make it better, but the skin feels the same. It's the inside that feels like a cheese grater.

"He hasn't left this room." The soft words come from the left side of my bed.

I turn my head, tears instantly collecting in my eyes when I make out Aunt Ruthie seated beside me, her Bible open on her lap.

"Aunt Ruthie." The words emerge as a croak, my mouth working uselessly to get out my gratitude, my relief that she's here. "You're . . . I . . . you . . ."

My shoulders shake, soft sobs racking my sore body. Hot, salty tears slip into the corners of my mouth. I lift my hand to reach for her, only now noticing the IV in my arm. Oh, God. What's wrong with me? What am I doing here?

"It's all right." She sets the Bible aside, crossing the small space between her chair and the bed to wrap a work-roughened hand around mine. She reaches into her pocket for a small handkerchief, dabbing at my tears. "You're okay, baby."

"But what . . . what's wrong with me?" I look over at Rhyson, still asleep. If our places were reversed, and I was in that chair, waiting for him to wake up, I'd be going out of my mind.

"Pneumonia." Aunt Ruthie brushes hair away from my eyes. "And exhaustion. And dehydration. You really did a number on your body, honey."

"Pneumonia?" I shake my head against the cool pillow. "That's not possible. I mean, I had a little cold. A cough."

"And a fever, too, right?" Her brows climb into the sandy brown hair dipping over her forehead, a little more salt in it than the last time I saw her. "Apparently your 'little cold' left unattended became a lot more."

How could I not know? How could I have missed that? I knew something was wrong, but I never imagined it was more than a bug I couldn't shake.

"How's Rhyson?" I whisper, still not ready to wake him. I know his concern will smother me like a blanket once he's up.

"How do you think he is?" Aunt Ruthie tilts her head to catch my eyes. "Worried and ornery. Making life difficult for everyone around here."

"That sounds about right," I mutter. "How long have I been out? How long have you been here?"

"You've been asleep for about a day. They sedated you. I got here a few hours ago." She inclines her head toward the man still sleeping to my right. "He had a fancy plane come get me."

"That was sweet of him. I—"

"Pep?" Rhyson's voice, faint from fatigue, interrupts our conversation. He blinks away sleep, pushing his hands up over his face and through his hair. He's swift to his feet, crossing over to the bed to grip my hand between his. "You're up."

He leans down, pressing his nose into my hair.

"God, I've been so worried, baby." His kisses feather across my face, one landing like rain on my lips before he pulls back. He glances up to meet Aunt Ruthie's curious eyes. Her mouth crooks into a small smile. "How long has she been awake?"

"Just now. You gonna yell at me for not letting you know sooner?" Aunt Ruthie turns amused eyes back to me. "This one seems to think yelling is how you get things done around here."

"Thanks a lot," he says. "That was supposed to be our little secret."

"I would buzz the nurse," Aunt Ruthie says. "But someone, I won't call any names, has been abusing the buzzer."

"I just buzzed her a couple times." Rhyson rolls his eyes and grins, not quite meeting my eyes.

"Mmmmmm." Aunt Ruthie walks over to the door, turning with her hand on the handle. "He's the boy who cried wolf so she won't come anymore when he buzzes. I'll go get her myself."

"You'll be back, right?" She's a balm to me. I didn't realize how much I missed her warmth and care until I had it pressed against me again.

"I'll be right back, honey." Aunt Ruthie winks at me and points a warning finger at Rhyson. "And you behave while I'm gone."

"The nurse would have come if she buzzed," Rhyson says. "I think she's just trying to give us a few minutes alone."

"So you haven't been making life hell for everyone being protective and unreasonable?" I rasp, struggling a little to get the words out. "'Cause that would be your MO."

"Of course I have." He grins even though his eyes are sober when he brings me water from the small refrigerator in the corner of the room. "I've had to be kind of forceful. They didn't want me in here since I wasn't down as an emergency contact or anything, and no one knew we were together. I didn't have much of a leg to stand on. If San hadn't vouched for me, I wouldn't even be in here now."

I know going through San to get to me always infuriates him. I watch his face while he tips water into the dry, narrow passageway of my throat.

"I'm sorry about that." I cough a little, barely getting the words out. "I completed the paperwork a few months ago when the tour started. We weren't even speaking, so of course I put San down and hadn't thought about it since."

"Yeah, of course. I get it."

He doesn't get it. It's all over him, from the tight lips to the stiffly-held shoulders. I could apologize more, but I know that won't ease the sting of feeling cut out.

"I was there." Rhyson tunnels his hands into the pockets of his pants. He's wearing Dickeys, which he never would under normal circumstances be caught dead in. So I assume he was at my concert in disguise.

"You were?"

The intensity of the look he gives me is almost too much. I don't know if it's what's in his eyes stealing my breath, or the infection lingering in my lungs, but I can't breathe until he looks away, down to the floor.

"Yeah, I was in the audience when you collapsed." He clenches his eyes shut. "Worst moment of my life, Pep. Seeing you fall. Not knowing what the hell was wrong. Not able to get to you or knowing even where you were."

"I'm so sorry." I whisper as much as my voice will allow, grabbing his hand, dipping my head to catch his eyes even though he doesn't want me to see the vulnerability there. "Rhys, I'm sorry."

"I can't believe I held you in my arms coughing, walking around with fucking pneumonia and didn't do anything about it. Didn't even realize it." He shakes his head, jaw clenched, and walks to the foot of the bed. "That's never happening again. I'm never trusting someone else with you again. Not even you."

"What's that mean?" I frown even though every part of me aches so much even that action takes effort.

"Meaning I can't even trust you to take care of yourself, much less think Malcolm would look after you." His stare accuses me. "How could you let this happen?"

"Are you mad at me?" I inch myself upright in the bed. "I'm in the hospital, and you're mad at me?"

"You can't love me the way I love you if you don't understand that." He stands, pacing at the foot of the bed and shoveling both hands through his hair. "Did you mean it when you said I'm yours and you're mine?"

"You know I did. Of course, I me—"

"Then how dare you be so damn reckless with what's *mine*?" He presses his palms to the table at the foot of the bed, leaning forward, his stare pressing me deeper into the pillow behind me. "You can't possibly get that and be so careless with your health. With your life."

"I wasn't being careless. I was working."

"For a tyrant. And I told you he didn't give a shit about you, but you ignored me. *Left* me to go on the road for him, and this is what happens."

"How can you be mad at me?" Tears blur and burn my eyes.

"How can I not, Pep? You're my fucking *life*. How can you not know that?" He drops his head into his hands, digging and twisting his palms into his eyes. "You're my life."

"And you're mine."

"Am I?" He shakes his head, turning away from me to link his hands behind his neck. "If that were true, we wouldn't be here right now."

"You've gotten to do this your whole life. Is it wrong that I want to take advantage of my shot? I finally get the chance to make it, and—"

"I don't give a damn if you 'make it' if it hurts you, Pep." He swings back around to face me, eyes tumultuous. "If it jeopardizes you, then you're right. I don't care about your career. There. I said it."

"How would you feel if I said that to you?"

"I'd feel like you had your priorities straight. That's how I'd feel."

"No, you—"

The door flies open, and a nurse wearing purple scrubs and a scowl walks in.

"I heard our patient was awake." She sets her fists on her hips and walks over to my bed. "Were you planning to argue her back to good health, Mr. Gray?"

Rhyson at least looks abashed, his eyes losing some of their heat when he glances back at me.

"I'm sorry." He blows out his frustration. "We were just—"

"Oh, the whole wing heard what you were just doing." She looks up at him from the blood pressure cuff she's wrapping around my arm. "Am I gonna have to ask you to leave?"

Rhyson doesn't answer, but takes his seat by my bed and starts scrolling through his phone. I'm not sure if it's his way of demonstrating he'll cooperate, or showing her he's not going anywhere.

"Your vitals are good, but the doctor will be in soon to look at you," she says to me. "How are you feeling?"

"Thirsty," I croak. "And really drowsy."

"We gave you some medication that kept you asleep because the best thing you can do to get better is rest."

She offers me the water again. Each sip irrigates my dry, scratchy throat, so I keep sipping until the cup is almost empty.

"Slow down, honey." She laughs a little. "It's time for more meds actually."

She chides Rhyson with a look.

"If he's going to upset you, he'll have to go."

"He won't," I rush to say. "I promise."

"If he can't follow instructions—"

"Please don't make him go." I'm about to cry again. Is it the exhaustion making me such a crybaby?

"Don't worry," Rhsyon says without looking up from his phone. "She won't make me go."

The nurse lifts a brow, meeting Rhyson's defiance with her own.

"You have some other friends who'd like to see you." Her stern eyes soften on me. "Is that okay?"

"Sure. That's fine."

She leaves, and neither of us speaks for a moment, the memory of our argument too fresh in the room.

"Do you have any idea what you mean to me?" Rhys finally asks, his voice quiet, but still rich with emotion. "There's no happiness without you anymore. This didn't have to happen. I'm furious with Malcolm. I'm furious with myself."

"Furious with me?" I ask softly.

He doesn't answer, but the air throbs with it. This caged emotion that has been waiting for me to wake up, finally unleashed in a torrent. Fear and desperation stand in his eyes like water, reflecting everything he's been through since he saw me collapse. I can't be mad at him. And I know he won't stay mad at me.

He gets up from the chair and steps close to the bed, leaning down to slide his arm under my back, scooping me close. He buries his head in my hair, gripping me like he's afraid I'll float away.

"God, Pep."

"I'm okay." I lay soothing strokes over the knotted muscles of his back. "Baby, I'm okay."

I hear him swallow, feel his arms tighten around me.

"I can't." He shakes his head.

He doesn't finish that thought, but I know. He can't go through that again. He can't be without me. He can't lose me. I know because that truth hums through my veins as sure as whatever is pumping through the needle stuck in my arm. We are pieces that have interlocked, carved to fit by fate or something I don't understand, but I know is real.

"I can't either." I push my fingers into his hair, gently nudging him far enough back so I can look into his eyes. "I don't ever want to again."

I lean up to kiss him, an innocent touch that flares with the desperate intimacy enshrouding us. He deepens the kiss, his hands drifting to my back, pressing me closer. Even with stale breath and two days on us, kissing him is so sweet.

The door opening startles us apart.

"For the love of God, man," San says. "She's got pneumonia. You can't keep your hands to yourself for five minutes? It's like *that?*"

I don't have a fever anymore, but my face fires up because it's not just San at the door. Aunt Ruthie's back, along with Bristol, Grip, Grady, Em, and a white-coated doctor, all witnesses to the mortification of our sick bed make out session.

Rhyson steps away, a sheepish grin crooking his lips. He looks back at me, mouthing a silent "sorry."

"The nurse said you wanted to see your friends." The doctor walks over to the bed, taking my wrist, checking my pulse. "I guess we should have knocked."

Grip snickers, a fist at his mouth to catch the sound. His eyes and the smile he gives me are warm. I'm not sure what Rhyson's told him since Grady's wedding when he set up our barn loft rendezvous, but he doesn't seem displeased to see us together again.

Bristol's glance pops between her brother and me like a rubber band. Her smile is stiff, and I see the concern in her eyes. It's not for me, though. It hurt me to see Rhyson undone the way he has been since I woke up. I suspect it's hurt Bristol to see him that way, too. And she knows it's because of me. When someone loves you, especially the way Rhyson loves me, you have so much power. Every breath you take, every beat of your heart holds sway over them. You're sometimes moments from crushing them without even trying. Without even knowing. I'm finally understanding that Bristol knows I have that power over her brother, and she's not sure she can trust me with it.

Sometimes neither am I. Even though he has just as much power over me, sometimes I'm not sure I can trust me with it either.

Everyone crowds around the bed, talking at once, asking if I'm okay. They tease Rhyson ruthlessly about being an irrational pain in the ass while I was sedated. He backs away, propping himself against the windowsill to give them room. Every time I look up, his eyes burn over me like fever, and I have to force myself to look away.

The doctor, Dr. Wells, finally asks everyone to leave so he can examine me more fully.

"When can I go home?" I demand. I feel weak, but so much better even than I have for the last few weeks. "I can recuperate at home, right?"

"I need to examine you, but based on what we've been seeing in your lungs, in your levels, that might be fine." He bends a look over his spectacles. "In a few days, as long as someone is there to take care of you."

"I'll make sure she follows all your instructions," San offers.

"The hell you will." Rhyson's sharp words slice into the conversation like it's butter.

The room goes pin-drop quiet, everyone holding their breath while San and Rhyson hold a stare.

"Let's work out the details of where she'll be going and who'll be enforcing doctor's orders later." Grady saves the day with his characteristic diplomacy. "Why don't we get out of Dr. Wells' way so he can examine Kai properly?"

Everyone drifts out the door with promises to check on me and hopes that I'll get better. Rhyson, San, and Aunt Ruthie remain. Before Dr. Wells can shoo them away, I need to clarify something.

"I want to go home," I say, my voice even and strong, despite the insistent fatigue pressing in the longer I'm awake.

"Of course." Rhyson grabs my hand. "Sarita will—"

"Not to your place, Rhys," I say softly, gently, before looking up at Aunt Ruthie. "I need to be in my mama's house."

Aunt Ruthie nods, pressing her lips tight against the emotion dampening her eyes.

"Okay." Rhyson takes a step back, shoving his hands into his pockets and heaving a sigh. "If that's what you want, then of course I understand."

He's studying his shoes, the muscles along his jaw tensed, brows lowered over his eyes.

"Think you could spare some time in the country with me?" I ask, stretching my hand toward him.

A huge grin breaks out on his face, and he takes my hand to his lips, kissing my fingers folded over his.

"I might be able to work that out."

Chapter NINETEEN

Kai

NOTHING IN THIS HOUSE HAS CHANGED but me.

The pencil dashes Mama made charting my height from childhood and through adolescence still mark the kitchen wall. The same white and green hand-made eyelet curtains hang at the window over the sink. Many a night after dinner, I'd stand here washing dishes, watching Mama cross the yard to her work shed out back where she canned vegetables from our garden, made her soaps, and jarred preserves. She could have done that here in the house, but I think she had Mr. McClausky build that little shed as an escape. As one of the few places she truly had to herself. With Glory Bee below, me sleeping across the hall, and Aunt Ruthie within snoring distance, there wasn't much room. I know because near the end, I felt these walls closing in on me. With death hovering over our little house and the demands of Mama's illness heavy on my back, there was barely room to dream. And when Mama could no longer leave her bed, I'd slip off to that little shed to see if there was any peace out there. To my dismay, all I found were shelves of Ball jars stuffed with fruits and vegetables, captured at their peak of freshness. I hope that little shed offered Mama more than that, but I've never been sure.

"You up here, babe?" Rhyson asks from the living room.

I heard him clomping up the steps that lead to our little place above the diner, but I was too caught up in memory to offer my help. Not that I'm much help. For all my blustering that I felt better and was ready to go home, my body is worn down. What the infection didn't ravage, exhaustion did. All bold and sure when I was stretched out in a hospital bed and freshly un-sedated, but I was embarrassingly weak the first time I tried to even get out of that bed. Aunt Ruthie had to help me to the bathroom. Rhyson left the room, faking a phone call, but I know seeing me like that made him furious.

I don't know how much time I have before he brings up Malcolm's contract, but I know it's not long. I seem to have quite a growing list of things I'm too embarrassed to share with him. First the sex tape from a one-night stand with a guy he detests, and now a bad deal I foolishly signed when we were apart, which I see no way out of.

Yay, me.

"Pep!" he calls again.

"Sorry." I go back into the living room, my legs still trembling a little from the climb up the stairs. "Let's put the bags in my room."

He follows me down the narrow hall leading to the room where I used to sleep, pausing by the room where Mama died. One thing in this house *did* change. Mama's old room is now an office of sorts. A desk on one side, littered with invoices and bills. Mama's old sewing machine, crammed in a corner, and baskets of what Mama used to call ribble rabble. Just crap you never can find the right place for. I don't think Aunt Ruthie even sews. She just probably can't make herself take that Singer down to Goodwill.

It's not the first time I've seen these rooms again. I was here for Christmas, and all these things were the same and Mama's room was already different. I think I feel it so profoundly this time because *I'm* so different. The girl who slept in this room listening to Rhyson's music never imagined he'd be standing by her bed.

"This okay?" He places my bags at the foot of the bed.

"Yeah, that's cool." I lift up on my toes, wrapping my arms around his neck, waiting for the familiar weight and heat of his hands to settle just below the curve of my hips.

"Where are you?" he whispers in my ear.

I know what he means.

"What do you mean?" I ask anyway.

"You're in your head or something." He toys with the end of the braid looping over my shoulder. "You okay?"

I nod because I can't put words to it yet. I would sound crazy if I told him I envy that girl with her simple life waking to make biscuits before sunup. That girl with the hope of a dream burning in her bright and strong. That girl who never considered sex tapes and sketchy contracts. Her life, though hard, was open and honest. With the tour behind me, Rhyson wanting to go public, and that sex tape still hanging over my head, I'm wrapped in lies. The girl I thought was so lost back then was in many ways much more sure than I am now.

"Really?" Rhyson searches my eyes. It's such a blessing and half a curse how attuned we are to one another. You tend to pay close attention to someone you're obsessed with, and we're happily obsessed with one another.

"I promise I'm fine." It's not a lie, but it's not the whole truth. Half-truths are becoming a habit.

"Coming here was a great idea." The palm of his hand cups my chin. "Fresh air. No commitments."

He leans down to drop a quick kiss on my lips.

"No worrying that someone will find out we're together." He pulls back, cocking one brow. "I don't have to pretend I'm not crazy about you here, do I?"

Instead of answering, I lift up to kiss him, my hands sneaking inside his leather jacket and under his t-shirt, gliding over the warm muscles of his back. I pursue the kiss, deepening it, making promises with my lips and tongue that my body longs to make good on. He squeezes my butt, brushes his fingertips across my breast, caresses my neck, rediscovering what's his as I rediscover what's mine.

The sound of Aunt Ruthie entering from downstairs and closing the door slows our kiss, little by little until we're just brushing lips and holding on. Rhyson pulls back, sucking in air, bracing his hands on my shoulders and caressing my throat with his thumbs.

"I'm gonna sleep on the couch." His eyes slip over the simple button down shirt clinging at my breasts and the curve of my hips in my jeans. "It feels like forever since that night in Berlin, and as I'm sure you noticed my dick is quite hard, but yeah. The couch. I may not share Aunt Ruthie's beliefs, but I don't want to disrespect them under her roof."

Just when I think I couldn't love him anymore, he goes and does or says something to prove I have no idea how much this guy holds my heart.

"Yeah. OK." I grab his hand and lead him over to the bed where I slept growing up. "Just lie down with me for a little while. Talk to me for a bit while I fall sleep."

He peers down at me, and I know he's searching my face for signs of exhaustion. He'll find them. The lines around my mouth. The smudges under my eyes. The heavy eyelids fatigue keeps dragging downward.

"Please."

I pull him to the bed with me, squeezing against his broad chest.

"I used to listen to your music in here every night before I'd fall asleep," I whisper.

"So in a way, I was with you back then." He smiles against my cheek.

"In a way, yeah."

"I want to be with you every step of the way." I can almost hear his hesitation. A pause that says so much before he voices it. "Kai, it doesn't have to be tonight, but we need to talk about your contract with Malcolm."

I knew this would come, but was hoping it wouldn't be day one.

"There's nothing to talk about. I'm with him for two years."

"But what are the terms?" he presses. "I'd buy your contract out. You know I would. I've wanted you on Prodigy for a long time. Malcolm mismanaging you on your first tour, compromising your health—"

"No one knew I was sick, Rhys. I didn't even know how much."

"Yeah, but—"

A light rap on the open door stops whatever he would have said. Aunt Ruthie stands at the entrance, her eyes moving between the two of us facing each other on the bed.

"You guys okay in here?" She leans into the doorjamb, one fist on her hip. "Ya hungry?"

Rhyson sits up, looking back and pushing a chunk of hair behind my ear, traces my eyebrows with his thumb.

"I think we're just tired." He smiles, some of the irritation from our contract discussion clearing from his face. "Especially this one."

"Well, get some rest." Aunt Ruthie turns to go.

"Could I get some sheets and a blanket for the couch?" Rhyson walks over to where Aunt Ruthie stands. Surprise flits across her face before she looks back at me on my bed.

"Sure," she says. "Oh. Kai, I know you're just getting back, but Mr. McClausky wanted to cook chicken in the pot for you tomorrow. He's the only one I told about you coming home."

"Chicken in the pot?" Rhyson looks between the two of us. "Is this a thing?"

"It's my favorite thing." My lips are almost too tired to grin, but I manage. "And, yeah, Aunt Ruthie, I'd love that. You can invite a few other folks you know won't talk about us being here or make a big fuss. I'd love to see everybody who was here for Christmas dinner."

"I was hoping you'd say that." Aunt Ruthie smacks her hands together, eyes bright despite the lateness of the hour. "I'll call 'em all in. They'll love seeing you. Well, I'm gonna turn in."

She blows me an air kiss.

"See you in the morning. Sleep as late as you want."

Aunt Ruthie leaves, and as much as I love Rhyson considering her beliefs, which were once mine, I want him crawling under the covers with me. Not to do anything other than hold me all night, but

I can tell it's important to him that Aunt Ruthie knows he's behaving. I have no idea why, but I love him for it.

He digs into my suitcase until he finds one of my vintage night-shirts, tossing it to me.

"Put that on and go straight to sleep. Dr. Wells won't be blaming me for your relapse."

A wicked, wanton imp possesses me for one last hurrah before I surrender to the sleep dragging at my consciousness. I slip one button and then another loose on my shirt until the lacy edge of my pink bra peeks out.

"Why don't you come put it on for me?" My raspy, barely-there voice sounds even huskier in the confines of my childhood bedroom.

"I don't think so." Rhyson leans out into the hall, looking in the direction Aunt Ruthie went. "There'll be plenty of time for that when we get back to LA."

"You're kidding, right?" My mouth falls open. We haven't made love in a month and he's serious. "But we—"

"Kai, I want Aunt Ruthie to like me." Fatigue and desire darken his eyes to slate.

"She does, Rhys, but I think she knows we sleep together. I was practically living with you a few months ago. I didn't hide that from her. I didn't have to."

"I know. I just . . . Let me do this, okay?"

I never thought I'd be the one pushing for sex. The thought of me pressuring Rhyson to sleep with me makes me smile all the way into my dreams.

Chapter TWENTY

RHYSON

THIS COUCH GAVE MY CHIVALRY A bad back.

I shift a little to avoid the spring poking my lower lumbar, but encounter a warm, curvy lump nestled against my chest. The smell of pears and cinnamon wafts up from the petite person squeezed between my body and the cushions.

"Pep," I whisper, more to myself than to Kai. This is how every day should start. For her to slip in here with me and endure this lumpy couch when she had a perfectly good bed up the hall tells me she feels the same.

I don't want to wake her. An investigative look over the top of the couch through the window sheers reveals the sky is still that just-past-dawn palette, faintly splashed with pinks and gold.

I want to keep things above board in Aunt Ruthie's house, but I have to squeeze Kai a little tighter to my chest. As sprawling and complex as my life can be sometimes, it really all boils down to this. To this girl huddled into me, sharing a blanket in the morning chill. I'll do whatever it takes to protect her from the likes of Malcolm. To keep her from guys like Dub. Anything to hold her right here this close.

"Guess she couldn't stay away," Aunt Ruthie says softly from the hall that leads to the bedrooms. "You two are like magnets."

Shit.

"Um, well, no. We didn't . . . I guess she wanted . . . Nothing happened."

I sound like some pimple-faced teenager from a John Hughes movie. I'm a grown man, and Kai's my girlfriend. And we sleep together. We fuck *really* hard, and I *really* love it. But under the steady stare of the closest thing Kai has to family, I want to strap a chastity belt on her.

Aunt Ruthie lifts the untamed line of her eyebrows, a small smile denting one cheek.

"I'll take your word for it," she says. "I'm getting coffee. Want some? Or are you going back to, uh . . . sleep?"

Kai's squished on the couch and would probably sleep a lot better and longer with me gone. I slide away, careful not to wake her, pulling the blanket up to her neck and following Aunt Ruthie into the kitchen.

The silence percolates in the dimly lit kitchen right along with the coffee. Aunt Ruthie seems content with it, pulling out eggs, milk, cheese, and bacon, humming a tune I don't know, probably some church song, but the quiet drives me a little crazy.

"I promise nothing happened," I blurt. "Last night, I mean. I just woke up and Kai was on the couch, but nothing—"

"Happened. Yes, you mentioned that," Aunt Ruthie slips in, handing me a mug of coffee. "Why do you care so much if I believe it?"

I clear my throat and sit at the square wooden table taking up a good bit of space in the small kitchen.

"You're the closest thing Kai has to family." I shrug, like my next words haven't knit a nervous ball of yarn in my stomach. "I want you to like me. To approve of me because one day I'll be asking for your blessing."

"My *blessing*?" Aunt Ruthie only bothers lifting one brow this time. "What kind of blessing?"

"To marry her." As soon as the words leave my mouth, that ball starts unwinding because that sounds so right.

"'Blessing's' an interesting word. You don't strike me as an especially religious or traditional man, Rhyson." Aunt Ruthie settles into the seat across from me, sheltering the steaming coffee mug between her hands, keeping her voice as low as mine. "Do you even believe in blessings?"

"No, I don't think I do, but she does." I take a sip of the coffee before continuing. "I've always been honest with Kai that I don't do religion. I don't really care about it, but I know it's important to her."

"Is it still?" Aunt Ruthie tilts her head, her eyes intent. "I wasn't sure. We haven't talked about it in a long time."

"I think Kai's figuring things out for herself like most people have to, but her faith is still in her heart."

"And where's your faith?"

"If I have any, it's in her."

"It's dangerous to love that way, Rhys." She shakes her head before taking another sip.

"Why?"

"Because none of us are perfect or live forever. We're just human beings who make mistakes and die eventually. When you love someone like that, so completely, they can hurt you without even meaning to. Kai's mama hurt me more than anyone ever has, and all she did was die."

I absorb those words through my skin, through my bones and to my heart. I get that. Kai and I laughed in Berlin over her being the most powerful person in my universe, but it's true.

"And as amazing as I think Kai is, she's not perfect. She'll mess up. We all do. Love her through her mistakes. That'll be the true test of it." She raises her brows over her mug. "Think you can do that?"

"I can do that." I nod, certainty settling over all my doubts because Kai loved me through my mistakes. I'd do that for her.

"Then you won't need my blessing." Aunt Ruthie breathes a

short laugh. "And if Kai's as in love with you as you are with her, she won't need it either. That girl is as stubborn as they come. In a lot of ways, Kai's more like her father than her mother."

Aunt Ruthie tips her head, brows up.

"Not that you could ever tell her that."

"What was he like? Her dad, I mean?"

Aunt Ruthie's long sigh makes the air heavy. She sets her coffee mug down, studying the dark liquid before answering.

"He was a good man who made a really bad decision and ruined everything." Aunt Ruthie runs a hand over her salt and sanded hair. "I can see that in people. How good people do really stupid things. We all do, but what he did, how he left them, was unforgiveable."

I don't want to be another man in Kai's life who hurts her with my bad decisions. Unfortunately, I already have.

"Did she tell you what I did?" I ask tentatively. "Why she left me?"

"No." Aunt Ruthie grins. "But you're a man, so I'm sure it was very stupid."

I can't help but grin back because in hindsight, getting *Total Package* to pass on Kai *was* very stupid.

"You're right. I was a Grade A imbecile, but I was only trying to do what's best for her, to help. She's not an easy girl to help, ya know?"

"Oh, I'm aware."

"And I want to protect her, to take care of her without smothering her, but I keep fuck—" My eyes dart to Aunt Ruthie's waiting expression. "I mean, I keep messing up."

Fucking and cursing—two of the things I'm really good at—are off limits in this house. The little smile she tries to suppress offers me some relief and emboldens me to go on.

"I'm in therapy, and I hope that'll help." I circle the rim of the mug with my index finger. "I've just never felt like this about anyone, about *anything* really, before. I'm not always sure how to handle it."

"Can I give you a little cheat sheet?" Aunt Ruthie waits for my nod before going on. "Don't just act out of what you think is *best* for her. You're not her parent. You're not her father. Think about what will show her that you love her and understand her. That's important to Kai."

It's a simple thing, but it forces Kai's words during our infamous fight back into my head.

"Do you have any idea how opposite of love that is?"

I can't say a light bulb clicks over my head. I don't know if it's a eureka, but I think that insight could be a light for my path, illuminating how I should go forward, one step at a time. I want to pay Aunt Ruthie ten years of counseling fees for it.

Who needs Dr. Ramirez?

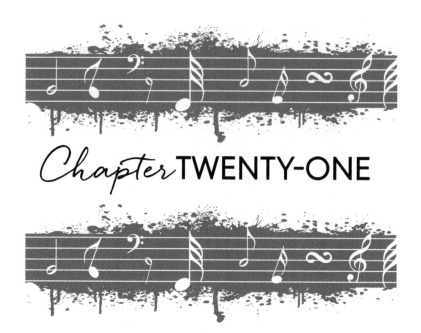

Chapter TWENTY-ONE

Kai

BY THE TIME I WAKE UP, shower, and make my way to the kitchen, the counters are loaded with raw chicken, fresh ears of corn, sweet potatoes, flour, and all the things that will make this day incredibly fattening and lots of fun. My boyfriend, the rock star, is peeling potatoes . . . and not very well. I better take that knife from him before he never plays piano again.

"Let me get that, baby." I reach for the knife, but he holds on.

"I got it." He leans up for a quick kiss before returning to the pitiful pile of stumps that used to be potatoes.

Aunt Ruthie levels a wide-eyed stare over his head, begging me to get him out of her kitchen.

"Um, Rhyson, maybe we should go check on things downstairs at Glory Bee," I say. "See if we can find a way to stay out of sight, but still help down there."

The awkward silence following my statement swells in the small kitchen.

"What?" My eyes flick from Rhyson to Aunt Ruthie. "Something wrong at the diner?"

"Well, we're taking the week off." Aunt Ruthie wipes her hands on the apron I gave her one Christmas.

"The *week* off?" My jaw drops. "Glory Bee has never been closed for a week."

"Exactly." Rhyson frowns at a particularly stubborn section of peel. "Aunt Ruthie's past due for a vacation."

"And if we close the diner while you're here, easier to keep your visit off the radar." Aunt Ruthie goes to the sink to rinse a few chicken thighs.

"Can you afford that, Aunt Ruthie?" I can't keep the concern out of my voice. If my presence here costs her something, I may need to find somewhere else to recuperate. I don't miss the quick look Rhyson and Aunt Ruthie exchange. A conspiracy if I ever saw one.

"Or maybe I should ask Rhys if *he* can afford it?" Hand on hip, I tilt my head and give him a meaningful look. Letting him know the jig's up. "What did you do, Rhys?"

He sets the knife and potato aside, standing up to wrap his arms at the elbows around my hips.

"What I always do." He kisses my eyes and then my nose. "Whatever it takes."

"What did you do, baby?" I repeat, but this time brushing the wild spill of hair back from his face.

"He asked me what it would take to close Glory Bee down for the week," Aunt Ruthie answers for him. "And he's covering our losses."

I glance over my shoulder at Aunt Ruthie, rinsing a big bucket of black-eyed peas, wearing her "no shame in my game" face.

"Unlike you," she says with a grin. "I have no trouble taking money from your rich boyfriend."

Rhyson's lips twitch almost imperceptibly, but I don't miss the satisfaction in his eyes. Still, his shoulders tense under my hands while he waits for my response. I know I'm stubborn and sometimes unreasonable, but this was sweet for Aunt Ruthie. And she really hasn't had many breaks since Mama passed. And none before.

"Thank you," I whisper, tipping up to kiss his chin.

For a moment, he's not sure what to say. He studies me an extra second before kissing behind my ear.

"Any time. Every time."

"It's a good thing, too," Aunt Ruthie says. "Already had a few reporters nosing around."

"What?" All softness drops from Rhyson's expression. "You didn't tell me that. I can get security here today."

"No need for that. We threw 'em off the scent." Aunt Ruthie shakes her head and scrunches her nose. "Closing the diner and keeping a low profile with just a few folks we know we can trust should be fine."

"It'll be fine," I assure him. "Everyone coming today will be a friend who won't say anything. We'll be in the backyard. It'll be fun. We'll show you all the wonderful things the country has to offer."

He tightens his arms around me, a smile softening his lips.

"I already got the best thing this place has to offer."

THERE ARE SOME DAYS THAT BUNDLE all your favorite things into a series of moments you'd live over and over again if you could. Today is one of those days. I'm surrounded by people I'd forgotten were my favorites, people I can tell aren't sure what to make of me now, but are trying to act normal. Trying to reconcile the little girl who sang in the choir and volunteered at the homeless shelter every Christmas Eve with the woman who's been on tour and in the spotlight. Whose well-documented relationship is speculated about on every blog and entertainment report Whose rock star lover sits right beside her at the picnic table behind our little house, and can' t keep his hands to himself.

It's subtle. Maybe. Probably not, but Rhyson doesn't seem to care, reveling in the chance to be open with his affection. Arm around my shoulder and kissing my hair while we watch the kids play kickball. Showing off for me and yelling "Did you see that?" across the yard when he beats Mr. McClausky at horseshoes. Weaving our fingers together on the table while he talks football with a few of the guys. This is Georgia, where college football is a religion, and the SEC its mightiest denomination. The men's fervor about it breeds humor in Rhyson's eyes and around his mouth, and the more they forget he's famous, the more he relaxes, seeming as at ease in a group of strangers as I've ever seen him.

"Now what's so great about this chicken in the pot?" He holds a golden crispy drumstick poised at his mouth.

"Oh, just taste and you'll see." I lick my lips, eyeing the food piled high on my plate. Yams, corn pudding, black-eyed peas, potato salad, and the centerpiece, my favorite chicken fried in a big old grease-filled black cast iron pot.

To call his first bite rapturous would not be an exaggeration. I've seen Rhyson in orgasm, and I'm a little insulted that his response to a drumstick doesn't look much different.

"That," he says, pointing to the chicken he holds in a death grip. "Is the best thing I've ever tasted."

"Good, huh?" I bite into the huge, crispy breast Aunt Ruthie set aside for me.

"Good is a paltry word for it." He digs in, groaning over every morsel until his plate is nearly clean.

"Kai, will you cook chicken in the pot for me when we get back to LA?"

"What?" I laugh and scrape the last vestiges of corn pudding from my plate. "Set up a big ol' black pot by your fancy swimming pool?"

"Why not?" He grins, reaching for his third piece of chicken. "Grip would love this."

"How's his project going?"

"Okay." Rhyson shrugs, wiping his mouth with the paper napkin. "I'm supposed to be executive producing it, so I'll have to get back to LA soon."

I'm determined not to let my disappointment show. I shred a roll into tiny pieces on my plate, eyes glued to the remnants of my meal.

"Hey." Rhyson cups my chin, gently tilting until our eyes connect. "Not for a few days."

"It's fine. I don't want you missing commitments because of me."

"You're my only commitment today," he whispers across my lips. I should be self-conscious about the eyes on us, but I can't make myself care. We haven't been all extreme PDA, but no one could miss that we're together. Between the sex tape and the fallout from the public fight we had, discretion has become such a habit for me. I pull back a little, hating the heat in my cheeks under his knowing look and grin.

The day is waning into late afternoon by the time we're all done. Stacks of Tupperware fill the small refrigerator in our kitchen once everyone has gone, and as much as I hate to admit it, I'm feeling every moment of this perfect day in my aching arms and legs. In my bones.

"I don't need you to tuck me in." I still can't fight back a yawn when Rhyson pulls the cover up and bends to kiss my forehead. "But you could lie down with me."

"You'll go to sleep quicker without my erection poking you in the back." He laughs at the face I make. "You know it's true and I can't help it."

"Rhys, you could—"

"Go to sleep, Pep." The smile falls from his face. "I'm afraid you overdid it today. Your meds will kick in soon, and you could use a nap."

"Okay, but don't let me sleep too long. There's still some day left."

My eyelids flutter and fall. I'll never use the word "exhaustion" carelessly again because I've never felt this bone-deep level of fatigue, punctuated by moments when you literally cannot fight sleep. It overtakes you. And just as I'm about to try one more time to persuade Rhyson he should lie down with me, I'm pulled under.

An hour, two—I'm not sure how much later, I wake up with the saltiness of tears on my lips. It's been a long time since I dreamt of my father, but he was in that dark well of fatigue I fell face first into. I don't remember all the details, but his face was clear. The day I sat in his lap, and he told me about the deepest of loves was so clear I could feel him tugging my pigtails and see my lavender tutu puffing around my little eight-year-old legs. Feel the bite of my new ballet slippers. I loved him so much, and that was the last time he held me. Why his betrayal and abandonment should still make me cry in my sleep after fifteen years, I can't understand.

I pull the sheet up to my face, wipe away the tears and toss my legs over the side of my bed, glad to find them less weak. The nap did me good, and maybe this surge of energy I feel is a mirage, but I'm pursuing it until it fades. I need to do something, and I know exactly where I want to do it.

"I'm going out to the work shed," I tell Rhyson and Aunt Ruthie, both huddled on the couch watching television. Rhyson never watches television unless I make him, so I'm curious to see what has him looking so enthralled.

"We'll be fine," he says, eyes barely leaving the screen to flick to me and then back again.

"It's awfully dusty out there, Kai." Aunt Ruthie's eyes remain fixed on the television, too, her words and attention absent. "Be careful. We're just catching up on the shows I recorded."

"What is this?" I step closer to the screen. *The Young and the Restless*? Are you kidding me, Rhys?"

"This stuff's fantastic," he says with a completely straight face. "Why didn't you tell me?"

"Um, because I haven't watched soaps since high school?" I laugh and shake my head, dropping a quick kiss on the beautiful mess of his hair. "I'll be out back if you manage to pull yourself away."

"Uh huh." Eyes back on the screen. This is so much fuel for me to tease him about later, I just let it go.

It's going to rain. Crossing the backyard, the rain sends its scent ahead of the storm, and the air is heavy with it, caressing my face like warm velvet. The sun is setting, painting the horizon with one last explosion of color, the last vibrant glimpse of daylight.

Mama's wind chimes still hang over the work shed door, and the slight breeze stirs them to sing a prelude for the storm. The door falls open, squeaking under my hand. Out of habit I thought I'd forgotten, my hand reaches blindly to the wall on my left, finding the light switch that doesn't even have a faceplate anymore. The stale, unstirred air confirms that no one's been here for a long time. I think everyone knew how special this place was to Mama, what a solace it proved to be, and after she was gone, just let it be.

The small mattress in the corner reminds me that I was her exception, the only one who ever joined her. Some days after school and dance practice and dinner and dishes, I'd come out here to watch her make things while I did my homework. The memory is so clear I almost see the younger version of myself, back pressed to the wall, legs crossed on the thin mattress, Trapper Keeper balanced in my lap, number two pencil in hand, one long braid hanging over my shoulder. We didn't even talk much. She knew I needed to get my work done, and I suppose I knew she needed the quiet to think. I rarely asked her about what.

The scents of Mama's hobbies collide, fragrant and varied, trapped in the unstirred air of this room all these months. I venture over to the shelves, still neatly lined with Ball jars, vivid with the colors of her fruits and vegetables. I kick off my shoes like this is holy ground and pick up a jar of her strawberry preserves. I was in the eighth grade when she won the blue ribbon for her preserves at the county fair. I was ten when she started making soap, selling it at the diner to make extra money to cover my ballet class.

Were these just hobbies? Things on the side to make extra money? Rituals that kept something sweet or fresh always on our table? There was a sadness that hung around Mama when she was out here that she rarely showed beyond that door. I don't know if it was a privilege or a burden that I saw it when I was here, diagramming sentences and learning about the Civil War.

Did she come in here to ponder what my father took from her? What she'd lost? Mama always sacrificed for my improbable dreams.

Not many actually make it the way I have, the way I am, but Mama always believed I would be a star. Her dreams, in comparison, were so modest. Be a good wife and mother. Make a home. Have a happy marriage. The irony of my dreams, so farfetched coming true, and her simple hopes being crushed doesn't escape me.

I pull down a jar of pear preserves. Strawberry won the ribbon, but pear was always my favorite. The Ball jar top untwists easily under my fist, the little lid popping back to free the scent of pears. I dip one finger into the sticky mixture, tasting the nostalgia of early mornings, biscuits smeared with preserves. Maybe it's been so long, or maybe this was a bad batch, but it leaves something slightly bitter on my tongue. Was it always there? Did I never notice? Did Mama stuff the isolation, the unhealed pain, the unrelenting loneliness into these Ball jars so that she could smile for the world beyond this shed? Is this where all her hurt went? Was I too young and self-absorbed to detect it before?

The wind chimes tinkle and the door opens, bringing no light now that the sun has set. I don't know how long I've been out here, but the frown on Rhyson's face tells me it may have been too long.

"You okay out here, Pep?" He leans a shoulder into the door, hands tucked into the pockets of his jeans.

"I'm fine."

I prop a hip against the worktable, watching his confident stride toward me. What must it be like to be Rhyson? So sure. So strong. I can't take my eyes off him, and he's not even trying to seduce me. As soon as he's close enough, I'm reaching for him, my arms slipping around his waist, my head dropping to his chest.

"You finished your soap operas, I presume?"

"You do not get to tease me about that." A chuckle vibrates in his chest, rumbling against my cheek through his t-shirt. "Aunt Ruthie and I were bonding."

"Over soap operas?" I lean back, smiling at my beautiful man.

"Whatever it takes." He reaches down to drop a kiss on my lips, the smile fading. "Bristol just called."

My smile fades, too. Work. LA. Real life. Scandal. Secrets. Crack the door and it all floods in.

"And?" The question lands on his chest since I won't lift my head to look at him.

"I promised Kilimanjaro I'd meet with them face to face when they came to LA to talk about a deal with Prodigy." He cups my neck, caressing the skin under my hair. "They arrive tomorrow and leave the next day."

"Of course you should go." It's so stupid to have tears in my eyes. I blink several times until they dry up, coughing a little to cover the tremble in my voice.

"You're coughing." His hand slips to the small of my back. "Should you be out here at night?"

"Rhys, I'm fine. I just coughed. I . . . it's okay." I run my thumb over the fullness of his bottom lip. "I'm fine. I want you to go back to LA. Kilimanjaro will be great on Prodigy, and I don't want you to lose them."

"I'll be back in a couple days."

"You don't have to." I lower my eyes to my toes, feet bare on the little rope rug Mama placed at the work table.

"I had a surprise getaway booked for us after the tour." He smiles at the shocked expression I know is all over my face. "Yep, but those plans were foiled."

"No one says foiled," I say absently, still processing the vacation I missed. "Where were we going?"

"I still have it tucked away, so I'm not telling you. I'll surprise you with it when you least expect it. Just you and me."

He leans down to brush his lips over mine. When he would pull back, I grip his neck, deepening the kiss, my tongue insisting, searching his mouth. The thought of losing him for even just a few days after so long without him squishes my heart in my chest. I fist his thick hair, my hands wandering down to squeeze his ass.

"Okay, Pep." His breath comes heavy, and he inserts a bit of space between us, but his cock bridges the short distance to poke my stomach. "Maybe we should get back to the house."

"Why?" My husky question hovers between us, our eyes locked, my desire as palpable as a touch. I haven't had him in over a month, and I know he thinks we shouldn't here at Aunt Ruthie's, but we should. I lift the t-shirt over my head, tossing it to the floor. Rhyson's eyes fix on my simple black bra, on my nipples poking against the silk, turgid and begging for his lips and tongue.

"Pep, I think—"

"Technically, out here we aren't under Aunt Ruthie's roof."

I slip one strap off my shoulder and then the other, undoing the hook at my back so it falls away, exposing my breasts to the air.

"Fuck, Pep." His words shake in the stillness.

"Make love to me, Rhys."

"You're exhausted. You're just getting over pneumonia." He swallows, his eyes ignoring the excuses and crawling over my breasts. "You . . ."

His words trail off as I unsnap my jeans, urging them over my hips and down my legs until only my black lace panties remain.

"I won't break." I grin up at him, feeling a little wicked on the cusp of screwing my boyfriend in the room where I did my high school homework. "But you can try."

I dip one finger into the jar of preserves, scooping up the thick juice. I reach up to paint his lips with it. Before he can lick it off, I tilt up on my toes, lashing away the sweetness with my tongue, rubbing my bare nipples into his chest. He groans, hands spanning my back to draw me closer. The hunger, delayed and put off by the tour and by my sickness, roars to the surface of our kiss. His palms skid over the small of my back and into my panties to cup my butt, skin to skin. Pear-sweet words fall from his lips to mine.

"Aunt Ruthie—"

"Isn't thinking about us when her soaps are on." I grip his dick through his jeans.

"Shit, Pep." He drops his head until our temples rest against each other. "If you keep doing that, I'm not gonna be able to stop."

"I don't want you to stop." I unsnap his jeans, slipping my hands into his briefs to touch him, cupping his balls and pulling on him. My knees almost buckle at the warm, silky strength in my hands. "I need you."

I need him pushing between my legs, rushing hot and liquid inside of me. I need his lips closing around me, sucking, licking, biting, tasting me like I'm as sweet as these preserves. Mostly I need him to chase away the half-sad memory of my mama in this shed. To kiss away the bitterness of her loneliness. The last traces of uncertainty remain on his face, and I'm determined to wipe them away.

I dip my fingers into the preserves jar again, eyes tangled with his as I smear the gooey thickness over my nipples. Rhyson's eyes, mist grey, go dark and hot, prickling my skin with heat.

"That's just not fair," he breathes, hoisting me by my waist up onto the wooden table.

His head lowers, lips closing over my breast until it disappears in his mouth, worshipping each nipple and lingering to suckle and bite. I grip the edge of the table behind me, want splintering right down my middle and spreading my thighs, a blatant invitation for him to take what unequivocally belongs to him. He presses his eyes tightly closed, one hand at my back, pushing my breasts up and into his mouth. I'm licked clean of the preserves, but he can't stop. I see it all over his face, hear it in the compulsive suckle, feel it in the rough tug of his lips over my breast. He moans like it hurts, but I see such deep pleasure on his face it pounds my heart and snatches my breath.

"The mattress." The words labor past my lips, barely making it. "Let's go to the mattress."

Rhyson looks up for just a moment, his dark eyes wandering to the wall where the mattress waits. He walks us there, my legs clenched around his waist.

"Aunt Ruthie's quilts are on the top shelf." I nibble at his bottom lip.

He sets me on my feet to grab a quilt, which I spread the over the mattress, feeling his eyes burning over my body in just my tiny panties. He swallows, his voice coming out rough in the quiet room.

"Are you sure, Pep? Just a few days ago you needed help to the bathroom. If I hurt you—"

"You won't. I'm fine." I grab his hand and squeeze so he feels my need. "I want you, Rhys. It's been so long."

"Damn right it has, but I can wait." His eyes search my face, looking for any sign that I'm not well, not ready. "If I need to, I can wait."

"But I can't." I lie down on the mattress, diving my fingers into my panties, emboldened by the desire he keeps trying to dam back. "I can't wait, Rhys."

I rub myself, my breath catching at the first touch. Rhyson's eyes fix on my fingers, back and forthing under the silk. I'm hot and wet and slick and swollen, every fire-tipped stroke tantalizing my heart right out of my chest. It's so good. So much better with him watching, but it's not him. Not his touch.

He drops down to join me. With his eyes fixed on my fingers, I take his hand, slowly pushing it beneath the black lace, inviting him to join me. He swears so softly it barely reaches my ears, but he meshes our fingers, the rough calluses on his fingertips a sweet abrasion over my clit.

I haven't been with many men, and I've never been this bold with anyone else. I may still hold onto a few secrets, things I'm not ready for Rhyson to know, but there are no secrets between our bodies. He knows every spot that sets me on fire. He knows that when he starts with one finger, it makes me gasp. That when he adds another, I have to bite my lip to stifle a scream. When he strokes me with his thumb and thrusts with his fingers, it's not long before I . . .

"Ahhh!" My back curves, heels digging into the mattress, the first orgasm stretching me taut as a wire. "Ohmygodohmygodohmygod. Rhyson."

"I could watch you come all day, Pep." He says it against my neck, scattering kisses over my shoulders, sucking my nipples, instigating another wave that takes me under, gasping, drowning, dying a little every time. Then resurfacing, coming back to life.

"Gimme your hand," he says. I offer him the hand that's clenched around a fistful of mattress. "The other hand."

His eyes slide down my body to where my hand lies just beyond my black panties, fingers still wet and shiny. Watching me watching him, he takes my fingers into his mouth, rolling his tongue over them until they're licked clean. He slides down my body, pushing my knee, gripping the back of my thigh and dipping his head between my legs, mouthing me through the panties before he coaxes them aside and then down and then off. Every lash of his tongue pushes me over that precipice again. My hands are buried past the knuckle in his thick hair. My legs flop open, a silent plea for him to take as much as he wants. And though it's so good my eyes roll back in my head, none of it is enough. None of it satisfies that longing at the very bottom of me that cries out to be filled.

"I need you, Rhys." Through barely open eyes I watch him. "*You*, baby."

I taste myself in his kiss before he turns me onto my side, nudging my knee up just a little bit. He's hot and hard behind me, an urgent press, but so gentle, so careful with me, guiding my thigh with his, angling me to his satisfaction before pushing in, a slow, sure thrust. The moment he fills me, my face twists with the pleasure of it. He grips my hip with one hand, the other reaching around, tilting my head up for a kiss. His hand wanders from my hip to my breast, thieving my breath. The whoosh of air from my mouth breaks our kiss. I turn my head into the pillow as he pumps into me from behind, a silent scream wrenched from me.

"Don't stop. Rhys, baby, don't stop," I pant into the pillow.

"What *is* this?" he breathes into my neck. "It's never been like this with anyone, Pep. I promise you that. Never."

"I know." I bite my lip to keep from crying out, even though we're alone out here. "I know."

"I need to see you." He flips me onto my back and plunges back in, almost too much, but my body stretches around him, eager and pliant. "Let me see you."

He doesn't just mean to look into his eyes when I come for him. Whatever this is, it shoves aside even our base desires, ignoring our limited understanding of intimacy and closeness. Winnowing down deeper and deeper until it hits bottom. Until it crash lands in our souls, and I can't even take it. My soul is flayed open, like he's peeled back every layer and laid me out. I know Rhyson feels it, too, his pace becoming more urgent. He rolls into me like thunder, pushing impossibly deeper until he hits *that* spot and my last reasonable thought flees my body. We are mindless together, a frenetic madness possessing our bodies, our cries mingling in the sweet-scented air until we both shake and tremble and clutch.

Every emotion coalesces into this joining, and I can't help it. I weep into his neck. Tears flowing, not just for everything this is to us, but for my mother who never had it. I know she didn't. She couldn't have. If my parents had this, my father never could have walked away. And mingled on my lips with the taste of our kisses, is the bittersweetness of everything trapped in mama's jars.

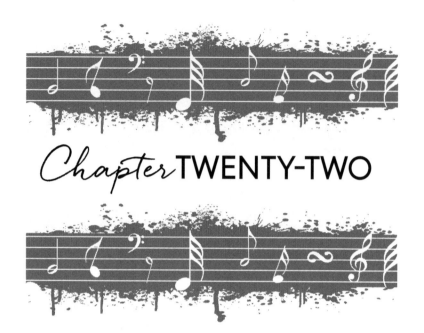

Chapter TWENTY-TWO

Kai

RHYSON IS AS RELUCTANT TO LEAVE my body as I am to let him go, but he finally does, stroking one wide palm over my leg, over my knee, my hip, my arm. The leisurely exploration of lovers, tinged with love and possession. With the tip of my finger, I trace an invisible heart over his thigh thrown carelessly over me. I don't care that it's heavy. I only care that he's mine.

The rain has finally come, ting-tinging the tin roof above us. The storm's breeze breathes through the wind chimes over the door outside, teasing them to tinkle in the quiet country night.

"Let's stay out here." I look up from his chest, my fingers tracing the striking angles of his cheekbones and the full lips. "I don't want to sleep on the couch."

"*You* could sleep in *your* bed and *I* could sleep on the couch." His laughing eyes and smirk tell me he knows good and gosh darn well I'm not sleeping without him the night before he goes back to LA. He just wants to hear me say it.

I sit up as if to go.

"Okay." I swing my legs to the floor and start to rise. "Sounds good to me."

He grabs my wrist, gentle and firm, one hand splaying across my hip.

"Look at you calling my bluff." The husky laugh behind me skitters shivers over my spine. "You know you're not getting out of here before morning."

I smile at him over my shoulder before settling my back against his chest. Our thoughts meet in the silence. It's amazing how perfect silence can be with the right person. His fingers trace my spine and over my shoulders.

"I had moonshine today," he finally says.

I turn over so I can see the smile I hear in his voice.

"Mr. McClausky?"

"Yep."

"And how was it?"

"It was hot going down and went straight to my head." One palm cups the side of my face. "Reminded me of you."

"Ha-ha-ha. Very funny. That stuff's too strong for you city boys. A few more sips and I would have had to carry you home."

"Oh, I would have loved seeing *you* trying to carry *me*."

"I'd figure it out." I drop a kiss on his lips, pulling back to grin when he would deepen the kiss. "So eager."

I send my fingers exploring the line between his abs.

"What's all that land for beyond the backyard?" He toys with my hair spilling onto his chest.

"That's Mr. McClausky's land." I sigh. "For now, at least. I'm not sure he'll be able to keep it. Property taxes. He'll probably sell a good chunk of it off in the next year or so."

"Would he sell it to us?"

I look up at him, my fingers stilling over the hard muscles under my hand. He's looking down at me.

"What do you mean 'to us'?"

"Us, you and me. We could build a place out there. I mean, we couldn't live here year round, but we'd have a place close to Aunt

Ruthie. We could include a home studio, so if either of us ever need to record, we wouldn't even have to leave the house. And the kids could—"

"Kids?" The word pops out in a higher octave. My heart hiccups between beats.

"You do wanna bear my children, right?" He frowns a little, but I can tell he's messing with me.

"Rhyson!" I sit up, twisting around to face him. "Stop acting like we've talked about all of this before. It's . . . it's a big deal. It's a *huge* deal."

"We have talked about it." He shrugs. "Kind of. We kind of have. Maybe I've thought so much about it, it feels like we have."

I'm blindsided by all of this. That he's been thinking all of this. I mean, yeah, once or twice he's *alluded* to our future, but this is so concrete. This is a *plan*.

"Can I tell you something without you freaking out?" He waits for me to nod a little dazedly, even though I'm halfway to freak out town already.

"I dream about our little girl." He laughs and shakes his head. "I mean, I know it's not *actually* our little girl, but it's the same girl every time, and I know she's ours. She's so real that I miss her when I wake up."

I'm almost afraid to ask questions in case this little girl becomes as real to me as she is to him. In case she starts haunting me, too.

"In your dream, what . . . what does she look like?"

He's slow responding, taking me in, his eyes becoming more tender every second I wait for him to answer.

"Like you. She looks like you." A self-conscious laugh accompanies the shrug of one shoulder. "And I guess me. She has my eyes, but they tilt like yours do. She has dark hair. I guess she's whatever my imagination dreamed up a combination of the two of us would look like."

I don't know what to say. His words have stolen mine. They're so sweet. He can be so sweet, his love like a warm blanket that enfolds me completely. Tears fill my eyes. He sits up, too.

"I know we just got back together, that we haven't been together that long." He takes my hand between his. "I hear all those excuses you and everyone else will give me. Just because it's not the right time, doesn't mean it's not *right*. When the time is right, I want to make this permanent, Pep. What we feel now, what we feel every time we're together, I'm never ever letting it go. You know that, right?"

I can't look away from those gorgeous grey eyes. Now that he's said it, I can't shake the image of a beautiful little girl, running around, this perfect meshing of him and me.

"Pep, you know that, right?" His fingers weave into the hair at my neck.

I nod, still a little dumbfounded. There are no words for the sense of rightness burgeoning inside me. If we felt right before, his declaration, his plans, his dream of our future solidifies my absolute devotion to him and commitment to us. I can't speak, so I lean into him, taking his lips between mine.

"Can I ask you another question?" he asks against my lips.

He's melted me into a pile of gooey submission. I'd give him just about anything right now, so I nod.

"What's your deal with Malcolm?"

I pull back to stare at him.

"Seriously, Rhys? That's what you want to talk about now?"

"We have to." He catches my chin and won't let my eyes go. "We can't talk about our future without talking about this deal. You collapsing, that can't ever happen again. And I'm telling you Malcolm won't change. He'll keep pressing you and pushing you past your limits. He'll disregard your health and well-being for his ends, and I can't have it."

He shakes his head.

"I won't have it, Pep. He told me at the hospital that you're locked into a bad deal with him. That for the next two years he owns you and there's no way to get out of it." The concern in his eyes unravels my defenses. "Is that true?"

I want to keep fighting on my own. To keep figuring things out for myself. It's what I've always done, but it all feels so heavy right now. I can't bring myself to tell him about the sex tape yet, but this I'll hand over to him, if only to feel a few ounces lighter.

"I didn't pay close enough attention." I lower my eyes from his intense stare, embarrassed that I was so naïve when he could have prevented this with half a glance at that contract. "There's not even a buy-out option. If I refuse to work for him, I can't work for anyone else for the next two years in anything related to entertainment. I can't even record a jingle for a radio spot. If I do, he'll literally get an injunction to shut it down. So I work for him or for no one."

"Yeah, that's what I figured." He sucks his teeth, exasperated. "He was so smug thinking it's all airtight."

"It is airtight, Rhys." I push the thick hair falling into his face back so I can see his eyes. "It's my fault, and it's okay. It's just two years, and I—"

"I can get you out of it," he cuts in, eyes alert on my face. "I don't want to lie to you again. When you forgave me, we hit the re-set button. Nothing but honesty between us going forward, right?"

The nasty memory of that tape intrudes between us, and he doesn't even know it.

"Right," I whisper, dropping my eyes. "Reset."

"So I want to be up front and above board about this. I have a way to get you out of this contract. It isn't conventional. It's pretty ruthless, but it's legal. I was so tempted to just do it, but I wanted you to know. I wanted you to have the choice this time."

He lifts my chin, palm warm against my face.

"I'll never go behind your back again."

The memory of Malcolm's condescending smugness sliming me onstage, his presumption of ownership, *little girl*-ing me stokes my anger.

"Do it."

Rhyson blinks a few times, obviously surprised by my instant agreement.

"Do you even want to know what it is?" he asks.

"I trust you." I shake my head. "Just get me out of it."

"And then you'll come home to Prodigy where you belong?" He scoops me into him, our naked bodies flush and warm, relief and happiness in his expression. "With me, where you belong?"

The intimate contact has me wanting him again, so I just nod numbly, ready to give him whatever he wants. A text alert from my phone shatters the intimate agreement building between us.

"Ignore it," I say, leaning in to kiss hm.

The persistent alert sounds again.

"We should make sure it's not Aunt Ruthie looking for us," he says against my lips as the alert pings against my ears a third time.

"It's gonna keep doing that," Rhyson says between kisses. "I'll silence it. Where's your phone?"

"In the pocket of my jeans, I guess." I turn onto my back, throwing my arm over my closed eyes. Whoever it is, they can forget about it.

"Be right back."

I peek out from under my arm when he rolls off the mattress, striding naked over to the work table, reaching down to retrieve my phone from the puddle of denim our jeans make. He talks about my ass, but what about his? God, he's gorgeous to me. Lean and tan and firm. The flex of muscles as he walks hypnotizes me. Every part of him hard and beautiful and mine as he walks back, frowning at the phone.

"Text from an unknown number." Curiosity flecks his voice as he studies the screen. "We probably shouldn't open it. Maybe a virus or something weird."

I jump off the mattress and stumble across the few feet separating us, diving for the phone he holds just out of my reach. His eyes flick from me to the phone for precious seconds while my heart melts down in my chest. I snatch it from his hand, the breath stuttering over my lips.

His frown, his eyes ask what's wrong with me, but I can't come up with anything. The panic swallows me up. I can't think straight. I'm a mass of self-preservation and fear. I clutch the phone and stumble naked over to the work table, turning away from him. His eyes sear the bare skin of my back, burning questions there I can't possibly answer.

I open the message, and my fears blossom into the worst reality. It's two messages from my blackmailer. The first is a link to a *Spotted* post.

Are they or aren't they?

The elusive Rhyson Gray and his ex-girlfriend, rising star Kai Pearson, have been mostly silent regarding the public spat that almost broke the internet a few months ago. Our sources suspect the romance may have quietly rekindled. Gray was spotted in Berlin with DJ Kaos just weeks ago, coincidentally (?) on the same night Pearson's tour passed through. And when Pearson collapsed last week during a performance, he rushed to her side at Cedars Sanai. Since her collapse, Pearson is nowhere to be found, and our sources confirm Gray hasn't been in LA since Pearson was released from the hospital a few days ago.

And then this picture really got us thinking.

It's a shot of Rhyson and me leaving the hospital. It was through the underground parking lot, what we were told was a private exit. Even still, we'd taken the precaution of pulling our hoods up. Just one tall hooded figure and a petite girl, barely clearing his shoulder approaching a black SUV, hand in hand.

What do YOU think Spotters?

The second text message is direct and cutting.

Unknown: I know he came to the hospital. If I find out these rumors are true, the tape goes live. How would your rock star ex-boyfriend feel seeing you doggy style with the man he hates? Think about that before you start "rekindling."

How could I have forgotten this feeling of helpless dread? I allowed the hectic pace of the tour, the drama of my collapse, and this idyllic time with Rhyson to lull me into denial. To forget that a madman is out to destroy the thing I hold most dear. Rhyson held that vile thing right in his grasp. My hands tremble at the thought of him opening that message and asking all the questions that would come with it. Even now his curiosity reaches me across the shed. He may as well be standing right over my shoulder his attention is so focused on me.

"Pep?" He asks from the mattress, back propped against the wall. "Everything okay?"

No. Actually I'm being blackmailed by some monster who, for whatever reason, doesn't want us together.

"I . . . it's fine."

"Who is it?"

"Um . . . San." I bite my lip as soon as the lie crosses it. "It's San."

"Hmmm." He sounds distracted, so I glance over my shoulder to see him studying his own phone. "He sent you the story?"

"The story?"

"Bristol just sent me a link to some *Spotted* post about us." He glances up, wearing a small frown. "Why's San's number unknown?"

"Huh?" That word oughta buy me a few seconds.

"You said it was San, but it was an unknown number."

"Yeah." I bend to slip on my panties and jeans, shoving the phone in my back pocket. "He's . . . on assignment. Sometimes he uses . . . yeah."

I look around the shed.

"Have you seen my bra?"

"I thought you wanted to stay here tonight?" He walks over, putting his hand over mine. "What's going on with you? Is it the story? We were going public anyway now that the tour is over."

"It's not that." I drop my forehead to his chest, at a loss. "I'm just so tired."

Tired of hiding. Tired of lying. Tired of keeping this from him, but desperate for him to never know. God, so desperate.

"Tired, we can fix." He bends, arms folding around my legs, under my knees, and lifting me up until I'm looking down on him, hands on his shoulders. He walks us over to the mattress, laying me down gently. He unsnaps my jeans again, sliding them down my legs. His eyes plumb mine, his hand pushing my hair back.

"Whatever's waiting for us in LA isn't here tonight." He lies down behind me, pulling Aunt Ruthie's quilt over us. "The whole world is out there. We're in here."

I wish I could tell him the outside world invaded our solace, that the ugliness of that sex tape sullied an almost spotless night. I'm so burdened. The truth rests on the tip of my tongue, a much-needed confession I can't manage to make. He leans over to give me one last kiss before we succumb to sleep, and it's that look he gives me that holds my tongue.

He loves me.

Do I make him feel this way when I look at him? Like I would die for him? Like I can't believe my good fortune to have him? Like I'll do anything to keep him as mine for always? Because his eyes tell me all those things.

And I'll do whatever it takes to keep that.

Chapter TWENTY-THREE

Kai

IN THE BRIGHT LIGHT OF MORNING, here on the porch, there are so few traces of the night Rhyson and I shared out in that shed. A fresh beginning crisps the air. The heavy, velvety pre-rain cloak has been shed. No breeze stirs the chimes out back, and only the faint caw of a bird here and there disturbs the quiet. If it weren't for the puddles lining the graveled driveway, I wouldn't even know the rain had come and gone.

One thing remains. The intimacy bred between our bodies still grips us. I stand in the strong circle of Rhyson's arms, and every time I look away I'm afraid I'll miss something. The last few days have drawn us impossibly, inexorably closer, and it's hard to imagine anything that could separate us. Except I know there is something. A nasty secret that could crack the very connection walling us away from the rest of the world every time we're together. Love, fear, regret, guilt stir inside of me. I'm as at odds with myself as early Spring, with its morning frost and afternoon heat. One thing is clear. I don't want him to go.

But a discreetly designer duffle bag rests on the top step, and there's a plane idling somewhere until Rhyson arrives, ready to take him back to LA.

"Two days." He leans down, cupping one side of my face and kissing the other. "I'll be back in two days."

"When are you taking me on that vacation? And where did you say we were going again?" I ask, faking innocent as best I can.

"You think that works?" He binds both my wrists in one hand, pulling me closer until his words mist my lips. "You think you can just bat those pretty eyes and I'm putty in your hands, don't you? You think you have me wrapped around your little finger, huh?"

That's the furthest thing from what I think since Rhyson is always trying to boss *me* around and control every aspect of my life, so I just stare at him, slightly stunned, even though he has to be joking.

He bends to whisper in my ear, dusting kisses down my neck.

"You're right. I'm totally wrapped, but I'm still not telling you."

"Just a hint?"

"Okay. I can guarantee you it's somewhere that won't require clothes and allows for a lot of open air fucking."

A laugh cracks my face open, and I throw my head back.

"You make it sound like a sport."

"Once you get your wind back, it will be," he says, his voice a husky promise.

I laugh into his neck, committing to memory his clean scent and the warmth, the strength of his chest under my hands. Clinging to the impression of his lips on me. I tip up, angling my mouth under his, opening him up for me. Sliding in to deliver the wordless message of how much I will miss him while he's gone. These last moments we have together are a cup, both bottomless and full, with this kiss running over the side, spilling out, dousing us with need and love.

The screen door opens behind us, and Rhyson jerks back, breaking the sweet, heated contact. He looks over my head, running his fingertips over his mouth, chagrin all over his face.

"Shit." He rolls his eyes at himself. "I mean, shoot. Morning,

Aunt Ruthie."

I can't bring myself to tell him Aunt Ruthie doesn't really care much about swearing, except in the house of the Lord. She and I are having too much fun watching him struggle with it. I glance over my shoulder to find her standing at the screen door entrance, and sure enough, her mouth sets in a firm line, but if you know her like I do, you see full-on mischief in her eyes.

"Morning." Aunt Ruthie steps out onto the porch, looking between the two of us. "Didn't hear you two come in last night."

Before I can answer, Rhyson starts stammering and umming.

"Um, well, we . . . we just kinda . . ." He looks at me for help. No freaking way am I helping him. Rhyson doesn't let anyone get to him, so to see him flustered by my harmless little Aunt Ruthie is too good to pass up. "I guess we just fell asleep in the shed, right, Kai?

"Did we *sleep?*" I ask innocently, pressing an inch closer. Swear to God, he jumps back like I'm a hot poker, giving me "what the hell" wide eyes.

"You slept in that old dusty place?" Aunt Ruthie shakes her head and shrugs. "Well there's some eggs and grits in the kitchen if you want to grab some."

"I just had some coffee. Thank you." Rhyson gestures to the duffle bag on the step. "I need to get back to LA for a couple days, but I'll be back."

"Be safe then." Aunt Ruthie turns her attention to me, most of the laughter at Rhyson's expense gone. "I'm going into town to run some errands. Thinking of clearing out some space in the office, giving some things to Goodwill. You might wanna look to make sure there isn't anything you want to keep."

The words run a tiny razor blade across my heart, nicking open places I thought were healed. By "office" she means Mama's old bedroom, where she drew her last breath. By "some things" she means my mother's things.

"I might take the sewing machine back with me." I shrug. "Not much else at this point, I don't think."

"Just check to make sure." Aunt Ruthie pats my shoulder and

gives it a squeeze.

"All right." I glance up at Rhyson when he grabs my hand, compassion and love in the look he gives me. Is he just naturally sensitive? His artist's nature? Or is it just with me? Is it that chain that connects us? A conduit that runs straight from my heart to his.

"This you, Rhyson?" Aunt Ruthie tips her chin toward the yard and a black Escalade sidling up beside the one Rhyson drove us from the airport in. We took a chartered flight here, so we didn't have many onlookers. I'd been so exhausted I didn't even question why none of Rhyson's security detail was traveling with him. I'd just enjoyed the privacy.

"Yeah, that's me." Rhyson meets the questions in my eyes with a small smile.

"Well, I'll see you when you get back." Aunt Ruthie gives Rhyson a hug, which makes him grin at me over her shoulder like he just got perfect attendance at vacation Bible school.

This man of mine.

"She likes you, Rhys," I tell him as Aunt Ruthie crosses the yard to her old Ford Tempo. "I've never seen you so . . . nervous with anyone before."

"Not nervous. Just . . . it's important to me, okay?"

"I know it is, baby." I peck his cheek. "Is that Gep?"

I shade my eyes, watching him and another hulky guy get out of the Escalade. The second guy drives away in the other SUV, almost identical to ours, and Gep leans against the truck, checking his phone.

"Yeah." Rhyson toys with my fingers.

"He just got here?"

"No, he's been here. He and another team member were staying in town." He gives me a hooded look. "He's pretty much always with me, even if you don't see him."

"In Berlin?"

"Up the hall, two rooms down. I only get so much privacy. You know that. And half the time the little I get is a bit of an illusion."

"At the beach?" The day had been so special. I hope Gep

wasn't hiding on a boat in the harbor watching with binoculars or something.

"That day it was just us." He links our fingers on his chest. "I promise."

He considers me for a moment before speaking again.

"We'll need to assign someone to you after we go public, Pep."

"To me?" I unlink our fingers to lay a hand on my chest. "I don't need security like you do, Rhys. I'm not that famous."

"Not to sound like an asshole, but I *am* that famous, and if you're with me, you need security." He pauses. "That's my life. That's *our* life, you know?"

"I don't want that until I really need it."

"You really need it as soon as everyone knows you're mine. I didn't push before, but now you have some degree of fame on your own, too." He bites the inside of his jaw, like he's weighing his next words. "You meant what you said last night, right? About our future? About kids? All of that?"

"You know I did." I say it so softly anyone else on the porch wouldn't even hear. Like it's our little secret from the world how committed we are to each other, and maybe I want it to be.

"You know me, Kai. Do you honestly think I'm gonna have you walking around some mall with my kids unprotected? At Whole Foods? The movie theater? That's not our normal. It doesn't work that way, and I need you to accept the way it *does* work."

It feels like my bottom lip has slid into a slight pout, but that would be childish, so I tighten my lips around any counterpoint I could come up with.

"Baby, please. I don't want to spend the last ninety seconds we have together arguing about something you know damn well I'm not caving on." He slides his palms down my back until they cup my butt, pulling me up onto my toes and into him. "Yield."

It's hard to be obstinate when he has me like this. When I can feel how much he wants me, how much he loves me. When I want, more than anything, to make sure he knows I feel the same. I flatten my elbows against his chest and nod. He drops a final kiss into my hair.

"Gep'll work out the details when you get back to LA. In the meantime," he says, reaching into his pocket and retrieves something, but closes his hand over his palm so I can't see what it is. "I have a parting gift for you."

"I get a parting gift when *you* leave?" I laugh, shaking my head. "And just for two days?"

"What can I say? I'm an extravagant guy."

He opens his hand, and my mouth falls open. Delight and shock mix up to spread a huge grin over my face. He has the little sheer bag containing all the broken pieces of the ballerina my mother gave me so long ago.

"Where'd you find this?"

"Find. Stole. Semantics. I *may* have opened some of the boxes packed in your room when you left on tour. I wanted something of yours while we were apart." He shrugs. "I wanted something of you with me."

That self-consciousness comes over him like it does every time he's thoughtful, like he's not used to how well sweetness fits him.

"I didn't know . . . still don't know . . . what it is," he continues. "But I figured something this broken worth holding on to had to be special to you."

It's so broken and so special my fingers tremble as I take it from him.

"I've been looking for it."

"I'm sorry, Pep." He frowns, palming the side of my neck. "I didn't even think about that."

"No, it's fine. It's a ballerina. Mama . . ."

My words evaporate as I remember the day my ballerina broke. The day Mama broke in our living room. I couldn't ever really put either of them back together after that. I slip the bag in my jeans pocket.

"I'm glad you had it with you," I say, leaning into him and turning to kiss his palm.

"Well, I'm returning it now that I have you back." He takes my chin between two fingers. "And not planning to let you go anytime soon."

He draws me up for a kiss that turns me liquid, his mouth searching out even any lingering sadness until I taste nothing but him, see and feel nothing but him. His kisses take me hostage. We cling to each other on the porch, slowing the kiss until we just share breath, his head pressed to mine.

"I don't want to leave you." He kisses my forehead. "But that plane won't wait forever, and Gep's getting this show for free."

I had forgotten the somber security guard still leaning against the Cadillac SUV, ostensibly checking his phone.

Rhyson moves to pull away, but I grip his neck, reaching up to whisper in his ear.

"I live you."

He pulls back enough to look at my face, and every promise and dream of our future from last night in the shed rushes back, filling up this moment that's just ours, even with Gep looking on. He nods.

"I live you, too, Pep."

Reluctance marks every motion as he grabs the duffle bag and starts down the steps. He walks backwards and keeps talking.

"What's the rest of your day look like?"

"I'm gonna try to make Mama's soap." My smile is a recipe, equal parts content and sad. "I'm down to my last bar."

"We can't have that. I need cinnamon pear in my life." His eyes grow more serious with every step carrying him away from me. "Take care of yourself 'til I get back, okay?"

I lean against the porch rail and nod, emotion crowding the words out of my throat. It's only two days, but after being apart, after last night in the shed, after these last few moments, two days feels like forever. He gives me one last smile and then turns to go.

Chapter TWENTY-FOUR

Kai

ONE OF MAMA'S OLD APRONS COVERS my jeans and t-shirt. My face mask protects me from the fumes as I stir lye into the water, gloves on up to my elbows. Heated essential oils wait in bowls. I'm starting to feel confident that I can actually do this when my phone buzzes.

Seeing San's name and picture on the screen makes me feel sick. I lied to Rhyson last night. Out and out *lied* to him when he asked about that unknown number. And I involved San in my lie. I didn't mean to, but the truth wasn't even an option, and before I knew it, the lie took over. Or rather I gave into it.

I lift my face mask and slip off my gloves to answer the phone.

"Hey, what's up?"

"You don't call. You don't write." My mind's eye can perfectly picture San's handsome smiling face. "You go off with your famous boyfriend on your chartered plane with your caviar, and forget all about the little people."

"Shut it. There wasn't caviar." I grin, tilting a bowl of oil to watch the light dancing over its surface. "And I *am* the little people."

"If you say so. How are you feeling, pipsqueak?" He keeps his voice light, but it's too deliberate. I know he's concerned. If Rhyson hadn't come home with me, he would have.

"I'm good. Really, San. Don't worry."

"Oh, I'll leave that to Rhyson. He worried enough for us all at the hospital. Have I mentioned what a pain in my ass he is sometimes?"

"You have once or twice, yes." I give into a grin because they're such *boys*.

"Did he see the *Spotted* piece?" His voice loses some of the humor.

"Yeah, Bristol sent it." I draw a deep breath, holding the phone between my ear and shoulder while I slap a glove into my palm. "I hope you're calling with some news on Drex."

"Actually, yeah, I am."

I freeze, death-gripping the phone with one hand and the glove with the other.

"What? Where? San, I have to talk to him. We have to figure this out." My words pop like pellets. "He . . . or someone sent me another text last night. It was a link to the *Spotted* piece and a message threatening to send Rhyson the tape if we get back together."

"Why that? I mean, I know Drex and Rhyson hate each other, but he'd have to know we'd suspect him first."

"Well, yeah, which may be why he's been in hiding and we can't find him."

"*Couldn't* find him." San pauses. "One of my sources saw him at a music festival in Topanga. Not playing there. Just walking around."

I drop my elbows to the work table surface, forehead resting in my hand.

"You sure it's him?"

"They sent me a picture from their phone. He had on a hat, but it was him."

"So we find him? Talk to him?" Anger bubbles under my skin. This lowlife thinks he can ruin my life? Thinks he can hurt Rhyson through me? I want to shove this lye down the front of his pants and burn his balls off. Tape that, you bastard.

"He lost him." San cuts in over my frustrated growl. "*But* it's only a matter of time. That was yesterday. Topanga's not a big place. He may be in a rental property up there. I have some *Spotted* researchers pulling records now to see if we find anything."

"Will they get suspicious?" I chew on my thumbnail. "Start asking questions?"

"I told them I was doing a piece on one-hit wonders."

I chuckle, imagining how Drex would respond to hearing himself described that way.

"Okay, good." I tip one of the Ball jars holding water to the side. "Maybe we're close to getting to the bottom of this."

"You could still tell Rhys," San says softly. "I think you should."

I press my eyes closed, cupping my hand over my mouth in case the scream building inside of me escapes. Rhyson can't ever see that—Drex pounding into me, grunting, holding my hips, grinning into the camera. It's a horror show, and I don't want him to have to get past it. I'll fix this so he doesn't *see* that every time he looks at me.

"We just got this breakthrough, San," I finally say. "I have it under control."

"And you say Rhyson has control issues."

That stings. Considering I asked Rhyson to go to family counseling to understand *his* control issues. There is no easy route here for me. I've already lied to him for weeks. There's no erasing that. Either I, at some point tell him about this tape, a mortification I can't even wrap my heart around, or I live with it invisible but looming between us forever.

"I gotta go." I hold my breath, silently begging San to recognize I can't take anymore. "Keep me posted. Let me know as soon as you find him."

"And you'll do what?" San demands, voice hardening. "Confront him? If he *is* the one blackmailing you, Kai, have you considered he's a criminal? That he's dangerous? That he'll stop at nothing to hurt Rhyson, and consequently you?"

"San, I . . . I don't know." I trap my trembling bottom lip between my teeth. "I'll figure it out."

There's a pause on the other end, like San holds the words in his mouth, deciding if he should release them or not.

Don't.

"Okay. Yeah," he finally says. "I'll keep you posted."

Once he's gone, I stare at the phone. I don't know what makes me do it, but I flick through my message thread, thumbing over texts from Rhyson, from San, from Ella, people who care about me, until I reach that first dreaded message months ago, from someone who must hate me.

I haven't looked at the clip since that first day. I tap it with my thumb, and the disgusting thing springs to life. A full color spectacle, loaded with grunts and pants and the lascivious looks Drex flashes at the camera every once in a while. For the first time, I make myself really study the girl being taken from behind by a stranger she just met in a house she's never seen before. It was a lonely night. Mama's first birthday since she passed. I wasn't used to that much alcohol. What I really wasn't used to was that much pain.

I toss the phone down hard to the work table, wishing it wasn't encased in the tough Otter Box. Wishing it would shatter.

"Enough of this," I mutter only to Mama's Ball jars.

I inspect the elements I've assembled to make her soap and realize I'm missing cinnamon. Mama kept some on one of these shelves to add to the essential oils. I'm pushing jars and bottles around when the wind chimes tinkle, disturbed by someone or by the wind, I'm not sure, but I assume it's Aunt Ruthie since no one else ever comes out here.

"Back already?" I ask without turning around. "That was quick."

The silence at my back prompts me to check.

It's not Aunt Ruthie. It's a man. Handsome, older, but just beyond his prime. Dark hair silvered in places. The years have sketched new lines around his mouth and a few dips in the skin over his brow, but if he's had hard times, he's not wearing them on his face. And that's just not fair since he caused the hardest times in my Mama's life.

He doesn't smile, and it's obvious he's not expecting one from me. He would never get one from me. His name stirs on my tongue, but I can't bring myself to say it. It's locked behind my teeth. The room tilts a little, and I wonder if I might pass out. I wonder if he is a figment of my imagination who will fade as soon as I say the name. I don't know if I force myself to say it because I want him to fade away, or to stay, but before I can think better of it, his name is in the air.

"Daddy?"

Chapter TWENTY-FIVE

Kai

WOULD I HAVE BEEN ANY MORE shocked if Mama had walked through that door, hailed by wind chimes? Alive and well? No, I don't think so.

My father is just as I remembered, only older. That's a stupid observation. Obviously he's older. I haven't seen him since I was eight, but he's still handsome. I see traces of myself in his lips and eyes. He still looks at me like he loves me more than anything. It was a lie then, and surely it's a lie now.

His name was all I could manage, that first startled breath of a word, and then nothing. All rational thought flees when you see a ghost. My fingers go numb, and the jar of cinnamon I'd just located drops and shatters on the floor.

I glance down at the pile of fragrant glass broken at my feet. I can't move. I don't bend to pick it up, clean it up. I just look from the mess at my feet back to my father. Neither of us makes a move toward the other.

"There was no one at the diner . . . the house." He thumbs back in the direction of Glory Bee. "I just thought I'd check to see if there was someone out back."

"What . . ." I have to stop for a moment, damming every emotion that would flood this room and drown us both. "Why are you here?"

He takes a cautious step into the shed, eyes exploring the shelves packed tight with jars and spices and all the things Mama needed. He scratches his eyebrow, which used to be a sure sign of nerves. Sometimes he'd do it right before he got up to preach. I don't know what it's a sign of anymore. Maybe now he just itches.

"I heard on the news that you were in the hospital." He takes two more steps in my direction. "I wanted to make sure you were okay."

Fury elbows my shock aside. Outrage tightens my fingers into fists and boils hot water just below my skin until it overflows, hissing when it hits the surface.

"And what did you think you could do?" I snap. "You didn't make sure I was okay when you missed my recital. That hurt. Or when I sprained my ankle at cheerleading camp, or broke my wrist in gymnastics."

"Kai Anne, I—"

"Or how 'bout this one? You weren't here when my mama was sick." My lip betrays a tremor, but I pull it tight. "I could've *really* used your help all those times, but you weren't there for any of it. So why the hell would you think I need you now?"

"Baby girl, if—"

"Don't you dare call me that." Like a riled bull, I force air through my nostrils. "My father called me that, and you're a stranger. I have no idea who you are."

"I understand you're angry." He shakes his head, his expression helpless at how understated that must sound even to his own ears. "Anger probably doesn't begin to cover it, but I couldn't just sit back and do nothing knowing you were in the hospital."

"I think you're very good at sitting back and doing nothing. That's exactly what you've done for the last fifteen years. Nothing.

And it's real convenient that you show up now that I'm on television and linked to a very wealthy man."

"You can't think . . ." He frowns. "I don't want your money, Kai."

"Good, because I don't have much of my own yet, and if I had millions I certainly wouldn't give it to you."

"Maybe this was a mistake." He directs his words and his eyes to the shed floor. "Carla just thought that—"

"Your mistress?" I slice into whatever crap he almost spouted about that whore he left my mother for.

Anger flashes in the glance he raises to me, but he quells it.

I thought so.

"My wife," he says softly. "We got married."

I grab the shelf to steady myself. He *married* that woman? That somehow makes it worse. She wasn't some hussy he ran off with on a whim. He *committed* to her instead of to us. He chose her over us.

Over me.

"I . . . I didn't realize that. I mean, I had no idea where you went."

"Vegas." He crosses over to the work table, picking up a mason jar and inspecting it. "We moved to Vegas."

"Please tell me you see the irony of the southern Baptist preacher leaving his family with his . . ." The word "whore" hovers over my lips. "Mistress for Sin City."

"Carla had some friends out there, and we just needed to get far away."

I bend to finally pick up the cinnamon splattered glass at my feet. As careful with my next words as I am with the shards in my palm.

"Far away from us, huh?"

He looks up, his eyes muddied with regret or some emotion he shields with his lashes before I can fully read it.

"Not from you," he says softly, swallowing visibly. He opens his mouth and then shuts it before trying again. "Leaving you was the hardest thing I've ever done, Kai Anne. It doesn't make it right, and I know you don't care, but—"

"Not so much don't care as don't believe it." I shuffle over to drop the broken glass into a trash can by the work table. Now only a few feet separate us, and there is some pitiful little eight-year-old ballerina in me who wants to fling herself into his arms, who is glad to see him after all these years.

Weak little snot. Sitting on that step in her ballet slippers waiting for him to come home. Waking up on birthday mornings wondering if a card would come. Every recital, secretly thinking this might be the one where he turned back up because he promised he'd never miss. And that little girl in her purple tutu and tights was always fool enough to believe him. Was it a secret hope, a hidden wish that if I made it big, he'd have to come? If I was a big enough star in the sky, it would draw him out from wherever he'd gone, and he'd have to come?

Looks like it worked.

"Mama's dead."

I say it just as much for my benefit as for his, a flat, harsh reminder that this man took everything from my mother, who deserves my loyalty. He may look like the man who sat me on his lap and read Bible stories to me, but he is actually the man who left my mother one afternoon and never looked back.

"I heard." His lips turn down at the corners, and when he lifts his eyes to me I see genuine sorrow.

"Did you ever love her?"

Did you ever love me?

"Of course I did." He shakes his head, shrugs the broad shoulders I remember thinking could carry the weight of the world. "Things got complicated."

"Really? Seemed simple to me. You were married and had a family. You don't fuck around and leave them for the church secretary." I offer a careless shrug of my own. "But hey, I was a kid. What did I know? Please enlighten me with your perspective. Tell me how very *complicated* it was."

"I deserve that."

"You deserve worse," I spit, clenching my teeth around a stream of vitriol that's been building in me for a decade and a half. "Mama deserved better."

"She did. Much better. I always knew she was too good for me."

"On that we can agree." I tap my foot against the trash can. Even now I have to fight the urge to apologize because he's the one who first taught me to respect my elders.

"It should have been simple, Kai Anne. It should be, but things got so twisted around." He leans against the work table and sighs. "I never wanted to be a preacher."

"What?" I frown, recalling all the Saturday nights I saw him bent over the Bible preparing for his Sunday message. "But you loved God. You loved the church."

"You're right. I did love God." He picks up my work gloves, flipping them from hand to hand. "I still do. And I loved the church, but I never wanted to lead it. Never wanted any of that. I came from generations of preachers. It was expected, and I was good at it."

He glances up with an adult honesty I never would have recognized as a child.

"It was the natural progression of things," he says softly. "My family wanted me to go to seminary. So I did. And then your grandfather wanted me to be his assistant pastor. So I did. And everyone wanted me to marry your mother."

He licks his lips and tosses the gloves to the work table before looking back to me.

"So I did."

"So you didn't love her." I want to wail because I know she loved him with her last lucid thoughts.

"I didn't love her the right way. I loved her the best I could with what I knew love to be." The callused hand he runs over the back of his neck makes me wonder what he does with those hands nowadays.

"Not the deep way?" My voice is hushed in this room with Mama's jars where I suspect she stored her loneliness. Where I think she sealed her regrets. "Is that how you loved Carla? Deep cries out to deep?"

He knows exactly what I mean. Surprise flits briefly across his face. Maybe he's surprised that an eight-year-old grasped that much about a Bible verse and that it stuck with me all these years. Did he really have no idea how much I adored him? How I lived for his every word? That I even felt a childish possessiveness of him with the people from the church who stole his time from me? I think of all the things I lost when he left, it's that feeling I mourn the most. That my daddy stood on the stars to hang the moon. I'm sure all girls lose it at some point. I'm sure many think they never will. I can testify that when it goes, it's gone forever.

"I guess you could say it was that deep cries out to deep kind of love." He looks down at the shed floor. "It feels almost blasphemous to say it, though."

"It should. To feel it for anyone other than your wife should feel like a blasphemy."

He only nods.

"I know it won't be enough, but I have to try to explain this to you." He sighs, a small smile on his face. "Just about everything in my life felt like a trap, but Carla made me feel . . . free. I felt like myself with her for the first time, even though I knew it was wrong. There had never been anyone I could bare myself to. I could share my darkest parts with, but she saw them and loved me anyway."

I hate that I know exactly what he means. I felt that with Rhyson almost from the beginning. My eyes settle on my phone on the work table. It holds my darkest secrets, and yet I've withheld it from Rhyson. If deep has ever cried out to deep, it does with us. The lies I've told, the secrets I've kept feel like such a betrayal I can barely stay in the same room with myself.

"All my life I hoarded my secrets and hid my true self from everyone around me." His eyes focus on something in the past or something inside of him, but not on me. "I did all the things they wanted, knowing it wasn't me. It wasn't right. I never learned to stand, so when things got tough, I hid and then I ran."

"You're right. It's not enough." Frustration rips the next words from my mouth. "You felt trapped? By the church? By the town? By mama? By me? What had you feeling so trapped, Daddy?"

"All of it." He closes his eyes and shakes his head. "You don't know what it's like to want more and be stuck here."

"I don't know what that's like?" I close the distance between us until I'm standing right in front of him. I'm no longer a little girl, but he still towers over me. I bang my fist on the work table. "I stayed in Glory Falls five years after I was supposed to be gone, and do you know why?"

I couldn't stop the tears if I wanted to, and I don't even want to try. He needs to see.

"I stayed because Mama was diagnosed with ALS." My voice breaks, catching on emotion. "And it was a privilege to take care of her 'til the day she died. I wouldn't trade one day of it. What you call a trap, I call *love*, Daddy. I realize now you wouldn't know the difference."

"Kai Anne—"

"Tell me, when you heard she died, did your sympathy card get lost in the mail?" My words ooze venom and disdain. "Along with my birthday cards and all the money we could have used to survive?"

"I sent your Mama money and she sent it back every time telling me to bring it myself. We *divorced*, Kai Anne. My address was on every letter. She knew where I was."

"That's a lie." I mean to screech it, but it comes out a creaky whisper.

"It's true. I tried a few times, but she told me to stop if I wasn't coming home."

"So you stopped because you were never coming home, right?" I blink at these damn tears that tell him too much. "And me? You never thought to reach out to me? See how I was doing?"

A mixture of emotions passes over his face. It looks like guilt. It looks like regret, but I don't know this man anymore, so I won't presume to know.

"I didn't know what to say after so long," he finally says. "I wish I had been strong enough to face my mistakes. To face the church and the community."

He looks down at his boots.

"To face you and your mama."

"I wish you'd been strong enough not to fuck another woman."

We both flinch at the vulgarity dirtying the air between us. The last time he saw me he was teaching me scripture, and we were bonded by love. Now all we have is this biological link and a collection of memories that feel like lies.

"Carla was pregnant," he says softly. "For a long time I resisted what we felt, but eventually, it was too strong, and we gave into it. When she got pregnant, I—"

"You have a family?" I cut in, so braced for his answer, the muscles in my back and neck and arms ache.

"Yeah, we had a little girl." I think it's involuntary, the smile and tender look that soften his rocky expression.

Jealousy rocks me. He stayed for her, but not for me. He chose them, but not me. He loves them, but didn't love me. Not enough.

"Pictures?" Tears water the question. "You have pictures of her?"

He flips through his phone for a minute and hands it to me. Photo after photo of him with his new family at ball games, during the holidays, on vacation. And then finally the one that punches right through my heart with brass knuckles.

His daughter, the little sister I've never met, at a dance recital, and him right there with her perched on his knee.

I just can't. I hand him the phone. I gulp back a knot of emotions that have gotten so tangled up over the years I can't separate the love from the hate, the bitterness from the regret, the resentment from the longing.

"There was a little girl who used to wait for you to come back." I sniffle, swiping at the tears that defy my every attempt to hold them back. "I used to think, if I just do well at this dance recital, if I just make the honor roll, if I get the lead in this play, he might come home."

I drop my head into my hands, tears slipping through my fingers, sobs tumbling past my lips.

"If I can just be good enough, he might come back."

I lift my head and laugh, cheeks wet.

"And I was right because here you are. I finally made it, and you finally came back, but you know what?" I look at him, even though the tears in my eyes make him a wavering line. "I may be good enough, but you're not."

It's his turn to be teary eyed. He opens his mouth and then clamps it closed. What can he say to me that will make it right? That will erase Mama's years of back-breaking work? Of denying herself so I could have? He wasn't worth her love. And even though maybe on some level, just about every step I've taken to get where I am was to prove something to him, to *draw* him back to me, he's not worth mine either.

"I think you should go," I choke out, turning my back on him, an echo of what he did to us all those years ago.

"Kai Anne, let me just say one thing before I go," he says, voice husky with tears. "I know you're mad at me, but I'm not giving up,"

"Oh, I think you will." A harsh laugh abrades my lips. "Giving up is what you do best."

"I understand if you want nothing to do with me, but you have a little sister who would love to know you. She's your only blood left in the world, after all," he says. "I'm leaving my number here on the table."

For a moment I think he's gone, and I almost let it all go, but then I hear one more broken whisper before he leaves for good.

"Bye, baby girl."

I train my eyes on the hands fisted around each other at my waist. I didn't get to see him leave the first time, and I don't want to watch him go now. I hold it together until the door closes behind him, and then like the ballerina Mama gave me years ago, I shatter. I'm strewn, my broken pieces so myriad, I could never put them back together into what they were before he re-entered my life. I cry for that little girl who held on to her delusions about her father for too long, and for my mother who loved wrong and only once in her whole life, and could never let go even when that love let go of her.

I sob for hours, or it could be only minutes. I shed a billion tears, or maybe it's just a few. This is a vacuum that has sucked away all sense of time and reality. In Mama's shed, I'm suspended in pain and lost in regrets. Hers. Mine. Daddy's. They're all here. I pour them all into this room, into these jars, and it's only once I'm empty that something begins to fill me for the first time. An understanding that I couldn't have had without this pain at the hands of my father.

Train up a child in the way he should go.

This, like so many of the lessons from my father's Bible, revisits me.

As a little girl I expected my father to do just that. To train me in the way I should go, but it's only now that he's unpacked his life, his mistakes, his weaknesses that I see he did exactly the opposite. Everything he modeled for me was all wrong, but in many ways, I was trained by his failings. Tutored by his mistakes.

Aunt Ruthie told me more than once that I'm just as much my father's daughter as I am my mother's. That I'm as much like him as I am like her. I didn't believe her until now. The secrets. The lies. The hiding. The running. All a latent legacy from my father that, under pressure, has sprung to life.

Hypocrisy scents the air and turns my stomach. I've asked so many things of Rhyson that I haven't been willing to do myself. I let my own fear and insecurity ruin our trust. The foundation he thought we were rebuilding, I've cracked with my lies and secrets. San tried to tell me. Rhyson learned from his mistakes and has done everything to show me, but it was coming face to face with my father that held the mirror up to me. My life for the last few months has been one huge blind spot with me overlooking all the ways I've done to Rhyson exactly what he did to me. I was blind to it, but now . . . well, now I see.

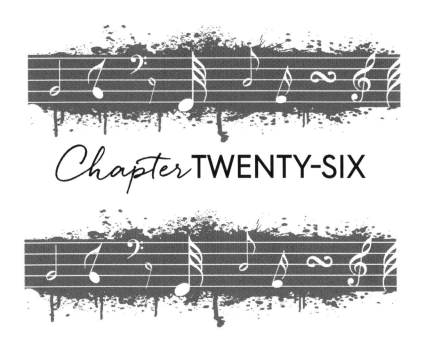

Chapter TWENTY-SIX

RHYSON

I MISSED A CALL FROM MY father.

I'm leaving the studio, debating whether to return or ignore the call. The missed call alert on my phone mocks me, daring me to respond. We've had a few more counseling sessions since that initial one, and things have thawed some between my father and me. My mother . . . still frozen.

I may never be able to say the word "frozen" again without laughing. I was only half-joking when I suggested animation for Kai's acting career. Yet another bridge we'll have to cross when we come to it. That one—nudity, sex scenes, all that shit with some other guy, even if it is acting—that bridge I'll burn. Got the match right here.

I don't even register that I've dialed his number until it's ringing. Only then do I realize it's almost midnight. I'm about to hang up when he answers.

"Rhyson, hey."

He sounds surprisingly alert and as strong as ever, even though I'm always shocked that he looks frailer than the man I grew up with.

He and Grady are identical twins, but now he looks like Grady's older brother. Em's keeping Grady young, and my mother's *got* to be aging my father. I feel weary after every session, and she and I barely look at each other in those.

"Dad, hey. Sorry to call so late. I didn't realize it was . . . well, I'm just leaving the studio." I barrel ahead with an apology before he asks for an explanation. "Sorry I missed yesterday's session with Dr. Ramirez. I didn't mean to blow it off."

"It's fine," he says. "But I wanted to call and make sure you were okay."

I hesitate, weighing how much deeper I want to allow him into my life. Kai's about as deep as you can get with me, so sharing anything about her would crack open that door between my father and me just that much more.

"My girlfriend, Kai, collapsed during one of her concerts. Not sure if you heard. It was on the news a lot last week. She was in the hospital."

"I did hear. I actually left you a voicemail checking to see if she was okay."

His concern startles me. I can't imagine him doing something like that years ago.

"Sorry. I didn't check all my voicemails," I say. "I kind of forgot about everything else. I went home with her to recuperate. I should be able to make next week's session. We'll have to see how she's doing."

"Maybe we could . . ." My father's voice goes somewhere I've rarely heard it go. To uncertainty. "Maybe we could have coffee or something when you get back. You know, meet outside the session."

Holy shit.

"Uh, we could do that." I tap the steering wheel. "Coffee's kind of public for me, though. Maybe you could . . . come to the house for dinner or something."

Thank God it's almost midnight, and there's hardly any traffic because this conversation requires my complete focus.

"Dinner?" Surprise tinges his voice. "Sure. I'd . . . well, I'd like that."

"Kai's a great cook," I continue before I think better of it. "Did I mention she's from Georgia? Can you believe I ended up with a girl from Georgia?"

"A Southerner, huh?" His laugh makes him sound freer than I've heard in a long time. Maybe ever. "You sure know how to pick 'em."

"And to top it off, she's a Baptist. As in church. Crazy, right? Anyway, they fry chicken in this big black pot, in like a foot of grease. It's the best thing you'll ever taste. I think I'm getting her a pot for our back yard."

"That sounds nice," he says, that smile still in his voice. "I'd love to come."

It's unspoken between us, but we both know I'm extending the invitation only to him. My mother . . . that's still another issue entirely.

"How about I call you when I get back from taking care of her? Or . . . I guess you could call. Or whatever."

"That'd be great." He pauses. "Thanks for calling me back, Rhyson."

"Sure. I mean, of course." I roll my eyes at myself. "Yeah."

Smooth. Real smooth. You're such a baller, Gray.

"Talk to you later, son."

I can't remember the last time I didn't flinch when he called me that. The fact that I don't gives me hope I wasn't sure I'd ever have.

I'm still processing our conversation when I walk into the house. It's completely quiet. I'm replaying every word I said to my dad, wondering if I should have said more, less.

I need to talk to Kai. She always helps me sort my shit. I wouldn't even be wrestling with this had it not been for her forcing me . . . *er, encouraging me* . . . to go to counseling. I'm dialing her number before I think twice about it, not even factoring in the lateness of the hour, the time difference, nothing. Just as I'm realizing it's about three in the morning there, and am about to disconnect, I hear my song *Lost* ringing up the staircase. The closer I get, I think it's coming from my bedroom.

I cross the threshold, and sure enough, Kai is curled up asleep fully clothed on my bed, the phone ringing by her side. She sits up groggily, patting the bed to search for the phone. I'm there before she can even get to it, pulling her up, sitting on the edge of the bed and straddling her over me, knees on either side of my legs.

"Hey, what are you doing here?" I bury my head in her hair and her neck, inhaling cinnamon and pear. "I mean, you're great to come home to, but I was on my way back to Glory Falls tomorrow night."

She nods into my neck, her fingers clutching my elbows, her slight frame pressing into me.

"I know." She lays her temple to my shoulder. "I needed to talk to you."

"You okay?" I tug on the hair streaming down her back until she's forced to look at me. I know what she looks like at peace. The tumult in those beautiful eyes fists my heart. "What's wrong, Pep? Aunt Ruthie?"

"No." She remains on my lap, but scoots back a little, legs folded under her thighs on the bed, arms crossed over her waist. "Aunt Ruthie's fine. She's good."

Her eyes drop again, so I palm her chin, tilting her face back up to me.

"What's going on?"

She closes her eyes and swallows, pressing her lips together.

"My dad came to see me."

Of all the things I would have imagined she'd say, that never entered my mind.

"Your *father*? Your real dad?"

"Yeah. He, um, saw on the news that I collapsed at the concert and was in the hospital. He said he wanted to make sure I was okay. When he heard no one knew where I was, he took a chance and checked Glory Falls."

"Wanted to make sure you were okay?" I squeeze her thighs, wishing I had five minutes alone with his no-show ass. "After all these years he just happens to get concerned when he sees you on *television*?"

She nods, her eyes unfocused over my shoulder.

"Exactly what I said."

"Hey." I tug her chin so she looks at me. "You okay? Talk to me. What did he have to say for himself?"

A tear slides down one cheek, and she swipes at it before it makes it very far. She tucks a chunk of dark hair behind her ear, a humorless smile on her lips.

"Not enough. He didn't say enough to make up for any of it." She sighs, folding a little to press her forehead to my chest. "Growing up, I used to think there was an explanation. Something we never could have thought of. Like, maybe he was secretly a spy, and for our sake, he had to go into witness protection. Only no one could know, not even us."

Her laugh is a short, dry bark in the quiet bedroom.

"But he was just weak. He fell in love with someone else and chose her over his family." She shrugs her slim shoulders. "A liar. A cheat. That's all."

I brush a hand over the dark hair tumbling around her shoulders and down her back. God, I hate that guy. The pain comes off her in waves, and if I could take it all, absorb it all into myself, I would.

"I'm sorry, Pep. I can't even imagine what you're feeling right now. That's a lot to deal with."

"He said he felt trapped in Glory Falls and never wanted to be a preacher. He felt trapped in their marriage, Rhyson."

She shakes her head, another tear sneaking past her eyelids.

"It would have killed Mama to hear him say that. I'm glad he never came back if that's all he had to say for himself."

She pulls back to study me, her eyes holding more than pain. Holding something I can't quite figure out yet.

"Maybe one good thing came out of his visit." She drops her eyes before looking back to me, even though it feels like she's forcing herself to. "My Aunt Ruthie used to say that I was more like my father than I wanted to admit. That I was just as much his daughter as I was my mother's."

I nod, not wanting to admit Aunt Ruthie basically told me the same thing.

"Maybe she was right." Kai bites her lip before going on. "Maybe the only legacy he has for me is the lesson of his mistakes."

"Okay." I frown a little, running a thumb over the high curve of her cheekbone. "Baby, what does that mean?"

"He said he hoarded his secrets, hid all the darkest things. The people who loved him most never really knew him. Not in the ways that matter. He said he ran when he couldn't face the consequences of his actions." She doesn't lift her gaze any higher than my chest. "He's a runner and a hider."

She closes her eyes, dropping her head to my chest.

"And so am I," she whispers.

Those few words cause a ripple in my peace of mind. Why is she talking to me about running and hiding and secrets? We're done with all of that. So why, when she raises her eyes to my face, does she look so damn guilty? So afraid?

A memory of San's face at the hospital flashes through my mind, that feeling I got that there was something he knew. Something I should know, but didn't.

"Kai, baby, what is it?" I nudge her face toward me, dropping a kiss on her lips. "You know you can tell me anything, right?"

"Yes, I know that now."

Now? I go still and then slide my hand up her slim back, feeling the tension in the muscles there.

"Rhyson, there's something I need to tell you. I should have told you before, but couldn't." She runs a hand through her hair, her expression agitated. "I just couldn't, but I should have."

"Pep, you're freaking me out here." I interlock our fingers. "What's going on?"

She draws a breath so deep, I'm not sure it will ever end before she looks at me, her eyes uncertain. How can she still be uncertain of me? After everything, still?

"Someone's been threatening me, Rhys."

The word "threaten" pummels me. Someone threatened her? Everything in me shouts for answers immediately, but I force myself to remain calm. To fake being reasonable.

"Who threatened you, Pep?" I ask quietly, my fingers tightening just a bit around hers. "Threaten how?"

She knows me too well to believe the calm façade. She searches my eyes until she locates the rage I'm carefully concealing.

"Please don't be angry with me," she whispers.

"With you?" I lean back, sliding my hands to her hips, securing her in my lap. It's bad enough I have to fake calm without having to solve riddles. "Pep, tell me everything now before I lose my shit."

"Someone sent me a . . . a tape." She drops her eyes and worries the corner of her mouth with her teeth. "A sex tape."

My mind races to all the implications of someone seeing us together. Why would they go to her with it when I'm the one with all the money?

"They came to *you* with our sex tape? But why—"

"Not you," she cuts in, eyes still averted. "You're not on the tape."

"But you just said . . ." My words die right alongside a chunk of my sanity. "Who? Who is on that damn tape, Pep?"

"It's me." She finally looks at me, tears gathering at the corners of her eyes. "It's me and Drex. From that night. I swear I had no idea he was recording us."

Her admission topples any semblance of calm and rationality I clung to. It all falls down. Rage rises. Finally, a legitimate reason to have Gep find a secret way to kill that piece of shit.

"So Drex is the one threatening you?"

Years of hatred and resentment wrap around the words, choking them like weeds in my throat. That viper has found ways to make life difficult for me since the day we met in high school. Him fucking Petra, that was one thing. Him sabotaging my first album release, that was another. And he's found dozens of ways through the years to piss me off, but this? Him threatening Kai with some bullshit tape from that one fucking night is too much.

"I don't know if it's him actually making the threats. I assume he has something to do with it obviously." Kai covers her eyes. "We've been looking for him, but he's disappeared."

"We?" Pieces of information begin clicking into slots, forming a clearer picture. "When did he threaten you? Yesterday when I left?"

She couldn't have let even a day go by without telling me this. Right?

"Pep?" She shifts on my lap, head lowered again. "When?"

"It was at the beginning of the tour." She directs the words down, unable to meet my eyes.

"Three months ago? He threatened you three months ago, and you're just telling me? What the hell?"

"We weren't together at first, and I . . . I wasn't sure what to do."

"You tell me. That's what you fucking do. Three months? And what about when we were together again? For the last six weeks you knew this and didn't even mention it?"

"I thought . . . I thought I could handle it."

"And what's he demanding? What are the terms? Money?"

"No, not money." She gives me a cautious glance. "Whoever it is only demanded that I not be with you."

Whatever I thought rage was, it was a pale imitation of the fury that pounds in my temples when she says that.

"Is that why you didn't want to go public?" I demand. "I mean the *real* reason, not the *lie* you fed me about not wanting to detract attention from your tour."

"I did what I thought was best, Rhyson, for both of us. To protect you."

"Bullshit. You did it to protect yourself. At least be honest with yourself since being honest with me obviously isn't important to you. And that sounds eerily like my rationale when I took matters into my own hands with *Total Package.*"

"I know. I made a mistake, too."

"You said we hit reset. We promised we wouldn't lie to each other, and that's all you've done for the last six weeks. I went to counseling with my parents for you."

"That was for you, Rhyson." She shakes her head, eyes barely holding mine. "You know it was the right thing."

"Not the point, Pep. I went into counseling with my parents, whom I haven't spent more than twenty-four hours with in over a decade, *for you*. So that you would know I'm serious about figuring out my shit. So that you'd know I'm serious about us having a healthy relationship, and you do this? Behind my back you hide this?"

I breathe in through my nose and out through my mouth a few times, truly struggling to bring my temper under control.

"I lied first. I know that. I deserved your anger, your silence." I take a moment before looking at her. "But when you said you forgave me, I never planned to lie to you again. We hit reset, and it meant the world to me. So finding out you lied—well, that spits on everything."

"Rhys, let me explain—"

"So this piece of shit contacted you three months ago." I can't deal with her right now. I need to focus on *him*. "What's happened since?"

"Well, you and I haven't been public, of course, so he hadn't bothered me at all." She closes her eyes, folding her lips in before continuing. "But then that *Spotted* piece came out the other day speculating about us, and he contacted me again. Texted me threatening to release the tape if I didn't stay away from you."

A threatening text?

"That unknown number in the shed?" I demand. "Was that him?"

She nods mutely, eyes afraid of the anger I know is building in my expression. It has to be because I can't hold it in any longer.

"You told me that was San." My voice has climbed to a yell. "You lied to my face. God, Pep, was any of that true that night? Has any of it been true? If you could—"

"How can you even ask me that?" Her voice shakes, then breaks over the words. "You know I meant every word about our future together."

"Yeah, and how did you plan to spend your future with me indefinitely pretending we aren't together?"

"I just needed some time to track down Drex so we could talk to him, rationalize with him, and now San has a lead so we—"

"San?" I interrupt. "He knew about this? Of course he did. Of course you'd tell him and not me. Trust him and not me."

"It wasn't a matter of trust."

She's too close. I can't stand for her to be this close when I'm this angry, like a flame that might scorch her if she's not careful.

"Get off me." Rage mottles the words so I repeat them when she doesn't budge from my lap. "Get the fuck off, Pep."

"No," she whispers into my neck, her fingers circling my wrist like she's prepared to hold on.

"Fine, if you won't move," I say, grabbing her hips and lifting her up and off me, dropping her on the bed, "I'll move you."

As soon as I'm clear of her, I reach for the phone in my pocket and start dialing.

"Who are you calling?" I hate the fear in her voice. The thing I hate most is that she's been living with fear for three months and didn't share it with me. Didn't let me protect her. Lied to me instead of trusting me.

"Dammit, Pep," I say through gritted teeth while Bristol's phone rings.

"That's me on that tape, Rhyson, not you." She stands on her knees in the middle of the bed. "I have a right to know who you're calling."

"No one says your name without thinking mine, Kai. So it may be you on that tape, but it affects me whether you like it or not, and if we—"

"What tape?" Bristol asks, voice gruff with sleep, from the other end. "This better be good, brother. What the hell?"

"Bris, how soon can you get to the house?" My eyes don't leave Kai's devastated face, shame burning a red spot in each of her cheeks.

It's quiet on the other end, and I can almost hear the cogs of Bristol's wheels turning as she brushes the sleep off.

"Twenty minutes."

"Make it fifteen. Gep, too. I'll explain when you get here."

I hang up, striding for the door to wait for them downstairs. I can't even look at Kai right now. I'm so furious with her. So . . . hurt by her. Is this how she felt when I pulled that stunt with *Total Package*? Betrayed? Split open? A raw wound salted with lies?

"I was just trying to handle things myself." She trails me down the stairs. "Can't you see I never wanted you to find out? To see me like that with him? God, even now just the thought of you seeing it makes me sick to my stomach."

"I get that, Pep, but you lied." I keep going, not turning to look at her. "For weeks you've lied."

"I wanted to find Drex to get to the bottom of it."

"And have you found him?"

"We're about to. One of San's contacts spotted him in Topanga a few days ago. We lost him, but we're close."

"Three months and that's all you have to show for it?" I turn to face her in the foyer. "Did it ever occur to you and your Scooby crew that Gep is a former CIA operative? That he *might* just have some connections that go beyond some trash rag television show's research department?"

She shakes her head, tears standing in her eyes.

"I didn't want you to see, Rhys. Didn't want you to ever know. You said you could never know details."

"That was before . . ." I let the words fall off. I know I said that, but to keep this from me? For this long? "How could you think it was okay to lie to me about this? Did you just think it would go away? What was your plan here?"

"Once San found Drex, I was going to talk to him and—"

"Talk to him?" I'm seeing red. "On your own? This scumbag who recorded you having sex with him and is now blackmailing you, a criminal act by the way. You were just gonna track him down and say please don't? Please stop? I wish you wouldn't do that? That was your fucking plan?"

"I was scared, Rhys. I messed up. I hate that one night with that idiot is ruining everything."

"That night and what happened between you and Drex isn't what's ruining everything. I don't blame you for that." I wave a hand in the abyss between our bodies. "Us. The lies and the deception.

That's your fault."

"I know that, and I'm sorry."

Her voice is so small. She is so small, and the thought of her putting herself in that kind of possible danger because she wanted to keep it from me when I'm the one who would literally lay down my life for her without a second thought . . . it infuriates me. Before I can tell her all of that, the front door opens, and Bristol walks in, punching in the alarm code from her phone. She lives close by, but she must have sprouted wings to get here this fast. She glances at the watch on her wrist.

"Seven minutes and several traffic violations later, here I am." She glances past me to Kai. "Gep's on his way. May take him a little longer, but he'll be here soon. What's going on?"

"We've got a situation." I glance at Kai, whose eyes are fixed on the marble foyer floor. "I'll explain when he gets here. I don't want to go through it twice."

I don't want to go through it even once, but we have to. It's probably good that Bristol got here so quickly. I don't know what I would have said if my fight with Kai continued. I still can barely make myself look at her, and it's not because of what we'll see on that tape. It's because she lied to me when I thought we had gotten past it. Because I fooled myself into thinking we had given ourselves completely to each other, and all this time she was holding back. All this time, she didn't trust me. And that makes me question every moment we've shared since Grady's wedding. And I hate that because those were the best moments of my whole life. And her lies cast a shadow over every one of them.

The three of us are brewing in a tight silence in the kitchen drinking coffee when Gep arrives. He looks fresh, alert and ready, like it's the start of a new day, not just past midnight.

"What's up?" Gep's calm tone soothes me just a little bit. Kai tried to handle this alone, but couldn't. I can. We can. We will, and I'll deal with her lies after I've destroyed Drex once and for all. I'm determined that on that dude's deathbed he'll still be thinking about what I take from him because of this.

"Someone's been blackmailing Kai." The words land with a thud into the kitchen quiet. Gep glances at Kai surreptitiously, but Bristol out and out stares at her, and the questions begin.

"With what? Blackmailing how?" Bristol demands of Kai, her eyes narrow. "And what the hell does this have to do with Rhys? How are you involved?"

Even though she's looking at Kai, I will answer her because as angry as I am with Kai right now, no one's gonna bully my girl. Not even my twin sister.

"I'm involved because she is." My voice is quiet, but so firm there is no doubting I'll lay into her if I have to. "And you're here to fix it. You're here to work on this problem as if it's my problem because it is."

Bristol presses her lips together and sits on one of the high stools at the counter.

"All right." She takes a sip of her coffee. "So let's hear it."

I make myself look at Kai, even though for the first time since we've met I don't want to. I've barely been able to take my eyes off this girl since that day in Grady's rehearsal room, and now when I look at her, she's covered in lies.

"Tell us, Kai."

She leans her elbows to the island in the middle of the kitchen, her eyes down, hair covering her face, and begins.

"About three months ago I got a text message from an unknown number." She pulls the hair behind her ear, showing me only her profile. "There was a link to a write up on the fight Rhys and I had, and a warning that we should stay apart or they would release this tape."

She glances up at me only briefly, but the connection between our eyes still runs through me like a volt. I want to turn it off, but even pissed off with her, I can't.

"It was a clip of me . . ." Her words die, and she gulps with eyes closed, before resurrecting the sentence. "A clip of me having sex with Drex."

"Shit," Bristol says under her breath, but loud enough for us all to hear. She drills a look into me until I finally have to look at her.

Fury and frustration pool in the eyes just like mine, reflecting some of what I'm feeling.

"You fucked that douchebag?" she asks Kai.

Kai nods, biting her bottom lip, the breath trembling over her lips before she answers.

"It was before Rhys and I met. I was a dancer in one of Drex's videos, and after the shoot wrapped we . . . well, went back to his place." Her eyes squeeze shut like she can't bear us looking at her. "I had no idea he was recording it, and I never . . . God, I'm so sorry."

Tears leak over her cheeks, and she doesn't even try to wipe them away they come so fast. I'm surprised when Bristol grabs a box of Kleenex Sarita keeps on the counter and walks it over to Kai. Everything in me strains to comfort her, but I just can't. I'm not past the lie, the deliberate deceptions and blocking me out of this when I gave her everything. And if I soften toward her at all, I'll lose focus. And right now my focus is a search and destroy mission.

"So he's disappeared." I take up where Kai left off as she wipes her cheeks and sniffs. "San's been looking for him, and they spotted him yesterday in Topanga. Obviously he's connected to this, but maybe not working alone. We don't know."

"What do you want to happen, Rhyson?" Gep asks quietly. "Blackmail is a crime, potentially a felony. We could contact the police."

"No," Bristol and I say in unison. I'm not even surprised. We may not be your typical twins, but in cases like these, we synch.

"This needs to stay as far off the books as we can keep it." I shake my head. "I don't trust the LAPD, not even a little bit. There have been too many leaks to tabloids. I can't chance this getting out."

"Yes," Bristol chimes in. "Even though Rhyson isn't on that tape, he's been linked to them both, and this would drag his name through as much mud as it would theirs."

"I want to make something perfectly clear," I say. "This isn't about protecting me. This is about protecting Kai, about making sure that damn tape never sees the light of day. Anything short of us finding the tape and destroying any and every copy in existence, short of finding out who is behind it, and destroying *them,* is failure to me."

"But Rhyson," Gep says. "If we do this off the books, we—"

"I said we keep this off the books." I back up my words to Gep with a cold look. "There isn't another option. No police. Less exposure. This motherfucker is fighting dirty with *my* girl, and as soon as we bring the police into it, we can't fight dirty back."

My words drop like a bomb, and for a moment it's complete silence. I glance at Kai, and she's looking right at me. I'm no less angry with her. I feel no less deceived, but she's still my girl. And protecting her is still the most important thing.

"I need to see your phone, Kai," Gep says, his eyes softer than I've ever seen them, his voice gentler. Gep is a hard ass recruited to the CIA before he even left college. I don't know half of what he's done, but the little I know would give me nightmares if I were him.

"My phone?" Kai's panicked eyes toggle between Gep and me. "Why?"

"I know it's tough, but I need to see the number the text and the video came from," Gep explains, firming his lips before speaking the next words. "And I'll need to watch the tape."

"No!" Kai's protest explodes into the quiet kitchen, and tears fill her eyes again. "I can't . . . no, Gep. Please no. Don't watch the tape. I'll answer any questions you have. I'll—"

"Kai, there may be something retrievable there," Gep interrupts softly. "And I need to see if there are any clues embedded in that video, if the link has anything traceable, IP codes, anything. Who knows what information we can get from that. It's the only smoking gun we have, and we need it to get to the bottom of this."

He glances at me, twisting his mouth.

"Especially if we aren't bringing the police into this."

"And we're not." I extend my hand to Kai. "Give me your phone."

One elbow on the island, she shields her face with her hand for a moment before lifting her head and walking over to me. She offers the phone to me, but when I try to take it, she doesn't release it right way, looking up at me, her eyes pleading.

"Please don't watch it." Her voice breaks on a sob she tries to clamp her lips over. "I know Gep has to watch it, but you can't. I can't . . . promise me."

I know what it costs her to ask that of me in front of Bristol and Gep. I can't explain why, but I have to see that tape. I *will* see that tape. If only to prove to myself and to her that I was a fool to think seeing it could ever affect how I feel about her. I can't promise her that I won't, because I know I will.

"Did you take your meds?" I pull the phone all the way from her fingers.

"Rhyson, please. I—"

"I can't have you relapsing, Pep. You had pneumonia and were in the hospital last week. You look exhausted." It's a habit to touch her, and I force myself not to push her hair back. Not to wrap my hands around her small waist. Not to dip and kiss her lips, as richly red as her mother's strawberry preserves. "Go upstairs, take your meds, and go to sleep."

"To sleep?" Her eyes stretch, mouth falling open. "I can't sleep with this hanging over my head."

"You have to." I allow myself one touch, a hand at the small of her back to turn her toward the back stairs, just above the curve of her ass, one of my favorite spots on her body. "I'll let you know if we need anything else."

There's more she wants to say. Protests she wants to make. Apologies in her eyes when she looks up at me over her shoulder. I see it all, and as usual, everything about her tugs me centripetally.

"We'll talk later," I tell her, looking away from the plea all over her face.

"Promise me," she whispers, eyes fixed on me and blocking out Bristol and Gep.

I don't know if she means promise we'll talk later, or promise I won't watch that tape. Her deceit builds up between us like a wall, each lie a stone to block the intimacy I've never wanted to resist until today. But today, I'm resisting it, and I'm not making her any promises, so I just turn away from her and hand Gep the phone.

Chapter TWENTY-SEVEN

Kai

IT'S THE CRASH THAT WAKES ME.

When I take the medicine, it drops me like a stone to the bottom of the sea, and I have to struggle to swim to the surface and break through. My body is still recovering from the abuse I put it through on tour. Not even the pneumonia, but the exhaustion. Even though the medicine imposes much-needed rest on me, I hate the way it makes me feel. My limbs are heavy and my tongue feels thick. Sleep clings to me, but the crash from below jerks me up and past the dreamless surface.

I've gotten spoiled waking up with Rhyson. Not because he's famous, but because he reaches for me in his sleep and makes me feel safe. Because he can't go two minutes without kissing me once he's awake. And waking up alone . . . well, it's not the same. I roll into the cold void beside me with its undented pillow and unrumpled sheets. He hasn't been here at all. I'd smell him. I'd know.

Still in my fitted t-shirt and jeans, barefoot, I stumble from the bed and out onto the landing. Another crash reaches my ears, and

Rhyson's voice, hoarse and rough, joins the chaos. Quietly, I make my way down to the first floor and then down another to his music room.

"Fuck!" Anger and frustration strangle the word in his throat. Another crash and more "fucks" and a few "shits" and "dammits" sting the air like hornets. I poke my head just a little around the wall. I can't face him right now, and judging by our last interaction, he doesn't want to see me.

The glimpse I have almost makes me gasp, but I catch it before the sound gives me away. Several of Rhyson's autographed guitars lay splintered and ruined at his feet. The side of his drum set is completely gone like a cannon blew it out. A growl, a low feral sound, rumbles in his chest as he stands drawing in labored breaths amidst the beautiful debris of his priceless instruments.

He watched the tape.

The thought sucker punches me, makes my head spin and leaves me reeling. I sink to the step, too ashamed and afraid to enter the room. To face him. So I sit there with the wall between us. Not just the wall, cool against the side of my face, but the wall of my betrayal and subterfuge.

After the crash and the destruction, there's a few moments of complete silence. So quiet I hear his heavy breaths in the wake of the storm. I'm just about to gather my courage and walk around that wall into the room, when the music begins. I haven't heard this song since Grady's wedding. It's a skeletal version of *My Soul To Keep*, but enough for me to recognize the song he wrote for me. He can't be playing this song and not thinking of me, not aching the way I am. I've run and I've hidden so many times before, but I have to come out of the shadows to fight for this man. The future he dreamed about, our future, is worth that.

Hearing the notes of my song in this tight, unnatural quiet after the violence of his anger hurts. It's like I'm in one key and he's in another. I've never felt this far from him, even when I wouldn't let him in.

I rest my head against the wall, helpless to move. I want to taste my tears, so I don't even check them as they roll over my cheeks and into my mouth. They are salty and taste of the recriminations I deserve. I'm not sure how long he plays. That first night months ago in Grady's studio Rhyson's music awakened something in me, and tonight it lulls me back to sleep.

THERE IS NO BETTER PLACE THAN this. Nestled against Rhyson's chest. The medicine still clouds my head, scrambles my thoughts, but I'm lucid enough to know I'm safe in his arms.

"Rhys," I mumble into his shoulder, and his arms tighten around me when he climbs the stairs carrying me. "I can walk."

"Is that why you were knocked out on the steps?" he asks softly. "Because you can walk?"

It's too dark for me to see his face clearly, but I'd like to imagine that smile he wears just for me is back on his face, even though I don't hear it in his voice.

"It's the medicine," I whisper, pressing into his neck, searching out his scent. "It makes me so groggy."

"You still have a lot of rest to catch up on."

I hold my breath when he reaches the landing, so afraid he'll take me to a guest room instead of the bedroom we share. Instead of the bed where I wake up beside him. I need it so badly. Just his arms around me tonight. Just his touch in the morning. Something that tells me he still wants me, that what he saw on that tape doesn't change any of that.

He sets me on the bed, turning on the bedside lamp. Our eyes catch and hold for a second before he drops his glance to the floor. His demeanor, his expression—everything about him is a KEEP OUT sign, when he's only ever been an invitation to come inside.

He pulls the fitted t-shirt over my head, slides my bra straps off my shoulders, reaches behind my back to undo my bra. The lacy black cups fall away, baring me to him. His eyes rest on my breasts like breath, so hot my nipples peak and tighten. I want him so desperately. To take him into my body. To reclaim him and yield to him. His thumb strokes my collarbone for a moment, a muscle bundling along the sharp line of his jaw, but that's all. He unsnaps my jeans and tugs them down my legs as efficiently and impersonally as my nurse in the hospital only a week ago.

He studies my Tuesday underwear for a moment. It's Thursday, and I know he's remembering our night in Berlin. The memory sizzles between us. I want to spread my legs and tempt him. See if my body still holds any sway over his, but I can't. When he comes back to me, it can't be for that. He peels the loose plain white t-shirt over his head, the rung of muscles in his stomach and chest chiseled and beautiful. A hint of the "v" at his hips just evident at the edge of his low-slung jeans. He pulls his t-shirt down over me, and I push my arms through until it covers all I want to offer him. Desire penetrates the fog floating around my head, his scent lingering in the shirt enveloping me. I can't take my eyes off him. I'm panting, the ragged breaths raising and dropping my breasts under the soft cotton, still holding his warmth.

He pulls back the cover, waiting for me to lie down, and then tucking the comforter under my chin.

"You've got a few hours left before it's morning," he says, his tone flat and wooden, despite the heat brimming from his eyes. "Get some sleep."

He reaches for the lamp switch, and I grab his arm, forcing him to look at me.

"Do you remember the first night we met?" I ask.

He nods slowly, his eyes filling with the same memory I'll never forget.

"You glanced up from the piano in Grady's rehearsal room and looked right through me." A bitter-tasting laugh lingers on my lips. "Or at least that's how it felt. Like you saw everything about me in a flash. It was like you brushed up against my soul. I know that sounds melodramatic, but it scared me half to death. "

"And you ran." He pulls back until my hand falls away. "I looked back and you were gone."

"Yes, I ran."

I grab my nerve and swallow my pride and press into the cold front he's been giving me since I confessed about the tape.

"I felt you, Rhyson. Even when I ran and resisted and said we could only be friends, I felt you. For the first time since that day at Grady's, I don't feel you. Not in that way that was so deep, so fast it felt like I knew you before we ever even spoke. It's the thought that we've lost that because of what I did that scares me. It's scarier to me than that tape coming out, than not getting to perform for two years. It's as scary to me as the day my mother died."

I pour it all out, spilling it into this room we've shared. He says nothing. After all that, after I peel back my skin, my flesh, my bone and bare my heart to him, he says nothing. I can't do this. I can't be this close to him and feel a million miles away. He just looks back at me unblinkingly.

"Kai, it's not gone." He shakes his head and runs a hand through his hair, disheveling it even more. "I just . . . get some sleep."

"Don't leave me." I don't want to beg, but I'd rather sleep on the steps with his music wooing me than in this California king without him. I fold the comforter back, opening a space for him in our bed. "Could you just . . . stay?"

He closes his eyes and swallows, emotion working the muscles in his throat.

"Nah, Pep. I'm not doing that. Not tonight. Not yet."

"Why?" My voice shakes, even though I try to steady it. "Is it because you saw the tape? And now . . . and now you see him when you look at me?"

He dips his head until our eyes are level, and I couldn't look away if I wanted to.

"I did watch that tape."

It's a pitchfork right though my heart, calling to mind what I know he saw on that video. Drex grinning like a salacious demon, slamming into me from behind. My breasts bobbing with every thrust. My dead eyes.

"Is that why you were breaking things?" I venture, afraid to hear his response, but waiting with bated breath. "Why you can't look at me?"

"I can't look at you, Kai, because you lied to me." His words come sharp and short like wood chips flying off an axe. "When I look at you, it's not Drex I see. I see lies."

His words land on me heavy with irony. I started down this path because I never wanted to lose that look in his eyes that's just for me. And it's my deception that may change the way he sees me forever. A painful backfire. If I could have that moment back, the one in the barn when I forgave him and our slate was clean, I would confess. I would tell him everything and trust his love. But I didn't, and now I'm living with the look in his eyes.

"Rhys, I forgave you because I loved you, but I didn't have to. We're not entitled to forgiveness. That's what makes it a gift." I make myself look his disappointment in the eyes. "I'm asking you for that gift, not because I deserve it, but because I need it. I need you to forgive me."

My words thaw something in his eyes. Not completely, but something softens. Something melts infinitesimally before he swallows and looks away, his frown almost a reminder to himself that it's too soon to let go of his anger. That it's too soon to relent.

"Yeah, you forgave me. After I texted and called you for two months with no answer. I just found out about your lies a few hours ago. Seems to me we're just getting started. Give me some time and let me focus on fixing this shit."

He turns to leave, and I hope the words that have always moved him won't fail me now.

"I live you, Rhyson."

He looks over his naked shoulder, one brow lifted.

"Aren't you the one who said sometimes love isn't enough?"

"I was wrong," I rush to say. "Rhys, I was wrong about that. If you love someone the way we love each other, it is enough. It *has* to be."

He starts toward the door, and I barely hear his last words, but I do.

"Well, now we'll get to see, won't we?"

Chapter TWENTY-EIGHT

RHYSON

BETWEEN THE STRAIGHT-BACKED CHAIR BY KAI'S hospital bed last week, the couch in Glory Falls, the dusty, lumpy mattress in the shed, and sleeping again under my piano last night, I haven't been in a bed in what feels like weeks.

I'm like a homeless person living in a mansion, minus the shopping cart. I sit up slowly, making sure nothing hurts. The floor is worse than Aunt Ruthie's couch. Just days ago I woke up with that damn cushion like a springy knife in my back and Kai curled up to my front instead of in her nice, comfy bed up the hall.

Only days ago I thought we were on the right track. In addition to being in the best place we've ever been in our relationship, or so I thought, she had given me permission to get her out of the shitty deal with Malcolm. She was coming to work with me at Prodigy. She promised to marry me when the time was right. We even talked about *kids*.

It was heaven that all went to hell with just a few words in a few moments. Words Kai should have said to me weeks ago. I know I had a strong reaction when I first found out Drex and Kai had a one-night stand. I understand her hesitation, but to lie to me for this long? To set a plan in motion . . . and I use the word "plan" loosely . . . that would leave me in the dark completely about something so important? A secret she would have kept from me forever? *That's* our problem, not the fact that someone is threatening her with a sex tape.

But damn if that video didn't cut through me like a scythe, leaving a curved trail of guts and emotions. I knew Gep would need to see it, but I wasn't sure I'd be able to. I only made it through a few seconds, but I wish I could take those seconds back. Like I'm gonna watch some punk ass fucking my girl for five minutes. Even if it wasn't Drex I couldn't do that. Each frame was a nail drilling into my eye, an anvil swinging at my head. And that smug smile on his damn face, I'll punish him for that. I'll punish him for making the tape at all. I've never felt this level of unadulterated hatred for anyone. Not even for him, but doing this to Kai goes too far.

Even if I can barely be civil to her right now.

I know I have to find a way to forgive her. She forgave me. I get it, but it doesn't change how betrayed I feel. How galling it is to know that once again she trusted San with something she didn't give me. That she held a threat in the palm of her hand in that shed and lied to me outright about it. Every time I'm with Kai I feel emotionally naked, like she has unrestricted access to every part of me. I don't want to hide anything from her, and that was only possible because I thought she felt the same.

But she didn't.

And I'm really struggling to get past how I deceived *myself* that she felt that, too.

When I saw her curled up last night at the base of the stairs from my music room . . . God, I just wanted to fuck her right there on the steps, to bury my body so deep there would be no room for even vestiges of anyone else. To exterminate all the termites chewing through my brain after seeing Drex with her in a way that only I should ever be with her. But I couldn't do it. Sex between us right now would do exactly what Kai thought it would have done before.

It would give us a false sense of intimacy. Give us a false sense of rightness. Because nothing is right, not right now.

In addition to the knotted muscles in my back, I'm starving. And there's not much time to eat. I have to hit this day running. Gep assured me he'd find Drex where San and his minions failed, and I need to be ready to move as soon as he does.

And when I find that motherfucker . . .

After a quick shower, the sight of Kai already in the kitchen truncates the thoughts of how I'll punish Drex. Several delicious scents hang in the air around her. The smell of strawberries from the jar of preserves open on the counter tangles with her cinnamon pear soap. I smell the toast popped up in the toaster mingling with the rich roast coffee brewing. The sweetest and most addictive scent is the most subtle—just Kai. Just whatever chemistry mixes in that tight, petite body to make her skin, unadorned, smell the way it does without soap, perfumes, or anything else. I can never get enough of it.

Kai's at the stove, back to me, so I have a few seconds to study her. Skinny jeans mold her toned legs and cup that round ass. Her favorite wedge-heeled Converse give her a few inches, but I know she still won't make it past my chin. A cropped Kelly green sweater flashes just a strip of her slim back, and I know when she faces me, I'll see her stomach, flat and subtly muscled. Her hair drapes over one shoulder, and I want nothing more than to have that dark, wavy mass poured over me while she takes the top and rides me until we explode into a hot Milky Way, lost in a galaxy where it's just us. The sweater hangs off one bare shoulder, and her skin is melted honey gold fitted over delicate bones. She's probably not wearing a bra, and any other day I'd send my mouth searching under that sweater and make love to her nipples until she collapsed in my arms, all weak knees and hungry hands.

Under all that beauty, I see her lies.

She turns to the refrigerator to grab orange juice and catches sight of me.

"Oh, hey." Pink tints her cheeks. "I mean, good morning. I didn't know you were up yet. I know you had a late night."

I don't answer and don't move, but her voice like molasses, thick and sweet, sticks to me, weakens my resolve. And if I speak or move, I might give away just how flimsy my defenses are against her, when she's not even trying.

"Um, there's breakfast." She gestures to the eggs and bacon and toast she's made. "I wasn't sure if you . . . well, if you'd want to eat, or if Sarita was coming. And I wanted to make sure you, well, had . . . yeah."

I would laugh at her rambling if I wasn't so gutted by what I saw on that tape. If I wasn't so furious with Drex and frustrated that I can't rip his throat out for threatening her and exploiting her. So I don't laugh, I just keep staring at her, not sure which move to make. Her eyes drop to the floor. She shifts her feet and shoves her hands into the back pockets of her jeans.

"Say something, Rhys." Uncertainty threads her words. "I can't deal with the silent treatment."

"Ironic since I did for two months." I shake my head and move toward the coffee on the counter. "A few hours and already you can't deal."

"I didn't mean it like that." She sighs and reaches up to grab a plate from a high shelf in the cabinet. The stretch pulls the cropped sweater up a little more to reveal just the bottom curve of her breast.

Dammit, no bra.

My mouth waters, and not for the food she's plating. I sit at the counter, gulping down the coffee, even though it's so hot it singes the lining of my throat. She sets my food down and takes the high-backed stool beside me, silently digging into her breakfast. Tension entombs the kitchen, sealing us in dead air and tight silence while we eat. After a few moments she tosses her fork onto her plate and takes a huge gulp of the orange juice.

"I thought it might . . ." Her words peter out, and she swallows. "I thought it might be better if I crash at San's for a while."

My fork hovers between the plate and my mouth for a few seconds. I drop it and swing my head around to stare at her.

"So you're running again?"

"I'm not running." She presses a shaky hand to her forehead, shielding half her face from me. "I just thought it'd be better for you. You obviously don't want me—"

"Stop right there," I cut in. "How the hell do you know what I want? How do you presume to know anything right now?"

"Well, you didn't want to be anywhere near me last night and you're barely speaking this morning. I thought you'd . . . I just thought it would make it less awkward while we figure things out."

"Do you have any idea how hard it was for me not to fuck you in half last night?" I demand, voice low and tight. "And even now, not to bend you over the counter? I want you all the time."

"Still?" she whispers, fear and hope twisting in her eyes.

"All the time," I reiterate, my words softer, but still fierce. "But I'm still sorting this out, Kai. I just found out about all of this last night. You can't just run every time we fight. If you hadn't been on tour, I would have been at your door every day begging you to take me back, even knowing you didn't want to see me. Knowing that you may have even hated me. It wouldn't have mattered. I'd rather live with your anger and disappointment every hour of every day than be apart from you. All I'm asking is for you to show me you'd do the same."

She's off the stool and standing right in front of me as soon as my last word hits the air, her scent wrapping around me. Her eyes connected with mine, setting me on fire. Her hands cup my face, forcing me to look at her.

"Then you've got it." The words are husky and breathless. "I want you to forgive me. I need it like air, Rhys, but I'll be here living with your anger until you're ready. I'll take whatever you think I deserve, just don't stop loving me."

It's a compulsion, my hands sliding down her waist to grip her hips, to pull her close. I press my forehead to hers, taking in her strawberry-scented breath.

"Pep, I—"

The door swings open, and Bristol walks in, dark hair scraped back, all suited up, stiletto heels clicking across the marble floor. Her steps falter for a second when she sees us standing so close. I reluctantly put space between Kai and me, returning to my breakfast.

"Morning, Bris." I grab Kai's orange juice and take a quick gulp to soothe the third degree coffee burn.

Marlon's right behind her, his face more somber than I've seen it in a long time.

"Marlon, what's up?" I take a bite of the toast smeared with preserves from Glory Falls. "Didn't know you were coming. Did I forget a session or something?"

"I called him." Bristol helps herself to a piece of toast and peers at the jar of preserves like it's under a microscope.

"It's strawberry preserves," Kai says with a tiny smile. "I have pear, too, if you want that instead."

Where Bristol hesitates, Marlon dives right in, grabbing two pieces of toast and loading them up with preserves. Grunting and nodding at how delicious it is.

"Grip's here because I thought you might need some back up." Bristol rolls her eyes. "Or at the very least a babysitter to make sure you don't end up in jail, and I don't trust Gep with that responsibility."

"Jail?" I stop chewing. "What the fuck?"

"We found Drex." My sister passes a glance between Kai and me. "Took Gep no time. Drex is in Topanga, just where San last spotted him."

I spring to my feet and scrape the remains of my breakfast into the garbage disposal, the satisfying grind only making me wish it was Drex's head I was shoving down that dark, greedy hole.

"Gimme the address." I lean against the sink, arms folded across my chest. I can't even look at Kai, who went completely still as soon as Bris shared her news.

"I hope it's okay that I caught Grip up on some of what's happening. Not all," Bristol says. "You can tell him what you like, but I don't want you going to see Drex alone."

I shrug, avoiding the sympathy and the questions in my best friend's eyes.

"Gep will be with me," I remind her.

"Gep's ex-CIA. Just as likely to water board Drex as you are, if it comes to that," Bristol says. "Besides, you need someone who will keep you, not just safe, but out of trouble."

"And you choose this pothead to keep me out of trouble?" A small smile quirks one corner of my mouth. A full on grin spreads across Marlon's face as he chomps on a piece of bacon.

"I'm all you got, dude." The grin slips a little, and he glances at Kai, whose head is bent over her plate. "You've wanted to kill him before, and I'm always the one who stops you."

Maybe not this time.

"There's something else you should know." Bristol heaves a deep breath before looking at me. "The rental property Drex has been hiding out in, it belongs to John Malcolm."

Kai's head snaps up, and her wide eyes find mine.

"What?" I run my hands over my face and through my hair. "Are they working together? Is he protecting him for some reason?"

"I'm still figuring that out," Bristol says, a grim, determined set to her lips. "But we'll get to the bottom of it before the day is over. That you can be sure of."

My wheels are spinning like a windmill in a tornado.

"Where are we with that other project we discussed a few days ago?"

"What other—" Bristol's eyes light up as her brain makes the same connections mine do. "Far. We're already far down the road with that project. I'm waiting to hear back from one last person. Should be done by the end of the day."

"Don't wait to hear. Wrap that shit up, and we don't have until the end of the day. Now that we've found Drex, that's at the top of your list." I push off the counter and nod my head toward the door. "Come on, Marlon. Let's go."

"Gep's meeting you there," Bristol says. "Don't go in without him. He was confirming one last thing with his techie friend at the CIA, but he knew you wouldn't wait."

"Damn right."

Marlon's out the door, and I'm right behind him, but I hesitate. Kai's been quiet since Bristol and Marlon arrived. I know this is tough for her. Not just me knowing about the tape, but my whole team knowing. My sister and Gep. Now Marlon. Shame highlights her cheeks, but she takes another bite of her toast like this isn't killing her. I cross over, tipping her chin until she has to look at me.

"Be careful," she says before I have the chance to speak. "Please don't do anything crazy because of me."

I bend until my lips are suspended over hers.

"You're the only thing worth doing something crazy for." I press a quick kiss to her lips. "Don't worry about it. About any of it, okay? Let me take care of this."

"I don't suppose I could come with you?" The question barely makes it past her lips, before I shoot it down.

"No way are you going anywhere near that douchebag."

She drops her head a little, nodding.

"I'm sorry I didn't tell you sooner." Her eyes flick to Bristol ostensibly consumed with making coffee a few feet away. "I know you're still angry with me."

"Furious," I whisper over her mouth, drawn to the sweetness beyond her lips despite my lingering hurt and anger.

She closes the few inches to kiss me deeply, sinking her fingers into my hair, gripping me until I couldn't move if I wanted to.

But I don't want to.

I wish I could forget about the tape and about John fucking Malcolm and just stay here and repair all that's broken between us. She hurt me, like I've hurt her in the past, but every kiss, every touch, carries a balm that soothes me back into wanting every moment I can have with her.

"When you can forgive me," she says, her breath coming hard, eyes melded with mine. "I'm yours."

The look I give her penetrates as surely as if I'm sliding up inside of her.

"Pep, you're already mine."

And then I walk away from her while I still can.

Chapter TWENTY-NINE

Kai

I F BRISTOL DISLIKED ME BEFORE, AND I'm pretty sure I can safely conclude that she did, she must hate me now. I clear the breakfast dishes so Sarita won't have to, putting away the preserves I brought back from Glory Falls. The quiet begins to suffocate me, and I struggle to breathe evenly.

"I didn't watch that tape, you know," Bristol says matter-of-factly from her stool at the breakfast bar.

I pause, mid-load of the dishwasher, to glance at her before turning around to fully face her. I'm not sure what to say to the woman who has never wanted me with her brother. Even with her back turned, I felt her attention on us when I kissed Rhyson like my life depended on it before he left. That's how it feels. Like my life depends on what happens next. I can make a name for myself. I'll get another shot at being a star. I can find another manager since things are kind of falling apart with Malcolm. Rhyson is the only irreplaceable thing left in my life, and the thought of losing him . . . it levels me. Everything is flat until I have his forgiveness, and not even

Bristol's prickly self will get a rise out of me.

"I'm gonna go clean up downstairs." I wipe my hands on a dishtowel, not addressing her comment. "There's a mess in the music room."

"You know he slept under his piano when you left?" she asks, eyes fixed on her coffee.

"What?" I pause at the kitchen door. "What do you mean?"

"I mean he was wrecked when you left him and wouldn't take his calls." Bristol sets her coffee down with a thud. "Thank God he had his tour to focus on those first few weeks, or he would have completely lost it. When he got back, though, we couldn't get him out of that room."

"I didn't know that he—"

"Writing songs about you," she presses on, eyes hard, voice brittle. "Missing sessions. Blowing off meetings. I've never seen him like that."

She pauses, dropping her eyes back to the breakfast bar.

"I never want to see him like that again."

"I don't want him like that, Bristol." I take a few steps until I'm standing in front of her. "He hurt me really badly, and I needed time to get over that."

"And now you've hurt him really badly. Will you give him time to get over it?"

"As much as he needs." I bite my lip, uncertain if it's the right thing to say now, but sure of my feelings. "I know you've never trusted me, and I get it. He's rich and famous, and I was a nobody from nowhere who out of the blue was all of a sudden your brother's girlfriend. I understand why you'd assume I wanted something from him."

"That about sums it up," she mutters.

"But I love him." I swallow my tears because Bristol doesn't strike me as a girl who respects any sign of weakness. "And he loves me. I have to believe that will be enough. That the way we love each other will be enough."

"Do you have any idea how special he is?" Her voice is quiet, her eyes probing mine.

"Of course I do. He's a genius."

"Not that shit. He's a good guy. With all he's been given, some-how he's managed to be a good guy." She shrugs her slender shoul-ders. "Probably Uncle Grady's doing."

"Yeah. He's a good guy." I twist my lips. "A great guy."

My guy.

"Don't hurt him again." Bristol lifts her lashes, her eyes a blunt warning. "Look, I want to trust you, but then I find out you fucked the guy who hates Rhys more than anyone, and that you hid a sex tape for three months. Not exactly endearing."

"I know it was bad judgment, not telling Rhyson."

"It was bad judgment fucking Drex."

She's not saying anything I haven't told myself a million times, but it still feels like she's a sword that just drew first blood.

"Yes, it was," I agree. "But Rhyson and I hadn't even met when that happened. The thing I most regret that I *could* have changed is keeping this from him for weeks. I never wanted him to see that tape."

I pause, studying the marble floor and gulping back shame.

"I know you didn't watch, but you know what's on it. Can you understand how desperate I was for the man I love to never see me that way?"

"But he has, right?" Bristol asks. "He watched it?"

"Yes." I look her right in the eye. "He saw it."

"And yet he's still racing off to handle this for you." She licks her lips and lowers her eyes to the coffee in front of her. "He still loves you."

"We love each other," I say softly. "I don't know how long it will take him to forgive me for lying to him. I don't know how long it will take him to trust me again, but I'll wait."

"I can't promise you that I'll trust you anytime soon." Bristol gives me frank eyes. "You may think I'm cold and that he's just my job. Hell, sometimes he thinks that, too. But he's my brother, Kai. I've seen that he'll always choose you, protect you. I hope you understand that I'll always choose him. That I'm here to protect him."

And just like that I like her. I mean, we're still from different worlds. She may never be the girl I grab a mani/pedi with, or tell my secrets to, but she loves Rhyson. Deeply. And that we have in common.

"Bristol, you say that Rhyson chooses me every time. I promise you that I'll choose him every time, too."

She stands to dump her remaining coffee in the sink and to grab her purse.

"You better." She looks at me unsmilingly for an extra few moments, and though she doesn't crack, her eyes soften just a little. Just enough. "Well, you heard him give me my marching orders. I'm gonna go. I have work to do."

And she's gone, eyes already glued to the phone that seems to hold the solution to any problem Rhyson ever has. She's Rhyson's fixer. Makes life smoother. I don't think I appreciated before how very good she is at it. I want to ask if she can fix Rhyson and me, if there's anything on that phone that will fix the mess I've made, but I know that's something I'll have to do myself.

What will it take to repair the damage I've done to our relationship? To our trust? Last night he wouldn't stay with me, but this morning he asked me not to leave. This stasis, this space between his love, which I don't doubt, and his anger, which I deserve, feels like a lifelong sentence, even though it's only been a few hours. Rhyson lasted months with my anger and my silence.

I'll give him no less.

Chapter THIRTY

RHYSON

IT'S NEVER BEEN THIS QUIET IN the car when it's just Marlon and me. We find something to talk about all the time, even if it's just Madden high scores or our music. He knows how I feel about Kai and how much I hate Drex. So a sex tape featuring the girl I love and the man I despise . . . yeah, I'd be at a loss for words, too.

"So did you watch it?" He finally drops the question into this vat of boiling silence. "The tape, I mean."

I'd rather have the quiet than this conversation.

"Uh, a little bit." My grip tightens on the steering wheel. I almost smile when I think about the first time Kai sat where Marlon sits now and told me her name was like my Porsche.

Kai Anne. Like your car. Cayenne.

From the beginning, she always made me laugh. If I'm a safe, she cracked me day one, and we were friends before we were anything else. We were friends when I wasn't sure that was all I could settle for. And we *trusted* each other with secrets we'd never shared with anyone else. How did that happen so quickly? So deeply? I want that back more than anything. She figured it out for me, and as much as the lies hurt, I'll figure it out for her . . . eventually. But first I have to eliminate these threats.

"Have you thought about what you'll do if it comes out?" Marlon asks.

"It won't come out. That's why we're doing this now, so it doesn't come out."

"It's possible, Rhys, that it will." Marlon pauses before going on. "I'm just asking if you've thought about how you'll feel if everyone sees Drex fucking your girl."

I shoot him a dark look and take a deep breath, glad the curving road gives me something to focus on besides my fury. The thought of anyone seeing Kai like that takes a chainsaw to the lining of my stomach. I must be bleeding inside. There's no way I can have pain like this without blood.

"If it was the girl I love," he continues. "I would tell the whole world to go fuck themselves. Who cares what they think?"

"Yeah?" I divide a glance between him and the road. "Easy to say when it's not you on the tape. I don't care if people talk about me, but people talking about Kai? Seeing her like that? That I can't take."

I shake my head, my heart straining with every beat at the thought of her humiliated that way.

"I'll do anything to keep that from happening."

"So this isn't to save your face? It's for her?"

"It's all for her." I frown at the road ahead. "I don't give two shits about anything else."

I think that night I found out she'd been with Drex, I thought it might change things. Honestly, with all the acrimony between Drex and me, the thought of him, filthy, dirty *him*, having her was like a needle threading through my brain, but I underestimated myself. I underestimated my love for her. Even I didn't know how deep it went. Though I'm disgusted by the video, nothing's changed in my heart. Not for *her*. Did I plant the seeds of her insecurity? Or water the ones her Dad planted when he walked away? Maybe I left her thinking I couldn't handle the truth because on some level, I wasn't sure I could. But this love, even after my lies and hers, is immutable. Unmoving. Lodged in my heart. Stuck in my soul.

"Damn, this girl's got you whupped." Marlon laughs, banging the dashboard with his fist.

"Like you're just now realizing that." I pull myself out of my head, out of my thoughts, to respond to him. "I could wring her neck right now for keeping all of this from me, but we'll work it out. She's the one, so we have to."

"How do you know?" His voice is softer somehow, and there's more than idle curiosity in his eyes when I take a second to search them.

"Remember your Uncle Jamal, and how he always used to tell us about girls?"

"The OG!" Admiration tinges Marlon's grin. "The man knows his pussy."

"That he does." I nod, sketching a quick grin of my own. Only Marlon would have me grinning when I'm on my way to pound Drex's punk ass into next week, and could barely breathe past my anger twenty minutes ago. "Remember he told us there was—"

"Basic and magic."

"Exactly. He said most girls think they're magic, but they're all basic until you meet that one." I shake my head, recalling the day I met Kai in Grady's studio. "I knew Kai was different the first time I saw her. I didn't have to sleep with her, had never even kissed her, and I knew she was magic."

I recognize how very whipped I sound, but there's nothing I can do about it.

"It's hard to explain," I add.

"I think I get it." Marlon shrugs, brushing a rough hand over the dreadlocks hanging past his shoulders. "I mean, that's how I kinda felt the first time I met your sister."

I nearly run off the road.

"Are you shitting me?" I swivel a glance his way. "Bristol? My sister Bristol?"

A heavy frown settles over his dark eyes.

"What? You think your sister's basic?"

"I don't exactly give it much thought with her being, you know, my sister." I hesitate because Marlon isn't serious about much other than his music. And I guess Bristol. "Are you for real? That's how you felt the first time you saw Bris?"

"Your sister's gorgeous."

"Of course she is." I shrug. "We're twins."

"And you're both *really* modest, too," Marlon deadpans. "She came to visit you and Grady on Spring Break her sophomore year from Columbia."

I remember that rare trip. She had to ask Marlon's name about five times.

"Man, she barely acknowledged your existence."

"She's playing hard to get."

"For a decade?" I do a brow lift. "More like never gonna get it."

"That joke will never get old, will it?"

"Sure, it will, if she ever goes out with you. So . . . probably not."

"She's driving me crazy." He holds his head like he would squeeze her out if he could. "She brought this Qwest thing to me. She wants to manage me so bad."

"Let her. You know she'll do a great job."

"Yeah, a *job*. I don't want to be her job."

"What do you want to be?" For once, I'm not going to tease him about my sister because I can tell he's serious.

"I want her to be my girl." He frowns at me. "You know that."

"I mean, you still fuck everything that moves, so I didn't think it was like *that*."

"I'm not a monk." He gives me a knowing look. "You telling me all those months Kai had you in the friend zone you didn't get it somewhere else?"

I shake my head. His grin drops.

"Not even a little bit o' pussy?"

"Not even a little bit." I shrug. "She was it for me. I didn't want anybody else. Haven't since the day we met. It wasn't like love at first sight or anything. I *grew* in love with her, but all the other girls just kind of disappeared."

"And when Kai told you no and friend zoned you so hard, did you give up?" Marlon demands.

"Nope. Failure wasn't an option."

"Well, then you understand why I haven't given up on Bristol yet."

"Frankly, I don't want you to get hurt." I sigh. "And as much as I love my sister, she could roll over you like a speed bump and never even feel you under her tires."

"I'll take my chances. I think she'd be worth it." His grin makes a brief appearance before fading. "Your girl's worth it, right?"

"There's not a chance I wouldn't take for her."

I slow down a few blocks from the address Bristol gave me when I see Gep's truck pulled off to the side. Once we're out of my truck and standing in front of him, I see the sober look on his face.

"What we got?" I demand. "He's in the house?"

"Yeah, he's there." Gep puts a firm hand on my shoulder. "I don't know exactly what we're walking into here, Rhys. It could be volatile. It's not too late to contact the cops."

"No cops." I slam my frown into place. "The circle of people who know about this is already larger than it should be. I can't risk exposing Kai like that. Some cop or clerk looking to make something on the side gets wind of this and sells to the highest bidder. No fucking way, Gep. We get to the bottom of this quickly and quietly."

He looks like he'll make another argument, and I'm braced to stand my ground.

"Gep, let's try it his way." Marlon leans against my truck, arms folded across his chest. "I've kept him from killing this guy since high school. I think I can do it one more time."

Gep's got about five seconds to concede before I go in there on my own. My fingers itch to wrap around that fucker's neck. I know Gep's job is to keep me safe, but my safety is the last thing I care about right now.

"Okay, let's do it." Gep taps on the tinted back right passenger window, and a guy I've never seen before dressed in UPS browns steps out. Gep gestures to him. "Our element of surprise."

We make our way silently up the steep driveway of the small house nestled into the side of the mountain. Gep and I step to one side of the door. Marlon steps to the other, and our fake UPS guy rings the bell. The door is barely cracked open, and as soon as I see Drex's face, I shove UPS out of the way and lunge for that asshole, pushing him back into the house. He slithers out of my grip and zips toward an open door leading to the patio. I'm on his heels and tackle him to the flagstones, sitting on his chest to keep him pinned. The fool has the nerve to laugh up into my face.

"If you're here for tips on how to fuck your girl right, I'm not telling you shit. Figure it out for yourself."

My body processes what he said before my mind does, immediately punching him in the face. His eyes glaze a little, but the smile pops right back like a demented clown.

"She was so tight and wet that night," he rasps. "Next time I'll let her suck my dick."

There is no stopping it. The momentum of my rage drags me into his face again and again and again. The sound of his flesh flattening under my fury brings me an unreasonable pleasure that drowns out the pain of my knuckles splitting, the flesh peeling back from my bones. That metronome that always marks my anger explodes, the tick tocking detritus littering my brain. I don't even notice when he manages to roll to the side, and my fist pounds full force into the flagstones beneath us. I barely feel the impact, adrenaline surging. I snatch him back, latching onto his throat. Bloodlust swells in my veins, hauling every savage instinct to the surface. I tremble with the desire to choke off his air supply for good.

"Rhys, man." Marlon pulls at me, and out of pure reflex I draw back to punch him, too, but catch myself. His eyes travel from my bunched fist to my face. "You gonna hit me now? Just be prepared for me to knock the living shit outtta you."

Hot, heavy breath forces past my lips. When I try to flex the fingers of my right hand, I can't. Since before I can even remember, protecting my fingers, my hands has been paramount. Our lives, my livelihood, *everything* always centered in my hands. And now it's a limp mass of bloodied flesh. Needles of pain stab my fingers. Panic feels like it may catapult my heart from my chest.

"Rhys, your hand." Marlon's worried eyes settle on my hand. "We need to get you to a doctor, like now."

I peer through the patio door into the living room where Gep has dragged Drex's sorry ass. Gep towers over him, and the look he gives him is deadly enough to pin him to the couch. I draw a calming breath and approach them.

"Later," I say to Marlon over my shoulder.

"Not later." Marlon grabs my arm. "Now. This is your hand, Rhys."

"I know." I pull away. "See if you can find some Aleve or something until we're done with this."

"Aleve?" Marlon whooshes a frustrated breath. "At least let me call Bristol so she can have a specialist standing by."

"Yeah, good idea. Dr. Mason's the one who examines my hands for the insurance policy. She should probably notify him." I turn to look at him. "Make sure she doesn't mention it to Kai."

Marlon holds my eyes for a moment before denting one side of his cheek with a smile.

"Always Kai."

Always Kai.

"Just find that Aleve for me."

I hold my injured hand, wincing as I join Gep and Drex in the living room. Drex offers me a bloody smirk, his face already swelling. He gestures to my hand.

"Looks like that hurts."

"So does your face. Shut the hell up."

Even bloodied and already swelling, his face manages to look smug. I have to look away because the urge to slam my probably-broken fist right through that expression is so strong, and I know we need the information Gep is trying to extract.

"Look, you've broken laws here." Gep rests meaty fists on his hips. "You recorded Kai, and God knows who else, without her knowledge and blackmailed her."

"That wasn't me." Drex's eyes take a leisurely path between me and Gep. "I mean, yeah I recorded her when we fucked."

He pauses to grin at me.

"But I'm not the one blackmailing her, and I'm not going down for it."

"Then who?" I frown, unable to let Gep take the lead for very long. "Tell us everything, you piece of shit."

"Ah ah ah," Drex tsks and shakes his head, eyes alight with hatred and satisfaction. "I'm the one with all the information. You better be nice to me."

"Nice to you?" Incredulity rolls a hollow laugh up my throat. "I'm going to destroy you either way. Your cooperation determines if I'll leave you any scraps of your pathetic career so you can at least book weddings and bar mitzvahs."

I lean close, almost close enough to sniff the barely-veiled panic that lurks just beneath his self-satisfied façade.

"Because make no mistake about it." I look straight into his eyes so he sees that I have every intention of backing up this threat. "You're through in this town. Done. I'll block every deal. I started the black-balling as soon as I saw that tape just a few hours ago. You're poison already and just don't know it yet."

"You can't do that." He says it, but I can tell he knows I can.

"Let's not play the game where you pretend to have any power in this situation, when we both know I'll come out on top."

"You always do, don't you?" Bitterness corrodes his words. "You always have."

"Is that what this is about? Your ridiculous jealousy since high school?"

"Everything came so easy to you, Gray." He shakes his head, hatred alive in his narrowed eyes. "I was the one person who didn't scrape and bow at your feet just because you were some piano savant in another life."

"You have no idea what my life was like. It certainly wasn't easy."

"Whatever." He shrugs, deliberately casual. Falsely calm. "At least I fuck your women first. If that's my only concession, I'll take it."

Gep grabs my arms, but I shake him off, staring back at Drex without making a further move toward him. This idiot thinks he knows my buttons? He has no idea.

"Here's the deal." I step directly into Drex's line of vision. "Like Gep said, you recorded Kai without her consent. It's illegal."

"And I wonder what the cops would find on your laptop?" Gep keeps his face straight, playing along since he knows I have no intention of bringing the police into this. "If we got a warrant to seize your cloud, would there be other women there recorded without their consent? We could build quite a case, and you could do some real time."

Drex's jaw clenches, and fear thins his lips.

"What do you want?" he asks after a few moments to contemplate that possibility.

"First, I want any and every copy of that tape so I can destroy it," I say immediately.

"I don't have it anymore." Drex leans back into the cushions. "I don't have any copy. I told you I'm not the one who's been threatening her."

"Who?" I try to keep my voice free of panic. Whoever has the tape could do anything with it. They just threatened Kai days ago. They could release it at any time. They could release it while I sit here with this idiot. "Who has it?"

Drex sits back and remains silent, looking around the cabin like it might offer some escape, but it doesn't. There is none.

"And we know this place is owned by John Malcolm," Gep continues. "How's he involved? Tell us everything or we get the cops in on this, and it gets messy."

Drex's eyes drift from me to Gep to Marlon and then back to settle on me. He heaves a sigh.

"Fuck it. I gotta save myself here." He shrugs. "When things blew up between you and your girlfriend, and she signed with Malcolm, I saw . . . let's call it an opportunity."

"Go on." Gep folds his massive arms across his chest.

"I called Malcolm and said I had something on his bright new star artist that I'd release unless he signed me, too. Got me some gigs. Gave me a shot."

I already see where this is going, and the thought of Kai being caught in their disgusting cross hairs makes me sick. Makes me furious.

"To my surprise, he wanted the tape for his own game." Drex laughs. "What'd I care? He told me to lay low for a few months because they'd be looking for me when he started threatening her."

"Why'd he threaten her with it? Why keep them apart?" Marlon demands, confusion on his face. "I don't get it."

"He didn't want Kai with me," I say softly. "He knew I wouldn't let him control her. He knew I'd get her away from him."

"He figured when she didn't take you back, things would die down. You'd give up and move on, and he'd have Kai for the next two years at least. Just another break up."

"But it wasn't just another break up." I shake my head. "Not to me and Kai. He underestimated us, I guess."

"Well, I don't even have the video anymore," Drex says. "He made a hard copy and deleted it from my cloud. I couldn't release that video now if I wanted to."

"And in exchange?" I demand.

"In exchange, I have a new record deal." Drex smiles, a grimy spread of his lips. "And even shows in Vegas this summer."

I don't have the heart to tell him that will never happen. Or maybe I'm just saving that for dessert.

"Call him." My words land in the room with atomic force.

"What?" Drex frowns. "He's never been up here. He'll suspect something's wrong. What will I tell him?"

"I don't care if you tell him he needs to come because the Easter Bunny has his eggs. You get that piece of shit here as soon as possible." I flick a glance to my security guard. "Or Gep here will call some of his friends. Did I mention he's ex-CIA?"

Our eyes lock, and he can hardly disguise his malevolence

toward me. That's fine because I can barely check mine for him, so we're even.

Reluctantly, he grabs his phone and makes the call.

Chapter THIRTY-ONE

RHYSON

"**W**HAT THE HELL DO YOU THINK you're doing, calling me?"

John Malcolm's voice in the living room booms loud and irritated enough to reach me in the bedroom.

"What's so urgent you broke protocol? Why am I here?" he demands of Drex.

"I had an emergency I couldn't discuss over the phone," Drex says, his voice as nervous and tentative as I've ever heard it. "Something that could jeopardize the whole plan."

"What?" Malcolm snaps

I step into the living room, Marlon and Gep right behind me.

"Not what. Who. Me."

I lean against the wall and slide one hand into my pocket, leaving the injured hand hanging limply at my side. The pain is nearly unbearable. It is obviously beyond the power of Aleve, and as soon as I handle this monster, Dr. Mason is waiting to tell me exactly how bad the damage is.

Malcolm's beady eyes stretch momentarily when they settle on me before swinging back to Drex.

"You idiot." His frown just gets heavier and his complexion ruddier with his anger. "If you've fucked this up—"

"No, you fucked up, Malcolm." I struggle to keep my voice even now that I'm faced with this manipulative bastard, responsible, at least indirectly for Kai's exhaustion and hospitalization. For the last three months she's been threatened and tortured and trying to fix this on her own.

"You fucked up when you interfered in my relationship with Kai," I continue. "When you convinced her to leave me. When you tricked her into a shitty contract. When you pushed her past her limits. When you had the audacity to threaten *my girl* with a sex tape recorded without her consent."

I draw a deep breath, reaching for the calming effects that never come.

"Oh, you've fucked up badly, Malcolm."

The shock of seeing me fades the longer he stands there, leaving nothing but the monster I always knew lurked just below his too-polished, fleshy veneer.

"You should be very careful with me, Gray." He laughs, sitting on one of the couches and pulling out a cigar to gnaw on. "I have Kai locked into a contract for the next two years. There's only plusses here for me. If I release that tape, my client will be even more popular. How many celebrities have been propelled from obscurity to infamy with a good sex tape? The guys are already eating her up. Imagine how hungry they'll be for her once they jerk off to that video a few times. I see nothing but possibility here."

He looks up at me, his smile cruel and lascivious.

"And Kai's sex tape is a good one. I've watched it over and over and over. Professional curiosity and due diligence, of course." He levels his stare at me, smile growing wider with every venom-tipped word. "Nothing to do with the fact that my client has an excellent set of tits, if you like them small. But that ass of hers makes up for—"

Before the next words leave his mouth, I've jetted across the short distance separating us, everything civilized falling away from me at the prospect of crushing his windpipe. I slam into a wall of flesh and bone, Gep blocking my access to this belly-crawling reptile.

"Rhys." Gep's huge hands shove me back by my shoulders. "He's pushing buttons. Don't let him get to you."

"Oh, is that your babysitter?" Malcolm asks. "Good thing he's here to keep you from doing something more stupid than you've already done."

I need to cut this short before I commit a real crime. Neither of these bastards is worth me spending even a day behind bars away from Kai. I take the seat across from him and lean forward to rest my elbows on my knees.

"I'm so many steps ahead of you, Malcom." My eyes don't stray from his. His smile slips almost imperceptibly, but I detect it because now I'm in tune to this bastard's every nuance.

"You're afraid to ask what I mean, but you should already know." I lift both brows, my mouth a straight blade on my face, flat and sharp. "You have a debt problem."

The confidence flickers on his face like a candle's flame, recovering from a gush of wind.

"Matter of fact, you couldn't even have financed Luke's tour without some help, and even with it selling out, your head still isn't above water."

"You're crazy." His voice is weaker, though. Fainter.

"You're very fiscally vulnerable right now. Digital has wrecked sales. And before Luke and Kai, you had a stable full of B-listers who never earned out. Everything you've built is held together by string and a group of investors." I shrug. "And not exactly the most loyal investors."

Malclom sits up, back straight, paunch poked forward.

"What have you done?"

"Just made some inquiries." I borrow some of his previous smugness for my smile. "And maybe some offers."

My smile evaporates.

"You will hand over to me any and every copy of that tape and you will release Kai from her contract, free and clear."

"Why should I?" he grits out. "I could launch her even bigger if that tape goes live."

"Except you'll have no money to launch." My face goes as stiff as caulk. "We've spoken to every one of your investors over the last few days, and each of them is prepared to withdraw their support from you."

"Why?" A low growl quivers his fleshy jowls. "Why would they do that?"

"Maybe they got a better offer?" I shrug. "Apparently, they'd rather have a cut in my label than do business with you. For some reason they seem to think I'm a better bet."

"You wouldn't do that." Malcolm frowns, confusion clouding his face. "You've always wanted all the creative control. All the control really. That's the whole point of you starting your own label. You wouldn't relinquish it before the label even gets off the ground."

"For her I would," I say softly. "Try me."

"How do I know you're not lying to me?"

"I expected you to want proof." I give my phone to Marlon because I can't negotiate with one hand. "Go to my email."

Marlon looks from my phone to my face and then to Malcolm before tapping the screen.

"Open the one from Bristol." I keep my face as expressionless as I can, but the pain in my hand only intensifies every moment this guy needs convincing. "Give it to him."

Malcolm studies the phone, eyes widening then lifting to narrow on my face. I know what he sees. Bristol has attached signed letters of intent from every one of Malcolm's investors.

"If you release that tape, it would be embarrassing for Kai." I keep my words low and smooth. "But you're right, she'd get past it. She's talented and beautiful and in some twisted way, it could make her more popular. You, on the other hand, will have nothing."

My face cements into implacable lines.

"You, on the other hand, won't be able to take advantage of any positive effects because I'll take everything from you." I nod toward the phone in his hand. "I'm just one email away from doing it already."

"But if I give you all copies of the tape and release Kai from her contract, this goes away?"

"And Luke." I level a hard stare at him. "I want Luke away from you, too."

"That's ridiculous. You'd leave me with nothing."

"Not nothing." I wave toward my phone still in his hand. "You'd have all your investors, and you'd have your freedom. We wouldn't prosecute you for blackmail."

"You can't prove a thing." His voice is more certain than his eyes.

"I'm sure Drex wouldn't mind testifying for me since some of Gep's hacker friends have already tapped into his cloud and found several sex tapes, none of which, I'm guessing, had consent." I turn to Drex. "Am I right about that?"

Drex swallows and drops his eyes to the floor.

"I won't let you get away with this." Malcolm struggles to get the words out past his rage.

"Let me?" My breath comes quick and shallow, anger rupturing the calm I'm barely holding on to. "At what point in this conversation did you become confused? I hold all the cards. Every scenario is one I've *designed*. Every outcome gets me something I want, even if that's just you broke and behind bars. Kai will weather any storm that comes with exposure. I'll make sure of that, but you won't."

Malcolm's marble eyes shift like a rat's from Drex to Gep to me and back again. A cornered rodent, looking for a way out. But there isn't a way out. I've blocked all his escape routes. Even though my hand is throbbing, discolored, and limp, I can't focus on the pain because I see how close he is to caving.

"And if I give you all copies of the tape—"

"And release Kai and Luke from their contracts," I insert.

"And release Kai and Luke from their contracts," he concedes, lips tightening and eyes slitting like a snake's. "Then you withdraw your offer from my investors? And I just go on about my business?"

I won't mention just now that I have wheels in motion to

undercut the contracts he has with the remaining artists on his roster. I won't mention it because he won't know I was behind it.

"Yeah. On about your business."

What's left of it.

Neither of these low life parasites will have much left by the time we're done, but at least they won't be in jail, which by all rights they should be. If it weren't for the public spectacle that would become for Kai, I would press for that. We don't always get everything we want precisely the way we want it, but I can live with this. Knowing Gep and Bristol, they're already setting up contingencies to protect our interests. This is as fixed as it will get for now. Now to fix my hand.

And then finally to fix things with Kai.

Chapter THIRTY-TWO

Kai

I WAKE UP PIECE BY PIECE, my body sounding no alarms, but languidly shaking sleep from one limb at a time until I'm fully aware. The bedside lamp I left on still shines a dim, soft arc of light across the bed. I'm huddled under the covers, basically the same position I passed out in after I took my meds. Bristol left to work on whatever she works on for Rhyson soon after our conversation in the kitchen, and I've been here at the house all day waiting for calls that never came. Information about what's happening. Confirmation that Rhyson is okay. I fell asleep alone and anxious.

But I wake up with him beside me. He's sitting up, shoulders against the headboard, his eyes pewter-dark and set on me.

"It's kind of creepy waking up to you watching me like that." I toss back to him the words he said to me what feels like a millennium ago in this very bed, hoping it lightens the air between us. "But I could get used to it."

One side of his mouth tips up a degree, but his eyes remain sober. I brace myself for whatever he has to say. If the tape is coming out, I can take that. It would be humiliating and debasing, but I can withstand that. If I have to stay with Malcolm for two years, I can endure that. Or if I'll be sidelined, unable to perform and back at the Note slinging overcooked burgers, I'll do that, too. Whatever the outcome that has him looking so serious, I can take it. As long as he doesn't say we're over. As long as he can forgive me for lying to him and keeping this all a secret. That is the only scenario from which I'd never recover.

"Do you remember the first time we made love?" he asks softly.

The question is like an arrow from overhead in the middle of a picnic. It ambushes me. It goes straight to the center of my heart. I can't keep up, my poor, half-asleep brain struggling to process this unexpected conversation. It's not the test I thought I'd be taking, but I think I have all the answers.

"Of course, I do." I don't sit up, but instead burrow deeper under the covers, searching his face. "On your pool table."

Half a smile crooks his lips.

"I'd never felt anything like that." He gives into the rest of that smile briefly. "I mean, the sex, yeah. But the closeness. I'd never felt that close to anyone in my life."

"Neither had I."

I hold my breath, not wanting to disturb this memory with anything from the present. That night went beyond flesh. I recognized him in my soul. In that deep place of which my father spoke, when that other person's soul is merely an echo of your own.

"Every wall I'd ever raised, every defense I had, you got past them all," Rhyson says. "You went deeper than anyone ever had. You peeled away every layer of skin, sunk through the flesh, and I felt you right next to my bones. For the first time in my life I felt fully . . . known."

Rhyson's smile fades, and his eyes drop to the hand in his lap.

"I wanted to give you everything that night. Money, houses, jewelry—you could have asked me for anything. I wanted to give it all to you."

I don't know what to say because I didn't want anything from him that night other than what he gave me. And more of it.

"Mostly I just wanted to give you all of me," he says. "But you ran from it."

Tears burn my eyes. I'd never thought of it that way. I'd been freaked out by my feelings. Afraid to trust him. Scared we'd ruin our friendship and that what we'd felt couldn't last because I'd seen love not last. I didn't want things to end that way for us.

"I was so scared, Rhys. I didn't know if I could trust you. If I could trust myself, but I got past that."

"Did you?" He frowns. "'Cause it feels like you still don't trust me. When you said we hit reset, I believed you. We said no more secrets, no more lies, but then you—"

"Lied." My voice barely slips through my lips. "And kept things from you, I know. I'm sorry."

"I didn't know how much it hurts. I didn't realize what I was asking of you," he says. "To forgive me after I'd betrayed your trust until I had to do the same. It's not easy."

"No, it's not easy." I shake my head, stealing a look at him. "But it's worth it. I think *we're* worth it, Rhyson."

He looks back at me for a moment as if weighing his next words.

"I want to be known, Pep, and I want to know you. Fully. I need to believe there isn't any dark part of me I can't trust you with, and I need you to believe the same."

He finally touches me. Thank God, he touches me. Even though it's just a brush of his fingers across my hair.

"Nothing will make me walk away from you." He shakes his head, the heat in his eyes smelting this moment down to something precious and raw. "Today I realized that I made you believe what happened between you and Drex might make me run. I don't want us to live like your father did, hoarding his secrets. Being known too late and by the wrong person."

"I don't want that either." I lean into his gentle fingers, wanting him to touch every part of me, seen and unseen. "God, Rhyson, you're all I want. That's what I know. Everything else can go to hell, but please forgive me, because you're all I want."

Everything in my body pauses, waiting for his response. Waiting to see if my words are enough to convince him.

"Somewhere along the way I failed you." He sinks his fingers deeper into my hair and sighs. "Somehow, I wasn't clear. I haven't made it abundantly clear that this—what I feel for you—goes nowhere. Maybe it was your good-for-nothing father that planted this insecurity inside of you. This sense that I might walk away, might leave, might love you less."

The look he gives me reaches in and squeezes my heart.

"Aunt Ruthie said it's dangerous to love the way we do because people die and aren't perfect." He smiles a little. "She promised me that you would make mistakes, and that the real test would be to love you through them. It's a test you already passed when you loved me through mine."

Aunt Ruthie has done an awful lot for me over the course of my life, but she may have just given me the greatest gift. One I didn't even know to ask for.

"You once told me there are at least two categories of forgiveness," he continues.

I nod into his hand, closing my eyes like a sinner waiting for atonement.

"My Daddy said that, believe it or not." I breathe something close to a laugh into the pillow that smells faintly of Rhyson. "In one of his sermons, and I still can't forgive him, so I'm not sure how much weight it should carry."

His fingers still in my hair for a few seconds, before moving again, lightly massaging my scalp and pushing the thick strands when they fall forward.

"What was that second category?" he asks.

My mind reaches for the conversation he and I had a few weeks ago. Reaches further back to the day I sat by Mama on a wooden pew, wearing my pink and white dress with roses she sewed on at the waist. I'd absorbed every word Daddy said like water, as truth. And as flawed as he was, as wrong and broken as he was, and despite his lies and his secrets, maybe there *was* some truth to what he said because I've never forgotten.

"It's that kind of forgiveness where you just love the person so much, you can't stand being apart from them. You have to forgive them because you'd do whatever it takes to restore the relationship."

I finally look up from under my mound of covers to find his eyes waiting for me.

He smiles just enough at me to let me know we'll be okay.

"That's the one."

I drag myself out of the covers and onto his lap to reacquaint myself with his lips, but stop when I notice his right hand beside him on the bed, wrapped and splinted.

"Rhys, what happened to your hand?" I'm horrified. I'm afraid to touch it in case I hurt him. I go to pull back, but his left hand pulls me closer so that I'm straddling him, knees folded under, pressed into his chest.

"Don't move." He leans into my neck, inhaling whatever scent I have left at this late hour. "Stay."

Tears blur my vision for a few seconds, but I blink at them so I can see him clearly. I force myself to speak past the sorrow and guilt searing my throat.

"Baby, oh God. What happened?" I palm his face, catching and holding his eyes with mine. "This is my fault."

"No." He shakes his head. "I lost my temper, missed Drex's face and hit a stone patio. My bad, not yours."

"Oh God." I cover my mouth, closing my eyes with tears trickling down my cheeks and over my fingers. "But you wouldn't have been in that situation if it hadn't been for me."

"Stop." He buries his face in my hair, his hand splaying over my back and soothing me when he's the one hurting. "*He* put me in that situation when he threatened the most important thing in my life, and I'd do it again."

I pull back as much as he'll let me, enough to peer into his face with the beautiful tired eyes.

"Your music, Rhyson." I shake my head helplessly, a sinkhole opening up in my belly as I consider the implications of this injury.

"What did the doctor say? Will you need surgery? What's the prognosis? Should we—"

"Stop." He presses a finger to my lips. "All great questions that I'll answer tomorrow. Right now, I'm exhausted. I just want to go to sleep. We can talk details tomorrow, but that tape is dead and so is your contract with Malcolm. I promise I'll tell you everything in the morning. Right now I just want to hold you."

I nod, sitting back on his legs a little to look at him. My fingers shake, but I reach for the hem of his t-shirt and pull it over his head, being mindful of his hand. I had fallen asleep again in my clothes, so I peel my t-shirt off next, my skin heating under his watchful stare. I scoot back until I can reach the buckle of his belt, undoing it, unsnapping his jeans and carefully tugging them and his briefs over his legs and feet until his long, lean body is completely naked. Standing, I strip off my jeans, my panties, my bra. I'm as naked as the day I was born when I lie back down on our bed. His eyes rove over me as hungrily as they always do, but oddly, as much as I know we want each other, this isn't about sex. I was doing more than stripping away our clothes. I was stripping away the last of my secrets, baring my soul to him. Baring his to me.

I press our foreheads together until I can whisper over his lips.

"I live you, Rhyson." My voice shakes with emotion. With acceptance. With gratitude that he's forgiven me. Assuring him that I've forgiven him. The words land on a slate that is finally completely clean.

He nods, eyes pressed shut and lips open over mine to make his words simultaneously a kiss, a confession, and a promise.

"I live you, too, Pep."

I explore the sharp, strong angles of his face and roam into the gorgeous mop of messy, burnished hair. I claim him with the pads of my fingers, with the palms of my hands. He is mine and I am his. Our darkest secrets, shared. Our deepest places, reached. We are completely known. Completely loved down to our very souls.

Epilogue

Kai

EVERY MORNING I'M AWAKENED BY AN ocean breeze. The wind whispers through the sheer netting encamping our bed, skipping across my naked shoulders and lifting the hair from my neck. Here in Bora Bora, we haven't glanced at our phones for the time, text messages—nothing. The ocean is my alarm, but this morning, something else lures me from sleep. It's music wafting from the deck into our bedroom.

I wrap the soft sheet around my breasts toga style, and notice the nameplate "Pepper" necklace hanging at my neck above Gram's for the first time. I touch it with a smile. I thought I'd lost it the night we fought and I ripped it away. Yet another thing of mine he held on to. Having it again makes my day before it even starts.

I shuffle across the bamboo floors that give glimpses of aquamarine beneath our overwater bungalow. Rhyson stretches out on a lounger, a pad on the deck beside him and harmonica in hand. He bends to jot down a few notes, sun-darkened and beautiful in just his board shorts, the coppery streaks in his hair deepened by our two weeks here.

His right hand is still paler than the rest of him, even though the cast has been gone for a few weeks. Guilt seizes my insides every time I imagine one of this generation's greatest musicians slamming his hand into stone for me. I've cried about it more than once, but I'm trying to forgive myself for something Rhyson insists wasn't my fault. The surgery was three months ago, so he's in very aggressive, well-monitored rehab. The insurance company's specialist will examine him when we return to LA next week. I think I'm more worried about it than he is. He does all the rehab exercises and keeps all of his weekly appointments. He even brought a small keyboard with us so he can practice some basic scales every day. The specialist advises slow and steady, and I can only pray that he regains full mobility. If he is any less of a pianist than he was before we met, I don't know how I'll forgive myself. I don't think there's a category of forgiveness for that.

"How's the hand?" I lean into the door, knotting the sheet under my arms.

He looks up from the notes he's scribbling onto a composition pad, his smile bright against his tan.

"Sixty percent of the time," he says, wiggling his fingers. "It works every time."

"It's too early for *Anchorman*." I laugh and roll my eyes.

"Will I ever stump you?"

I pretend to think about it, tilting my head and tapping my chin.

"Probably not. You're the better musician. At least give me movies." I flick my chin toward his hand. "So you think you'll be ready for the Boston Pops come Fall?"

Even though he doesn't talk about it much, I know he regrets not being able to accept the invitation to play with the famous symphony orchestra this summer. Of course, they extended the offer to whenever Rhyson Gray is good and ready.

"We'll see where I am with the album." He glances at his hand, shrugs. "And everything."

A cloud passes over the sun, temporarily dimming its brightness, just like this moment dims all that's bright in our life. We have so much, but a full recovery for his hand is what I want most.

"Is that the harmonica I gave you for Christmas?" I ask, needing to change the subject, gesturing toward the small instrument in his lap.

"It is. Come here." He extends his arms for me to join him on the sun lounger. A smile stretches wider across my face and the shadow lifts the closer I get. I climb on top of him, locking our bodies at the center.

"Are you writing something for the new album?" I nuzzle into his neck.

"Uh, no. Not for the album. Something else."

"Vegas?" I pull back to peer at him.

Prodigy is holding an artist showcase in Las Vegas soon. Grip will preview songs from his new album. Kilimanjaro will perform a few songs they've been doing at festivals. And Rhyson will introduce me as Prodigy's newest signed artist.

"No, not for Vegas." He gives me a careful glance. "You still thinking about inviting your sister? About meeting her while we're there?"

My teeth snap together. I decided I'd like to meet my sister, the only blood I have left in the world besides my father, but I'm not sure what I want with *him*. His betrayal, not just of me, but of Mama, cuts so deep, I just don't know if it will ever fully heal. I'll take it one day at a time. The same way Rhyson takes his relationship with his parents. His father came over for dinner right before our vacation, and I was amazed by the growing ease, maybe even affection, between them. They talk at least once a week outside of their sessions with Dr. Ramirez. His mother . . . I don't know why that relationship remains frozen, or if it will ever thaw, but I don't think she'll be coming to dinner any time soon.

"Pep, Vegas?" Rhyson's raised brows remind me I haven't answered him.

"Yeah, I want to meet my sister when we're out there." I shrug. "We'll see what happens with my dad."

I nibble and lick the strong tendon in his neck, wanting to shift away from something I'm not certain of to something I absolutely am—our connection.

"So what *are* you working on?" I ask, my voice dipping to a provocative whisper.

"This is what I'm working on." He presses my butt until his erection grinds between my legs even through the sheet. "You wanna collaborate?"

My husky laugh is his answer, and I unknot the sheet so it falls away, kicking it to the floor. It took me a while to get used to the "private" part of private island, but after days of walking around naked, not another person in sight, I got it.

My breasts are already heavy and begging for him. There's an ache building between my legs that only he can satisfy. I spot a tray of fruit on the deck beside his lounger. Pineapple, limes, mangos— our meal every morning.

"I'm ready for breakfast." I snatch one of the lime halves, poising it over his chest and squeezing the juice over his nipples. My lips and tongue slurp at the juices running over the muscles in his chest and abs, his grunts and groans more music to my ears than the tune that woke me up. Fingers steady, I pull back the Velcro strip on his board shorts, sliding them over his hips and down his legs. I grab another lime half and squeeze it over the powerful thighs, licking and nibbling my way to the most sensitive part of him. Grabbing one more lime, I squeeze the juice over him, my mouth watering in anticipation.

"Hmmmm." I catch and hold his eyes, licking my lips. "Breakfast of champions."

I pull him into my mouth, the tart juice and the tanginess of his body mixing on my tongue like liquor, inebriating, slowing my motions as I bob my head over him languidly, taking my time.

"Dammit, Pep," he growls above me, fingers tangling in my hair, urging me to take him so deep he fills my throat. "Baby, just like that."

I keep going until I'm frantic, squeezing his butt, pushing him as deep as I can, determined to have him spilling down my throat, but he pulls out, bringing me up.

"No." I try to push my way back down. "I want to, Rhyson."

"But I want *you*," he whispers against my neck. "Let me have you."

I sit up over him, watching as he squeezes lime juice over my breasts, rivulets running over the muscles in my stomach, disappearing between my legs. He chases the juices with his tongue, taking his time gathering every drop, sucking my nipples into his mouth so tightly they prick with a hint of pain in the pleasure. He licks tenderly at the faint marks he left on me last night.

"Was I too rough with you?" He looks up from his task, lips never leaving my skin, knowing he wasn't.

"No, it was perfect." I gasp when he finds the juices between my legs.

He lays me back on the lounger, spreading me until my feet are on either side flat on the deck and I'm wide open for him. He squeezes another lime over the pulsing spot between my legs, watching as the juices trickle inside of me.

My eyes stretch and then clench shut when he spreads me, licking me clean of the citrus juice, his tongue dipping inside, his teeth nibbling at me like I'm a delicacy. Seeing his dark head working between my legs, the velvety tongue licking into my crevices, the sound of him drinking my juices with the lime like a delicious cocktail—it's too much. A moan rips through me, and I'm shuddering with an orgasm so strong it's like a wire pulling my back into an arch. And all the while he never leaves me, keeps licking and nipping and sucking at me.

I'm still trembling, my body still quaking when he lies back on the lounger and pulls me on top. I sink onto every inch of him, fitting our bodies like lock and key, my feet on the floor, both of us gasping into each other's mouths at the perfect union. I ride him with the sun beating down on my shoulders and back, my fingers gliding into the sun-kissed hair at his neck. He controls the pace, keeping it slow and deep, one hand gripping my hip and the other clamping my neck.

"I love you, Pep," he pants at my breasts, dusting kisses over my nipples and then taking one fully into his mouth, sucking hard and long until sensations ricochet through my body, the sweet, rough pull of his mouth toppling me over the edge again. This time he follows, the force of this storm throwing his head back as our hips collide, our bodies slamming into one another with a passion so violent there's nothing to do but scream, our hoarse voices soaring into the air with no one to hear but us. Our bodies making a symphony for just us two. Making an opus of our love.

I push my fingers into his hair as our motions slow to nothing, as the storm subsides, tears gathering at the corners of my eyes. I bite my lip, dropping my head to his shoulder.

"I didn't know there was love like this," I say, barely able to catch my breath. "I don't ever want to lose you. It would kill me to lose you, Rhys."

Even with the tape settled and destroyed, even knowing it won't ruin us, all the ways you can lose a person sometimes still haunt me. The way my mother lost my father. The way Pops lost Grams. The how wouldn't matter. Losing Rhyson would leave a huge, unsealable hole in my heart forever.

"You won't." He pushes me up a little to suck my nipples, sliding his palm down my back, slipping a finger between the cheeks of my butt, indulging in the intimacies, the liberties of lovers. "You can't ever lose me."

"Promise."

"Hey, there's no losing, not really." He pulls back to search my face. "Remember the words to the song at Grady's wedding?"

He traces the prayer wrapping around my ribs, swallowing hard against the emotion that makes its way to his face.

"No matter what happens, my heart and my soul, I give them to you. They're yours to keep."

"Yours to keep," I echo back to him, threading our fingers together.

"The only thing that's true, that's real, is this, Pep." He pulls my other hand over his heart, pressing his hand over mine. "So you don't have to worry about losing me. You *can't* lose me. My soul is lodged that deeply in yours. I'm completely yours."

I collapse against him, our hands over our hearts a holy press between us.

"You asked me what I was writing on the harmonica when you came out." He pushes the hair over my shoulder.

I nod, pulling back to look at his face.

"I didn't think you were ready to hear what I was writing, but I'm going to tell you anyway." He glances down and then up, watching my face closely. "It was a song for our little girl. The one we're going to have one day. The one I dream about."

Shock and hope roll through me. Too much to even process.

"I told you before I don't need rings or ceremonies to know you're mine." He draws a deep breath, his chest swelling against mine. "But I *want* them. With you I want it all. I want the spectacle of a day that's all about us. I want you coming down an aisle and me feeling completely unworthy. I want you having my babies and me kissing your stretch marks."

"Stretch marks?" I shake against him laughing. "Boo to stretch marks."

"And I'll give you silver chewing gum paper for our twenty-fifth wedding anniversary." He laughs into my hair. "And Gold Bond medicated powder for our fiftieth."

"You're ridiculous." I laugh even though tears roll over my cheeks and down my chin, christening the space where our bodies touch.

"And we'll get so old that people forget about us. Forget we were ever famous. Forget our music. Hell, we'll get so old together that I might even forget our anniversary date, but it'll be okay. We'll get so old that the only thing I remember from this life is you. And if there's a next life—"

"There is." I cling to that. Maybe I've discarded my faith somewhere along the way, and I'll pick it back up when I'm ready, but I do know I'll see Mama again. "There has to be another life, Rhyson."

"Then in the next one," he says, eyes filled with infinite promises.

"I'll find you again."

"Find me," I whisper back with a smile.

"Do you remember that scene from *Cold Mountain*?" He pushes all my hair back so that he sees my face clearly. "When Nicole Kidman says 'Isn't there some religion where you just have to say three times "I marry you," and you're man and wife?'"

I can't hold on to my smile because this moment feels as sacred as what we'll do in a church one day real soon.

"I marry you." My voice quakes with the beauty of the declaration. "I marry you. I marry you."

His eyes burn across my face with the sweetest heat, with assurances of his love, with the certainty of forever.

"I marry you." He ordains my lips with a kiss, soft and tender. "I marry you. I marry you."

Neither of us saw this kind of love growing up. Between his parents, he saw nothing more than a business arrangement, between mine I only saw a broken promise, but we made our own way, made our own love.

We've made our own vow, and this one we'll keep.

THE END

About the Author

'M A WIFE, A MOM, A writer, and an advocate for families living with autism.

That's me in a nutshell. Crack the nut, and you'll find a Southern girl gone Southern California who loves pizza and Diet Coke, and wishes she got to watch a lot more television. You can usually catch me up too late, on social media too much, or FINALLY putting a dent in my ever-growing To Be Read list!

I love connecting with readers. These are a few ways we can stay in touch!

Let's stay in touch!
You can find me on Facebook, Twitter, and Instagram.

Other BOOKS BY *Kennedy Ryan*

SOUL SERIES
My Soul to Keep, Book 1

THE BENNETT SERIES
When You Are Mine
Loving You Always
Be Mine Forever
Until I'm Yours